Jean Dubreuil, Ephraim Chambers, John Bowles, Carington Bowles

The Practice of Perspective

An easy method of representing natural objects according to the rules of art

Jean Dubreuil, Ephraim Chambers, John Bowles, Carington Bowles

The Practice of Perspective
An easy method of representing natural objects according to the rules of art

ISBN/EAN: 9783337390747

Printed in Europe, USA, Canada, Australia, Japan

Cover: Foto ©Andreas Hilbeck / pixelio.de

More available books at **www.hansebooks.com**

The PRACTICE of PERSPECTIVE

OR, AN EASY

M E T H O D

OF REPRESENTING

NATURAL OBJECTS

According to the RULES of ART.

Applied and exemplified in all the Variety of Cafes; as LAND-
SKAPES, GARDENS, BUILDINGS of divers Kinds, their *Appendages*,
Parts, and *Furniture*.

With RULES for the Proportion and Pofition of FIGURES,
both in DRAUGHT and RELIEVO.

Alfo the Manner of conducting the SHADOWS, produced either by natural or artificial *Luminaries*; and Practical Methods of DRAWING after Nature, when the
Procefs of Rules are not underftood.

A WORK highly neceffary for

P A I N T E R S,

ENGRAVERS, | STATUARIES,
ARCHITECTS, | JEWELLERS,
EMBROIDERERS, | TAPESTRY-WORKERS,

And others concerned in DESIGNING.

The Whole illuftrated with One Hundred and Fifty COPPER-PLATES.

Written in FRENCH by a JESUIT of *Paris*. Tranflated by E. CHAMBERS,
Author of Cyclopædia, or, An Univerfal Dictionary of Arts and Sciences.

The FOURTH EDITION.

If you would proceed immediately to the Practice *of* Perfpective, *without engaging in*
the intricacies of the Theory; *the* JESUIT'S PERSPECTIVE *will anfwer your purpofe.*
Wolfius in Element. Mathef. Tom. II. P. 1048.

L O N D O N:
Printed for JOHN BOWLES, at the Black Horfe in *Cornbill*, and
CARINGTON BOWLES, in *St. Paul's Church-Yard.*
[Price bound Twelve Shillings.]
M DCC LXV.

THE

P R E F A C E.

THE Art of PERSPECTIVE is moſt elegant and agreeable: It affords great entertainment to men of leiſure, and is the very ſoul of painting; without which a PAINTER can never be a maſter in his profeſſion. It is this muſt conduct him in the diſpoſitions, heights, and proportions of his figures, buildings, and other objects. It is this muſt ſhew him what colours are to be deep or faint, vivid or dull; where each is to be applied; what parts to be highly finiſhed, and what ſlightly touched; where light is to be beſtowed, and where diminiſhed. In a word, it is this begins and compleats the painting. Without the aſſiſtance of PERSPECTIVE, the beſt maſter muſt make as many faults as ſtrokes; eſpecially in buildings with their enrichments. In which particulars I find ſome reputable painters ſo greatly defective, that this has been one conſiderable motive to my undertaking the following work: Wherein their errors will be ſhewn, without naming the authors; and novices inſtructed how to avoid the like. The moſt conſummate maſter is tied to the ſtrict obſervation of theſe rules, on pain of pleaſing none but the ignorant: And an indifferent painter may be told this to his comfort, that if he make himſelf a thorough maſter of them, he will be able to do wonders.

THE ENGRAVER in copper can no more excel without PERSPECTIVE, than the painter; as having every thing to expreſs with the graver that the other performs with his pencil. From PERSPECTIVE he muſt learn where to lean heavily, and where lightly

A 2   on

on his graver; what strokes must be sunk deep, and what soften-
ed. And his occasion for this art is more important, as his pieces
multiply to a much greater degree than those of the painter;
and, if artfully performed, will spread his praise more: But, if
otherwise, his failing will be the more notorious, and each print
be a monument of the author's ignorance.

THE SCULPTOR and STATUARY must here learn the heights
both for the high, low, and middle sight; the slopes and incli-
nations of buildings, and other bodies; the angle for the point
of sight; and the proportions and dimensions of all objects, near
and remote.

BY the same art the ARCHITECT must learn how to make
his designs intelligible in a little compass: How to raise
one part, and leave the other in its plan, to shew the whole
conduct and effect of his work. By the way, having mentioned
architecture, I must observe of how much consequence it is, for
such as practise PERSPECTIVE, to understand the fundamental
rules of that science; the finest pieces of PERSPECTIVE being
those of great and magnificent buildings, raised according to
the order of columns; the beauty whereof depends on their
just measures and proportions, which must be represented with
the greatest exactness, otherwise they will shock and offend the
eye. Ignorance in these things is not excusable, considering with
how much ease they may be learned in *Vitruvius, Vignola, Scamozzi,*
and some others.

To know the orders of columns and their characters, is not
enough: A draughts-man should likewise understand all the
usual dimensions of buildings, and the several parts; as doors,
windows *, chimneys, &c. how to dispose them to receive the
light to advantage, and that no part may appear maimed,
useless, or ill supported, and that there be a symmetry and pro-

---

* Halfpenny's Practical Architecture, in 12mo, price 4 s. illustrates, by various useful
tables, the exact measures and proportions of the five orders of columns, with doors and
windows adjusted to them.

portion running throughout the whole. Without fuch regu-
lation, a piece of PERSPECTIVE, in which noble ftructures have
a place, inftead of pleafing the eye, will offend it.

GOLDSMITHS, EMBROIDERERS, TAPESTRY-MAKERS, ENAMEL-
LERS, and even JOINERS, and others who have occafion to make
defigns, are under the ftricteft obligations to attain the knowledge of PERSPECTIVE, if they would be eminent in their pro-
feffions.

MANY who defired to improve themfelves by the ftudy of
this art, have affured me, that they were difcouraged by the
great number of lines which moft authors make ufe of to form,
and find the places of their objects. Others have been deterred
by numberlefs obfcurities in the rules and operations, and often perplexed from the inftructions not being immediately
annexed to the figures. Now thefe complaints have warned
me to be more clear and methodical in my inftructions, and
to place them fronting the copper-plates, fo that the Reader
may have both the rule and the example in his eye at
once. Through the whole I have accommodated myfelf to
the capacity of learners; not perplexing them with too many
demonftrations, nor ufing any words but fuch as may be readily
underftood, at leaft in the definitions. With the fame view I
have followed the common cuftom of attributing qualities to
certain things which really have them not. Thus, in confider-
ing diftance, or removal, I have been forced to fay, contrary to
my own fentiment, that it is the Pupil which receives the rays
from objects, as if they terminate therein; whereas it is paft
difpute, that vifion is performed on the *Retina* at the bottom of
the eye; and that the rays only pafs through the pupil in the
way thither: Which, to fome people, will appear a new language, and not eafily to be conceived. However, being affured
that fuch a piece of knowledge imported but little to the practice of PERSPECTIVE, I have attributed to the pupil what really
belongs to the bottom of the eye, the proper place of vifion,

where

where the images of all objects are formed; though there are others who refer this to the cryftalline. The Reader who requires farther fatisfaction in this point, may confult *Aquillo Scheiner*, and *Des Cartes*.

THOUGH I have ftrained every nerve to render the fcience eafy, I do not doubt but there are feveral will find fome difficulty at the beginning. But whoever can furmount the firft difficulties, may reft affured he will eafily underftand and practife the remaining rules, provided he takes care to mafter one rule well before he turn over the leaf to another. The rules, in fome meafure, depend on each other: And a little trouble, at firft, will be abundantly recompenfed by the future eafe accruing from it.

IT will appear from the following table, that this work alone fuffices to carry you through all the ftages and degrees of PER-SPECTIVE, and to perform every kind of draught; having recourfe to the feveral rules, and collating them together, to furnifh out the performance required. No doubt it muft be agreeable to any one, who defires to produce a compofition of his own, to find immediately rules that will anfwer his purpofe: His fatisfaction, affuredly, muft far tranfcend that of barely copying the defigns of others; and, in cafe he be obliged to copy any other, he will do it with much more eafe and pleafure, when mafter of thefe rules, in which inftructions are given for every thing that can occur. I take great pleafure in making new defigns, and inventing new figures; which I fhould have made public, as my predeceffors have done, but that I was willing every perfon fhould participate in the pleafure of compofing from his own fancy; having furnifhed him with all the means requifite thereto. Such as chufe to decline that trouble, will meet with defigns enough ready to their hand in *Marolois*, *Vredeman*, *Urieffe*, and others, who have fhewn the politenefs of their genius in this way.

So

So many fine performances, I doubt, have helped to render many of our painters too lazy to learn to do what they find ready done. All they afpire at is to copy them as well as they can; which were excufable, did they know how to do it with judgment: But their way is to copy without underftanding the rules of proportion and beauty, or, in other words, the rules of PERSPECTIVE. And hence it is, that we have often as many different points in a painting, as there are objects, lines, and returns. Some of them will let you fee the bottom of an ob-ject that fhould only fhew the top; and others, rather than be defective, will fhew both. Others again, having feveral figures to fhew in a painting, will make them all of the fame height: Though fometimes they vouchfafe to difpenfe with that rule, and make thofe in the fore-part lefs than thofe behind, to give room, as they tell us, for the hind figures to be feen: Which is to overturn both art and nature at once.

As to the order of this work, I have divided it into five parts. In the FIRST are delivered a few definitions, demonftrations, and reafons, which need no great ftock of mathematics to be underftood, and yet give a deal of light into the fubject. Thence I proceed to fhew the nature of the point of fight, points of diftance, accidental points, front point, and fide point; vifual rays, diagonals, parallels, perpendiculars, and bafe line. The previous knowledge of which things is very neceffary to the eafy underftanding the inftructions that follow. In the SECOND PART * I give the methods of fhortening and diminifhing plans divers ways; with feveral forms of pavements, which ordinarily ferve for the foundations of Perfpective Draughts. Having given fufficient inftructions for putting all forts of planes in PERSPECTIVE, I proceed, in the THIRD PART †, to the elevation of divers objects, beginning with the eafieft, which are cubes, and other bodies of feveral fides or faces. Thefe are followed by

* See Page 19.   † See Page 42.

walls,

walls, doors, windows, cielings, vaults, and ftair-cafes of divers
forms; all without ornaments, or mouldings, that the rules
might be lefs perplexed with a number of lines which fuch
enrichments would have rendered neceffary. After fhewing
all the buildings in their fimplicity and nakednefs, I go on to
furnifh them with columns, cornices, and other ornaments,
which add a majefty and grace. The houfes all built to the
roof, I fhew how to put them in PERSPECTIVE with variety
of coverings: Then proceed to the infides, and give rules for the
furniture, moveables, &c. Thefe are followed by inftructions
relating to ftreets, gardens, trees, walks; which are pleafing
objects, and render the draughts very entertaining. This part is
clofed with two or three contrivances for drawing after nature,
when the rules of PERSPECTIVE are not underftood. In the
FOURTH PART * is given the meafures and proportions of figures,
their poftures, fituation, and horizons, both for flat paintings
and relievo's. The FIFTH and LAST PART † confiders natural
fhadows, whether projected by the fun, torch, candle, or lamp.

WHEN the PERSPECTIVE of a building, garden, range of trees,
palifade, or the like intermixed with figures, is intended, I
would recommend it to you, to fketch out what relates to the
PERSPECTIVE with a pencil in the firft place; which done, you
will proceed with more affurance to fix the heights of figures,
and other circumftances.

ONE thing fome people will find to cenfure in this work,
namely, That the points of diftance in all my figures are too near
the point of fight. But if this be a fault, it is a voluntary one.
For my defign being to teach, it was neceffary every thing fhould
be fhewn, and the reader led to fee where fo many lines were to
terminate; otherwife he would have been left to his own con-
jectures. It is fufficient that I direct the learner to place them
farther off; and even fhew the laws and occafions thereof. Nor
can it be fuppofed I fhould have fcrupled making them more
remote, had not other confiderations prevailed with me: One of

* See Page 122.   † See Page 129.

which

which was, to render the book as fmall, convenient, and cheap as poffible. Had I followed the advice of fome of my friends, I fhould only have given a fingle inftruction in each leaf; which would have fwelled the book to about thrice its bulk, without rendering it a whit the more intelligible.

SOME people affect to conceal the names of the authors they have followed; and, as has been well obferved of a certain one, pilfer from private perfons what they give to the public. For my own fhare, I confefs, that having propofed to write a little treatife of PERSPECTIVE, I was willing to fee as many authors as I could on the fame fubject; nor made any fcruple of borrowing from any of them what I found to my purpofe, with an intention of making an open reftitution of all my private thefts to the public. The firft writer of any account is *George Reich*, in the Tenth Chapter of his works. The next, *Victor*, a canon of *Toul*, who gives us a number of good figures, but is too fparing in his inftructions. After him comes *Albert Durer*, who has left us fome rules and principles, in the Fourth Book of his *Geometry*. Then *J. Coufin*, who has an exprefs Treatife on the Art of PERSPECTIVE, wherein are many valuable things. After thefe come *Dan Barbaro*, *Vignola*, *Serlio*, *Du Cerceau*, *Sirigaty*, *Solomon de Caus*, *Marolois*, *Vredement*, *Uvrieffe*, *Guidus Ubaldus*, *Pietro*, *Acolty*, the Sieur *de Vaulizard*, the Sieur *Defargues*, and lately Father *Niceron*, a Minim: All whom I have read, one after another, and not without admiring their great and happy induftry in the fervice of the public; efteeming it fufficient honour for me to imitate what they have done, and to be the unknown copift of their works. Befides thofe already recited, there are many others whom I have never feen; which multitude of authors muft be allowed an argument of the great efteem the art has always been in, as well as the fuperior regard paid to it by the prefent age. On this confideration, I cannot doubt but the following work will be favourably received; efpecially as it brings along with it feveral new rules and inftructions, for putting in PERSPECTIVE any of the objects our fenfes are ordinarily converfant about; and, by confequence, of truly performing whatever relates to that Art.

a   A TABLE

A

T A B L E

The feveral Parts and Members whereof any PERSPECTIVE
DRAUGHT is to confift.

PERSPECTIVE muft begin with plans, and, of courfe, with
fuch as are the moft fimple and eafy; among which is the
fquare, or cube. The method of making the plan is fhewn in *A Cube view'd in Front, and Angle-wife.*
page 19, and that of its elevation in page 44, 49. If an angular
view be required, its plan is given in page 20, and its elevation
in page 50.

To raife the walls of a houfe, or the palifades of a garden, &c. *Walls and Palifades.*
fee the plans and elevations, page 51, 52.

Such as require the infide of a hall, or chamber, in a front *Infide of a Room. The Walls.*
view, muft take the fame page 52 for the walls; the following
page for the doors; page 54 for the windows; and page 77 for *Doors. Windows.*
the chimney. The pavement they will find in page 31, 32, 33, *Chimney. Pavement*
and 34. The ceiling is fhewn in page 55, 56, 57, and 58. If a *Ceiling.*
door is to be open, you have your inftructions in page 53, and
the page following gives a window or cafement open. The
fame rules are to be obferved when there are two or three ftories
over each other, as in page 76. To afcend to thefe ftories, ftair-
cafes are furnifhed in page 82, 83, and 84. *Stair-cafe.*

Houfes viewed on the infide are ufually feen furnifhed with
moveables; moft kinds whereof are fhewn in page 96--103. The *Moveables.*
proportions of figures to be placed therein are found in page 122,
123, 124, 125.

To fhew the infide of a church, the plan muft be put in per- *Infide of a Church.*
fpective, according to the inftructions in page 37, or 41. The
walls to be raifed, from page 51. The windows are conftructed *Windows.*
by the fame rules as the arches of page 62, or 54. Pillars and pi- *Filafters.*
lafters are to be taken from page 48. Columns from 87. A vault, *Columns. Vault.*
or vaults, from page 68---72. And a dome, or cupola, from *Dome.*
page 74, 75. To enrich it with cornices, mouldings, and other or- *Cornices and Mouldings.*
naments, have recourfe to page 88---92. For altars, to page 104. *Altars.*

For outfides of buildings: The doors and windows are per- *Outfides of Buildings.*
formed as in the infides, fee page 53, 54, and 106. When raifed

a 2   to

Cornice. to the proper height, the method of roofing and covering them will be found in page 107, 108. And if a cornice or other orna- *Galleries.* ments be required, you have them in page 88---92. Arched galleries, both within and without fide, are fhewn in page 63, 66, and 67.

Street.   If a whole ftreet be required, you muft multiply the houfes *Houfes far off.* on either fide, as in page 109. When houfes are made pretty deep within the draught, fee page 110. In large fquares, &c. *Pyramid.* a pyramid may be erected, as in page 144. Or fome ftatue, figure, or a pedeftal, as in page 91, and 124.

Buildings viewed by the Angle.   When a building is to be viewed by the angle, you may take its plan from page 19, 30, and 111. and manage the elevation as taught in page 50, and 111. which give rules for doors and windows therein.

Gardens.   Gardens in perfpective are exceeding agreeable. Their plans are *Arbours.* to be made as in page 35, 38, or 113. If arbours be required, you *Palifades.* are fupplied from page 60, or 61. If palifades, look to page 51, *Alleys of Trees.* and 52. And if you prefer a grove, thicket, or walk planted with *Fountains.* trees, page 112 furnifhes variety of each. If fountains, or jets d'eau be wanted, page 29 gives a bafon, and its elevation is performed as in page 73. For fquares, or beds, fee page 35, or 38. For polygons, 45, or 46. For placing ftatues, or figures in a garden, take the meafures from page 122, or 125. For grotto's, or niches, fee page 74. For an afcent out of one garden into an- *Steps.* other, you have divers forms of fteps in page 78, 79, 80, 81. In fine, you are at liberty to chufe whatever pleafes your fancy, and may range them all in the fame piece, provided you avoid confufion, and obferve the due fymmetry and proportions.

Shops.   If you would have open fhops, without any fixtures, you are furnifhed in page 55. If you require them fitted up with draw- *Boxes.* ers, boxes, &c. look to page 95, and 105.

Amphitheatres.   Amphitheatres were anciently of more ufe in paintings than at prefent, for which reafon I have chofe to omit them: And yet fhift might be made, by taking the plan in page 29, and adding more circles, according to the number of ftories intended. To raife the ftories, you are to ufe the line of elevation in page 75.

Fortifications.   For fortifications, you have the method of diminifhing their plans in page 39, and the method of raifing them in page 114.

Shadows.   To give the fhadows to bodies of all kinds, both thofe occafioned by the fun, candle, and torch, is fhewn from page 129, to the end of the book.

    See particulars in the following Table of Contents.

T H E

THE

CONTENTS.

A pave-

CONTENTS.

PART IV.

Measures and Proportions of Figures.

PART V.

Methods of finding the natural Shadows
of Objects, projected either by the
sun, candle, torch, or lamp.

Shadows

9

SOME

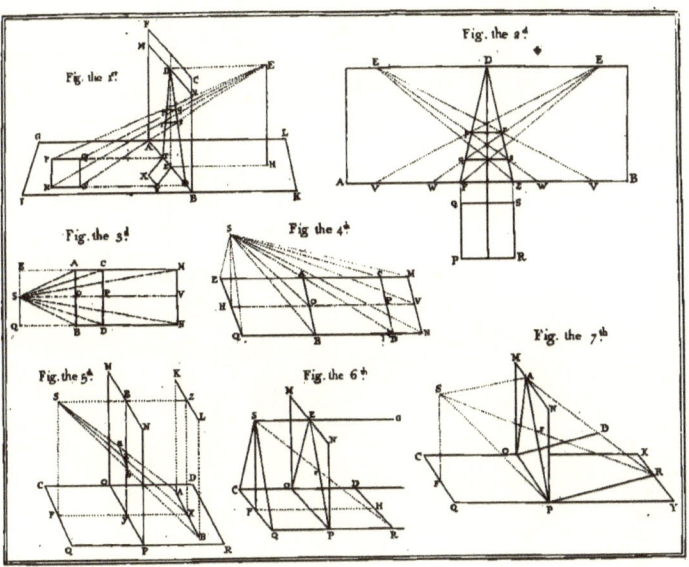

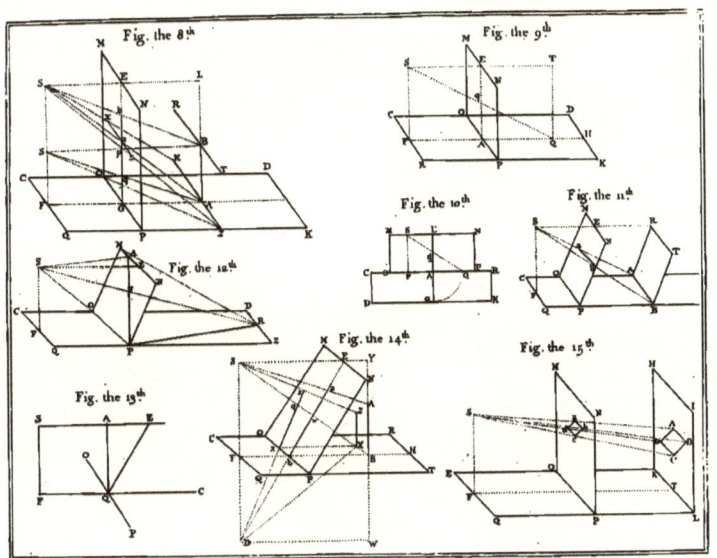

Fig. the 8th

Fig. the 9th

Fig. the 10th

Fig. the 11th

Fig. the 12th

Fig. the 13th

Fig. the 14th

Fig. the 15th

THE

THEORY

OF

PERSPECTIVE.

By *James Hodgson*, F. R. S.

DEFINITIONS.

1. **P**ERSPECTIVE is the art of defcribing on a plain furface the true reprefentation or appearance of any given object, as feen from one determinate point for any given diftance and height of the eye.

2. The perfpective table, or plane, is that furface whereon the picture of the object is formed, according to the rules of perfpective, as A B C F. *See Fig.* 1.

3. The geometrical or ground plane is that furface whereon the perfpective table is fuppofed to ftand, as G I K L.

4. The height of the eye is equal to the length of a perpendicular let fall from it to the ground plane, as E H.

5. The diftance of the eye from the picture is equal to the length of a perpendicular drawn from the eye to the perfpective table, as E D.

6. The common fection of the perfpective table with the ground plane is called the ground line or fection, as A B.

7. The horizontal line is a line in the perfpective table or picture, parallel to the fection or ground line, and of the height of the eye above it, as M D N.

8. The principal ray is the line drawn from the eye perpendicular to the table, and is therefore equal to the diftance of the eye from the table, as E D.

C

9. The

9. The diſtance of any point in the ground plane from the table is a perpendicular drawn from that point to the ground line or ſection, as Q T.

10. Direct parallel lines are ſuch as cut the ground line or ſection at right angles, as Q T and S O.

11. Oblique parallel lines are ſuch as cut the ground line or ſection at oblique angles, as X T and Y Z.

12. Tranſverſe parallel lines are thoſe lines which cut the direct parallel lines at right angles, as P R and Q S.

13. Radial lines, or viſual rays, are ſuch as run up from po:nts on the ground line, and unite in ſome certain point in the horizontal line, namely, either in the point of ſight or in an accidental point, as D T, D Z, D O.

14. The point of ſight is that point in the picture, which is found by drawing a perpendicular from the eye to the perſpective table or picture, in which all the direct rays concur, as the point D.

15. The accidental point is that point in the picture, where lines that fall obliquely on the ground line or ſection, but parallel amongſt themſelves, unite or concur as the direct rays do in the viſual point, as the point E. *See Fig*. 2.

16. The point of diſtance E is a point in the horizontal line of the table or picture removed as far diſtant from the viſual point D in the 2d figure, as the eye at E in the firſt figure is diſtant from the table or picture A B C F, namely, D E.

17. The point of incidence is a point in the ground line or ſection, where a perpendicular let fall from any point in the geometrical plane interſects it, as the point, T or Z. *See Fig*. 1.

18. The perſpective of any point is that point in the picture, where the viſual ray drawn from the eye at E to any point, as P, in the geometrical or ground plane, interſects the picture or table, as the point p.

19. The perſpective of a line is the common ſection of the table or picture, and the imaginary plane formed by an infinite number of rays flowing from the eye at E, and falling upon every point of the line R S to be repreſented, as the line r s.

20. The perſpective of any plane figure is the ſection of the cone or pyramid of rays, whoſe vertex is the eye, and baſis the figure propoſed, made by the plane of the table or picture.

21. The perſpective of any ſolid upon the table or picture is the aggregate of the perſpective of all the planes whereof the ſolid is compoſed.

22. The optic angle, under which any object appears, is formed by two lines drawn from the center of the eye, to the two extremities of the object, and here it is to be noted, that the moſt convenient diſtance of the eye, from the Extremities of the object ſhould be nearly equal to the longeſt dimenſion of the object, whether breadth or height.

For as the beauty of perſpective depends upon the point of diſtance, ſo the eye ought never to be placed too near the object, nor too far from it, but at a convenient diſtance ; and never nearer to the object than one half of the largeſt dimenſion, for in this ſituation the viſual angle will be a right angle or 90 degrees ; and as this is the largeſt angle that the eye can well diſcover at one caſt, ſo if it

be

be made lefs than 45 degrees, the object will be too much contracted, and the vifual angle will be fo fmall that the returns in buildings would not be diftinguifhed, and the whole would appear confufed, and therefore when the vifual angle is about 60 degrees, which agrees with the above mentioned limitation, then the object is feen with the utmoft advantage, and confequently in all perfpective defigns they ought to come as near this fituation as poffible.

23. When the projection of any object is made on a plane parallel to the horizon by rays parallel and perpendicular to the fame plane, the reprefentation of the object in this cafe is called the *Ichnography* of the figure propofed, whence the bafe, bottom or platform, whereon a body or building is erected, is called the ichnography of that building, fo that to project the ichnographic reprefentation of any building is to draw the exact ground plot of the fame building; thus the geometric ichnography of a column is a circle, of a pedeftal is a fquare, &c.

24. When the projection is made on a plane perpendicular to the horizon by rays parallel and perpendicular to the plane upon which the object is reprefented, the reprefentation in this cafe is called the *Orthography* of the figure propofed; thus the upright front of any building or object is called the orthography of that object or building, fo that to draw the orthographic reprefentation of any object or building, is to draw the exact front of the object or building as it really is and appears to be.

25. But when the reprefentation or projection of any object is made by rays flowing from the feveral parts of the object, as the front, top or bottom, fide or fides, and uniting in one point where the eye is fuppofed to be placed, the Reprefentation of this object (upon a plane placed before the eye ftanding at right angles to the line drawn from the eye perpendicular to the object, and) formed by the interfection of the feveral rays with this plane, is called the *Schenography* of that object, fo that to draw the fchenographic projection or reprefentation of any object, is to draw the projection or reprefentation of the feveral parts of that object, as they will appear to the eye fituated at a convenient diftance from the object upon a plane placed perpendicular to the horizon, and in a proper fituation to receive the object; and how this is to be done, is the proper bufinefs of PERSPECTIVE.

A X I O M S.

1. The common interfection of two planes is a right line.

2. If two right lines meet in a point, a plane may pafs through them both.

3. If two or more right lines are parallel to each other, they will all be in the fame plane ; that is, if a plane pafs through any two of thefe, it will pafs through all the reft.

4. If two or more parallel right lines are cut by another right line, there may be a plane that will pafs through them all.

5. If two parallel planes are interfected by another plane, their interfections will be parallel to each other.

6. Lines

6. Lines parallel to the fame right line, or to parallel lines, are parallel one to another; conceive the fame of parallel planes.

7. Every point in any right line is in any plane that line is in.

8. A fpace feen under a lefs angle appears lefs, and the fame fpace feen under a bigger angle appears bigger, and confequently fpaces feen under equal angles are equal amongft themfelves.

Note, In this *Axiom* we fuppofe the fpaces viewed ftand at right angles to the axis or principal ray iffuing directly from the eye, or, which is the fame thing, that they are parallel to the perfpective table, for in other cafes, where the diameter of the object is inclined to the table, it will not hold good.

THEOREM I.

If the eye be placed any where between two parallel right lines, the farther thefe lines are produced from the fight, the nearer they will feem to approach each other. See Fig. 3.

Let S reprefent the feat of the eye, E M and Q N the two given parallel lines, and S V the axis or principal ray, through the points A, C, and M, draw the lines A B, C D, and M N, perpendicular to the principal ray S V, and thefe lines will be parallel and equal to each other. Alfo from S, the point of fight, let the rays S A, S B, S C, S D, S M, S N, be drawn.

Demonftr. Becaufe the right angled triangles SQB, S Q D, have the perpendicular S Q common to them both, but have the bafe Q D of the triangle S Q D, greater than the bafe Q B of the triangle S Q B, therefore the angle S D Q of the triangle S Q D, will, be lefs than the angle S B Q of the triangle S Q B; confequently the angle P S D, which is equal to S D Q, will be lefs than the angle O S B, which is equal to S B Q, and confequently the double of the angle P S D, or the angle C S D, will be leffer than the double of the angle O S B, or the angle A S B, wherefore the line C D, will appear lefs than A B, by the 8th axiom, and confequently the points C, and D, of the parallels E M, and Q N, will appear to the eye placed at S, nearer than the points A and B of the fame parallels E M, and Q N. After the fame manner it may be proved that the line M N, which is placed farther off from the eye at S, than the line C D, will appear lefs than C D, and confequently the points M, and N, will feem to approach nearer to each other than the points C and D, which are nearer, and that the fame line M N, being placed at a greater diftance than S V, from the point of fight, will appear leffer, and confequently the points M, and N, in the laft Situation will feem to approach nearer to each other than in the prefent fituation, and thus fucceffively, till at laft the line M N will appear indefinitely fmall, and the Points M and N will feem to come together.

Let us now fuppofe the eye, fee *Figure* the 4th, placed above the plane paffing through the given parallels, and let E M and Q N be the parallels themfelves.

From H, the middle point of the line E Q. erect the perpendicular H S, equal to the height of the eye above the plane, then will S be the place of the eye; from

from the point S draw the rays S E, S Q, S A, S B, &c. Now becaufe the angles S E A, and S Q B are right angles, the hypothenufes, or rays S A, and S B, will be longer than the perpendiculars S E, and S Q; and inafmuch as both triangles have the fides S E, and S Q, equal to each other, it follows that the angle Q S E will be greater than the angle B S A, and confequently the line A B will appear lefs than the line E Q, by axiom the 8th, and the points A, and B, will feem to be nearer to each other than the points E and Q, and by the fame way of reafoning it will follow, that the angle D S C will be lefs than the angle B S A, confequently the line C D, will appear lefs than the line A B, and the Points C, and D, will feem to come nearer to each other than the points A, and B, &c. which was to be demonftrated : And the fame confequences will follow if we fuppofe the point S placed below the given plane of parallels.

Let us now imagine a plane, as E M N Q, to pafs through the parallels E M, and Q N, it is manifeft that to the eye placed in the plane itfelf, or above or below it, as in *Figure* the 4th, the two extremities M and N, which are fartheft from the eye, will appear the neareft to each other, and the farther they are produced the nearer they will approach, till at laft being indefinitely produced, they will feem to meet in a point, and the diftance will vanifh.

And the fame confequence will follow in whatfoever fituation the plane is placed, whether it be perpendicular to the horizon, or parallel to it, or inclined to it at any given angle.

Hence we fee why rows of trees, of columns, of pilafters, why walls and the fides of buildings contract themfelves and feem to grow narrower and narrower the farther they are extended from the eye.

Hence we fee the reafon why floors and pavements of buildings feem to rife upwards towards the eye of the fpectator, as is very vifible in long rooms or galleries, and why the cielings feem to fink gradually downwards towards the eye, whilft the fides of the fame building feem to come clofer and clofer, that the right Side feems to approach towards the left, and at the fame time the left Side feems to approach towards the right Side, each dimenfion growing leffer and leffer, and approaching nearer and nearer, the longer the room is, till at laft, if the length be indefinite, they will all vanifh into the vifual point.

Hence we fee the reafon why the horizon appears higher than really it is, and that the convex furface of the fea to an eye placed upon it appears curved and protuberant, and different from what it really is itfelf. And,

Hence we fee alfo the reafon why ftatues and pictures placed at a confiderable height above the eye, alfo why ornaments placed upon the tops of churches or other public buildings appear fo much fmaller than really they are, as well in breadth as in height, and hence are drawn rules for giving them their due proportion of magnitude according to the feveral ftations alloted them, alfo for portraits drawn upon cielings or fet up at any confiderable height, and for a great variety of appearances too many here to enumerate.

Now inafmuch as the vifible magnitude of the lines A O, C P, M V, fee *Figure* the 3d, or their doubles, namely the lines A B, C D, M N, are as the tangents of the optic angles, A S O, C S P, M S V, to the feveral radii S O, S P,

S P, S V, or to their feveral diftances from the eye, it follows that the vifible magnitude of any object increafes or decreafes in its various approaches to or removes from the eye in a reciprocal proportion to its feveral diftances from it : And hence,

The vifible magnitude of any body being given, and its diftance from the fpectator, the true magnitude of the fame body may be found ; and on the contrary, the true or real magnitude of the object being given, its vifible magnitude at any given diftance may be determined ; and hence we are taught to find of what magnitude any object ought to be made to appear of a given bignefs at a given diftance.

These laws extend to objects that are placed above or below the eye, as well as to objects that are placed upon the fame horizontal plane with the eye, provided they be placed at the fame diftance from the eye; but if they are erected perpendicularly over the plane, their altitudes muft be increafed in the proportion of the difference of the tangent of the angle of elevation, and the tangent of the fame angle of elevation increafed by the optic angle of the figure when viewed upon the horizontal furface, and confequently the higher any object is placed above the eye, the greater will be the difference between the tangents of the feveral angles of elevation, and the tangents of the fame angles of elevation increafed by the horizontal optic angle of the figure, and confequently the greater muft the real magnitude of the object be made lto appear of the fame bignefs as if it was placed upon the fame horizontal plane with the eye.

T H E O R E M II.

If any line in the object be parallel to the ground Line, its perfpective in the picture will be parallel to the ground Line alfo.

Let M N O P, fee *Figure* the 5th, be the picture or perfpective table, S the place of the eye, and A B, parallel to the ground Line O P, the line to be drawn in perfpective.

From S, the place of the eye, to the extremities A and B of the line A B let the vifual rays S A, S B be drawn to cut the perfpective table in the points a and b. If thefe points a and b be joined together by the right line a b, I fay this line a b in the table, which is the perfpective of the line A B, the given object, will be parallel to the ground Line O P.

Imagine a plane as K A B L, to pafs through the line A B, and to ftand at right angles to the plane C D R Q, now becaufe the lines a b, and A B, are the common interfections of the parallel planes M N O P, and A B K L, by the vifual plane S A B, they will be parallel by the 5th axiom, but A B is parallel to the ground Line O P by hypothefis, therefore its perfpective a b in the table will be parallel to the ground Line alfo, by the 6th axiom, which was to be proved : And inafmuch as the fame confequence will follow in whatfoever place of the plane C D Q R, the line A B is feated, provided it be parallel to the ground Line A B, or at whatfoever diftance from the eye the plane C D R Q is fixed, it follows that all lines that are parallel to the ground Line of any picture will, when drawn

in

in perfpective, be parallel to each other and to the ground Line alfo. Again, becaufe the triangles S a b and S A B are fimilar, S X, will be to S x, as A B to ab, but S X, is to S x, as S Z to S E ; therefore, by a fimilitude of ratios, a b will be to A B as S E is to S Z, that is, the length of the perfpective line in any picture is to the length of its original line, as the diftance of the eye from the picture or per-fpective table to the diftance of the eye from the plane of the original object.

T H E O R E M III.

The perfpective of any line, that is perpendicular to the ground Line in the ori-ginal plane, will, when drawn on the perfpective table, run up into the point of fight.

Let S, fee *Figure* the 6th, be the place of the eye, M N O P the perfpective table, M N the horizontal line, E the vifual point, O P the ground Line, and P R the given right line cutting the ground Line O P at right angles in the point of incidence, P, I fay, if from P, the point of incidence, to E, the vifual point, the line E P be drawn in the picture, the perfpective of every point R in the given line P R will be found fomewhere in the line E P, in the picture.

Produce the lines S E and R P to G and Q, and draw the line S Q.

Becaufe S G and Q R are parallel, and the line E P interfects them both in the points E and P, they will all be in the fame plane S Q R G by the 4th axiom ; and becaufe the point of fight S, and the point R will be always found in this plane, the perfpective of the point R will always be found in the common inter-fection of this plane S Q R G, and the plane of the perfpective table M N O P that is in the line E P, and confequently in the point r, where the ray S R drawn from the eye at S to the given point R in the line P R interfects the line E P drawn from the point of fight E, to the point of incidence P, and confequently if the point R were placed in the point P, the point P will be the perfpective at the point R, and the farther the point R is removed from the point P, the higher will its perfpective r be in the table, and the nearer will it approach to the vifual point E, till at laft, being removed at an indefinite diftance from the point of In-cidence P, it will be projected in the vifual point E, and confequently the line E P in the picture will be the perfpective of the right line P R, drawn perpendi-cular to the ground Line O P in the original plane, and indefinitely produced; which was to be proved.

After the fame manner it may be proved that any other right line, as O D, indefinitely produced, that cuts the ground Line at right angles, will be reprefent-ed in the perfpective table by the line E O, drawn from the point of fight E in the table to O, the point of incidence or point where the line O D cuts the ground Line.

Whence it follows, that all ftraight lines in the original plane, that cut the ground Line at right angles, will, when drawn upon the perfpective table, meet or interfect each other in the point of fight.

T H E O R E M

T H E O R E M `IV.

The perfpective of any line in the original plane, that cuts the ground Line at oblique or unequal angles, will be found in that right line that is drawn from the point of incidence P, *to the point A in the horizontal line of the table, which is found by drawing a line, as* S A, *from the eye at* S, *parallel to the original line* P R, *till it interfect the horizontal line of the table* M N. See *Fig.* 7.

Becaufe the lines S A and P R are parallel by hypothefis, and A P interfects them in the points A and P, they will all be found in the fame plane S A P R by the 4th axiom, and confequently the perfpective of the point R will be found in the table in the point r, where the ray S R fhall interfect the line A P, the common in-terfection of the plane S A P R, and the perfpective table M N O P, and if the line P R be indefinitely produced from the point of incidence P, that is, if the point R be removed at an indefinite diftance from the point P, its perfpective will be in the point of the table at A, that is, the line A P will be the perfpective ap-pearance upon the table of the line P R produced indefinitely.

After the fame manner it may be proved, that any other ftraight line, as O D, indefinitely produced will be projected on the perfpective table into the right line A O, drawn from the point of incidence O to the point found A, whence it follows, that all ftraight lines that fall ohliquely on the ground Line, yet if they be parallel amongft themfelves, they will all unite or interfect each other in fome point in the horizontal line, and that point is called the *accidental* point ; and to find it,

From the eye point S, draw a line parallel to the original line upon the hori-zontal table, and where this line cuts the horizontal line it will give the accidental point.

Hence it follows, that if the eye be placed any where in the line A S, produced from A towards S, as far as you pleafe, the fame converging lines on the table will be the perfpectives of the fame parallels in the ground Plane, and hence innumerable points of fight may be affigned for viewing the fame picture, and hence we have a folution of that perfpective paradox, That the fame reprefenta-tion of any original object will be projected on the table in the fame lines, though the eye fhould change its place and diftance.

This propofition is of very great ufe, and therefore ought to be thoroughly un-derftood, it being the main and principal foundation of all the practice in per-fpective and indeed the preceding or third *theorem* is nothing but a particular cafe of this general propofition.   Though I have given it a place by itfelf for order's fake, fince when the lines on the original plane fall at right angles upon the ground Line, the point of concourfe of thefe rays will be found by drawing a line from the eye perpendicular to the picture, and this will neceffarily give the point of fight to which all the lines, that fall perpendicularly upon the ground Line on the original plane muft neceffarily tend ; as has been proved in the third *theorem.*

And

And inafmuch as the line drawn from the eye to the point of diftance upon the perfpective table muft neceffarily form an angle of 45 degrees, with the principal ray or the horizontal line, the containing fides of the right angle being equal, it follows that the diagonals of all fquares, one of whofe fides is parallel to the picture, and all other lines that form an angle of 45 degrees with the ground Line, will have the point of diftance upon the table for their point of concourfe; and where, if produced upon the table, they will all center.

T H E O R E M V.

The projection or perfpective of any line, that is perpendicular to the horizontal or ground Plane, will on the picture or perfpective table be perpendicular to the ground Line.

Let N M O P, in *Fig.* 8. reprefent the perfpective table, C D K Q the horizontal or ground Plane, S the place of the eye, and A B the line to be projected, which in the prefent cafe is fuppofed to be perpendicular to the horizontal plane C D K Q: imagine the plane R T Z X to pafs through the line A B, and to be parallel to the picture M N O P; now becaufe S B A is another plane interfecting the two former planes, their common fections, or the lines A B, a b, will be parallel to each other by the 5th axiom, but A B is perpendicular to the horizontal line X Z, therefore a b, if produced to G, will be perpendicular to the ground Line O P, which is parallel to the line X Z, the ground Line of the plane R T Z X. w. w. d.

And fince the fame confequence will follow if the line A B be fet upon any other point in the horizontal table, it follows that the perfpective reprefentation of all lines, that on the ground Plane are erected perpendicularly, will when projected on the perfpective table be perpendicular to the ground Line and parallel to each other. And inafmuch as the line a b is to the line A B, as S b is to S B, that is, as S E is to S L, it follows that a b, the perfpective of A B, is to its original A B, as S E, the diftance of the eye from the perfpective table, to S L, the diftance of the eye from the plane of the original object.

Again, through the point a in the picture, the perfpective of the point A in the ground Plane, draw x z parallel to the ground Line O P, to cut the rays S X, S Z, in the points x and z, then will x z in the picture be the perfpective of the line X Z on the ground Plane, and becaufe, by the fimilitude of the triangles s a x and S A X, it will be as A X is to a x, fo is S A to s a, and fo is S E to S L, and fo is a E, to a S, and fo is a b to A B; whence it follows that x a is to X A, as a b is to A B, that is, any perpendicular on the ground Plane is to its perfpective in the picture, as any parallel on the ground Plane is to its perfpective in the fame picture, fuppofing the Perpendicular and Parallel at the fame diftance from the picture; whence it follows, that if the Perpendicular and the Parallel are both of the fame length, their perfpectives in the picture will be of the fame length alfo. And this is a property of no fmall ufe in the practice of perfpective; for the
D length

length of any original parallel or perpendicular being known, it will be eafy by the help of a fector to give any part of a fcenographic projection its due dimenfions in any fituation upon the table.

Again, if from any point S, in the line S F, confidered as the place of the eye, rays, as S p B, S q A be drawn to the extremities of the perpendicular A B, becaufe A B is to p q, as S B is to S p, that is, as S B is to S b, that is, as A B is to a b, it follows that p q, and a b are equal: wherefore the diftance of the object and the eye from the table, continuing the fame, the perfpectives of the fame perpendiculars, are equal to each other, whether the eye be placed at a greater or lefs height above the horizon.

P R O B L E M I.

To find the feat in the perfpective table of any given point in the original or ground Plane, the height of the eye, its diftance from the picture, and the diftance of the original point from the table, being given.

Let N M O P, See *Fig.* 9. reprefent the table, S, the place of the eye, S F its height above the ground Plane C D K R, S E its diftance from the picture, Q the original point in the horizontal plane C D K R, and A Q its diftance from the perfpective table.

From S, draw the line S E, parallel to the horizon or perpendicular to the table, to cut the table in the point E, the vifual point in the table, and from Q, draw the line Q A perpendicular to the picture M N O P, to cut the ground Line in the point A, the point of incidence. Now if a plane as T S F Q. be imagined to pafs through the lines, S T, F Q. it will cut the perfpective table in the line E A, their common interfection; and in this line of the table will the perfpective of the point Q be found, and confequently in the point q, the interfection of the diagonal S Q drawn from S, the point of fight, to Q, the given point on the ground Plane. Let us now imagine the plane of the perfpective table to revolve about the line E A, the common interfection of the two planes till it coincide with the plane S T Q F, as in *Fig.* 10. then will the point Q in the horizontal table coincide with the point Q in the ground Line, the point S or feat of the eye, in the plane S F Q T, will coincide with the point S in the horizontal line of the perfpective table, and at the fame diftance from the vifual point E as it was from the perfpective table: In *Fig.* 9. in the like manner, the diftance of the point Q. in the ground Line O P, will be as far diftant from its point of incidence A, as it was in the horizontal plane from the fame point A, for by this revolution of the plane of the perfpective table, the points S and Q revolve about the centers E and A, and confequently always keep the fame diftance from them, but the line E A, the common interfection of the two planes M N O P, and S T Q F becoming now the axis about which the plane of the table revolves, remains the fame immoveable, and confequently the feat of the point Q in the perfpective table, remains in the fame place as at firft before the plane was fuppofed to revolve, and is therefore the true perfpective place upon the table; which being allowed, we fhall have this general rule

For finding the feat in the perfpective table of any point in the horizontal table; (See *Fig.* 10.) Namely,

1. From Q, the given point in the horizontal table, draw the line Q A perpendicular to the ground Line, to cut in the point of incidence A.

2. Set off the diftance A Q, of the point Q, in the horizontal Plane, from the ground Line O P, from its point of incidence A in the fame ground Line, to Q.

3. From E, the point of fight, to A, the point of incidence, draw the ray E A, and from S, the point of diftance, to the point Q in the ground Line laft found, draw the diagonal S Q, and where this interfects the ray E A, laft drawn, as in the point q, it will give the perfpective in the table, of the given point Q in the ground Plane.

Now as every line is bounded by points, and every furface by lines, and every folid by furfaces; hence we are taught how to draw the reprefentation of any given object upon the perfpective table. And indeed the laws here laid down and demonftrated are fo general, that whofoever underftands them readily will fee the reafon of every ftep taken in drawing the fcenographic reprefentation of any original object upon any vertical perfpective table.

THEOREM VI.

If the perfpective table be inclined to the plane of the horizon at any given angle, the perfpective of any original line, that is parallel to the ground Line, will in the perfpective table be parallel to the ground Line alfo.

Let M N O P, in *Fig.* 11. reprefent the perfpective table, inclined to the horizontal plane C A B Q, at an angle equal to M O A; let S, be the place of the eye, and A B a line parallel to the ground Line P O, whofe perfpective is to be drawn; from S, the eye, let the vifual rays S A, S B, be drawn to the extremities A and B of the given line A B, to cut the perfpective table in the points a and b; now if thefe points a and b are connected together by a right line a b, I fay, this right line a b, which is the perfpective of the original line A B, will be parallel to the ground Line O P.

Imagine a plane as R A B T to pafs through the given line A B, and to be parallel to the plane of the table M N O P.

Now becaufe the lines a b, and A B, are the common interfections of the parallel planes M N O P, and R A B T, by the vifual plane S A B, they will be parallel to each other by the 5th axiom; but the original line A B is parallel to the ground Line O P, by hypothefis, therefore a b, its perfpective in the table, will be parallel to the fame ground Line O P alfo, by the 6th axiom. w. w. d.

Hence it follows that all lines whatfoever that upon the ground Plane are parallel to the ground Line, their perfpectives upon the picture will be parallel to the ground Line and to each other alfo.

D 2 *THE-*

T H E O R E M VII.

In any inclined plane, the perfpective of any line in the original plane, that, being produced, will cut the ground Line at oblique angles, will be found in the right line that is drawn from the point of incidence P, *See Fig.* 12. *to the point* A, *in the horizontal line of the table, which is found by drawing a line as* S A, *from the feat of the eye at* S, *parallel to the original line* P R, *till it interfect the horizontal line of the table* M N.

Becaufe the lines S A, and P R, are parallel by hypothefis, and A P a right line interfecting them both, therefore a plane as S P R A will pafs through them all, and therefore the perfpective of the point R, will be found in the table in the point r, the interfection of the diagonal S R, with the line A P, the common interfection of the plane of the table M N O P, and the plane A S P R; confequently, wherefoever the point R be taken, in the right line P R, its perfpective will be found fomewhere in the line A P, and confequently the line A P, in the table, will be the perfpective of the line P R indefinitely produced; fo that in whatfoever part of the horizontal plane the line P R be taken, provided it always forms the fame angle with the ground Line, its perfpective upon the table will be always found in that right line which connects its point of incidence P on the ground Line, with its accidental point A, in the horizontal line.

If the line P R cuts the ground Line at right angles, its parallel S A will interfect the table in the point of fight E upon the table; wherefore in inclined planes, as well as vertical planes, as all lines that are perpendicular to the ground Line in the horizontal plane, when drawn on the perfpective table, do run up and unite in the point of fight, fo all other lines in the ground Plane that cut the ground Line when produced at unequal angles, will if they are parallel to each other, when projected on the perfpective table run up and unite in one common point; whence it follows, that the height of the eye and its diftance from the inclined plane being known or given, the perfpective reprefentation of any original ground Plane is drawn on the inclined table by the fame method, and after the fame manner as it is done upon vertical tables.   Let it therefore be required in

P R O B L E M II.

To find the length of the principal ray intercepted between the point of fight, and the ground Line; or which is the fame thing, the height of the eye in the inclined table, and its diftance from the table, the perpendicular height of the eye above the horizon, and the inclination of the perfpective table, being given.

Let O P, fee *Fig.* 13. reprefent the ground Line, F Q C a line drawn at right angles to it, S the feat of the eye, S F its perpendicular height above the ground Plane, and Q E the inclined plane forming an angle with the horizontal plane equal to the angle E Q C.

From

From Q, the point of incidence of the line E Q, in the ground Line, draw A Q perpendicular to the ground Line, and through S, the feat of the eye, draw S A E, parallel to the line F C, to interfect the line Q E in E ; then will E be the point of fight in the inclined plane, Q E the height of the eye, and S E the fpace between the vifual point E and the point of diftance S, whence the perfpective of any ground plot may be drawn on that plane.

THEOREM VIII.

In any inclined plane, as M N O P, *fee Fig.* 14. *if from* E, *the point of fight, through the point* b, *where the bafe* F B, *of the eye's perpendicular height* S F, *cuts the ground Line of the table, a line as* E b, *be drawn, and produced till it cut* S F, *the line drawn from the eye at* S, *perpendicular to the horizontal plane* C Q O P, *produced downwards in the point* D, *I fay, the perfpective of every line perpendicular to the horizontal plane, will be found in that right line in the table that is drawn from the point* D *through the point of incidence made by a perpendicular drawn from the bafe of the elevated line on the horizontal plane to the ground Line of the inclined table.*

Let M N O P be the inclined perfpective table, O P its ground Line where it interfects the ground Plane C R T Q, S the feat of the eye, S F its perpendicular height, E the point of fight in the table, A B a line perpendicular to the ground Plane, whofe point of incidence b, is coincident with the foot b of the principal ray E b drawn on the table ; now if the lines S F and E b are produced till they interfect each other in the point D, I fay, that if from this point D, through any other point of incidence, as x, in the ground Line, a right line as D x z be drawn, the perfpective of the line Z X erected perpendicularly over the horizontal plane, whofe point of incidence in the ground Line is x, fhall be found in this line z x in the table.

Becaufe the lines S F D and A B W are parallel by hypothefis, a plane as S A B W D F will pafs through them, and becaufe the eye is feated in this plane in the point S, the perfpective of the line A B will be found upon the table in the line E D, the common interfection of the two planes, which line produced muft neceffarily cut the perpendicular S F, produced downwards in the point D, fince they all lie in the fame plane S Y W D.

Now if from this point D, a line as D x be drawn through x, the point of incidence of the line Z X, erected perpendicular over the horizontal plane C R T Q, I fay, the perfpective of this line Z X will be found in the line D z x.

For becaufe the lines S D and Z X are parallel by hypothefis, a plane as S Z X D will pafs through them both ; and becaufe the eye is feated in this plane at S, the perfpective of the line Z X will be found on the table in the line x z, the common interfection of the two planes, which being produced muft neceffarily cut the line S D in the point D, the interfection of the fame line S D with the plane of the inclined table produced, whence the perfpectives of the lines A B and Z X on the table, will be the lines a w, and z q, intercepted between the rays S A, S B, S X, and S Z flowing from the eye to the top and bottom of the given perpendiculars A B, and Z X.

9 And

And af.er the fame manner may the perfpective of any other line elevated perpendicularly over the horizontal plane be drawn on the table.

For if we imagine a plane to pafs through the line S D, perpendicular to the horizontal plane indefinitely extended, and at the fame time conceive this plane to
revolve about the line S D as an axis, it will during the courfe of this revolution
pafs through every line that ftands perpendicular to the horizontal plane, and the
fucceffive interfections of this plane with the plane of the table will be the fucceffive perfpectives of the feveral perpendiculars it fhall happen to pafs through ;
and as all thefe lines muft neceffarily center in the immoveable point D, as being
common to every fituation of the revolving plane, it muft neceffarily follow, the
eye remaining alfo immoveable, that the perfpective of every line that is perpendicular to the ground Plane, will be found in that line in the table which is produced by drawing a line from this point D, through the point of incidence in the
ground Line, made by a perpendicular drawn from the bafe of the given elevated line to the ground Line of the inclined table ; which was to be demonftrated.

Hence and from the rules demonftrated in *theorem* 6 and 7. the practice of
drawing the perfpective of objects of any kind upon inclined tables is eafily ·
deduced.

By viewing the figure, it is evident that the greater the inclination of the plane,
the leffer will be the angle S D E, and the farther will the point D be removed
from the horizontal plane C R T Q, till at laft when the plane becomes vertical
the point of interfection D vanifhes, and the lines E b D and S F D become parallel, whence, as has been proved in the 5th *theorem,* it follows that all lines that
are perpendicular to the horizontal plane will, when projected on the table, be perpendicular to the ground Line alfo.

Again, the farther the point of fight S, is removed from the table, the greater
will be the diftance of the point of interfection D from the horizontal plane
C R T Q, till at laft the eye being fuppofed at an infinite diftance, the line S F D
will be removed at an infinite diftance from the picture, alfo the point of interfection D will vanifh, and the elevation of all lines perpendicular to the horizontal
plane will become perpendiculars to the ground plane of the table, which is
the foundation upon which the *Military* or *Bird's perfpective* is founded.

Again, the leffer the inclination of the table M N O P, the nearer does the
point of interfection D approach to the point F in the horizontal table, the foot
of the eye's perpendicular, till at laft when the inclined plane M N O P, coincides
with the horizontal table C R T Q, the angle of incidence vanifhes, and the
point of concourfe D coincides with the point F ; whence it follows,

That in all horizontal or optical projections, the perfpective of every line that
is erected perpendicularly over the horizontal table, will be found in that line of
the table which is produced by drawing a line from the foot of the eye perpendicular through the bafe of the elevated line ; whence it follows, that the perfpective of all lines that ftand perpend cular upon the horizontal plane, will, if produced, unite or center in one common point, namely the point where a line let
fall perpendicularly fhall interfect the horizontal table.

7   T H E O R E M

T H E O R E M IX.

If the plane of any original figure be parallel to the table, its perspective will be similar to its original, alike, and alike situated.

Let S, see *Fig.* 15. be the seat of the eye, M N O P the table, H I K L the plane of the original figure A B C D.

I say, if the planes M N O P and H I K L are parallel, the perspective appearance a b c d upon the table shall be similar to its original A B C D.

For from S, the point of sight, draw the rays S a A, S b B, S c C, and S d D.

Because the planes M N O P, and H I K L, are parallel, S A B is a visual plane intersecting them, therefore the common intersections a b, and A B will be parallel, therefore A B will be to a b as S B is to S b: And again, because S B C is a visual plane intersecting the same parallel planes, therefore their common intersections, namely the lines B C and b c will be parallel, therefore B C will be to b c, as the same ray S B is to the ray S b, wherefore by equality of ratios a b will be to b c as A B is to B C; after the same manner it may be proved that b c is to c d, as B C is to C D, and c d is to d a, as C D is to D A, whence the perspective figure a b c d is similar to its original A B C D; which was to be proved: Whence it follows, that the optical or horizontal perspective of all plane figures that are parallel to the table, will be similar to their originals; that is, that the perspective of square figures parallel to the horizontal or perspective table, w'll on the table be square, also the perspectives of circles will be circles, of hexagons will be hexagons, &c.

Whence and from the last corollary of the preceding *theorem*, the reasons of all the appearances in horizontal perspective are manifest, and as all shadows are nothing else but horizontal projections of the several objects, the candle or luminous body supplying the place of the eye; hence it follows that every horizontal projection of any object elevated above the plane, is the projection of the shadow of the same object, and consequently the rules given for forming of one will serve for forming the other. And inasmuch as the immense distance of the sun is infinite with regard to any terrestrial object, hence it is that the rays that flow from the sun to form the solar shadow are supposed to be parallel; and hence it is that every orthographic perspective of any object elevated above the plane of the horizon, is the projection of the shadow of the same body, and consequently in drawing of one, you draw the other also ; and these several shadows, when drawn upon the scenographic table according to the rules of scenographic projection, will exhibit upon the same table the shadows of all objects drawn upon the picture.

Again, inasmuch as the practice of horizontal perspective proceeds after the same manner as does the practice of scenographic projections, so in *problem* the first, p ge the 10th,

If we suppose the eye in *figure* 10th in S, the point of distance in that case, and F Q to be the distance of the eye from the given object, the demonstration for one will hold good for the other, and consequently, in proving the operation in one, you prove the operation in the other also.

Though

Though my principal view in this tract has been to render the demonſtrations plain and conciſe, and the number of *Theorems* as few as poſſible, yet at the ſame time I have endeavoured to make them ſo general, that I may venture to ſay there is ſcarce any operation made uſe of in the practice of the ſeveral kinds of *Perſpective*, but what may be accounted for by ſome one or other of the preceding laws : This, together with the following treatiſe, which I look upon as one of the beſt practical books of its ſize that has appeared in the *Engliſh* language, will, I hope, make the whole as compleat and uſeful a piece as can be compriſed in ſuch a volume as this is.

PRACTICAL PERSPECTIVE.

PART I.

SHEWING THE

DEFINITIONS

AND

PRINCIPLES.

OF

PERSPECTIVE.

E

Definitions, Names, *and* Terms *of the* Points, Lines *and* Figures *ufed in the following Work.*

A Poi n t is that which is conceived to have no parts ; fuch as A, *Fig.* 1. There are three kinds of points ufed in perfpective, called *points of fight* or *view, points of diftance,* and *contingent* or *accidental points.*

A L i n e is a length without breadth ; fuch is A B, *Fig.* 2. There are five principal lines ufed in perfpective, namely, 1. The *line of the bafe,* called alfo the *line of the plane,* or the *terreftrial line,* as C D, *Fig.* 3. 2d. The *perpendicular* or *plumb line,* which, falling on another, makes the angles * on either fide equal : fuch angles are faid to be *right* ones, and the line fo falling on the other called a *perpendicular* thereto. Thus, in *Fig.* 3. A B and E F, falling on C D, and making right angles in B and G, is a perpendicular thereto. 3. The *parallel lines,* which, being continued on the fame plane to infinity, never meet; as the lines N and O, *Fig.* 6. The *horizontal line* is no more than a line drawn parallel to the *terreftrial lines* ; as fhall be fhown in its place. 4. The *diagonal line,* which is that drawn acrofs a figure, from one angle to another ; fuch is K L, *Fig.* 10. 5. The *occult line,* which is either drawn in dots, or dry, and is fuppofed not to appear when the work is finifhed ; fuch is O N, *Fig.* 2.

A r i g h t A n g l e we have already faid to be that formed by a perpendicular. It is here reprefented apart, by E F G, *Fig.* 4. to fhew what it is the more diftinctly. There are two other kinds of angles, which comprife all thofe that are not right ones : the firft, called *obtufe,* are fuch as are greater than a right angle : as H L M, *Fig.* 5. The other, *acute,* are lefs than a right angle ; fuch is H I K in the fame figure.

A T e r m is the extremity or bounds of any thing : thus the points A and B, *Fig.* 2. are the *terms* of the line A B.

A F i g u r e is comprehended under one or more terms; thus 7, 8, 9, 13, &*c.* are *figures.*

A S q u a r e has its four fides equal, and its four angles right ; fuch is A B C D *Fig.* 7.

A P a r a l l e l o g r a m, or long fquare, has its four angles right, but not its fides equal ; fuch is C D E F, *Fig.* 8.

An E q u i l a t e r a l T r i a n g l e confifts of three equal fides ; as G H I, *Fig.* 9.

The S e c t i o n or I n t e r s e c t i o n of two lines is when they run acrofs, or cut each other in a point, as in *Fig.* 11. where A B and C D cut or *interfect* in E.

A C u r v e L i n e is that which goes indirectly, or about, from one point to another; fuch is L M, *Fig.* 12.

A C i r c l e is a plain figure, comprehended under one fingle line, called the *circumference,* to which all lines drawn from the center are equal; fuch is B C D, in *Fig.* 13. And the point A in the middle thereof is called the *center.*

The D i a m e t e r of a circle is a right line B C, paffing through the center A, and dividing the circle into two equal parts.

A R a d i u s is any right line drawn from the center of a circle to its circumference, as the line A D.

An A r c h is any part of the circumference, as B D C.

The C h o r d of an arch is a right line drawn from one end of an arch to the other; as B C is the chord of the arch B D C, and B D is the chord of the arch B D.

Every A r c h of a circle is meafured by its chord; thus B D is the meafure of the arch B D, and B C, the greateft of all chords, meafures the arch B D C.

An O v a l, or E l l i p s i s, is an oblong figure, comprehended under one crooked, regular, but not circular, line ; fuch is E, *Fig.* 14.

A s p i r a l, or V o l u t e, is a line found by a revolution about one or two centers ; fuch is F, *Fig.* 15.

---

* An angle, the aperture or inclination of two right lines meeting in the fame plane, is u'ually ex-preffed by three letters; the middle letter fhews the angle, and the other two the lines that make the angle; as in *Fig.* 5. H L M is the obtufe angle L, and H L K, is the acute angle L.

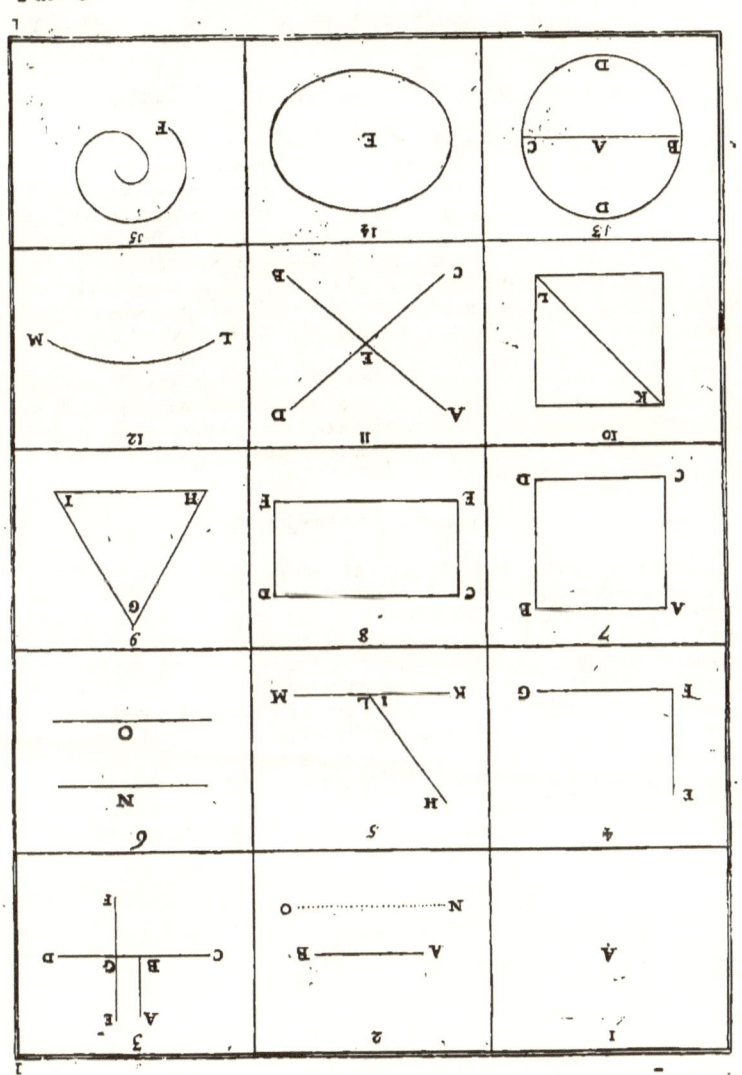

SEQUEL *of the* Definitions, Names, *and* Terms.

A TANGENT is a line, which being produced only touches or razes an object, figure, or line, without cutting it: thus the lines A B are *tangents* to the circle C, in the points D D. I here add two kinds of lines, which have the fame denominations as the former, and yet have different effects, on account of the point of view: for the angle E A B is to be efteemed a right angle, and all the lines C C C, &c. to be efteemed as perpendiculars to the plane, as D F is; and the lines A B, G I, and H K, as perpendiculars to the the terreftrial line. All the lines drawn to the point of fight, whether from above or below, or from either fide, are called RAYS, or VISUAL RAYS.

A PLAN, ICHNOGRAPHY, or GROUND-PLAT, is a firft draught or defign of a work, reprefenting the traces or paths of its foundation on the ground, fo as to exhibit the extent, divifion, and diftribution of its various parts, in their feveral magnitudes and proportions, refpectively, at one view. This is what I have reprefented in L and M.

A POLYGON is a figure containing feveral angles; as L.

A DEGREE is a fmall arch or portion of a circle. Every circle is fuppofed to contain 360 degrees, and an arch is eftimated by the number of thofe degrees it takes up. Thus N O is an arch of 90 degrees. Aftronomers fubdivide each degree into 60 minutes, and each minute into 60 feconds, &c. But fuch fubdivifion has no place here. It is enough we know that degrees are thofe little divifions in the circle N O P Q, whereby all angles are meafured. To know their quantity, an arch is defcribed, having its center in the point of the angle. From them we derive an eafy method of making all forts of polygons, namely, by dividing 360 by the number of angles the figures are to confift of. Thus, for inftance, if I would make a fquare, divide 360 by 4, the quotient is 90, which gives the right angle N M O: and fo for the reft. Such as are unacquainted with arithmetic, will find geometrical methods of doing the fame in *plate* IV.

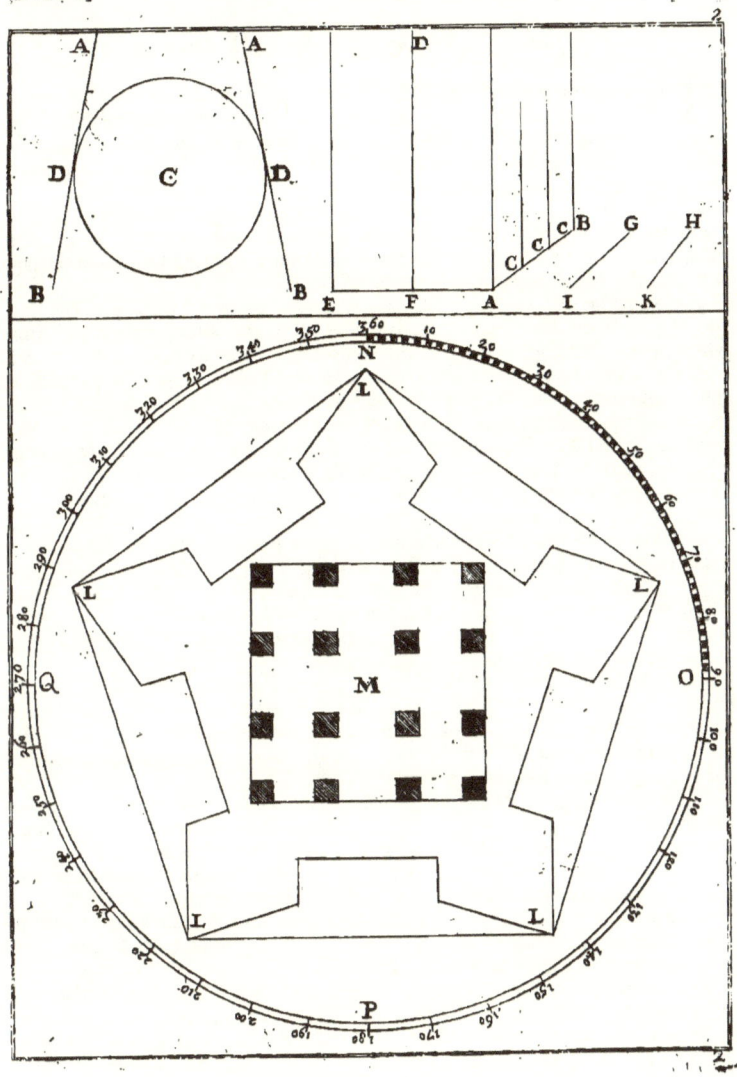

Methods of describing the Lines *and* Figures.

1. **T**O *raise perpendiculars:* If it be in the middle of a line that a perpendicular is required, open the compasses to more than half the length of the
line, and setting one foot in the point A, *Fig.* 1. with the other strike little
arches both above and below, as F and F : Do the like at the point E, and the
two intersections of those arches will give a perpendicular to the line A E.

2. *If the line be at the top or bottom of a draught or paper,* so that arches cannot be struck both above and underneath, divide the line into two, to get the
point G, *Fig.* 2. and from the two extremes of the line, make arches intersecting
each other in H ; then draw a line from H to G.

3. *To raise a perpendicular at the end of a line,* as at the point I of the line
I K, *Fig.* 3. there are divers methods : The first is that already delivered. But
where room is wanting, one leg of the compasses is to be set in the point I, and
with the other a large portion of a circle L M is to be struck, and the compasses,
thus open, to be set on the point M, and with the other leg the circle to be cut
in the point N, half the arch M N being set off from M towards O, gives the
right angle O I K. Or, without seeking for half the arch M N, from the
point N, describe an arch P Q; then, laying a ruler over the points M and N,
draw a line, cutting the arch P Q in the point P, and raise a line from I to P;
which is the perpendicular required.

4. *Or thus:* If you would raise a perpendicular from the point P, *Fig.* 4. take
a point at pleasure over the line P S, as the point Q, and from this point describe a circle passing through the point P, and cutting the line P S in some
place, as S ; then from S draw a line through Q to the circumference of the circle
T, and the point T gives the extreme of the perpendicular T P. A just square
shortens all these operations.

5. *To let fall a perpendicular* from a given point : From the point, as A, *Fig.* 5.
describe the arch B C, cutting the given line E F in the points G H, from which
points describe two little arches above or below, cutting each other in the point I;
then, from the point A let fall a line through I to the line E F, and it will be
the perpendicular of the given point.

6. *From a point given at the end of a line, to let fall a perpendicular:* Suppose the
given point K, and the line L M, *Fig.* 6. from K draw a traverse line at pleasure,
cutting the line L M in some point, as N; divide the line K N into two equal
parts, and from the middle point O, draw an arch through K; and from the
point P, where the arch intersects the line L M, draw the perpendicular K P.

7. *A parallel line,* if truly drawn, will be a tangent to semi-circles drawn from
points assumed in the other line : thus F G, *Fig.* 7. is parallel to H I, because it
only touches or razes the semi-circles L and K.

8. *To divide a line into equal parts:* Suppose the line be A B, draw another parallel thereto, either above or below it, as C D ; and on this last, which is either
to be greater or less than that to be divided, set off as many parts as A B is to be
divided into, for example, into seven ; from the first and last of these divisions
draw lines through the extremes of A B, intersecting each other in some point, as E;
from which point drawing lines to all the divisions of the line C D, the line A B
will be divided into seven equal parts.   4

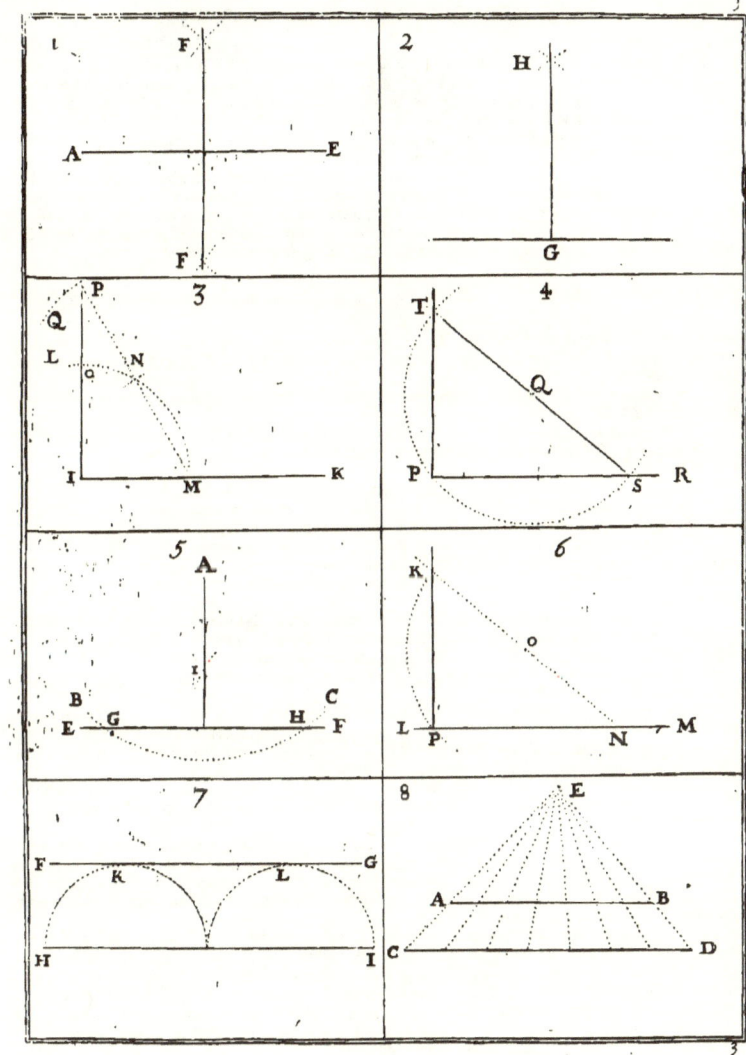

METHODS of Describing the Figures.

1. A Line as A B, Fig. 1. being given to form a square on, set one foot of the compasses in the point A, and extending the other the length A B, describe the arch B C ; then from the point B describe another arch A D, interfecting the former in E, and from E set off half the arch E A, or E B outwardly, to D and C ; to which points drawing lines from A, B, &c. the square is formed.

Or thus : upon the given line A B erect a perpendicular A C equal to A B; then, taking the length A B in your compasses, set one foot in B, and with the other describe an arch : the like being done from the point C, the intersection of the two arches will be the point D, which gives the square A B C D.

2. To describe a parallelogram, or long square, on the term E, of the given line E F. Erect a perpendicular either greater or less than the same, as E G ; then taking E G in your compasses, set one foot in F, and with the other describe an arch ; take also E F in your compasses, and setting one foot in G, describe a second arch, cutting the former in H : this will give you the parallelogram required.

Of Circular Polygons, which are Figures of several angles inscribed in circles.

3. To describe an equilateral triangle : The compasses being open to the radius of the circle, set one foot in the point A, describe the arch D E, and draw a right line D E, which will be the side of the triangle D E F.

4. For a square, draw two diameters at right angles, and join their extremes ; thus you will have the square A B C D.

5. For a pentagon, or five-angle, draw two diameters, and take D G, half the semi-diameter D I, and from the point G, with the interval G A, describe the arch A H ; the chord of which is the side of the pentagon.

6. For the Hexagon, or Six-Angle, the semi-diameter is the side of the hexagon.

7. For the Heptagon, or Sept-Angle, take half a side of the equilateral triangle.

8. For the Octagon, or Eight-Angle, take half a quadrant of the circle.

9. For the Enneagon, or Nine-Angle, take two thirds of the semi-diameter for the side ; as E B.1

10. For the Decagon, or Ten-Angle, divide the semidiameter into two in the point G, and from G, with the interval G A, describe an arch A B; the part of the diameter B C will be the side of the decagon.

11. For the Undecagon, or Eleven-Angle, draw two diameters at right angles, and from the point A, with the interval of a semi-diameter, describe an arch B C ; then from the point of intersection C, draw a line to E ; the portion C D will be the side of the undecagon.

12. Dodecagon, or Twelve-Angle, divide the arch of a hexagon, A B, into two equal parts; the chord of the moiety will be the side.

13. An Oval is formed divers ways; in all which the figure is either a compound of several portions of circles, or it is one line drawn from two centers. The most usual methods are these : having described a circle, and drawn two diameters therein, as A B C D, from the points A B we draw two other circles equal with the first ; then from the point D we draw a line through the center of the last circle to the circumference E : this done, setting one foot of the compasses in D, and with the other taking the interval E, we describe an arch E F. The like being done on the other side, the oval is formed.

14. For a rounder Oval, draw a single line, and from A, as a center, describe a circle, the intersection whereof with the right line in the point B, will be the center of another circle. Now, to form the oval, take in your compasses the whole diameter of one of the circles, as from A to F, and in one of the intersections of the circles, as D, setting one foot of the compasses, with the other draw the arch G H : the like do from the point E.

15. Otherwise we have an easier and a more useful manner of describing ovals than any of the preceding ones ; the same rule serving for all forms, long, narrow, broad, short, &c. thus : set two nails or pins in a right line A B, to serve as a center, and about these tie a thread of the length and width of the oval required, as A B C; hold the thread tight with a pen or pencil, and turn it about till you arrive where you began. If you require it a long one, set the centers the farther apart ; and observe the contrary for a short one ; for if the nails stand close together, the figure will be a circle.

16. For a Spiral, or Volute, take two points in a line A B ; the points to serve, one after another, as centers, For instance, having drawn the semi-circle A B, set one foot of the compasses in B, and open the other to the length B A, and describe a semi-circle A C; then setting one foot in A, take the interval A C, and draw the semi-circle C D; and this continuing as long as you please, still shifting centers. Vignola gives us another method.

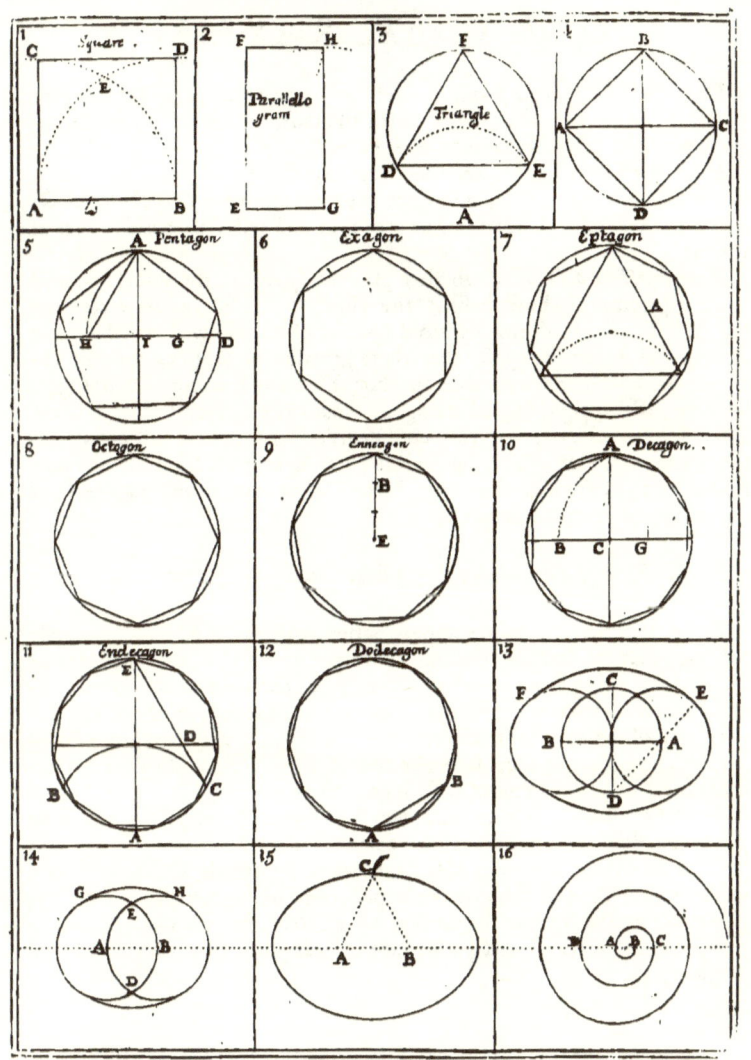

Of the VISUAL RAYS.

IF an object be a single point, it sends only one visual ray to the center of the eye; and that ray is called the axis, or central ray, as being the most vivid of all rays : such is A B.

If the object be a right line, the visual rays form a triangle, as C A D, whose base is the line C D, and sides the two extreme rays A D and A C; A B is the central ray. If the line was seen end-wise, it would appear as a point.

If the object be a surface, whether plane or spherical, the visual rays will make a pyramid, whose basis is the object C D E F, and its vertex the eye A. The rest of the pyramid consists of visual rays; of which the central A B is the strongest, the others growing weaker, as they are removed farther therefrom, though they still retain a competent strength, till they make a right angled triangle. Such as go beyond this, become so feeble, that they appear very confusedly, so that to have distinct vision, the extreme under which an object is comprehended, must, at most, subtend a right angle in the eye. If the surface was viewed edge-wise, it would appear no more than a line.

Why a Piece of Perspective *is seen better with one Eye than with two.*

Some hold that all objects appear better with one than both eyes ; alledging, that the sight is rendered more penetrating by the visual rays of the shut eye being determined to the other ; inasmuch as all powers become more vigorous when united, than when dispersed. Accordingly, say they, one of the eyes being closed, the whole visive virtue before diffused through both, is now supposed to be collected into one ; and this reinforcement must necessarily render it stronger, more piercing, &c. than both.

Be this as it will, it is certain, we see a piece of perspective with one eye better than with both. The reason is, that the central ray, in this case, is directed to the point of sight where all the radials of the piece unite and center, which is what shews a picture in its highest perfection. It is for this reason that we do not say, *the points of the eyes,* but, *the point of the eye,* as insinuating, that perspective is most pleasing when viewed by a single eye.   4

1. fig

A
A
A

C   F
B
B
C   B   D D   E

2. fig
A

G   B   P

First DEFINITION.

PERSPECTIVE is the art of reprefenting objects feen through fome tranfparent medium, which the vifual rays penetrate in paffing from the feveral points of the object to the eye. Accordingly, whatever is feen through any thing, as through air, water, clouds, glafs, and the like, may be faid to be feen in *Perfpective*. And fince we. fee nothing but through thofe mediums, it is certain all we fee is in perfpective.

The end of perfpective is to exhibit objects upon a plane, fituate between the eye and them, for example, on the plane E F G H, to reprefent the objects A B C D, in the points I K L M.

The better to conceive this, fuppofe an object A B C D on the ground, and a fpectator's eye in O, if a tranfparent body E F G H be placed between the two, the interfections of the vifual rays with the perpendiculars Q R S T, will give the figure I K L M, fuch as the object appears on that plane. Perfpective, therefore, confifts altogether in the interfections of lines: whence it is, that *Marolois* always calls any thing put in perfpective, the *appearance of the fection*; fince the plane E F G H cuts the vifual pyramid A C B D and O, and gives I K L M for its fection.

The reafon of thefe fections is, that one fingle line determines nothing; but there are two required to cut one another, to give a point. Now, as it is evident, that between our eye and an object there is always a right line, or ray, that can never be wanting : but to get the other, which is to cut it, it is neceffary we conceive, that from our foot as a center, there are a number of lines, or rays, continually flowing to the angles of the objects we fee; as from P to the angles A B C D : all which rays being cut by fome tranfparent plane, as E F G H, the rays P B, P A, P C, P D, which before were horizontal, are now erected and become perpendicular : P B, for inftance, becoming Q M, P D becoming R L, &c. For if they continued horizontal, the vifual rays would never interfect them, till they both met in the object itfelf. It is for this reafon we always fuppofe a plane, which, reflecting the rays, gives them an occafion of interfecting, and fo of finding the points to form the appearances of objects.

Second DEFINITION.

ICHNOGRAPHY is the plan of any work, on the view of it, cut off by a plane parallel to the horizon, juſt at the baſe or bottom of it. A geometrical plan, as that in page 2, exhibits the various parts in their juſt proportions, and their different magnitudes may be aſcertained by the uſe of a ſcale. A perſpeꞓtive plan, is one conduꞓted and exhibited by degra-dations and diminutions according to the rules of perſpeꞓtive; thus ABCD is the *Ichnography*, or perſpeꞓtive plan, of a ſquare body.

Third DEFINITION.

ORTHOGRAPHY is the delineation of the front or fore-ſide of an ob-jeꞓt, as an houſe or a cube, &c. Or the elevation of any objeꞓt, as a houſe or a cube, &c. direꞓtly oppoſite to the eye. Thus E F G H is the *ortho-graphy*, or fore-part, of a cube. As the *ichnography* repreſents the plan, the *orthography* repreſents the ſide oppoſite to the eye.

Fourth DEFINITION.

SCENOGRAPHY exhibits the objeꞓt quite raiſed, and perfeꞓt, in the front, top, and that ſide which is viſible from the ſituation of the ſpeꞓtator's eye. Thus I K L M N O P is a *Scenography*, or perfeꞓt cube. This is the whole objeꞓt compleat, and comprehends the plan and front as parts

The ſum of what has been defined is, the *Ichnography* of a building, &c. repreſents the plan or ground work of the building. The *Orthography*, the front or fore-right plane. And the *Scenography*, the whole building, front, ſides, height and all. Preferring the more familiar terms, for the future, I ſhall call the *Ichnography* P L A N, the *Orthography* F R O N T, and the *Scenography* ELEVATION.

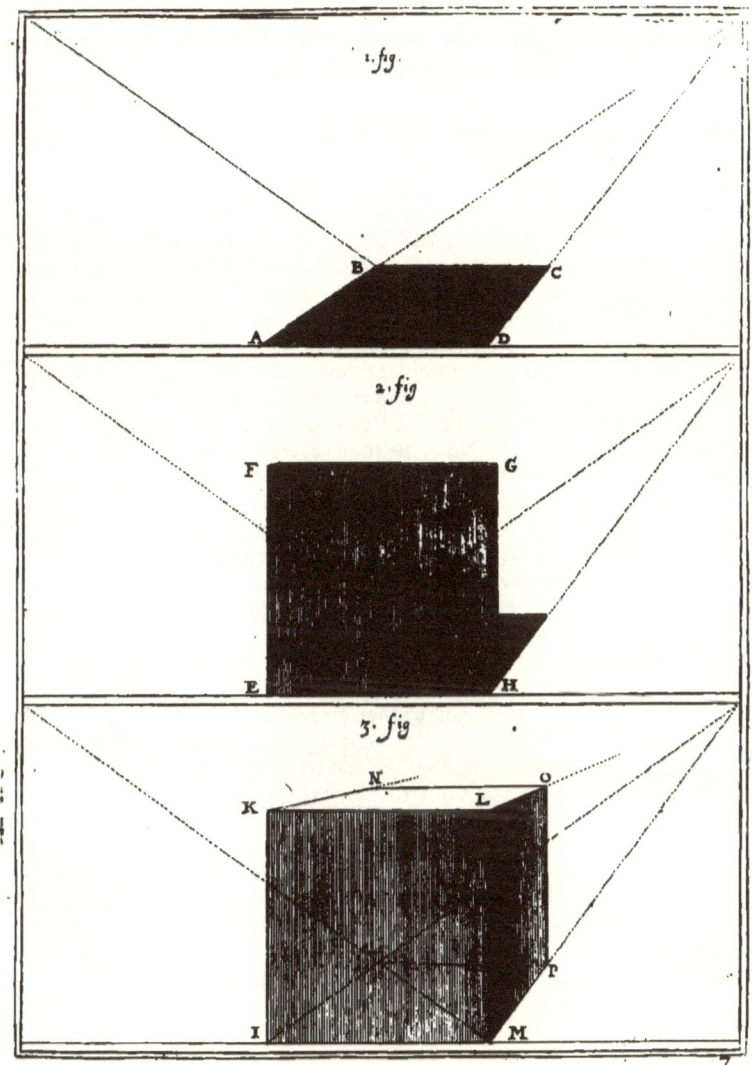

Why Objects *appear the nearer each other, as they are more remote from the Eye.*

THIS figure may help to folve a queftion of fome difficulty. Suppofe a fpectator's eye in the middle of a line at +, it is evident, that if it would fee the two extremes thereof, A and B, it muft take in a femi-circle V X, whofe center is in the eye itfelf, and whofe central ray is the line + T. By taking in this femi-circle, it will perceive the objects on eithe r fide, and in fuch manner, as that thofe fartheft off from A will appear to approach towards the center T, and thofe on the fide B feem to approach likewife.

Now it is afked, whence it is, that objects ranged on ftrait lines fo wide afunder, fhould feem to approach and join each other, and that whether the ranges are fituated fide-wife, or one over the other ?

The anfwer is in few words. All objects appear under the vifual angle they fubtend at the eye. Now, be they columns, trees, animals, or any other things placed on the fide A, K the remoteft will feem to border on the center T, by reafon they are feen under an angle, or ray, that is near thereto. The ray + K, for inftance, being much nearer the central ray T, than is the ray + C or + D, of confequence muft appear nearer to it. If the range of objects was prolonged, they would ftill approach nearer the central ray T, till fuch time as they feemed contiguous, and only to form one point therewith.

Now, in perfpective, the fides A K and B S do not continue parallel, but become vifual rays, which contract themfelves till they interfect each other in the point of fight, and by that means give the diminutions of ob-jects. Thus, for inftance, in the fecond figure, the eye being at a diftance capable of feeing the line A B ; from the two angles A, B, arife two rays, which proceed to the point of fight T ; which rays A T and B T receive the interfections the point of diftance makes with the objects, which all the while contract themfelves proportionably ; as will be fhewn in the defcription of diagonals and their fections. By fuch means the whole pa-rallelograms A K B S, and all the objects on either fide become reduced into the narrow compafs A V, B X: and if the eye were more remote, that fpace would be ftill fmaller, fince the farther an object is off, the fmaller it appears, as will be made appear in the following page.

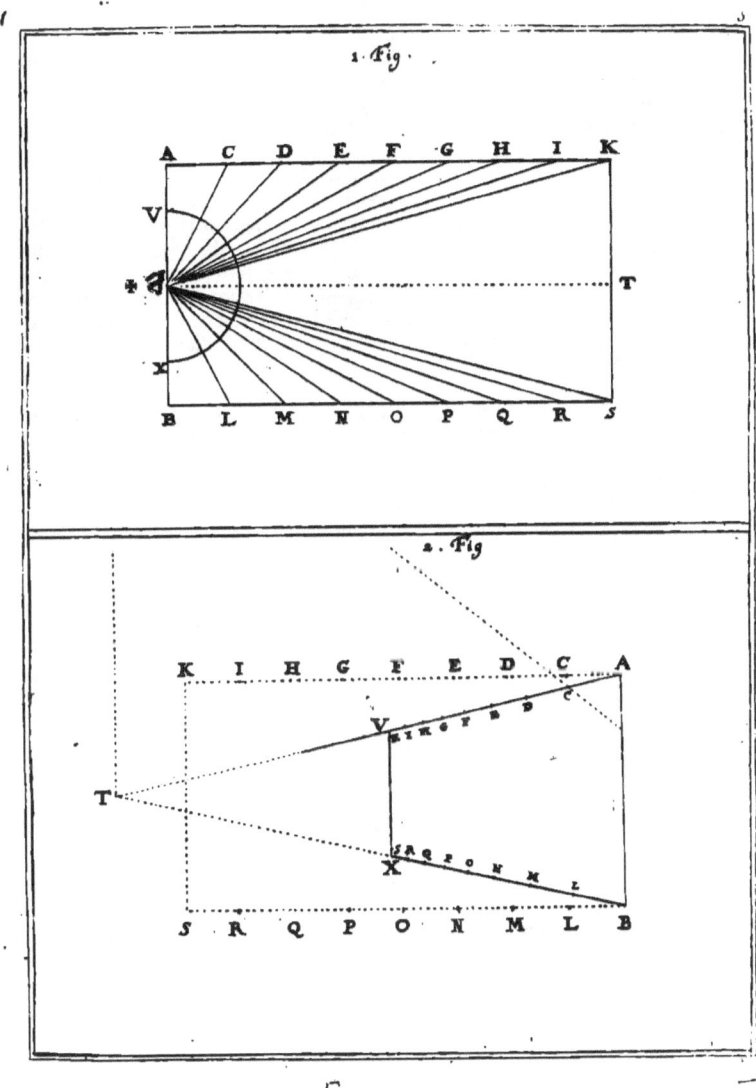

1. Fig.

2. Fig.

Why Objects *appear the smaller as they are at the greater Distance.*

I have already obferved, that objects appear large or fmall according to the angle wherein they are feen, and that this angle is taken at the eye, where two rays drawn from the two extreme points of an object meet. The eye A, for inftance, viewing the object B.C, will draw the rays A B and A C, which give the angle B A C. But an object viewed under a greater angle appearing large, and another under a lesfer angle, little ; and among equal objects, thofe at the greateft diftance appearing under the fmalleft angle, it confequently follows that in all perfpectives the remoteft objects muft be made the fmalleft. To illuftrate this by an example, if the eye be in A, the object B C, which is the neareft, will appear the biggeft, becaufe feen under the greateft angle ; and the fecond, third, fourth and fifth objects, though of equal magnitude, will all appear fmaller and fmaller, inafmuch as the angles under which they are feen, diminifh in proportion as the objects recede. If the eye were removed into M, K L would appear the largeft ; and B.C, in this latter cafe, feem no bigger than N O.

The fecond figure is a fequel of what I have advanced. For, fuppofing the apparent magnitude of objects, to be fuch as is the angle they are feen under, it follows, that if feveral lines be drawn between the fides of the fame triangle, then will all of them appear equal. Thus, all the lines comprifed between the fides O N, O P, of the triangle N O P, will appear equal to each other ; and as objects comprehended under the fame angle feem equal, fo all comprehended under a greater angle, feem greater, and all under a fmaller, fmaller.

Thus much premifed : if there be a number of columns, or pilafters, to be ranged in perfpective on each fide of a hall or church, they muft of necefsiry be all made under the fame angle, and all tend towards one common point in the horizon O, *fig.* 3d. For inftance, the eye being placed in A, viewing the firft object D E ; if from the points D, E; you draw the vifual rays D O, E O, they will make the triangle D O E, which will include the columns D E, F G, H I, K L, M N, fo as they will all appear equal in magnitude.

What has been faid of the fides, is likewife to be underftood of the cielings and pavements ; the diminutions of the angles of remote objects, placed either above or below, heirg governed by the fame rule as thofe placed laterally. I need not therefore add any thing farther; unlefs, that care be taken there be as many fquares or divifions between the remoteft objects as between the neareft : for in that cafe, though diftant objects be clofer as they are farther from us, they will appear in fome meafure to preferve their diftance; thus, in B C, D E, the interval between the four neareft columns, there are fixteen fquares, and no fewer than fixteen between the four remoteft K L, M N, *fig.* 4.

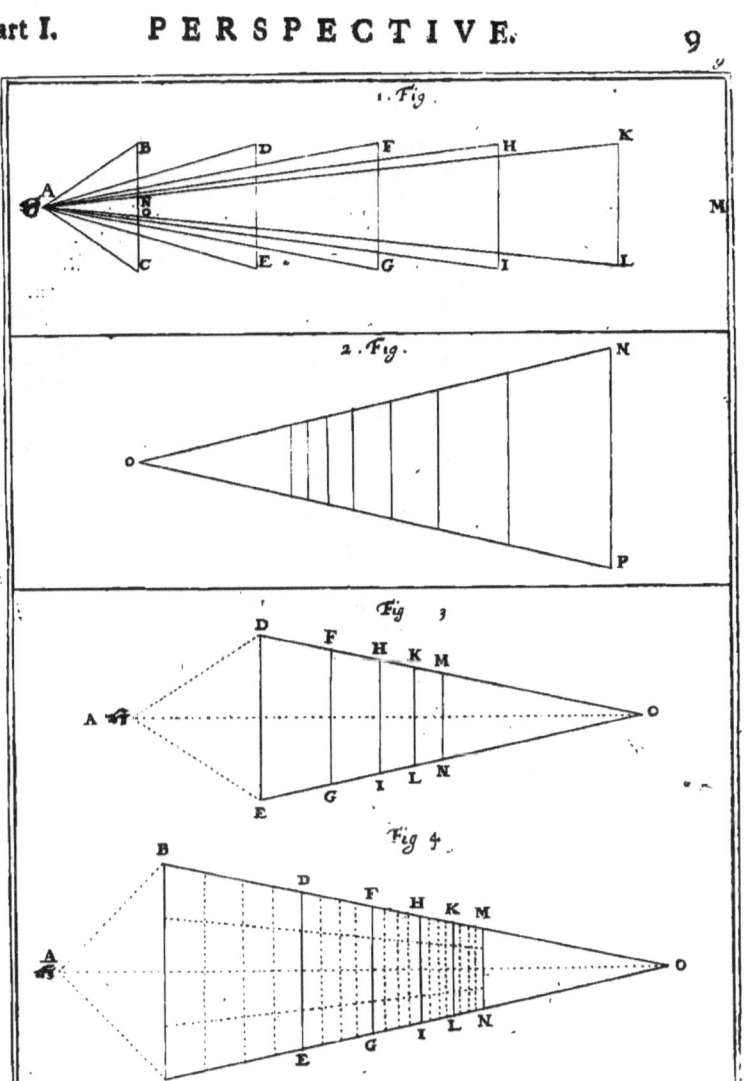

The Obfervations of the former page, applied to practice.

I T follows from what was faid in the foregoing page, that if you join two triangles, as in the laft figure but one, for the fides, and two others, of the laft, for the top and bottom of an object, all four will terminate in one fingle point A, which is the point of fight, wherein all the vifual rays meet. And this will give a proof of what I advanced, namely, that objects diminifh as they remove; the lower objects rifing, the upper falling, and the lateral clofing or approaching nearer to each other. An example of all which you have in *Fig.* 1. which exhibits, as it were, depths and diftances falling back, and receding from us, though all the parts of the defign are in fact equally near the eye, being all of them drawn on the fame plain furface; but this ingenious effect is produced, and the appearance of a diftant view procured, by comprehending and diminifhing the objects within the triangles.

The trees in the lower figure being ranged by this rule, have the fame effect as the columns, &c. The two rows are each of them comprehended within the fide-triangle, and diminifh as they approach the point of fight A. The third or bottom triangle, is the earth between the trees, and the fourth or upper one, is the air; and thus an elegant defign, highly entertaining the eye, is eafily conftructed.

I fhall next fhew, how you are to proceed in putting any plane body, or other figure, in perfpective.

Fig. 1.

Of the HORIZON.

WHAT we call the HORIZON, in perfpective, is only a line given us by the height of our eye. Thus, if we be raifed on an eminence, as is the man in the firft figure, our horizon will be high. If we ftand only on the plane, as reprefented in the fecond figure, the horizon will be our own pitch. And if we be feated, as is the third, the horizon will be low. So that it is the horizon fhews how high the eye is above the ground.

This, in effect, is the principal article in a picture, and that which directs and gives law to all the reft ; both as to the flope and inclination of buildings, and to the meafures and heights of the figures. This has occafioned a little difpute among our beft painters ; fome of them affert, that all paintings fhould have their horizon in the work itfelf, and that perfpective allows, where the painting is raifed very high above the eye, that it have its particular horizon. Others do not allow of a fecond horizon, but always ufe the natural one, where-ever the painting be placed ; as imagining that the whole height and breadth before them is, as it were, one large painting, from which that which is raifed above ought to take its meafures. The refpect I bear to the patrons of each opinion will not allow me to determine between them ; efpecially, as feveral good authors have tolerated both. But if my own fentiments were afked, I fhould make no fcruple to profefs myfelf of the opinion of thefe latter, becaufe every thing in the painting will thereby appear the more natural.

In this horizontal line are always found the points of fight and diftance, and fometimes the contingent or accidental point. It is this line that terminates the view, and which, to our apprehenfion when at fea, or on a large plain, feparates heaven from earth : it is always parallel to the bottom of the piece, or the plan the object is placed upon. Hence it appears, that nothing ought to be placed above the horizon, but what furpaffes the height of the eye ; and if an object be fo high as that it furpaffes this horizon, the plan of the fame object muft be placed below it. Thus, a tree or mountain may have its top above the horizon, but its bottom muft be a good deal below it.

Whatever is below the horizon fhews its top ; but in objects ever fo little above it, the top is invifible. Thus the two blocks A, B, placed on the ground of the firft figure, fhew their tops, by reafon the horizon is over them ; but in thofe of the fecond figure C, D, the top does not appear ; and much lefs in thofe of the third figure : yet, in reality, they are all of the fame height, fo that it is the horizon makes all the difference.   1

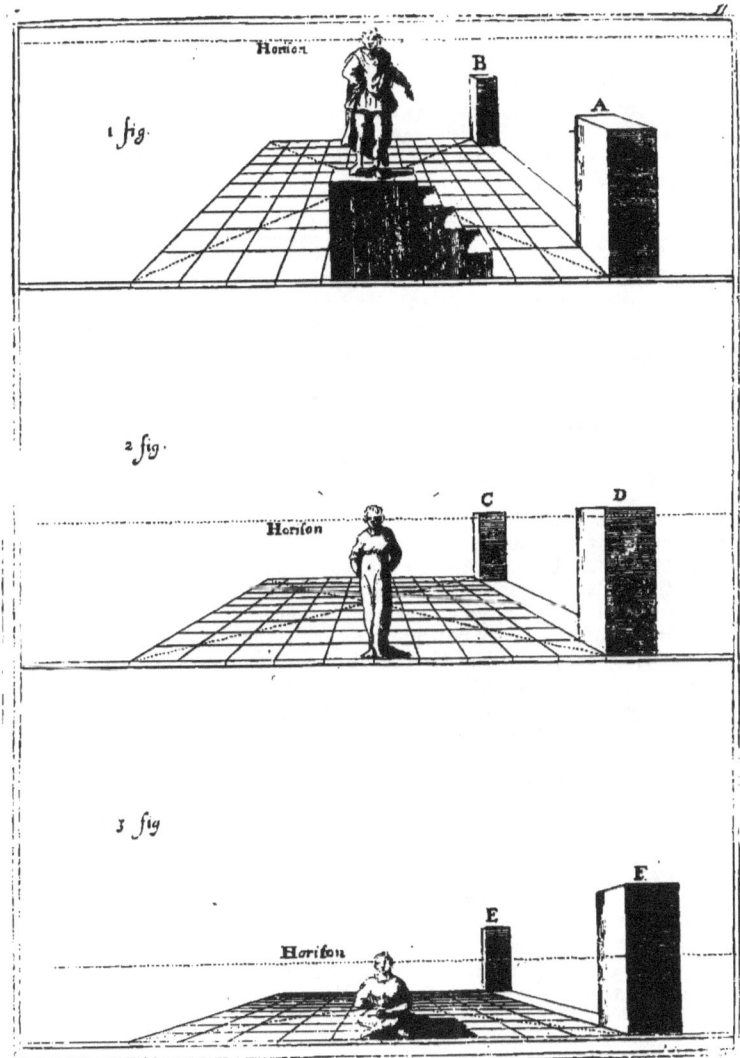

Of the Terreſtrial Line.

THE Terrestrial Line, Base Line, or Line of the Plan, is the bottom line of the drawing or plan. This is always parallel to the horizon, as is ſeen in A B of the firſt *Figure*, F G of the ſecond, and N O of the third. It is the firſt line drawn for the plan of a place; and whereon all the meaſures are to be ſet, as will hereafter be ſhewn.

Of the Point of Sight.

THE Point of Sight is a point in the axis of the eye, or in the central ray, where the ſame is interſected by the horizon; or in other words, a point in the horizontal line where all the viſual rays terminate. Thus the point E in the firſt figure is the point of ſight in the horizon C D, wherein all the viſual rays meet. It is called the *Point of the eye*, or *ocular Point*, becauſe directly oppoſed to the eye of the perſon who is to view the piece. It is alſo called the principal point, or point of perſpective.

Of the Points of Diſtance.

POINT of Distance, or Points of Distance, is a point, or points (for there are ſometimes two of them) placed on the horizontal line at equal diſtances on each ſide from the point of ſight. They are thus denominated, by reaſon the ſpectator ought to be ſo far removed from the figure, or painting, and the terreſtrial line, as theſe points are from the point of ſight. Thus H I being the horizon, and K the point of ſight, L and M are points of diſtance, ſerving to give all the ſhortnings. Thus, for example, if from the extremes of F G, *Fig.* 2d. you draw two lines to the point K, and from the ſame points draw two lines to the points of diſtance M and L, where theſe two lines G L and F M cut the lines F K and G K, in the points X and Y, will be the line of depth, and the ſhortning of the ſquare, whereof F G is the ſide and baſe. The lines drawn to the point of ſight are all viſual rays, and thoſe to the points of diſtance, all diagonals.

Of the Accidental Points.

CONTINGENT, or Accidental Points, are certain points, wherein ſuch objects as may be thrown negligently and without order, tend to terminate in the horizon. They are called accidental, becauſe they are not drawn to the point of ſight, nor the points of diſtance, but meet accidentally in the horizon as the ſituation of the objects happen. Thus, for inſtance, the two pieces of wood X and Y terminate in the points V, V, V, V, in the horizon P Q, not in the point of ſight which is R, nor in the points of diſtance S and T. Indeed ſometimes the objects are ſo ill diſpoſed, that theſe points muſt be made out of the horizon, as I ſhall have occaſion to ſhew hereafter. They ſerve particularly in the apertures of doors, windows, ſtair-caſes, and the like.   4

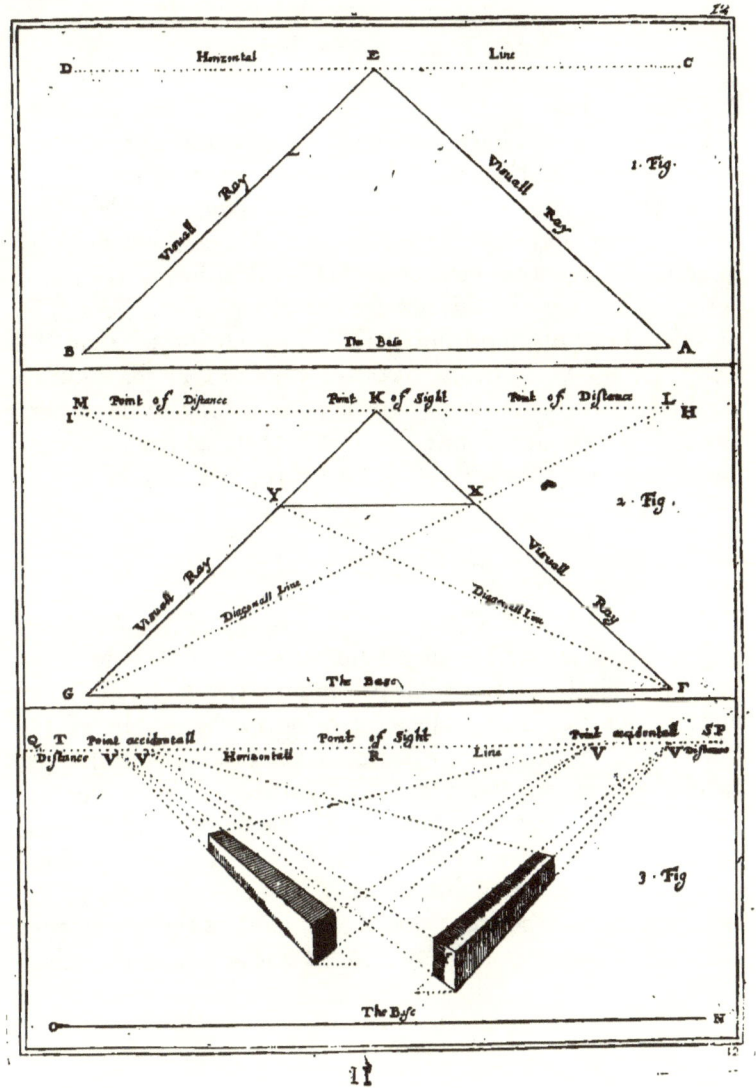

D .... Horizontal .... E .... Line C

1. Fig.

Visuall Ray   Visuall Ray

B   The Basis   A

M Point of Distance   Point K of Sight   Point of Distance L
I   H

Y   X

2. Fig.

Visuall Ray   Visuall Ray

Diagonall Line   Diagonall Line

G   The Base   F

T Point accidentall   Point of Sight   Point accidentall P
Distance V V   Horizontall   R   Line   V   Distance

3. Fig

O   The Base   N

Of the Point *of the* FRONT.

THE point of DIRECT VIEW, or of the FRONT, is when we have the object directly before us, and not more on one fide than the other ; in which cafe it only fhews the fore-fide, and, if it be below the horizon, a little of the top too, but nothing of the fides, unlefs the object be polygonous. Thus the plan A B C D is all in front, and, if it were raifed, we fhould not fee any thing of the fides A B, or C D, but only the front A D. The reafon is, that the point of fight E, being directly oppofite thereto, caufes a diminution on each fide ; however it is only to be underftood where an elevation is the object, that the front or forepart can only be feen, for, if it be a plan, it fhews the whole, as A B C D.

Of the SIDE POINT.

THE point of OBLIQUE VIEW, or of the SIDE, is when we fee the object fideways, or aflant. In viewing the object obliquely, it prefents us two faces, or fides ; and the point of fight, inftead of being in the middle of the horizon, as in the former inftance of the point of direct view, is now placed in the fide of the horizontal line. For example, if the point of fight be in F, the object G H I K will appear athwart, and fhew two faces, G K and G H ; in which cafe it will be a fide point. The practice is the fame in the fide points as in the front points ; a point of fight, points of diftance, &c. being laid down in the one as well as the other.

4

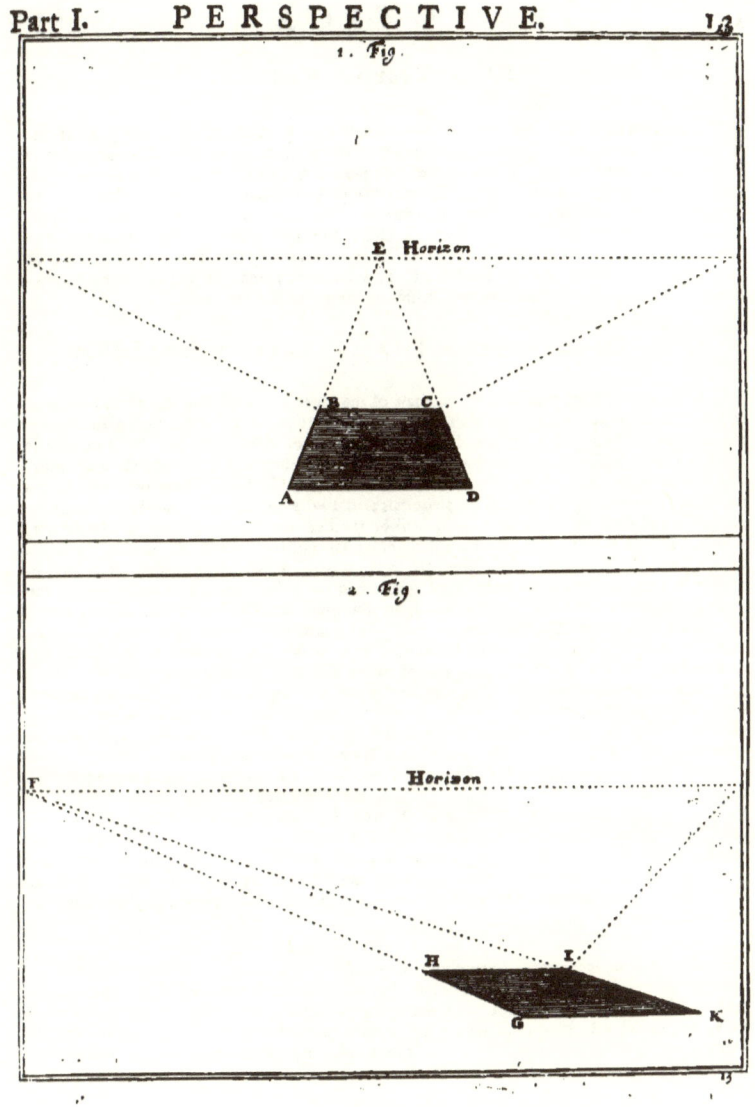

Of the Visual Rays.

IT is an univerfal rule, that all the lines, which in a geometrical plan, are perpendicular to the terreftrial line, be always drawn to the point of fight, when the fame plan is to be put in perfpective. Thus, in the little plan A O, O B, *Fig.* 1. A B is the terreftrial line, to which all the lines Z, Z, &c. are perpendicular. But if the plan be to be thrown into perfpective, and either a greater or a lefs line than that of the plan be pitched on, for example, the line A B, *Fig.* 2. which has the fame number of divifions as the fmall one ; from the feveral divifions Z, the lines are to be drawn directly to the point of fight **By** Such lines are properly denominated radials or vifual rays ; and the laft of them, the extremes, as being drawn from the extremities of the terreftrial line A B.

Of the Diagonals, *or* Diametrals, *and their* Sections.

It is likewife a rule, that all the diagonals of the fquares in a geometrical plan, be drawn to the point of diftance when the plan is put into perfpective. Thus, in the little plan *Fig.* 3. the diagonals, G O and F O, are drawn to the points of diftance, when the fame plan is exhibited in perfpective, and thereby the fhortnings or diminutions of the objects are procured. For example, if from the extremes of the bafe line F G, *Fig.* 4. lines be drawn to the points of diftance L M, they will be diagonals ; and where thofe lines interfect the extreme rays F K and G K in the points O, O, will be marked out the diminution of the fquare, whereof F G is the fide. And where thefe diagonals cut the lines Z, Z, &c. in the points Q, Q, &c. parallels to the bafe line are to be drawn, which will give the diminution of all the fquares, and the fame number of fides as in the little plan. The more remote the points of diftance are from the point of fight, the more the objects are diminifhed ; hence the beauty of a perfpective depends on fixing the points of diftance, at a proper diftance from the point of fight. On this account, I have added *Fig.* 5. with a diverfity of intervals between the point of fight, and points of diftance, to evince the truth of what is juft now obferved. Suppofe then R to be the point of fight, and R S, R S, the extreme rays ; if the point of diftance be at T, it will cut the ray S R in the point V, which will give the diminution of the fquare, whereof S S, is a fide. But it would be ridiculous to fee a fquare fo extravagantly deep, occafioned from the point of diftance T being fo much too near the point of fight R. The leaft fpace in any-wife allowable, is for the point of diftance to be removed from the point of fight, half the breadth of the whole draught or perfpective ; (fuch as is the diftance of X from R, *viz.* equal to that from the central ray C, to S ;) by reafon fuch a diftance makes a right angle at the fpectator's eye. It, would, however, be ftill more agreeable at 1, the line in that cafe cutting the fquare at 2 ; and it would be better yet at 3, cutting the extreme ray at 4 ; and beft of all at 5 ; being then remote enough, and making the fquare fhorter at 6 : the reafon thereof will be affigned in the next page.

It may be demanded, why, throughout the courfe of this work, I have put the points of diftance fo near the point of fight, when they have fo much better effect at a greater diftance ? The anfwer is, that the book not being intended to be viewed merely out of curiofity, but to inftruct, it was neceffary every circumftance fhould be feen, that the various methods of practice might be the better conceived. For this reafon I have included as much of the feveral operations as poffibly I might.

6

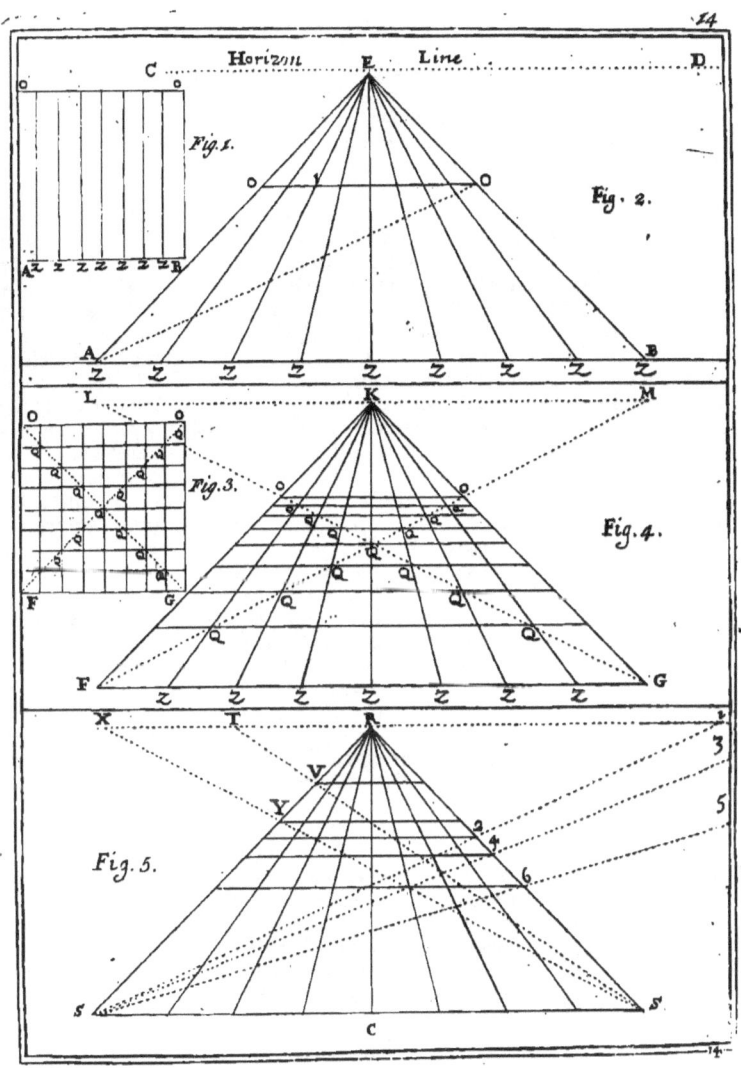

Of the D I S T A N C E, *or* R E M O V A L.

I Have already obferved, in fpeaking of the' vifual rays, page 5, that the eye
cannot commodioufly take in more of them, than are included in a right angle:
that is, that the fight does not receive the forms of objects fully and diftinctly,
when the rays tranfmitted from their extreme points, extend beyond a right angle.
The reafon is, the pupil being nearly in the center of the eye, does not well admit
more than a quadrant of a circle, fo that whatever rays exceed that portion, are
either not feen, or produce only a dim confufed effect. On this account, objects are
feen to greater advantage under an angle lefs than a right angle rather than greater;
for inftance, two thirds of a right angle, or fixty degrees, but not lefs, becaufe the
rays, in fuch cafe, being fo ftraitened become indiftinct, the angle being little more
than a point in the pupil. To fhew this difference in figures. Suppofe the plans and
fquares the fame as in the laft figure, and the fpectator's eye at the diftance of T
from the terreftrial line; the oppofite figure demonftrates it would be neceffary
the angle fhould open much farther, to fee the extremes Y, Y. If it only opened
to a right angle, the eye could not fee all the figure, as T for inftance could not
fee beyond the points V, V. Whence would arife a very faulty perfpective, inafmuch as what would exhibit a fquare, will now only form a parallelogram. The
neareft diftance for the eye is in the point X, which is the juft meafure of a right
angle comprehending the whole piece Y Y. If the diftance be carried ftill farther
back from the point of fight, it will be ftill more agreeable, as in I, where the
angle will be only 72 degrees. If it be brought back as far as Z, it will be in
perfection, inafmuch as the rays being now lefs dilated, have the more force, and
exhibit objects with the greater vivacity. But I would never choofe to go beyond
five, for the reafon already infinuated, that the angle then dwindles to a mere
point. Too much care cannot be taken in the difpofal of points of fo much importance; with regard to which it muft be efteemed a certain rule, that the diftance be at leaft equal to the fpace between the direct ray and the corner of the
perfpective. + R, for inftance, is the direct ray and X + the leaft diftance,
which is equal to + Y. This meafure being taken, muft be fet off each way from
the point of fight to fix the points of diftance, as here from R, to S, S; or only
one way, as in the following page, for a fide point.

Thus much we learn from reafons that regard the eye; but experience furnifhes
another noble rule, which may be general too, provided it be ufed with judgment,
namely, that having chofe the place where the perfpective is to be made, you are
to determine from what quarter it is to be feen to the beft advantage; then taking
the diftance from this place to the terreftrial line, fet off this interval, by a little
fcale, from the point of fight to the point of diftance, provided it be not too remote. Which is a circumftance that will require fome difcretion, to avoid the
inconvenience either of placing it too near, or too far off.

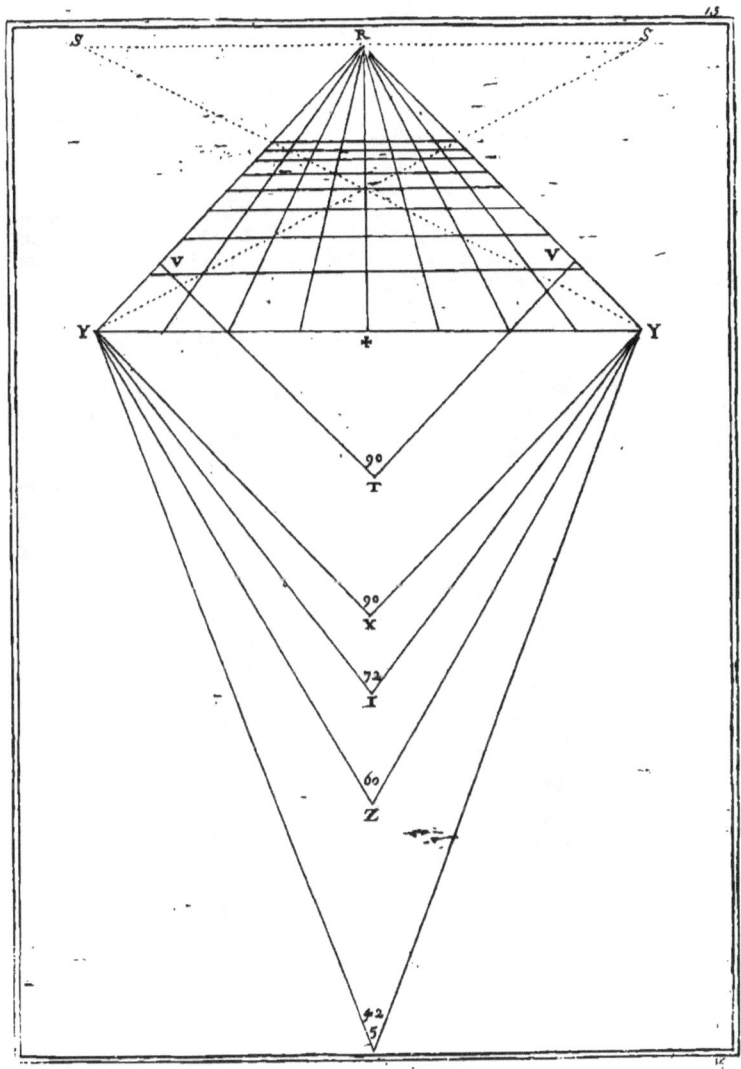

OBSERVATION I. *Relating to the* Side-point.

THE rules for the front point, are not varied in drawing the points of the sides, they are both founded on the same cause, which always produces the like-effects. *Fig.* 1. will sufficiently shew, that the method of practice for the side point, is the same as for that in front. Set off the division on the terrestrial line A B, and if the point of sight be supposed in C, and the point of distance in D, from the several points of division draw the rays to C, then draw the diagonal line A D, and you will have the interfections Q. Q. &c. which give the diminutions of the squares in the same manner as those in the preceding plates. The rest will be learnt from the following rules.

OBSERVATION II. *Of the* Depths *or* Hollowings.

A perspective may be sunk to any depth, by making new terrestrial lines and diagonals in the following method. For example, *Fig.* 2. from the terrestrial line E F, draw to the point of distance H I, the diagonals E I, F H, and where they interfect the visual rays E G and F G, in the points K, K; the diminution of the first square will be. Now, if we take this line K K for a new terrestrial line, and from its extremes K, K, draw diagonals to the points of distance; where these cut the same lines E G and F G, namely in the points L, L, will be the diminution of the second square, which will have as many divisions and squares as the first. Again, if we take this line L L, and repeat the same operation, we shall have the diminution of the third square in the point M. And if we begin again with this, we shall have a fourth; and so on, till we arrive at a point, which will be a length that will appear prodigious. By such means, it is easy either to sink the perspective plan deeper, or to shorten it. Thus, if you would have the depth, twice its width, proceed as already directed, by drawing new diagonals at K, K: and if you would have the depth but half the width, a line drawn at N, at the interfection of the diagonals, will give your request.

Since it is infallibly certain that as many visual rays as cut the diagonal line, so many squares of depths you have; it follows, as has been already hinted, that you may give the perspective what depth you please. For if, instead of drawing the diagonal from the ray F to the point of distance O, you draw it from Q, you will want two squares of the other diminished square R; and if you would have two squares more than the square R, draw a line from the same point O, cutting two rays, to V: if you desire four, take X; if six, Y; and if the intire square, Z: which is very easy, when well understood.

1 Fig
C
D
A
B
2 Fig.
H
G
I
M
L
L
K
K
N
E
F
3 Fig
O
Z
Y
X
R
S
F
Q

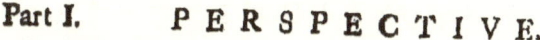

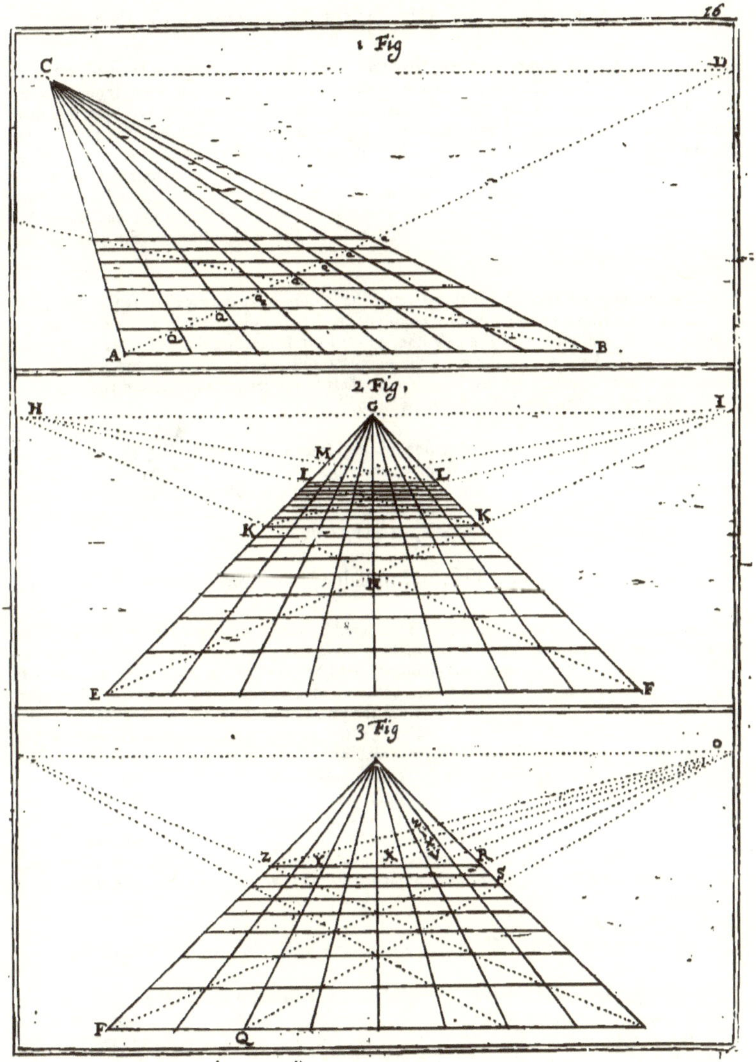

OBSERVATION III. *Of the Measures upon the* Base.

B Y the base line alone, one may give any depth, and in any part of the perspective at
pleasure, without the use of squares; which is a very expeditious way, though some-
what difficult to learn. I shall, however, endeavour to make it understood, because I shall
make frequent use thereof. For an example, *Fig.* 1. Suppose B S the base line; the point
of view A; and the points of distance D, E; if now you would make a plan of a cube, of
which B C is the side, draw two occult, or dotted lines, from the extremes B C, to the
points of sight. Then, to give the breadth, take the same measure B C, and set it off on
the terrestrial line C F; and from F draw a line to the point of distance D; and where this
line intersects the first ray C, in the point G, will be the diminution of the plan of the
cube B H G C.

If you would place the cube farther towards the middle, take the measure B C, and tranf-
fer it on the base line to the distance required, as I K; and to attain the depth, set the
fame as you would have it on the base line, as L : from L measure the width, as L M; then
from L and M draw occult lines to the point of distance D, and from the points N O,
where those lines intersect the ray K, draw parallels to the terrestrial line, and you will have
the square Q P O N in the situation you wanted.

You may set the cube on the other side of the square, by transferring the measure of
the side to W S on the base line, from whence draw the rays S A, W A, and perform the
operation as already directed. The cube B H G C is here transferred to V, by lines drawn
from the points C, D, to the point of distance E. The interval M T, intended for a
border, is shewn in the narrow figure X, as being very near.

OBSERVATION IV. *Of the* Base Line, *and a single Point of Distance.*

S I N C E the depths and widths may be procured by means of this base line, we need not
give ourselves any farther trouble in the making of squares; as shall be shewn in this example. Suppose a row of trees, or columns, is to be projected on each side; on the base
line lay down the place, and the distance between them, with their breadth or diameters,
as A B C D E F G, then laying a ruler from the point of distance O, to each of the points
A B C D E F G, the intersections it makes on the extreme visual ray A H, will be the
bounds of the objects desired. To set them off on the other side, upon the ray G H;
set one foot of your compasses on the point of sight H, and with the distance H G, strike
an arch: The point wherein this cuts the ray G H, as in N, will be the corresponding
bound. Thus N will be the same with M, and so of the rest; through which drawing
parallels, you will have the breadths. And as for the length, make it at pleasure; setting
it off from A, for instance, to P, and then from P drawing a line to H; and where this
cuts the other parallels, will be formed the plan required: which you may make either round
or square.

OBSERVATION V. *Not to deceive one's self in the Measures.*

N E V E R put any objects that are intended to be within the plan, on the side of the point
of distance, where you are to draw lines for managing the depth. Thus, suppose A B the
visual ray whereon the measures are to be marked; if you would produce the points C and
D through the same, do not draw the lines from the point of distance E, but from that
opposite thereto, F. Or if C and D were on the inside, as G and H are, you should not
draw from the point F, but from E; by reason the line of intersection is found between the
two. Consequently, the two will cut each other in the same points I, K.

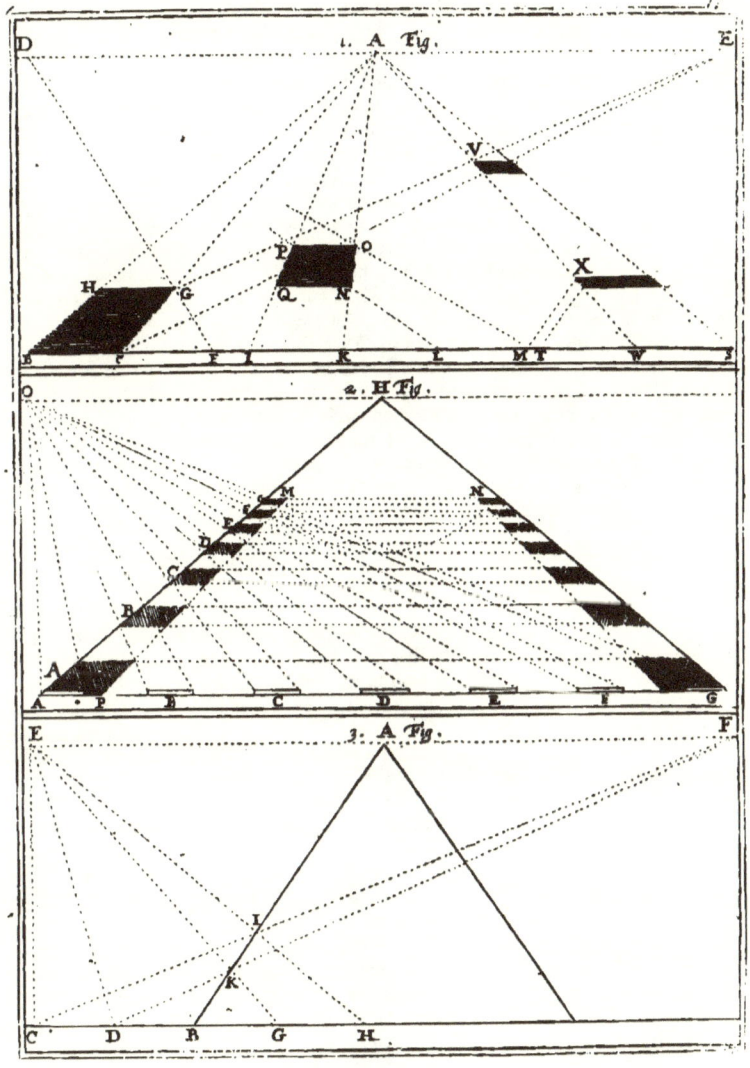

Observation VI. *Of a single Point of Distance.*

THE artist is sometimes so straitned for want of room on the place on which he exhibits his draught, that it is impossible to make above one point of distance. On which occasion, such as have been always accustomed to two, find themselves at a loss. This I am now to recover him from, and to give him to understand how a single point suffices for the operation. Suppose, then, we have a pavement to make of square stones, and that we have already drawn all the visual rays to the point A; to get the diminutions of them, draw lines to the points of distance, the interfections whereof will give us points for parallels to be drawn through. But here being only one point of distance, name-ly B, draw the single diagonal stroke C B, to cut all the visual rays. Then mark the same interfections on the opposite rays, for the drawing of parallels. Set, as already directed, one foot of your compasses in the point A, and sweep the other through all the interfections, as I P. This however is only advifeable for what is to be viewed in front; another method is to be given for plans to be seen sidewise, *viz.* set one foot of your compasses on the bafe line, and with the other take the interfection you want to transfer, as D, and set it upon the per-pendicular O E, marking the extent thereof, as F; then draw a line from D to F, and you will have the same as if there had been two points of distance. And so of all the other interfections.

Observation VII. *How to perform without making Use of* the Diagonal.

IF one would use the extreme ray G H for the line of interfection, the objects K L M N O must be set on the bafe line, and from them, lines are to be drawn to the point of distance I; which is here to be removed as far as possible that the diminution of the perspective may have the better effect. For if that point were too near the point of sight G, the objects would be too flat; I mean, for example, that a square would appear a parallelogram. Then from the point I draw lines to the several objects K L M N O, and mark the interfections thereof on the ray G H, and through thefe interfections draw parallels to the terrestrial line, as here P Q, &c. This method is not much in ufe, though some set a value on it.

Observation VIII. *Other methods of* Shortning or Diminifhing.

IF you chance to be straitned for fpace on the plane you draw upon, and can-not remove the point of distance far enough; from the foot of the ray R S erect a perpendicular T S, which will receive the interfections, and give a greater diminution. And if you would have the diminutions still more, draw a flope line, as X, which by means of its inclination, will give the interfections still clofer. Then, to draw the parallels, you have nothing to do but set off the line X or T on the foot of the ray, as in V; and from thofe points draw parallels to the terrestrial line.

I

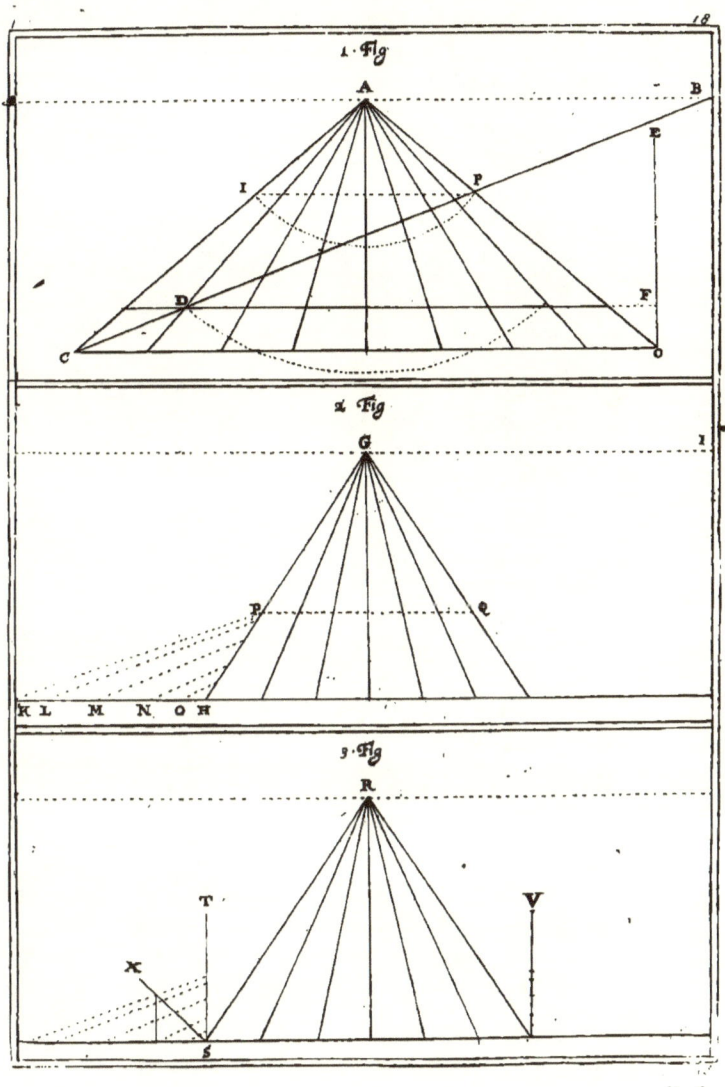

PRACTICAL PERSPECTIVE.

PART II.

SHEWING THE

METHODS

OF PUTTING

PLANES

IN

PERSPECTIVE.

Of Planes *viewed directly, or in Front.*

FROM *Obfervation* III. and IV. page 17, as well as from the elevations that follow ; it will appear that my intention is not to ufe geometrical plans, in order to the drawing of perfpectives. That being a double labour ; and there being fcarce any Painter would give himfelf the trouble, feeing I teach him to do the fame thing, by the ufe of the terreftrial line.' But as there is no rule fo general, but has its exception; fo there are certain figures which cannot be put in perfpective without the ufe of fuch plans. Befide, the confufion a man would be under, fhould a plane be given him to be exhibited in perfpective, if he had not been inftructed how to proceed. Therefore I am induced to give the following rules; which may fuffice to fhew how any plane that can be required, or even imagined, may be put in perfpective.

1 *To fhorten, or diminifh a fquare*; as A B C D. From A and B, to the point of fight E, draw the lines A E, B E: and from the fame angles A and B draw two diagonals F B, A G; and the points H and I, where they interfect the rays A E and B E, will give the fquare A B C D, diminifhed in A H I B. To do it without the geometrical plan; draw a line from B to F, or from A to G; or fet off the line A B on the terreftrial line; as in B K; and from K draw another line to F : which will give the fame interfection I, on the ray B E.

2. *To diminifh a fquare viewed by the angle* D. Having defcribed the plan A B C D, continue the fides D A, and D C, to cut the bafe line in H, and I : from the points H, and I, draw lines to the points of diftance G, and P; and from the angle B, of the fquare which touches the bafe line, draw to the fame points two others B G, and B P; their interfections being joined will give you the fquare K L M B. To do without the plan : fet off the diagonal D each way from the middle point B; as to H and I, and draw the diagonals as before. But in either cafe no line is to be drawn from the point of fight, O.

3. *To diminifh a Circle.* Draw a diameter S T, perpendicular to the ground-Line, and another R Q at right angles, which will divide the circle in four equal parts : a fquare A B C D defcribed about the faid circle, and drawing the diagonals A D, B C, will divide it into eight parts : from each of thefe points O, O, &c. draw perpendiculars to the ground-Line, and from each of their interfections with the faid ground-Line, draw lines to the point of fight H; and where they are interfected by the diagonals A K, and B I, make points ; the two laft of which, M N, give the fquare, which is to be divided into four, by diagonals, interfecting each other in the point P. Laftly, from the extremes of this crofs, draw curve lines through the faid points, which will give the form of the circle in perfpective. This method may ferve for fmall circles ; but for large ones we fhall give another method, more exact.

4. This figure is a compound of the two firft; which is all we need to fay about it.

5. This too depends on the two firft; only here is a lift, or border, going round, which the others have not. To put the lift in perfpective: from the four rays A B C D draw lines to the point of fight G; and where the inner rays B C interfect the diagonals A F and D E, draw parallels to the bafe-line; and you will have your defire.

The fixth is the fame as the fecond ; except that it is furrounded with two borders.

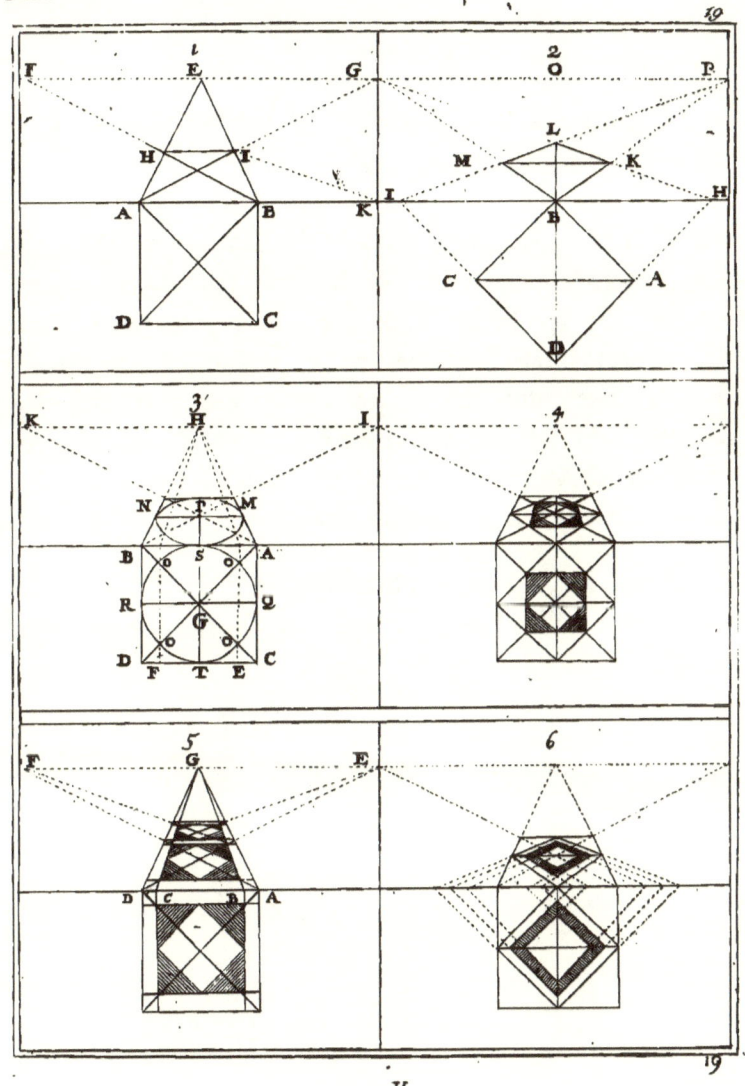

The perſpeƈtive appearance of P L A N S *viewed obliquely, or ſide-wiſe.*

THESE plans, being much the ſame with thoſe already diſpatcht, are to be managed after the ſame manner. It would be loſing time to repeat the method of operation how they are to be diminiſhed in perſpective; a bare inſpeƈtion of the figures and lines ſufficing to ſhew, that all the difference between theſe and the former, conſiſts in the ſituation of the objeƈts, which are here ſhewn laterally, and there in front.

All the A A A's are points of ſight, and the B B B's points of diſtance. The ſide-point has been deſcribed, page 16th.

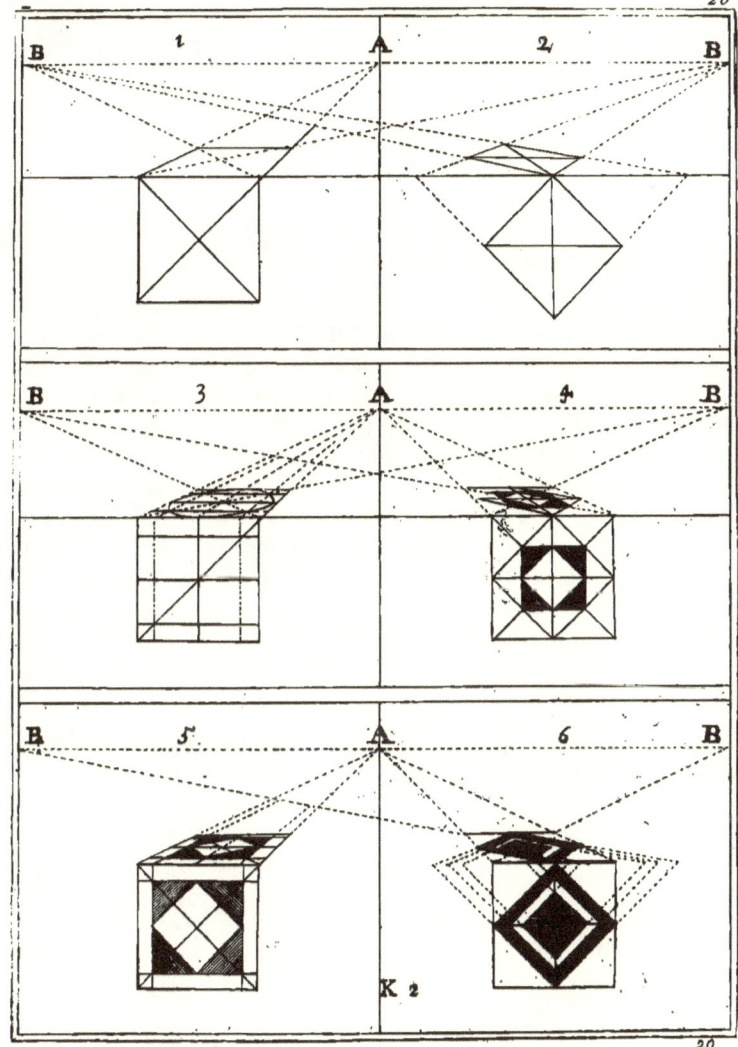

The Method to find the perspective Appearance of a
TRIANGLE.

TRIANGLES, according to the order of numbers, ought to pre-cede squares; but, according to reason, they are to come after them in this work, as being more difficult to put in perspective. Not on account of the plan, which is easy enough, as only confisting of three lines joined together, but on account of the obliquity of its sides.

I come now to apply some of the observations, page 17th, relating to the measures on the base line A B: for, to exhibit this triangle in perspective, whose base 1. 3. is parallel to the fundamental line A B, from all the angles thereof, 1, 2, and 3, perpendiculars are to be drawn to A B. Then setting one foot of your compasses in the intersections, with the other set off the distances of the parts of the object from the terrestrial line, along the same line, by striking arches, as from 2 to 2, from 3 to 3, &c. This done, having drawn another base line in ano-ther place, as here under E F, transfer the measures from A B to E F, and to the point of sight C draw lines from the points 1, 2, 3, &c. Lastly, having pitched one point of distance D, draw lines thereto from the other points of depth, 1, 2, 3, &c. And between the intersections made by these with the visual rays, lines, being drawn, will give the triangle required.

If you would give it the lift or breadth, repeat the same over again for the several inner points thereof; only using other figures to prevent confusion; as, next to 1, 4; next 2, 5; 3, 6, &c. Then drawing perpendiculars to the point C, and between the points where they inter-sect the others, draw lines as you see in the scheme.

The equilateral triangle, such as that here described, is inscribed in a circle, that is a circle may be drawn about it, every side subtending 120 degrees.

Note. The same operation will serve for all sorts of triangles.

I

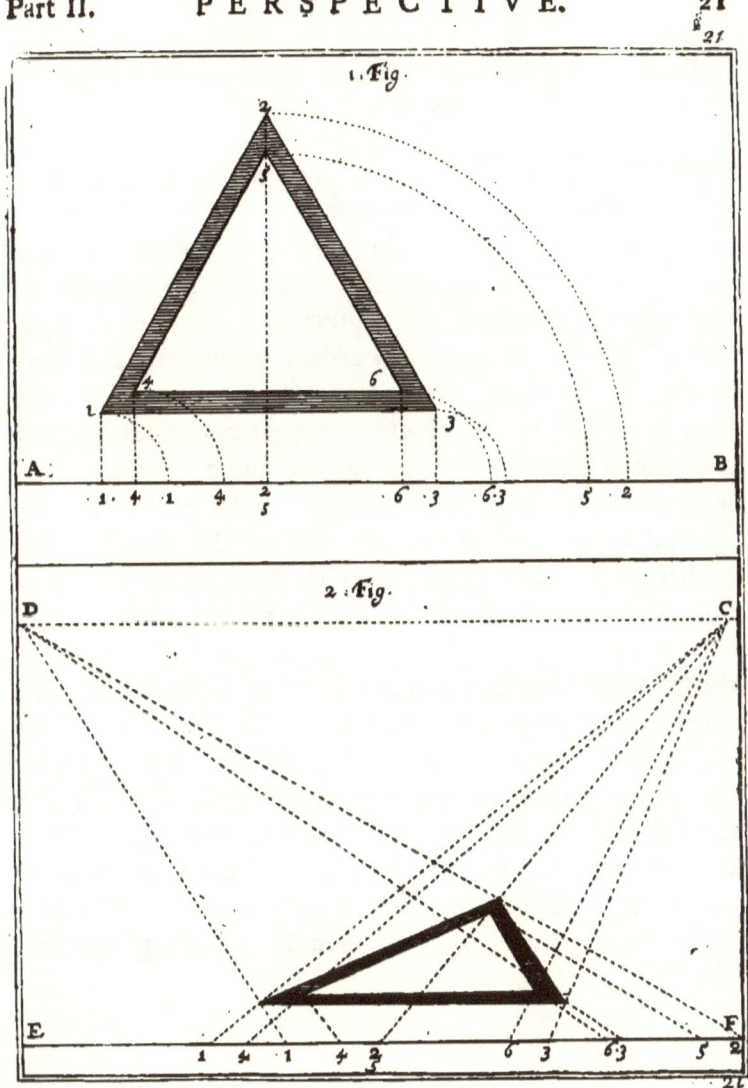

To exhibit a PENTAGON, *or figure of Five-Angles,*
in perfpective.

THE way to conftruct a pentagon is to defcribe a
circle, and divide it into five equal parts, of feventy-
two degrees each. Then, for putting it in perfpective, the
method is the fame as has been fhewn for the triangle, as
will appear in viewing the figures and the lines of operation. The lift or breadth is added, becaufe when I come
to treat of elevations, inftances will be given in objects that
have broad edges. The exterior pentagon muft be firft
compleated on the bafe line, and the inner one afterwards,
by the fame method of proceeding. The reader was inftructed herein, in drawing the rim of the triangle in the
former page. The point of fight, both of the front and
fide, is A ; the point of diftance B; the vifual rays, which
are the perpendiculars drawn from the angles of the plan to
the bafe line, are drawn to the point of fight A ; and the
other rays that give the diminution, and the place of the
angles, to the point of diftance B. As 2 cuts the ray marked 2, which gives the angle 2, 4 gives the angle 4 ; and
fo of the others. All the reft is clear enough ; regard, however, is to be had to one thing, that all the angles tend towards the center 6 : for this reafon the center is to be marked in the plans in perfpective, as well as in the geometrical
plans.

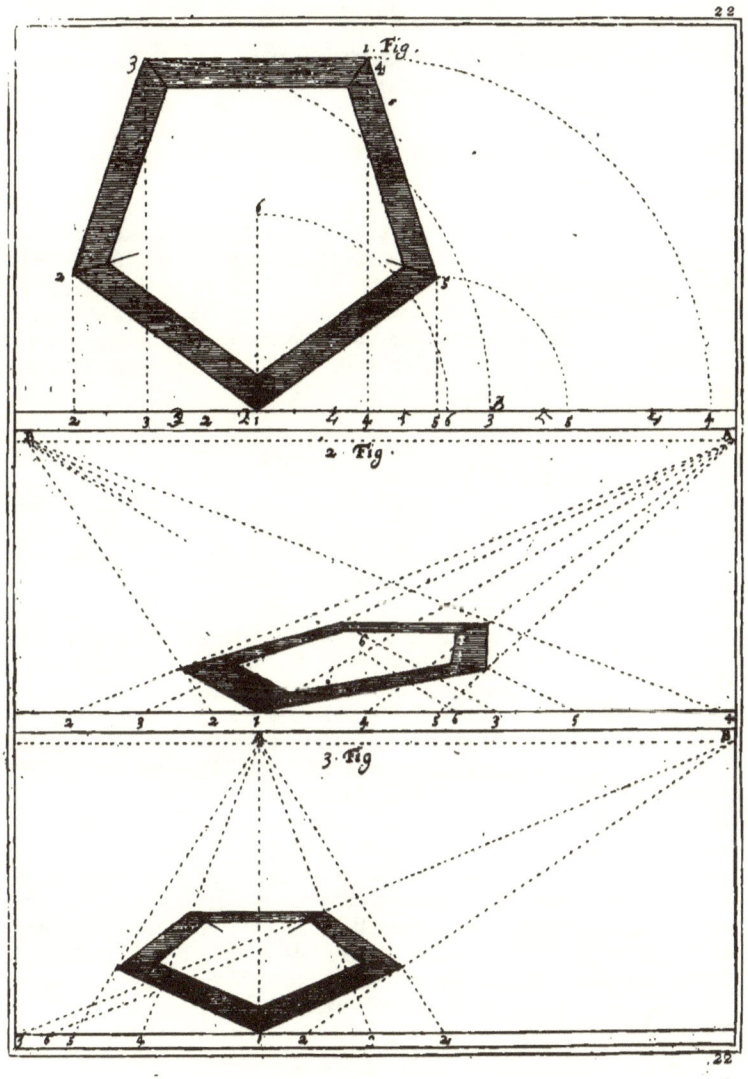

To find the perspective Appearance of an HEXAGON, *or Figure of Six-Angles.*

THE HEXAGON is a plane with six angles, and as many sides. If the sides be equal, it is a regular hexagon, and the easiest to describe of all the polygons, (figures of more than four sides and angles) by reason the same aperture of the compasses, which circumscribes it within a circle, is the measure of its sides, *viz.* 60 degrees each. In other words, the side of a hexagon is equal to the radius of a circle circumscribed about the same. As to the putting it in perspective, the method does not at all differ from that of the triangle, or pentagon; either when single, or with the lift or thickness, A is the point of sight, and B that of distance.

Since I have a good deal of room in this page, I think it not amiss to give a brief method of putting the lifts or thicknesses of all polygons, regular or irregular, in perspective. And the present hexagon shall serve for an example of this proposition. Suppose the exterior lines of the plan of *Fig.* 3. to be only laid down, and it were required to give it a lift or thickness within: to do this in perspective, lay your ruler along the sides, and make points in the horizon where it cuts the same; thus laying it along the side A B, it will cut the horizon in C; then laying it along B D, it will give the point E; and the like of the other sides. Before you proceed any farther, draw occult lines from the several angles through the center F, which lines are to receive the intersections that give the diminutions. Such dispositions made, set the breadth of the band or lift on the base line, as A H, and draw the first breadth to the point of distance G, and where the line G H cuts I, will be the bound of the thickness of the first side, which is to determine for all the rest. For from this point a line is to be drawn to the point corresponding to this side C, and the intersection of this line with K will give the diminution; from the point whereof drawing a line to the point E, corresponding to the line B D, you will have the diminution for the point L, which serves for the last side L M. Then transferring all the same measures to the other side, you will have the figure complete, by the formation of the inner hexagon.

Hereafter we shall have occasion to give another method.

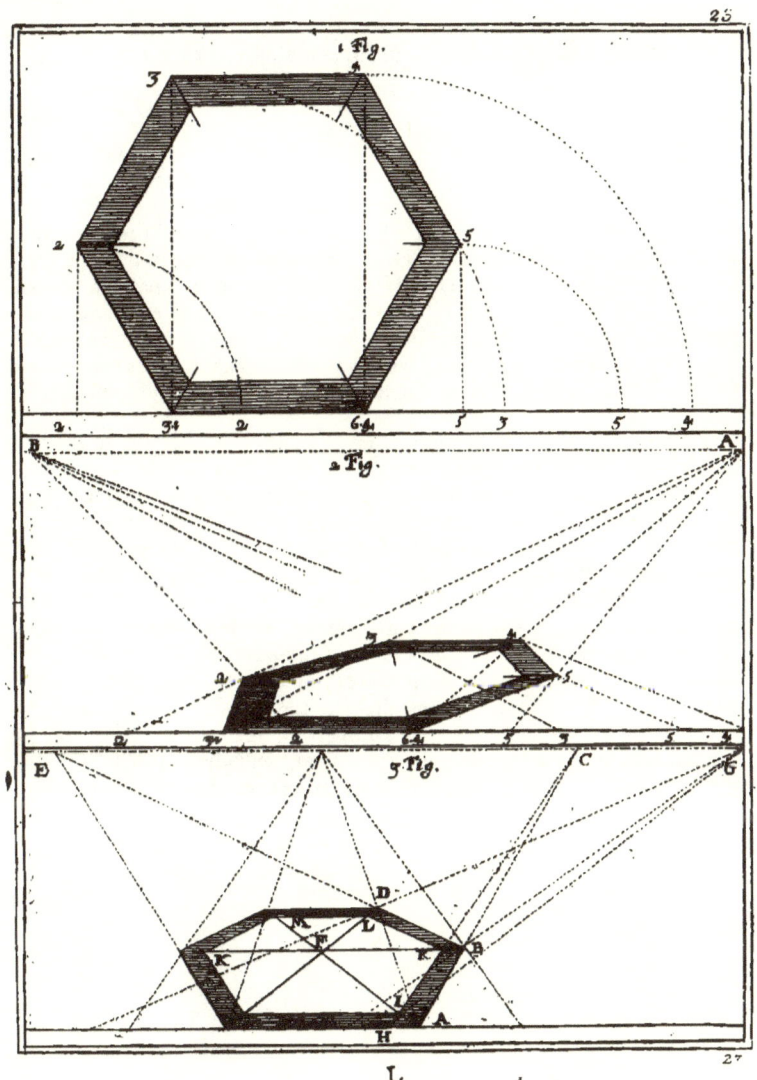

To exhibit the perfpective appearance of the HEPTAGON, *or figure confifting of feven fides and feven angles.*

THE HEPTAGON is formed within a circle, as the other polygons are ; in order to which the circle is divided into feven parts,
each fide fubtending 51 deg. 25 min. and fometimes more. The method of putting it in perfpective is the fame with that of the preceding
ones, as to the perpendiculars falling from the angles to the bafe line,
which are all drawn to the point of view A ; but as to the diminution,
and the lines that give the points of the angles, it is different, and rather
according to the feventh *Obfervation*, page 18; though I do not abfolutely
approve that, as thinking the eighth *Obfervation* the better. But to condefcend
to fuch as do ufe it, and fhew them that it does not diminifh enough.

Having drawn perpendiculars from the angles of the plan to the terreftrial line, as in the preceding cafes, a perpendicular is to be made on
one fide, as A B, to receive the interfections of the parallels drawn through
all the angles. Thus, the firft angle being placed on the terreftrial line
of 2 and 7, I draw a parallel through both, cutting the perpendicular
in C. After the fame manner, the angles 3 and 6 give the interfection
D, and 4 and 5 the interfection E. This line A B, thus divided, muft be fet
off the bafe line of the plan to be diminifhed, beginning to put the point
B in F, as in the figure. Then making the other divifions C D E, and
from thefe drawing lines to the point of diftance O, from the interfections of the extreme ray draw parallels to the terreftrial line, and where
thefe cut the rays that bear the numbers of the angles, points are to
be made, which, being joined by right lines, will give the figure defired.
As to the thicknefs, or lift, it is to be made after one of the preceding
manners.   9

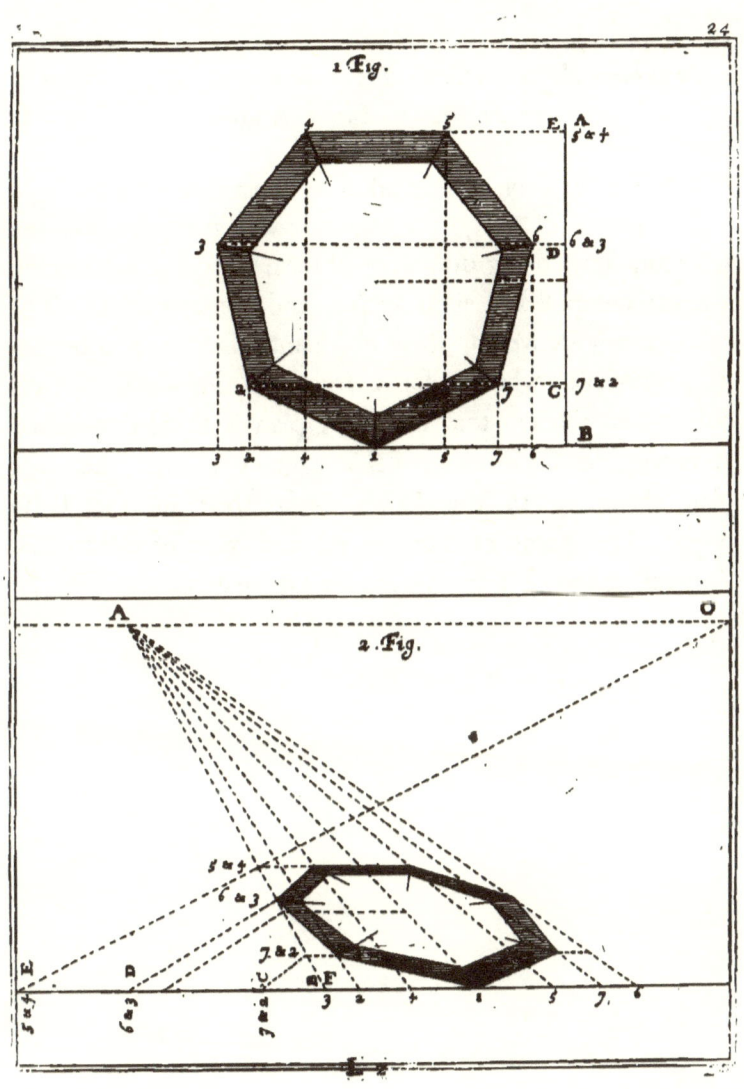

To exhibit the perfpective Appearance of the O C T A GON,
or Figure of Eight Angles.

T HE octagon is formed of a circle divided into eight
parts, of forty-five degrees each, from the divifions
whereof, lines being drawn, will form an octagon, that is,
a figure compofed of eight angles, and as many fides. The
rules already delivered, fhew abundantly how it is to be put
in perfpective, whether for a front or a fide view. I fhall
only obferve here, that the front plan is to be diminifhed
according to *Obfervation* VIII. page 18, and the fide
plan according to the VIIth *Obfervation* in the fame
page. The point of view is A, and that of diftance B.
The reft is too obvious to need an explanation.

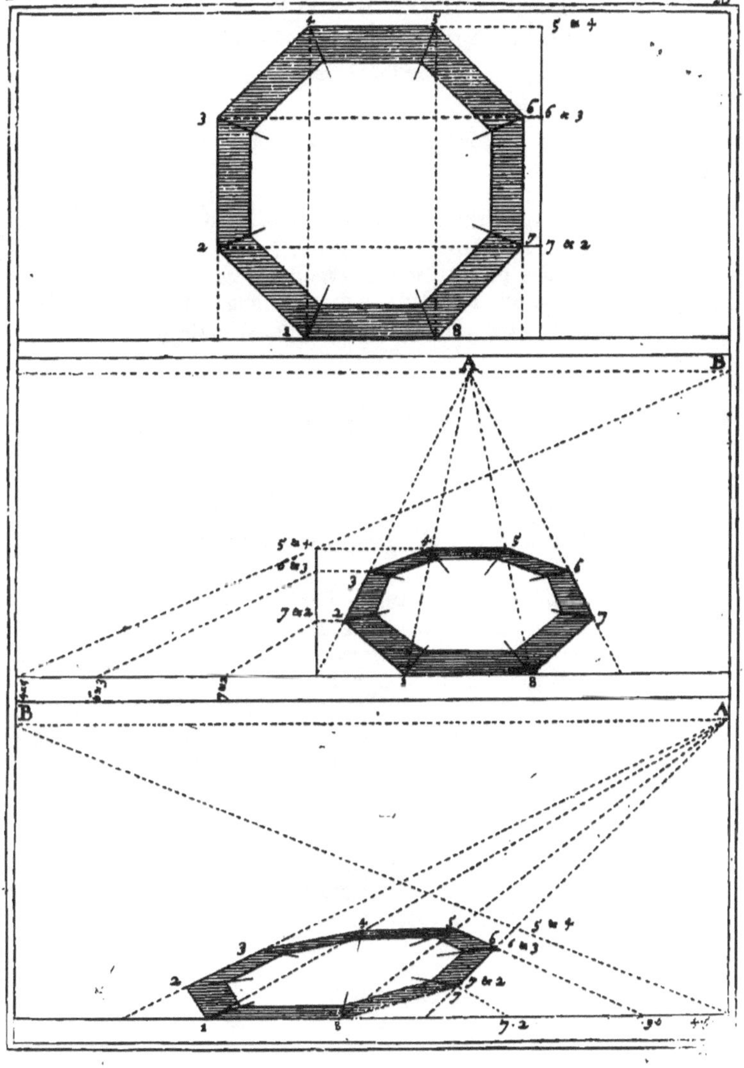

4
5
5 & 4
3
6
6 & 3
2
7
7 & 2
1
8
A
B
5 & 4
6 & 3
3
7 & 2
2
6
7
1
8
B
A
4
5
5 & 4
3
6
6 & 3
2
7 & 2
7
1
8
7.2

Another Method *for exhibiting the* OCTAGON *in perſpective.*

THIS method of conducting the OCTAGON was invented by
Serlio. The practice is thus: having found a ſquare ABCD the
ordinary way, divide the baſe line CD into ten parts, and, leaving three
on each hand, from the third of either ſide E and F, draw lines to the
points of ſight, G, and through the interſections of thoſe lines with the
diagonals O, O, draw parallels to the terreſtrial line, cutting the ſides of
the ſquare in the points H, I, K, L: then joining the points E H, I E,
FK, LF, by lines, you will have an octagon, as in the preceding figure.

❁ ❁

To find the perſpective appearance of the HEXAGON,
or figure of Six Angles, *by the above method.*

THE ſame *Serlio* has contrived a like way of managing the HEX-
AGON. Suppoſe, as above, a ſquare ABCD, and the baſe
line AD divided into four parts, from one of which, on either ſide E
and F, draw lines to the point of ſight H; then through the interſection
of the diagonals, which is the middle of the ſquare G, draw a parallel to the baſe line, cutting the ſides of the ſquare in I K; laſtly, drawing lines through theſe points E, I, E, and F, K, F, there will be found
a hexagon.

I ſhall ſay nothing of the octagon, *Fig.* 3. viewed ſidewiſe; ſince, as
it has been ſo often repeated, the method is the ſame as for that viewed
in front, *Fig.* 1: the operation is plain and ſimple, the lines drawn at
Fig. 3, ſhew it at the firſt inſpection.

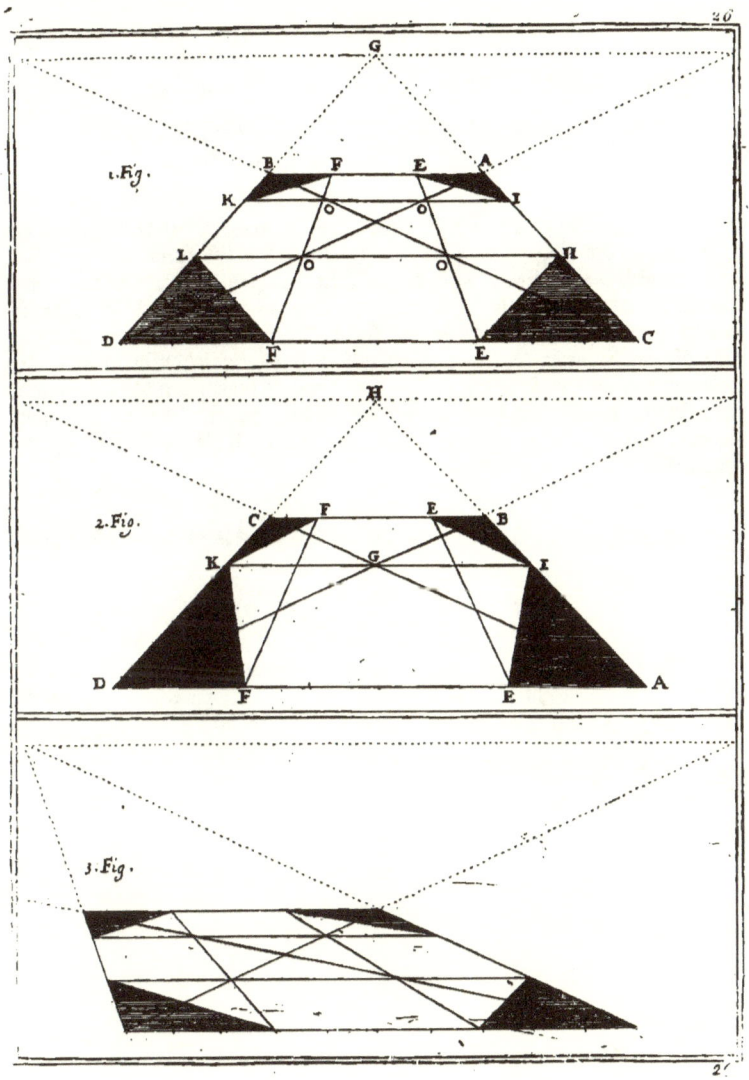

Of the Double O c t a g o n, *or the method of adding breadth or thickness to an octagon, by the operation of the circumscribed square.*

S UPPOSING a fingle octagon already made, if it is required to have it double, or to give it a thicknefs, or lift, proceed thus. Set the breadth or thicknefs you are willing to give it, within the fquare which circumfcribes the octagon, as here at A B; and from thefe points draw lines to the point of fight C; and where thefe lines cut the diagonals, as in O, O, draw parallels D D, which will form a fort of band within the fquare; laftly, draw occult lines from angle to angle, interfecting each other in N; and where they cut the lines of the inner fquare, namely, in the points E, F, G, H, I, K, L, M, will be the bounds of the inner octagon.

✿✿✿✿✿✿✿✿✿✿✿✿✿✿✿✿✿✿✿✿✿✿✿✿✿✿✿✿✿✿✿✿✿

Of the Double H e x a g o n.

A N hexagon circumfcribed with a fquare, will receive a lift, or inner hexagon, by the fame method of operation. It would be needlefs to repeat particulars, fince the figure will clear any doubts that may arife.

The octagon viewed fidewife, is managed precifely as that viewed in front; the point of fight is A, and that of diftance B.

1 Fig.

2 Fig.

3 Fig.

M

✿◉✿◉✿◉✿◉✿◉✿◉✿◉✿◉✿◉✿◉✿◉✿◉✿◉✿◉✿◉✿◉✿◉✿◉

To exhibit the perfpective of a CIRCLE.

IF the circle be fmall, you are directed, page 19, to an eafy method of projecting it, by circumfcribing a fquare about it. If the circle be large, take the following method, which *Serlio* has directed. Set one foot of your compaffes in the middle of the fundamental line, with the other defcribe the femi-circle A Z B, divide it's periphery or circumference into any number of equal parts at pleafure. You will fee in the procefs, that the more of thefe divifions, the eafier it will be to form the circular lines, from the junction of which the circle receives it's appearance. The femi-circle A Z B is here divided into eight parts, which is the ufual practice. From the feveral divifions Z Z, &c. perpendiculars are raifed to the bafe line in the points E E, &c. this done, the two diagonals are to be drawn to the points of diftance, which are here removed beyond the compafs of the plate, but which are to be fuppofed, as ufual, in the horizon. Thus you get a fquare A H I B ; and this fquare thus formed, draw lines or rays from all the points E towards the point of fight, as far as the line H I, and through the interfections of thofe lines with the diagonals, draw parallels ; then, beginning in the middle of one of the fides of the fquare to make a point, as *a*, connect it by a circular line with the oppofite angle *b*, and proceeding thus with arches from angle to angle, according to the direction of diagonals through the points *a b c d e f g h i k l m n o p q*, you will have your circle in perfpective.

By this method, it is apparent how any curvilinear figure may be projected on a plane, and therefore how neceffary it is, to have this rule of the projection of the circle very familiar, becaufe of the frequent ufe thereof in columns, vaults, arches, apertures of doors, windows, &c.

9.

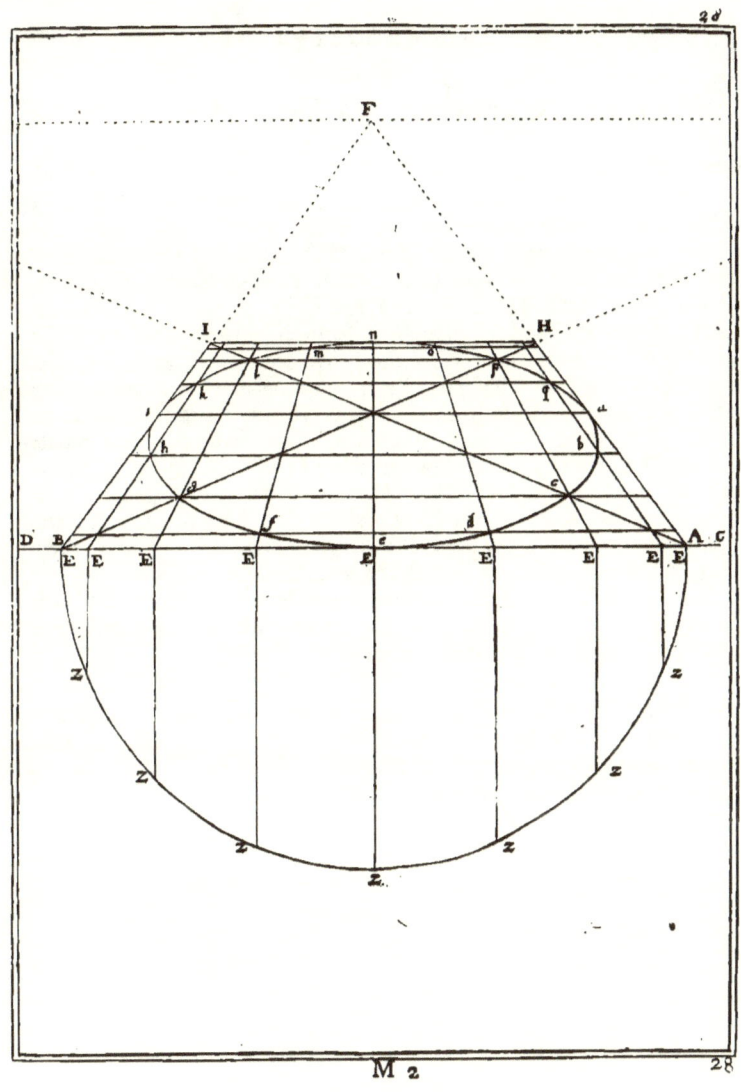

✿✿✿✿✿✿✿✿✿✿✿✿✿✿✿✿✿✿✿✿✿✿✿✿✿✿✿✿✿✿✿✿✿✿✿✿✿

To exhibit the appearance of a Double CIRCLE.

THE outer circle is fuppofed the fame that I have juft now been deſcribing; and it is required to give it a thicknefs, or lift, by making another within-fide thereof. Thus, give it any breadth at pleafure, as, for example, A C: from G the center of the outer femi-circle, deſcribe the inner one C D, which you are farther to divide, like the great one. Thefe divifions are eafily procured, by drawing lines from the divifions of the great femi-circle to the center G; the interfections of thofe lines with the inner femi-circle at l I I I, &c. are the points of it's divifions. From thefe points raife perpendiculars to the bafe line A B, and, to prevent confufion, let thefe laft lines be dotted. This done, proceed by drawing lines from the new points C I I I I D on the bafe line, towards the point of fight F, as far as the line H K, and through their interfections with the diagonals draw the two parallel dotted lines M N, which will give the breadth the circle is to have at G Q. and it's furtheft diminution. Laftly, draw lines from all the angles on which the great circle is produced, towards the center, and the points wherein they interfect the dotted lines *a b c d e f g h i k l m n o p q,* will be the points, which, connected with curve lines, will form the inner circle's circumference.

A perfon who fhould defire a plan of three, four, five, or fix circles in perfpective, muft lay them all down in the geometrical plan after the fame manner as the fecond femi-circle is done in this example; and then obferve the fame method of procefs.

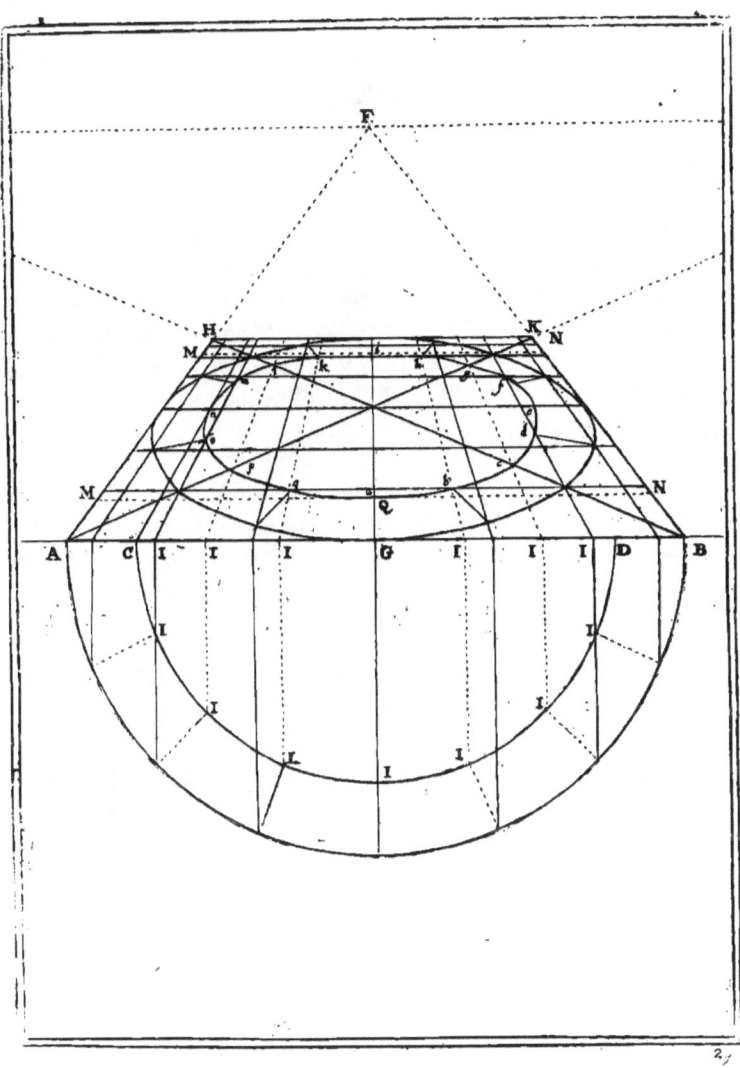

To exhibit the appearance of the PLAN *of a* Square
viewed Angle-wife.

IF it be required to draw a 'fquare, viewed by an angle directly
oppofite to the eye, there is nothing more requifite than to fet off
the diagonal of it upon the bafe line; as here A C is equal to the diagonal of the geometrical plan of the fquare to be projected. Then
from the points A and C to draw two lines to the point of diftance D,
then to fet off the meafure of the line A C on the bafe line towards
A E, and from E A to draw lines to the point of diftance F, and the
three interfections of the lines H I K will be the bounds of the fquare
defired, *viz.* A I H K.

When fuch a plan is to be divided into feveral parts, lay down the
number of divifions required between the points C and A, and the fame
number on the other fide A E; and from all thefe points draw lines to
the points of diftance; as in the prefent figure, which has eight fquares
on each fide, and fixty-four in all.

If in the fame plan, thus viewed by the angle, inftead of the divifions in the firft figure, it were required to have little plans in the four
corners, as four lodges, columns, trees, or other objects, fet the width
of each on the bafe line, as B D, E A, on the neareft fide, A F, G C,
on the other fide; from which points drawing lines to the points of diftance H I, their interfections will give the four plans K L M N required.

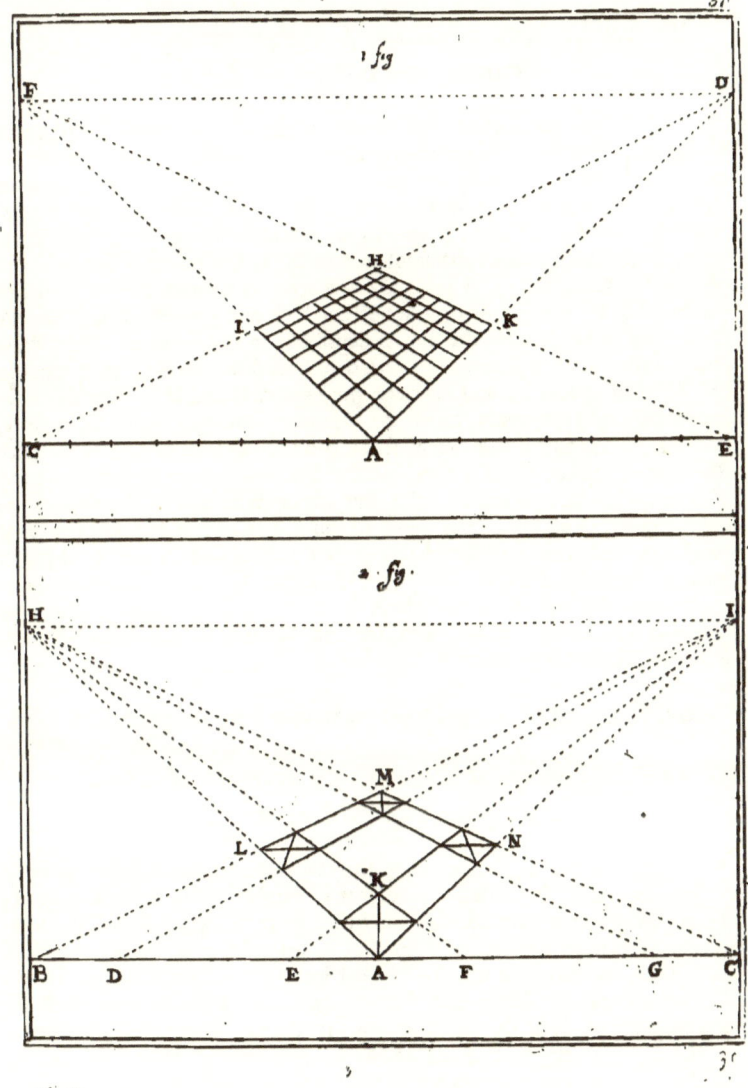

To exhibit the perſpective of a Pavement *of* Square-
Stones, *viewed by the* Angles.

NOW we are about places viewed angle-wiſe, it may not be amiſs
to ſhew how the pavement of a hall, church, or other place, is
:to be conducted. Having drawn the horizon parallel to the terreſtrial
line A B, the point of ſight C, and the points of diſtance D and E,. divide the baſe into as many parts as you would have ſquares; then draw
lines from the extremities thereof A and B, to the point of ſight C, and
from the ſame points A and B, draw two diagonals to the points of
diſtance D E, the points of interſection F G will give the ſquare of the
hall, and through them the line of depth H I is to be drawn. Then draw
lines from all the diviſions of the baſe line A C and B C, to the points
·of diſtance D and E, and between the rays A C and B C, you will have
your deſire; as appears from the figure. But here ariſes a difficulty,
namely, how to fill the vacant ſpace B B and G I, A A and H F, with
the ſame ſquares; for it is ſuppoſed the baſe line cannot be prolonged any
farther. On ſuch occaſion, take the meaſure of one of the ſquares, as
G K, on the line F G, and ſet it off on the ſame line H I as often as it
·will go, and you will have the points L M N O P Q and R, through
which drawing lines to the point of diſtance,· you will have the ſame
·ſquares as before; ſuch are thoſe here marked with dots. The ſame
method of ſetting off the meaſures on the line of depth, will be ex-
·emplified in other pavements hereafter.

❀❀❀❀❀❀❀❀❀❀❀❀❀❀❀❀❀❀❀❀❀❀❀❀❀❀❀❀❀❀❀❀

To exhibit the perſpective of a Pavement of Squares
encompaſſed with a Liſt *or* Fillet.

THE method of managing this ſecond pavement with a band
around it, is the ſame with that of ſingle ſquares viewed in front;
I ſhall therefore decline to waſte any time in teaching it, ſince I have already given ſo many figures thereof. It may be proper, however, to
add, that the baſe line is to be divided into unequal parts, as A, B and
C, becauſe of the fillets, and lines to be drawn from all theſe diviſions
to the point of ſight D, and through the points where theſe are interſected by the diagonals A E, and G F, parallels to the baſe line are to
be drawn. By this very plain operation will be produced the appearance
of the pavement ſhewn in the oppoſite figure.   4

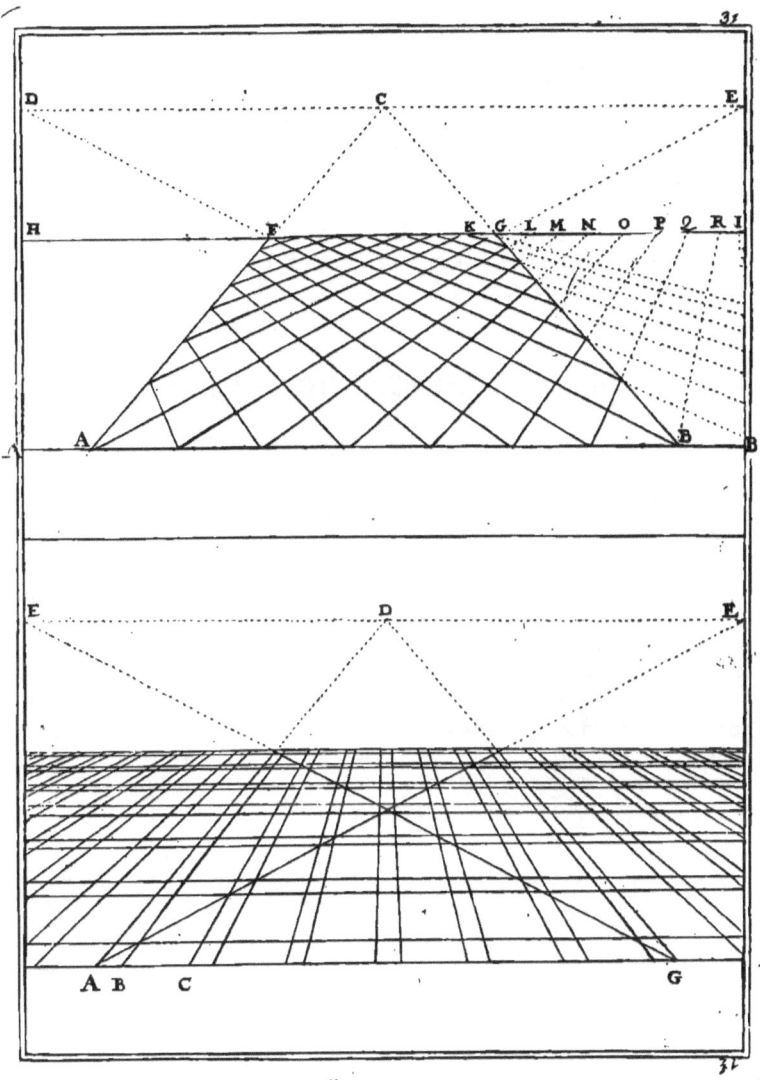

N

To exhibit the perfpective appearance of Pavements
viewed angle-wife, encompaffed with a band or fillet.

FOR fuch kind of PAVEMENT, the bafe line A B is to be divided
into unequal parts, the largeft whereof are to be for the fquares,
and the fmaller for the band or fillet ; and from all thefe divifions, lines
are to be drawn to the points of diftance E F, As has been already
directed in fingle fquares.

❀❀❀❀❀❀❀❀❀❀❀❀❀❀❀❀❀❀❀❀❀❀❀❀❀❀❀❀❀❀

To exhibit the perfpective appearance of Pavements *of*
Squares *viewed in front, encompaffed with bands, or*
fillets, whofe fquares are divided by the angle.

FOR this fourth kind of pavement, the fame method is to be
taken as in the fecond, by fetting the meafures of the firft range
of fquares and fillets on the bafe line, and from thofe points to draw
the lines according to former directions. Then to make the inner
fquares which are feen angle-wife, nothing more is required than to
bifect the loweft fide of each fquare of the firft range, and from thofe
points, as A, B, C, D, E, F, G, draw lines to the two points of diftance, and their interfections with one another will produce the feveral
inner fquares or lozenges throughout the plan.

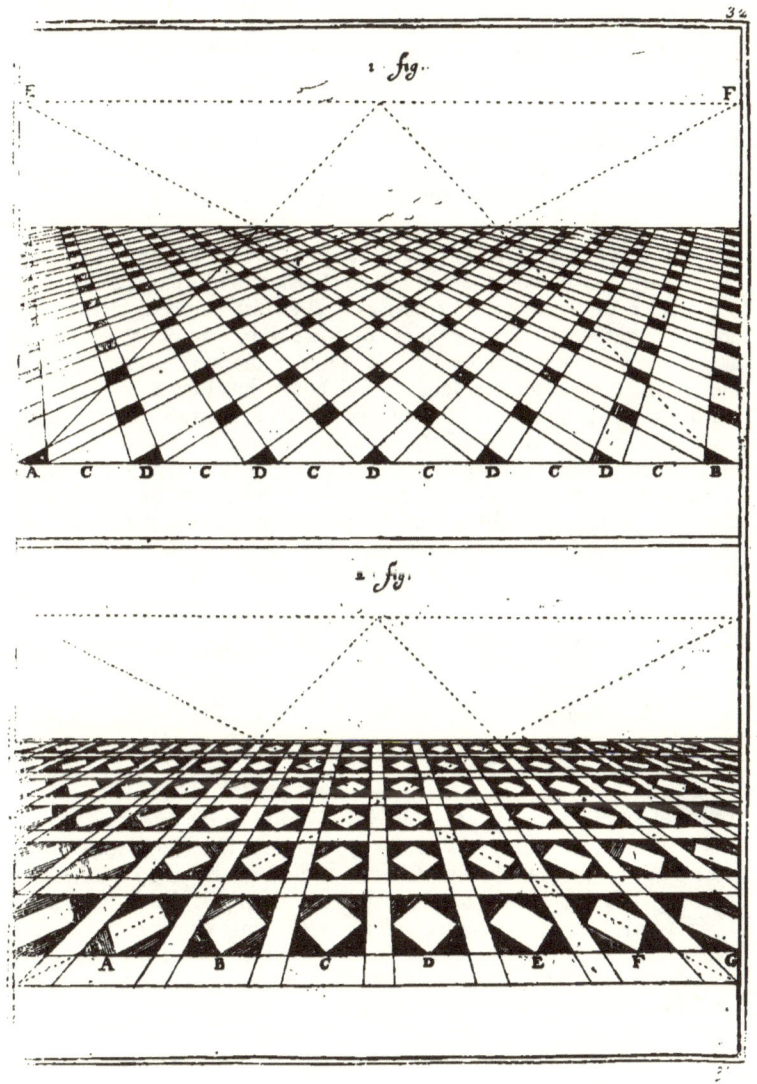

To exhibit a pavement *of* Squares *viewed angle-wife,*
with chains *of* Squares *feen in front.*

I Shall fuppofe the perfpective, or diminution of the fquare, by drawing the line of depth, to be already done, that I may fave the trouble
of too frequent repetitions in the enfuing pavements.

To manage this fifth fort of pavement, divide the bafe line into
equal parts, to anfwer the number of fquares, and from the points of
the fquares to be divided in front, as A B C, draw lines directly to the
point of fight, and from the points of thofe to be feen obliquely, draw
lines to the points of diftance, but without marking them through
the chains.   After all the fquares which are thus viewed by the angle
are drawn, the fquares of the chains will be eafily formed by parallels
from the oppofite angles of the oblique fquares on either fide.   As
for example, from the angle D and E draw the parallel line F, and fo for
all the reft, as is fhewn by the figure.   Care is ftill to be taken, that
there be always the fame number of fquares between the chains ; as
here we have three between A B.   The meafures on the bafe line,
rightly laid down, will prevent any error of that kind.

To exhibit a pavement *of* Squares *in front,* *with* chains
of Squares *angle-wife.*

THIS fixth fort of pavement is performed much after the manner
of the preceding, by dividing the bafe line into equal parts,
according to the number of fquares, and from the points of divifions
drawing lines to the point of fight, to form the bands or chains
G H I ; yet fomewhat more in it, care being taken to make the
crofs there is, of the fame breadth as the others that tend to the point
of fight O, and that there be the fame number of fquares between the
vacuities.   The reft is obvious enough.

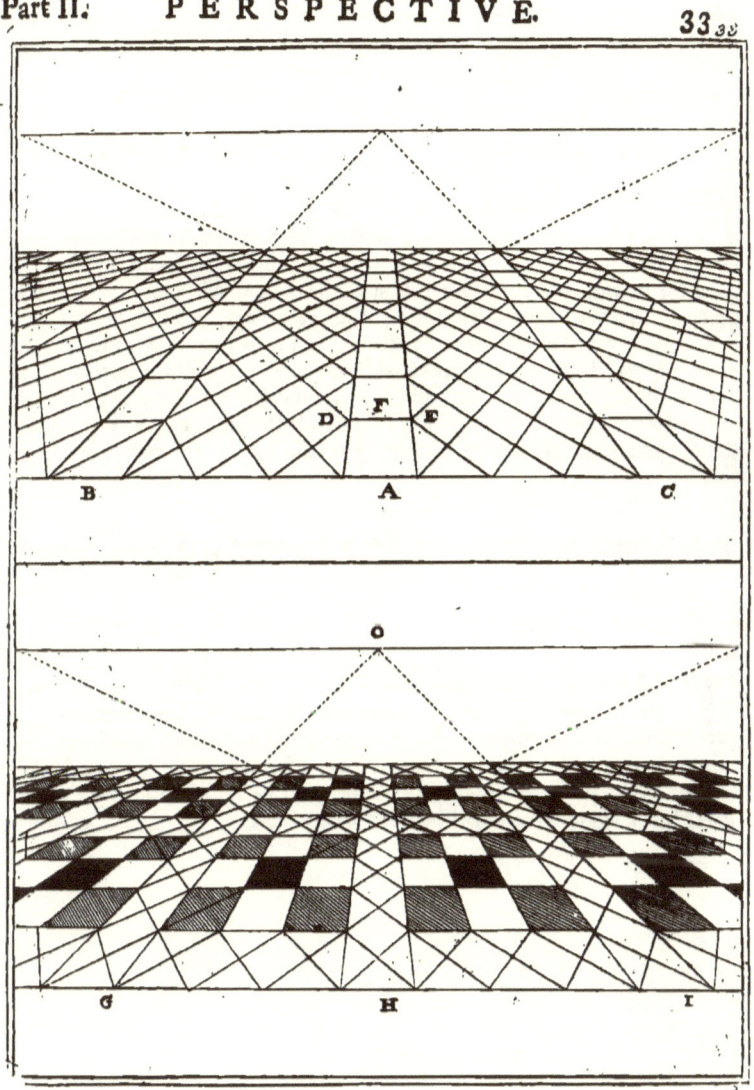

To exhibit a pavement *of* Octagons *intermixed with* Squares.

I should never have done, was I to give all the varieties of pavements: invention would find endlefs employment in their conftruction. This feventh inftance is obvious enough; all I add it for, is to open the mind, and furnifh occafion for the contriving of others. All that is required to produce this kind of pavement, is to divide the bafe line into a number of parts equal to the number of fquares to be formed, as has been already directed. Of which fquares a certain number is to be taken, as here nine, five whereof are full, and the reft only halves; the full ones give the infide of the figure 1 2 3 4 5, and the diagonals of the reft, 6 7 8 9, give the fides : the reft is evident.

❀❀❀❀❀❀❀❀❀❀❀❀❀❀❀❀❀❀❀❀❀❀❀❀❀❀❀❀❀❀❀❀

To exhibit a pavement *of* fingle Squares *viewed in front.*

THIS form I have put the laft, not as being the moft difficult, for in reality it is the eafieft of all, and the very beginning of perfpective, but to intimate that it is the moft ufeful and neceffary ; the others being feldom added but by way of ornament, and this ferving as the foundation whereon any folid is to be raifed, and the elevated parts made appear. As will be fhewn hereafter.

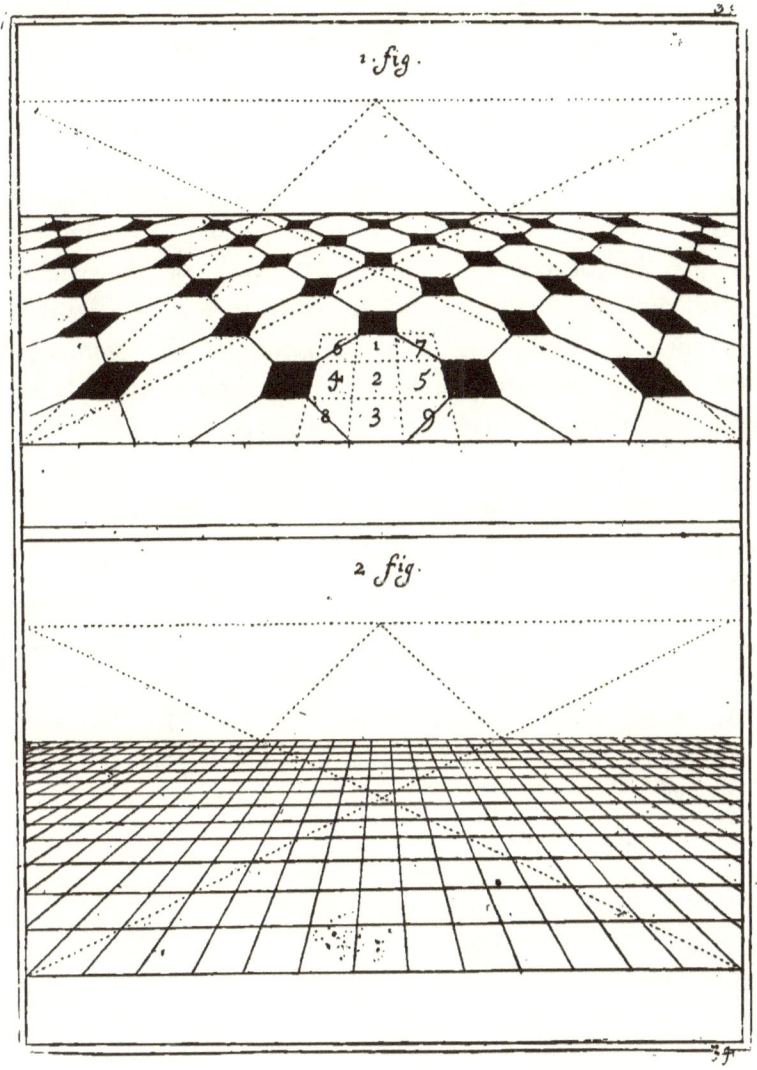

Plan *of a* GARDEN *in perfpective.*

WHAT we have been obferving, is confirmed by this plan, which shews with what facility the projection is made by the foregoing rules. For, drawing lines from all the divifions on the bafe line to the point of fight, the diagonals will give the depth of the whole plan, and the diminution of all the little fquares. Laftly, marking the walks, borders, and figures of the geometrical plan in the correfponding fquare of the projected plane, the whole parterre will be found in perfpective.

. Let the plan given you to put in perfpective, be of what fort foever, the readieft way will be to draw a fquare about it, and divide that into feveral leffer fquares. For after the grand fquare, with all the leffer ones, are projected by the ordinary rules, you have nothing farther to do, but take care that every part is comprifed in the fame number of little fquares in the diminifhed plan as in the geometrical one, and the figure of the one will be exactly found in the other.

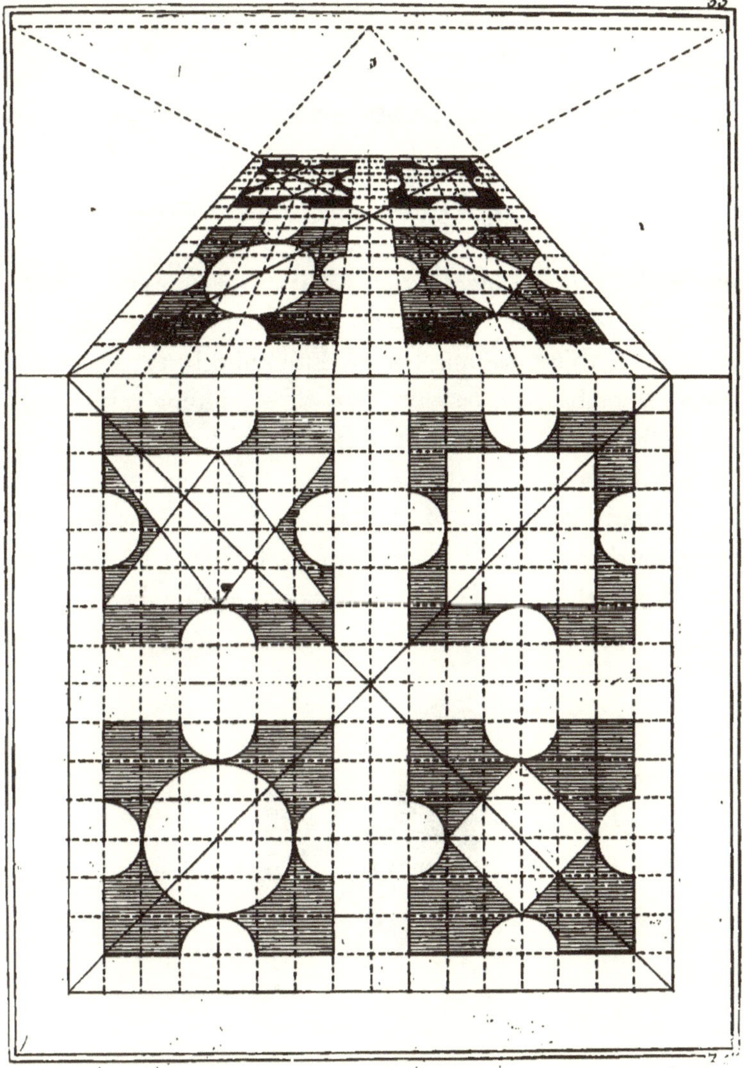

✿✿✿✿✿✿✿✿✿✿✿✿✿✿✿✿✿✿✿✿✿✿✿✿✿✿✿✿✿✿✿✿✿

Plan *of a* Building *in perspective.*

SERLIO, in his treatise of Perspective, sets a
great value on this method of putting plans in perspective, as a thing of singular use in architecture, whereby a
person is enabled to shew one part of a building raised, and
the rest in platform. But this method for exhibiting the
projected plans of buildings, being the same with that I
have already laid down for a garden, I need not say any
thing farther thereof: the figure is sufficient for the rest.
And from this one figure measures are easily taken for any
other, either more easy or difficult ones.

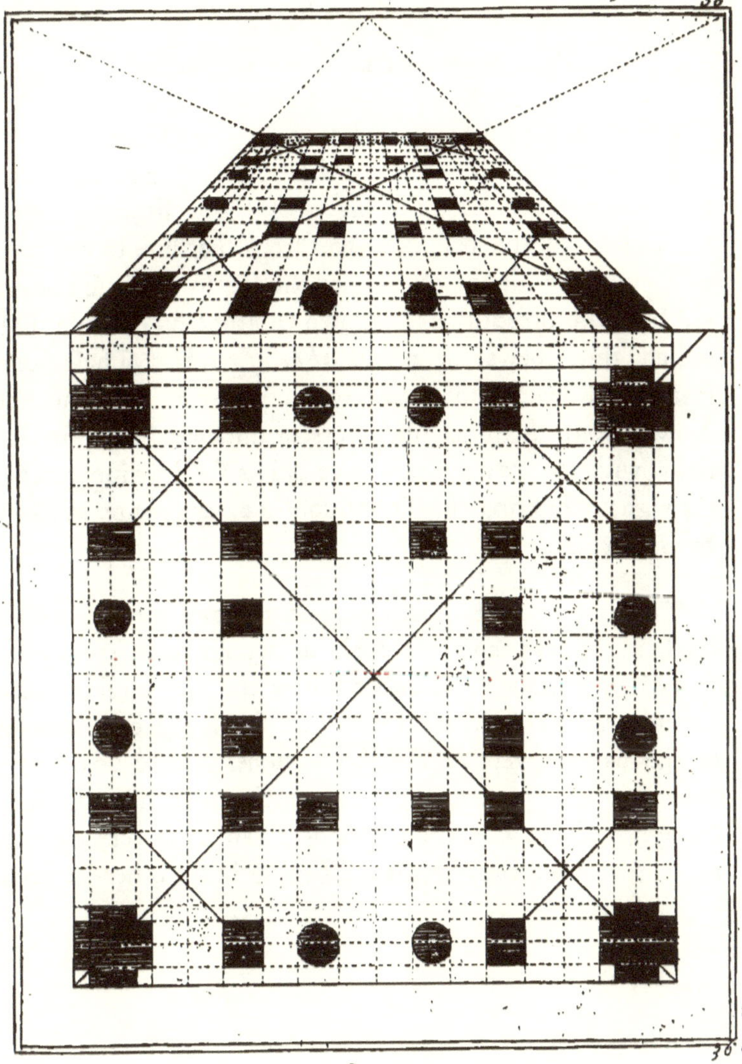

Plan *of a* C H U R C H, *in perfpective.*

THIS plan is conducted according to *Obfervation* VII. page 18. That is, all the fides perpendicular to the bafe line, as are here the places of the walls and pilafters, are drawn to the bafe line, and from that line to the point of fight ; and all the other fides parallel to the bafe line, as are here the breadths, *&c.* drawn to a line on one fide, O P, which thus fhews the points *abcdefghikl.* Thefe points transferred hence upon the bafe line as *a b,* &c. and lines drawn from them to the points of diftance, their interfections with the extreme ray, give points for drawing parallels through, exhibiting the diminution of every thing: as fhewn by *a, b, c,* &c.

This method of diminifhing on the extreme ray is practifed by many; and yet fuch as would take my advice, fhould let it alone, and rather follow the method directed in *Obfervation* VIII. where a perpendicular is raifed on the end of the bafe to receive the interfections, and to obviate the defect of the prefent method, which does not diminifh enough, unlefs where the points of diftance are very remote: for in that cafe, the effect is the fame as in the other methods.

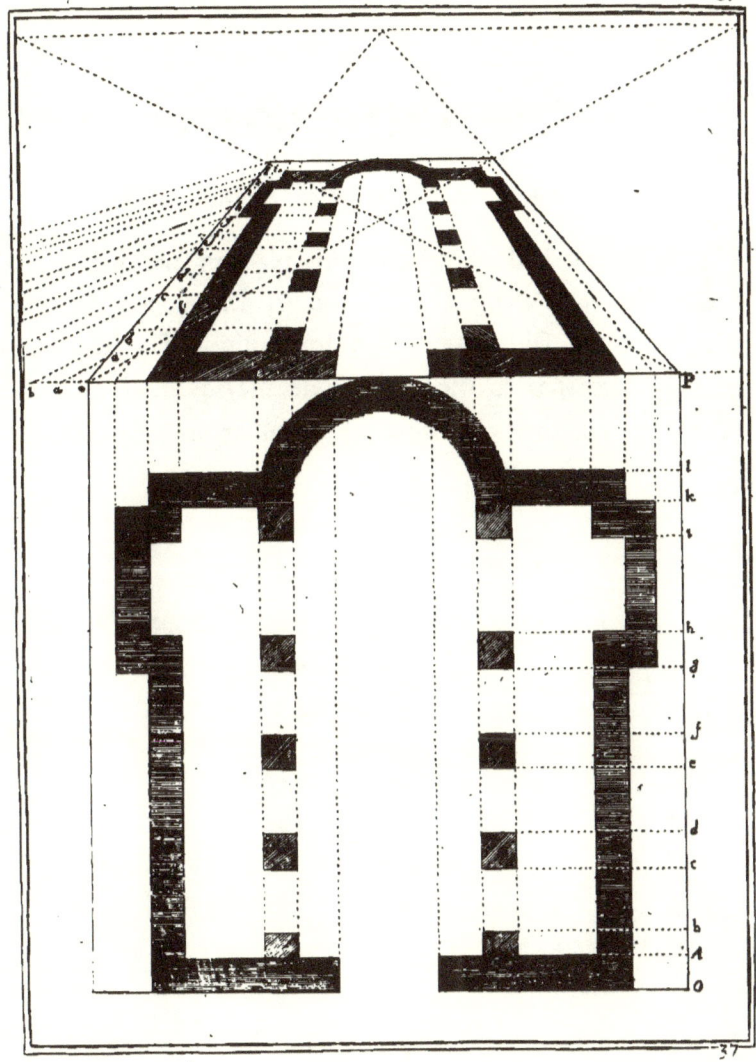

✿✿✿✿✿✿✿✿✿✿✿✿✿✿✿✿✿✿✿✿✿✿✿✿✿✿✿✿✿

PLAN *of a* House *with a* Garden.

THE method of putting this plan in perfpective, is the fame with that of the garden alone; fo that what is there faid may fuffice for both. My defign in putting it here, is to fhew, that one may diminifh all forts of plans, whether confifting of equal or unequal parts.

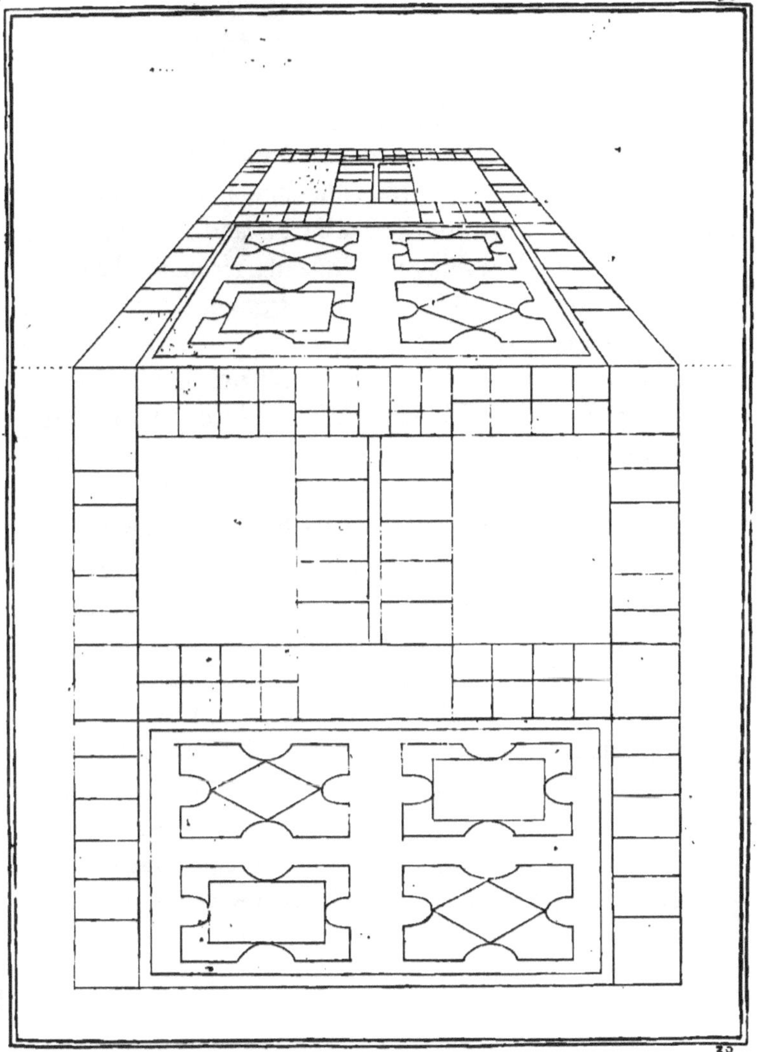

Plan *of a* FORTIFICATION *in perfpective.*

TO put a FORTIFICATION, or other plans of the like kind in perfpective, the VIIth and VIIIth *Obferva-tions*, page 18, are to be ufed. The fame in effect is the method already laid down for the CHURCH and HOUSE, pages 37, 38, namely, by raifing perpendiculars from all the angles to the bafe line, and producing rays from their interfections with the bafe line, to the point of fight; and from the fame angles drawing the parallels to the terreftrial line, and marking the divifions on a fide line, A B. Thefe divifions being transferred thence to the bafe line, and lines drawn from them to the point of diftance, we fhall have the line of interfections C D. But, becaufe there is not room on the plate to put it on the bafe line, I have added it underneath the figure, as in A B. Laftly, having fixed the point of diftance in E; draw lines thence to all the divifions of A B, cutting the line of interfection C D in fo many parts; which line, C D, with its divifions, is to be transferred to the bottom of the extreme ray, in the perfpective plan, or rather fet on each fide, as D D; and from all the points of the lines D C, D C, draw parallels, or only mock-points, on the ray proceeding from the angle of the plan belonging thereto. Which points, connected by lines, give the figure required.

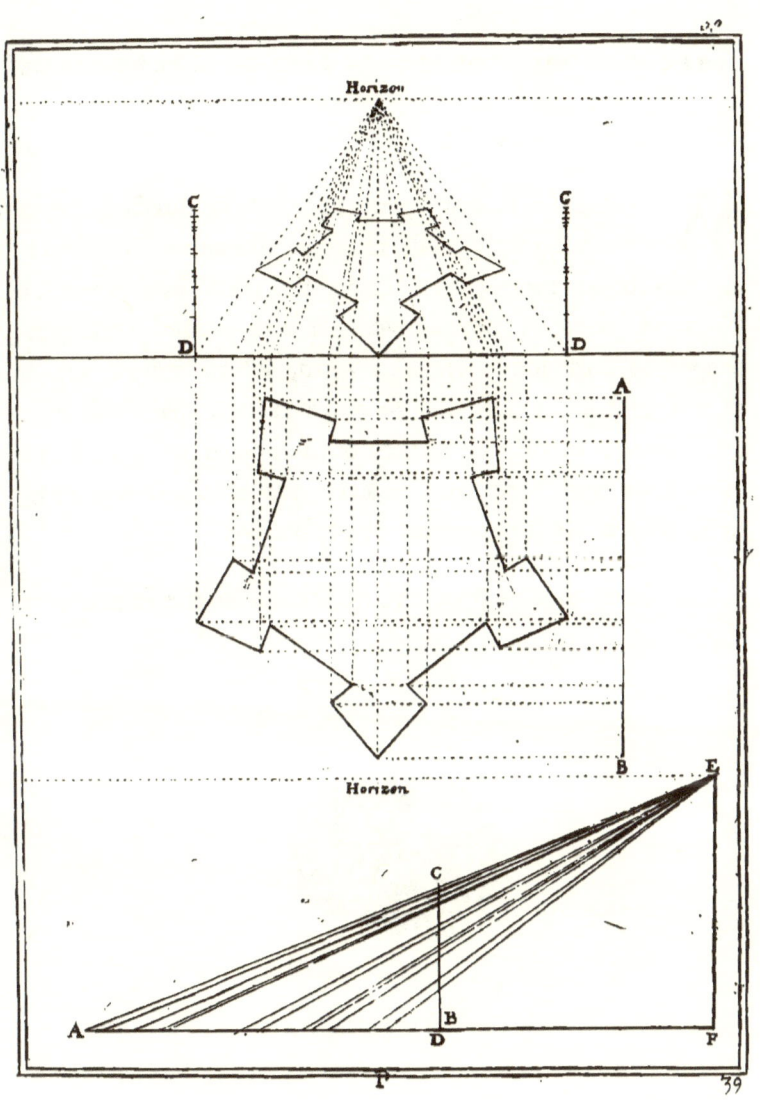

❀❀❀❀❀❀❀❀❀❀❀❀❀❀❀❀❀❀❀❀❀❀❀❀❀❀❀❀❀❀❀❀❀❀

An irregular Plan *and* Figure *in* Perſpeᴄtive.

WHOEVER can perform what is directed under the laſt article, will find no difficulty in project-ing any other figure, that being the moſt intricate of all kinds of plans in perſpeᴄtivc. It was judged, however, proper to add ſome irregular form, which might appear at firſt ſight to be difficult, in order to ſhew that theſe rules are adapted to all the variety of poſſible figures, and that every form and ſhape, in whatever view or aſpeᴄt it is to be ſeen, may eaſily be projeᴄted in perſpeᴄtive.

The lines in this plate are marked as in the former : to repeat the operation is needleſs.

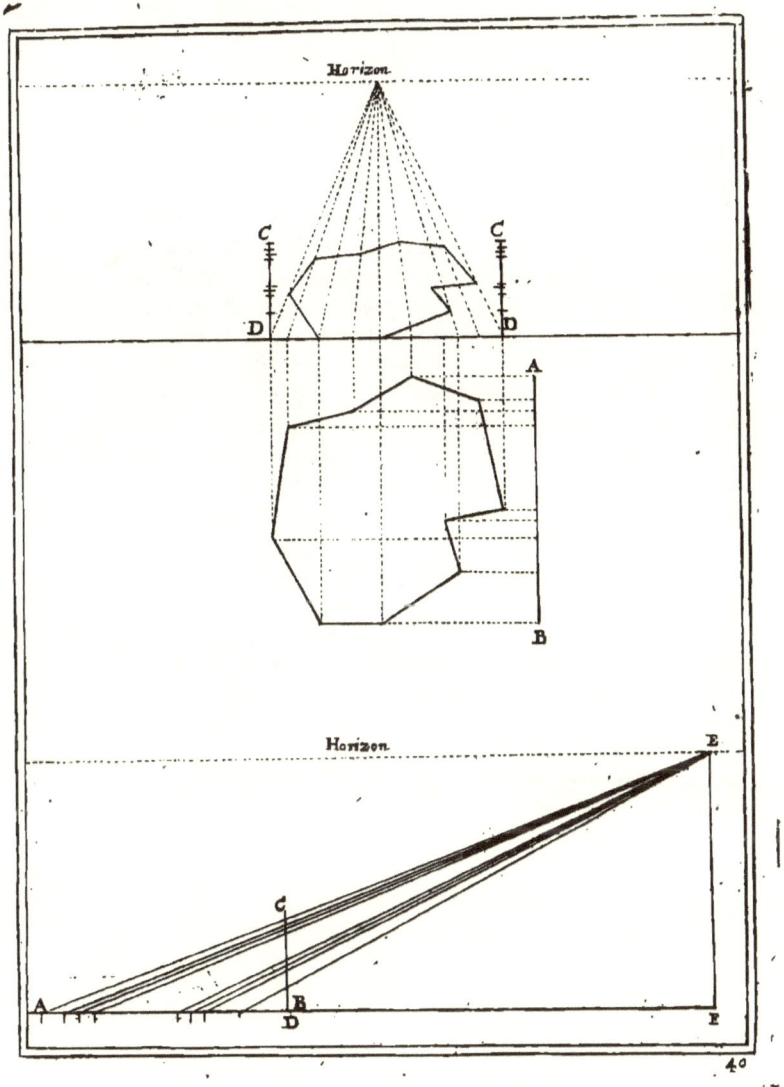

Another plan *of a* CHURCH, *in Perfpective.*

THE manner of projecting the perfpective of this plan, fhould feem very different from what I have hitherto delivered, by reafon of its different difpofition ; but that I own is a thing done defignedly, to fhew that though there be diverfe ways and manners of operation, they are all reducible to one. For this projection, in effect, is the fame with what I have already prefcribed for fortifications, irregular figures, and other plans, with only this difference, that the parallels to the bafe line are there marked on a fide line, and here, on a line in the middle of the plan. But the fame effect is produced from each method ; for drawing lines from all the divifions of the middle line B L to the eye A, you will have the line of interfection B C, which is upon what may be called the bafe line D E.

To put the geometrical plan in perfpective, transfer the whole length of the terreftrial line D E to any place at pleafure, as D E in the perfpective plan, and fet off the height of the eye A F ; then, putting the line of interfection B C either in the middle, or on one fide, draw parallels to the bafe line through all its divifions to the extreme rays D A, E A, and fet the breadth of the pilafters D K on the bafe line ; then drawing a line from K to the point of fight A, the points wherein it interfects the parallel lines will be the widths of the pilafters.

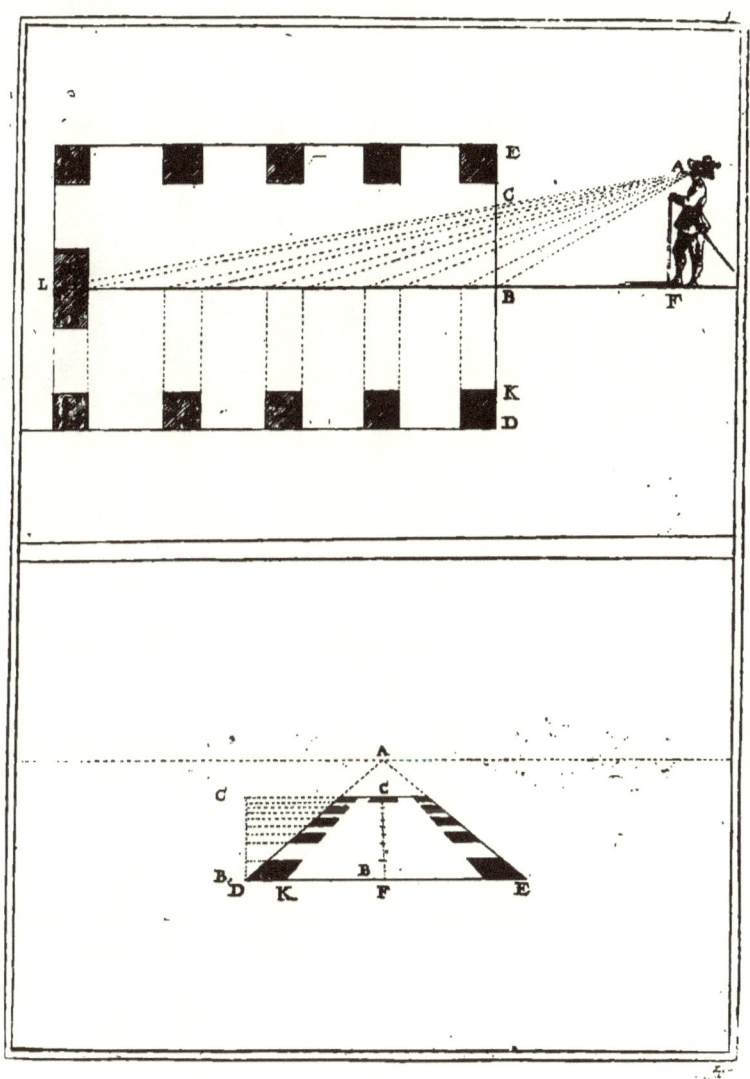

RULES

FOR

ELEVATIONS.

PART III.

Preliminary inftructions *neceffary to the following methods.*

T H E reader is by this time fufficiently inftructed in what relates to Ichno-graphy and Planigraphy, confidered as the foundations of Orthography and Scenography.

Orthography, I have already defined to be the elevation of the fore-right plane or front of any object, the elevation of the face or front, &c. and Sceno-graphy the elevation of all the parts. See the DEFINITIONS, page 7.

To make myfelf more intelligible to fuch as are not verfed in the ufe of thofe words, I purpofe, as already promifed, for the future to call Ichnography the *Plan*; the Orthography, the *Upright* or *Elevation* of the front; and Sceno-graphy, the *Elevation* of the whole.

Here it is to be obferved, that elevations never give the eye all the angles of the plan, and that the quantity of fides, or angles which appear to the eye, depends on the afpect or view the object is taken in. Thus, if it be viewed in front, as the figure A, it will only fhew one fide, though the plan hath four. If it be viewed by the angle, it will fhew two, as B; but never more, in what-ever view it be taken. I fpeak of fquares; for as to objects of many fides, they may fhew three, four, five, and more.

When objects decline ever fo little from the point of view, they are feen by the angle, and of confequence muft fhew two fides. And ftill the farther they are removed from the point of fight, the more of the fide they fhew; thus the fide K E fhews more of itfelf than C L, though their thicknefs be equal.

Another thing to be obferved is, that the lines which are parallel to the hori-zon when the object is viewed in front, as C D E F of the door in *Fig.* 1. be-come a vifual ray when the fame object is viewed a little obliquely. Thus C D E F, which in the upper figure ftands in front, becomes a vifual ray in that underneath. And, on the contrary, the lines which are rays in the upper, be-come parallel to the bafe in the under. As to perpendiculars, they always con-tinue perpendiculars in whatever view the projected bodies are exhibited.

9

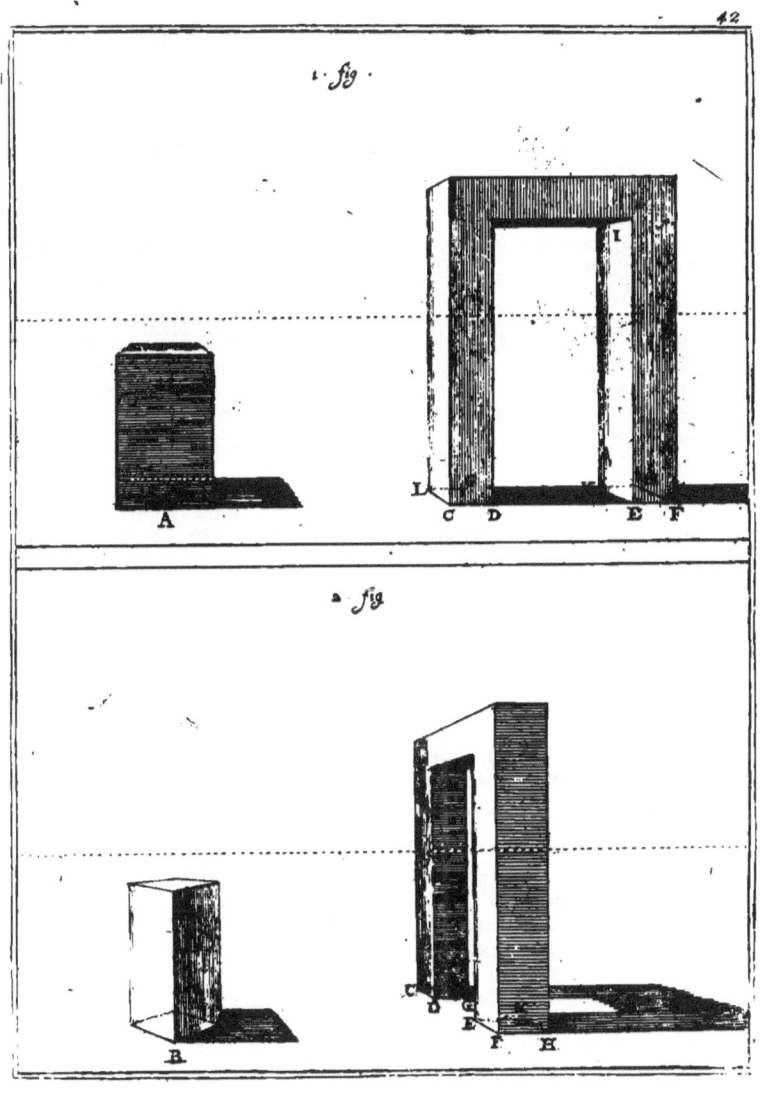

1. fig.

2. fig.

Q

Of the Line *of* E L E V A T I O N, *ferving to give the* Heights *of all Kinds of* Objeƈts *in all Parts of the* Plan.

T H E ufe of this line is of the laft importance, infomuch, that whoever is perfeƈtly mafter thereof, will fcarce meet with any difficulty in raifing any kind of elevation.

As in the putting planes in perfpeƈtive we made ufe of the bafe line ; fo in elevations, another line is to be ufed to direƈt us, and carry the proper heights to all the objeƈts to be raifed.

This *line of elevation* muft be perpendicular to the bafe line A B, which is always the firft line of the plan, and that next the eye, and of confequence the fitteft to carry the meafures to the feveral objeƈts in the plan. On this account the line of elevation C D, is raifed perpendicularly on A B, as the other lines in the plan fhould be. Infomuch, that it is to be remembered as a rule, that whenever, in the courfe of this work, mention is made of perpendiculars, it is to be underftood of perpendiculars to the bafe.

Since this line of elevation is to receive and give the heights of all objeƈts to be raifed on the plan, it muft have the fame horizon with the plan. Therefore, from the foot of this line (which is placed either on the right or left) a line is to be drawn to fome part of the horizon, though what part does not matter, the effeƈt being the fame in all. In this figure, the line of elevation is C D, and from C the line is drawn to the point of the horizon in E ; or it might be drawn to the point of fight, if one pleafed. I have here put the line of elevation on either fide, and the point different in each, to fhew that it will anfwer any where.

If from the point H, which is in the plan of the fecond figure, you would raife a line of two feet height, fet two equal parts on the line of elevation, which you hold equivalent each to one foot, fuch is here C F ; and from C drawing a line to the point E, you will have an elevation of two feet between the two lines C and F.

Now, to give the fame height of two feet to a line raifed from the point H, from H draw an occult line parallel to the bafe line, till it meet the line C E in the point I ; then from the point I ereƈt a perpendicular I K ; this will be the height of the line required, which is to be taken hence in the compaffes, and fet off from H to L.

If a line likewife two feet high were required to be drawn from the point M, the fame operation being repeated, you will have the perpendicular N O, which will be the height required from M. Laftly, performing the fame for the point P, you will have the perpendicular Q R for the height of a line of two feet from the point P.

The fame rule will give a height of 3, 4, 5, 10 or 20 feet ; all required being to fet fuch heights on the line of elevation, from thofe heights to draw lines to the point in the horizon, as E, and to proceed with the reft as above.

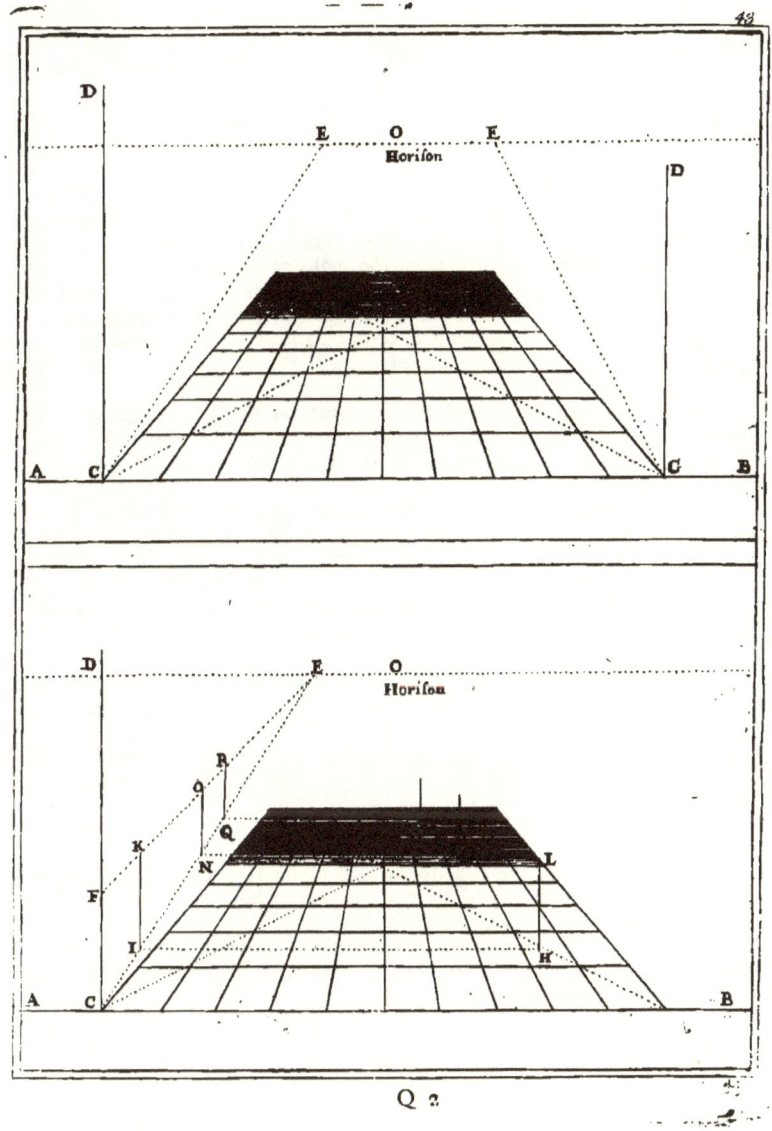

To exhibit the ELEVATION *of a* Cube *in* Perfpective.

HAVING projected the plan according to the preceding rules, and raifed the line of elevation as F L, fet off the height of the cube thereon, namely F M, and from the points F and M draw lines to the point of elevation E. From the feveral angles of the plan A B C D, draw parallels to the bafe line, till they meet with the line F E, and from the points of interfection F and H, erect perpendiculars F M and H K; then taking thofe meafures in your compaffes, fet them perpendicularly upon the angles of the plan; thus, taking the height F M, fet it on the two perpendiculars raifed from A and B, which will give you A G and B G; then taking the height H K, fet it on perpendiculars raifed from C and D, which will give you C O, D O; laftly, joining the right lines G O, O G, the cube will be raifed.

Or, if you draw parallels to the bafe line from M and K, their points of interfection with the perpendiculars A G, B G, C O, D O, will be the altitude of the cube, and thofe points connected by ftraight lines will complete its figure.

For the elevation of any figure whatever, always draw lines from the feveral angles of its plan, parallel to the bafe line, till they cut the line drawn from the foot of the line of elevation, and proceed in all refpects as directed for the cube, and you will find there is no figure however difficult and irregularly formed, but will be thus brought into its perfpective. Examples of which I fhall give in the polygons following.

The fecond figure is another cube, raifed after a fomewhat different manner from the firft. The procefs I fhall defcribe in few words, being nothing contemptible.

Having difpatched the plan the ordinary way, from the feveral angles thereof, B C D E, erect perpendiculars; and on the firft of them, B C, fet off the given height of the cube, namely B A, C A; then from the points A A draw lines to the point of fight F, or to the points of diftance G H, and the points I and L, wherein they interfect the perpendiculars of the angles D and E, will give the line of depth, and the top of the cube perfectly raifed.

This latter method is much lefs univerfal than the former, which has always been in ufe among the oldeft authors; yet has it fome advantages which I fhall have occafion to touch upon hereafter.

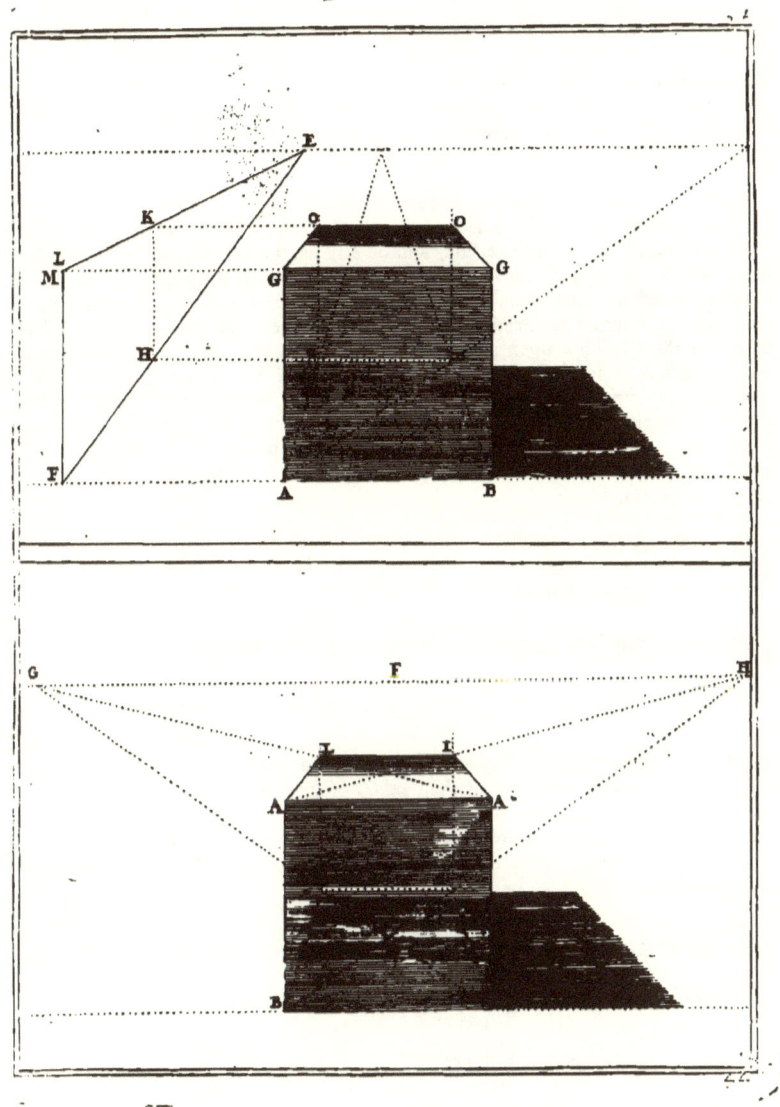

To find the Elevation *of a* TRIANGLE.

I Now proceed to fhew with how much eafe all kinds of figures may be raifed in perfpective. Of thefe, polygons, or figures of many fides, are the moft difficult. I fhall therefore choofe to exemplify in thefe; and, to obferve fome order, will begin with the moft fimple, the TRIANGLE.

Having formed the plan, as already directed, page 21, where is fhewn the method of drawing it with a ledge or lift; the line of Elevation, as juft now intimated, muft be fet on one fide, and of any height at pleafure, for example B A, which we fuppofe to be three feet; then from all the angles of the plan drawing parallel lines, parallel to the bafe line, to the line B E, and from the points of interfection erecting perpendiculars between the lines A E and B E, fet off all their heights upon the feveral angles, whence the parallels proceed. The height A B for inftance, on the angles C and D, which will give C R and D S, the height N P on the angle Q, which will give Q Y. Then for the inner angles, fet F I on G and O which will give G T and O V, and N L fet on K will give K K. Laftly, connecting the points R, S and Y, and again the points T, V and X, by right lines, you will have the triangle in its proper thicknefs, &c.

By drawing lines parallel to the bafe line, from the points A I L P, the points of their interfection with the perpendiculars raifed from the angles of the plan, will give the angles of its elevation.

✿✿✿✿✿✿✿✿✿✿✿✿✿✿✿✿✿✿✿✿✿✿✿✿✿✿✿✿✿✿✿✿✿✿✿✿✿✿✿

To exhibit a PENTAGON, *or* Five-angle, *in perfpective.*

THE PENTAGON, I have faid, is a figure with five fides, and as many angles; and have directed the method of forming its projection, page 22. As to the making its elevation, I fhould lofe time to defcribe it, the figure hereto annexed, with the lines drawn from its angles, and from the perpendiculars of its altitude, fhewing abundantly that its method is the fame with that of the cube and triangle.

✿✿✿✿✿✿✿✿✿✿✿✿✿✿✿✿✿✿✿✿✿✿✿✿✿✿✿✿✿✿✿✿✿✿✿✿✿✿✿

To exhibit the elevation of a HEXAGON, *or* Six-angle, *in perfpective.*

THE HEXAGON is a figure with fix angles, and as many fides or faces, as already obferved, pages 23, and 27. where I have given its diminution. The method of raifing it is obvious enough from the figure.

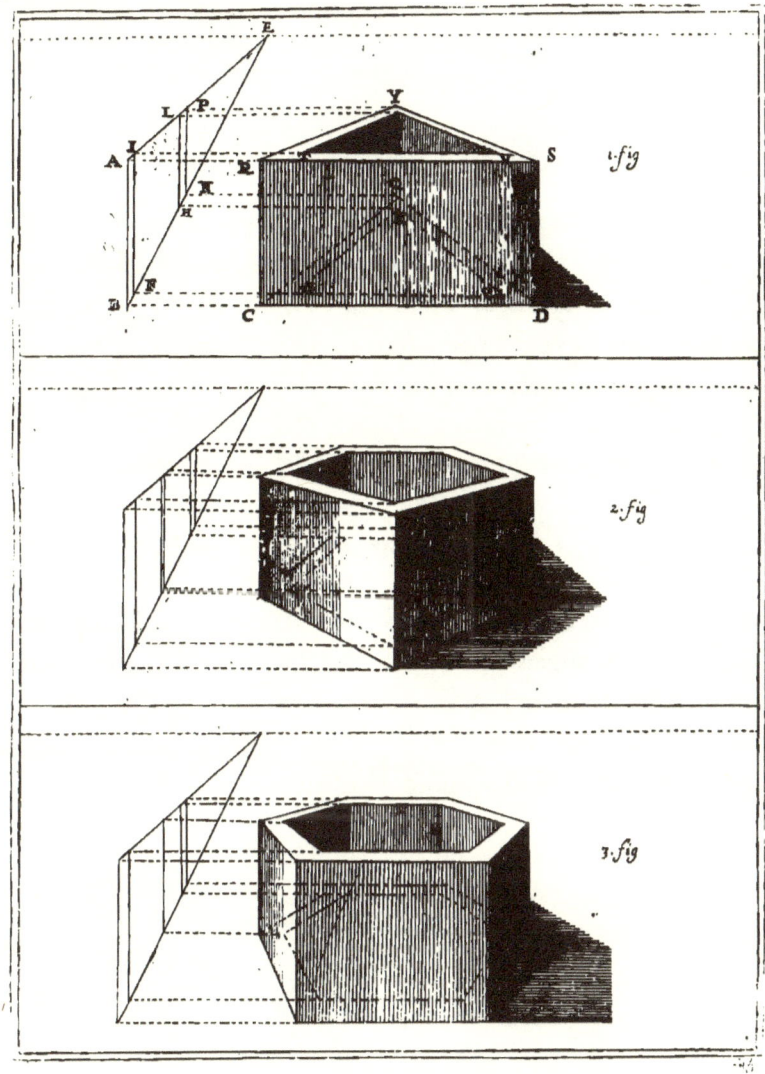

1. fig

2. fig

3. fig

The Heptagon, *or* Seven-Angle, *in* perspective.

THE Heptagon is a figure with seven sides and angles; the manner of describing it, and of putting its plan in perspective, I have already given in page 24. Its elevation is performed after the same manner as that of the triangle, as appears from *Fig.* I.

❖✿

The Octagon, *or* Eight-Angle, *in* perspective.

THE Octagon is a figure with eight sides and as many angles, as represented in pages 25, 26. where the reader will find different ways of putting the plan in perspective. Its elevation is to be procured in the same manner as that of the preceding object.

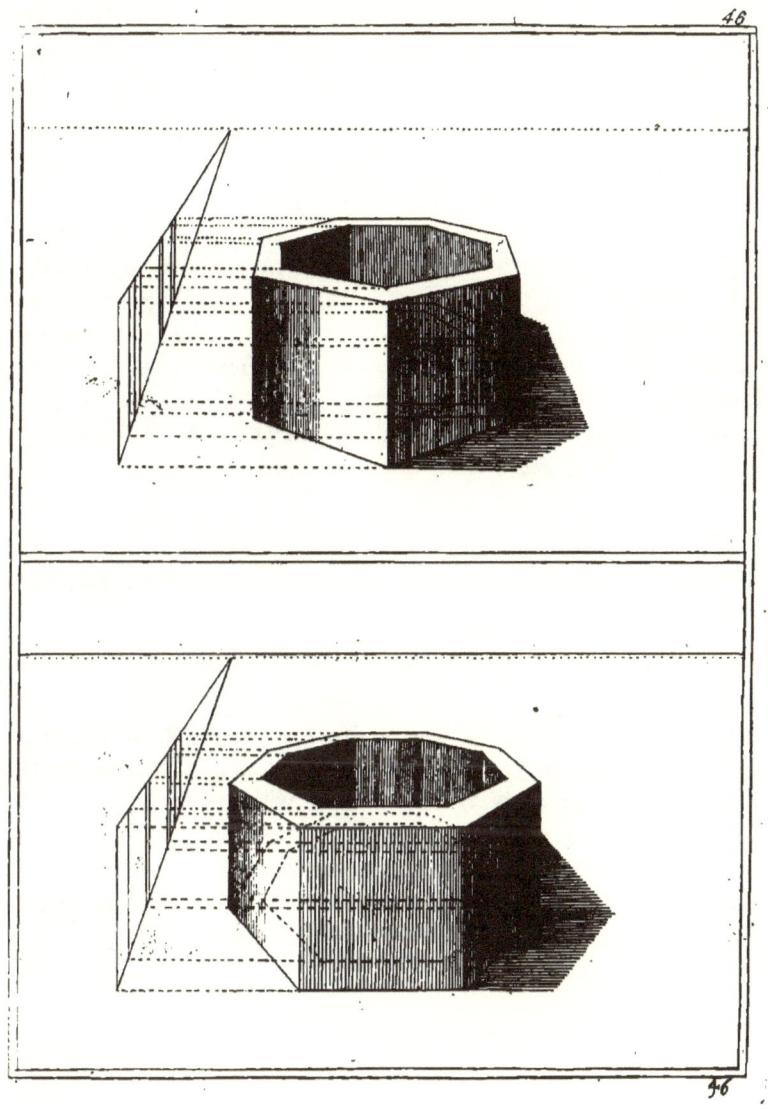

R

A Double Crofs *in perfpective.*

THIS and the following figure I add from the Sieur de *Maralois*, who has given them a place in his works according to the method I have already laid down.   The truth is, it would be fomewhat difficult to put them in perfpective any other way, by reafon of the multiplicity of their angles; but in this method all is eafy, by only raifing the heights from all the angles of the plan, *&c.* as already obferved of polygons, and is evident from the figure.

A Stone fluted, *or* channeled ftar-wife, *in perfpective.*

NOT having given the plan of this figure among the other plans, I have judged proper to add it underneath.   The geometrical plan is eafily made, as being only a circle whofe periphery is divided into fix parts and the divifions joined by right lines, leaving a point between each two; as, for example, between 1 and 3, leaving 2; and from 2 to 4, leaving 3; and fo of the other.   The reft is obvious from the fecond figure.   3

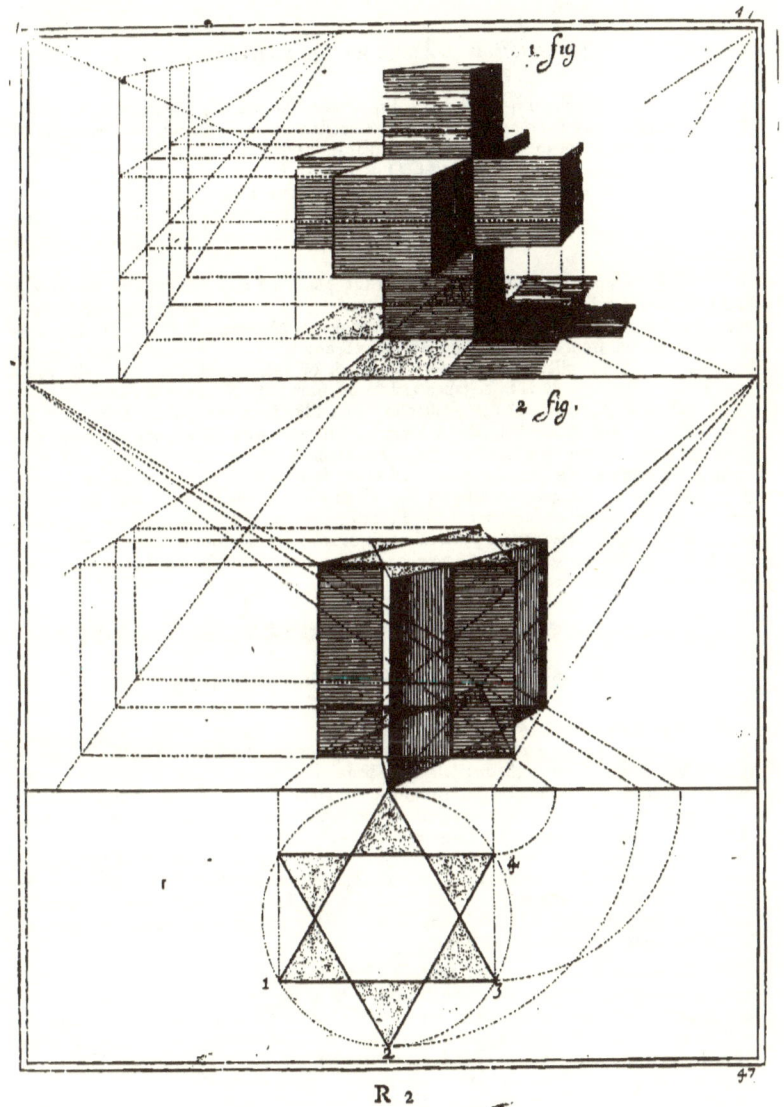

1. fig

2. fig.

To exhibit PILASTERS in perspective.

IN the raising of columns, pilasters, walls, or the like objects, which are to be of the
same height, there is no need of a line of elevation; it is sufficient to proceed as in
the second method for the cube, page 44, that is, having raised perpendiculars from the
angles of the plan, as here from A B C D of *Fig.* 1. set the height desired on the first
or second perpendiculars, as A F or D E; then drawing a line from E to the point of
sight F, to this line all the perpendiculars from the angles from the inner side of the pilasters are to be raised. In which case, the pilasters G and H will have equal altitudes to
the first.

If one choose not to make use of squares in the plan, the measures must be laid on the
base line, and rays be drawn thence to the point of sight F, and other rays for the diminutions to the point of distance K. Thus, for example, L M being a side of a pilaster, rays
are to be drawn from the two points thereof, L and M, to the point of sight F, for the
breadths of all the pilasters; and for the depth of each, as they are intended to be
square, the distance L M is to be taken and set off from L to N; then drawing a line to
K, it will give the depth of the pilaster in O; lastly, from the points L M O erect
perpendiculars, and proceed as above directed. If you would have the width of two
pilasters between one and another, set them accordingly on the base line, and after
making the depth of the second pilaster equal to the first, as here P Q, from the two points
P Q draw lines to the point of distance K, which will give the points R S on the ray L;
and from S draw another short parallel S T, cutting the ray M F; lastly, from the three
points R, S and T, erecting perpendiculars, proceed as in the former case. A third and
fourth pilaster, &c. are to be added after the same manner, still observing the same measures
on the base line as in the first figure.

❀❀❀❀❀❀❀❀❀❀❀❀❀❀❀❀❀❀❀❀❀❀❀❀❀❀❀❀❀❀❀❀❀❀❀❀❀❀

To exhibit PILASTERS viewed by the angle.

I HAVE already observed, page 17, that the plan of squares is formed by drawing
lines from the divisions of the base line to the point or distance. As to the elevations,
the method is the same with that just described. For having set the height A B on the
first perpendicular, lines must be drawn from the point B to the points of distance C D,
which will intersect and give the heights of the other perpendiculars raised on each side.
Then giving the distances required between the two pilasters, which are two squares, raise
the second; and by the same rule the third. Their heights will be found by drawing
a visual ray from the point B to the point of sight E, the intersections whereof with the
first perpendiculars in the points F and F, as also the intersections of other lines from F
and F to the points of distance C and D with the other perpendiculars, will give the
heights required, as in the first pilaster.

These pilasters which are raised without plans, must have their measures on the base
line, as if they were to have the same breadth with those viewed in front. Accordingly,
the breadth G H must be marked, and a ray be drawn from G to the point of sight E,
which will give all the middle points, or diameters. Then setting the same breadth from
G to I, from the three points G H I draw lines to the points of distance C D, which
form the first plan. On this plan erect perpendiculars, on the first whereof set off the
height, as G K, and from the point K draw lines to the points of distance, which will
give the shortnings of the perpendiculars of each side. For the second pilaster, do the
same with the points L and M: and for the third, with the points N O. The rest is
evident from the figure.   I

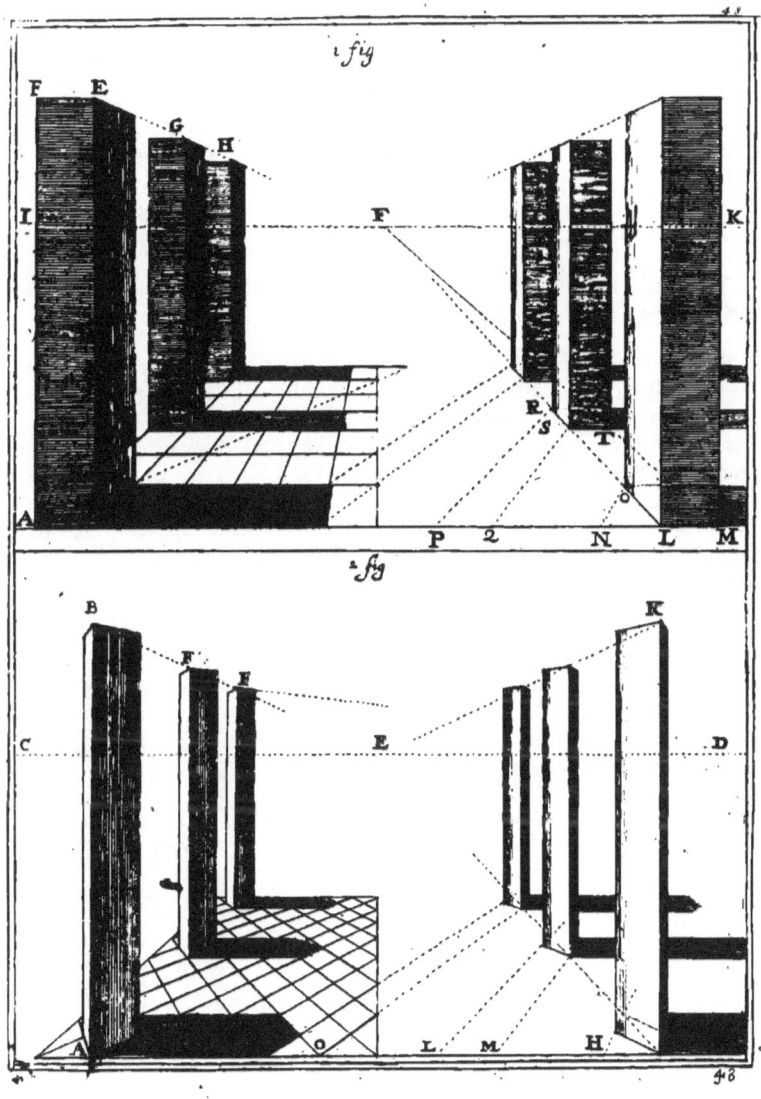

Effect *of the* Difference *of* HORIZONS.

THE higher a man is raifed above an object, the more he fees of the upper part thereof; of confequence the lower he is, the lefs he fees; and if he be underneath it, he only fees the bottom part, and nothing of the top.

The firft propofition is evident from *Fig.* 1. the fecond from *Fig.* 2. and the third from the laft.

The firft and fecond cubes are formed after the manner already delivered. The third are alfo produced by the fame rules, though they may appear fomewhat more difficult, by reafon the object is feen overhead; but inverting the paper, or painting, and drawing lines to the point of fight A, and points of diftance B and C, as in the former methods, you will have the fame facility in exhibiting them. I fay nothing of objects viewed fide-wife, as having fo often repeated, that the method is the fame as thofe in front. To render the practice of putting them in perfpective more eafy, I have added in the next plate two figures, the one a bare out-line, the other fhadowed farther.

Before we quit this third figure, it is to be obferved, that the lownefs of the horizon is the reafon we fee the bottoms of objects, as D E F, whereas of the two others, GH, placed in the horizon, neither top nor bottom can be feen. Not the top, by reafon of the lownefs of the horizon; nor the bottom, becaufe they are the horizon itfelf.

There are abundance of painters faulty in this point, inconfiderately fhewing the tops of objects, even where the horizon is very low.

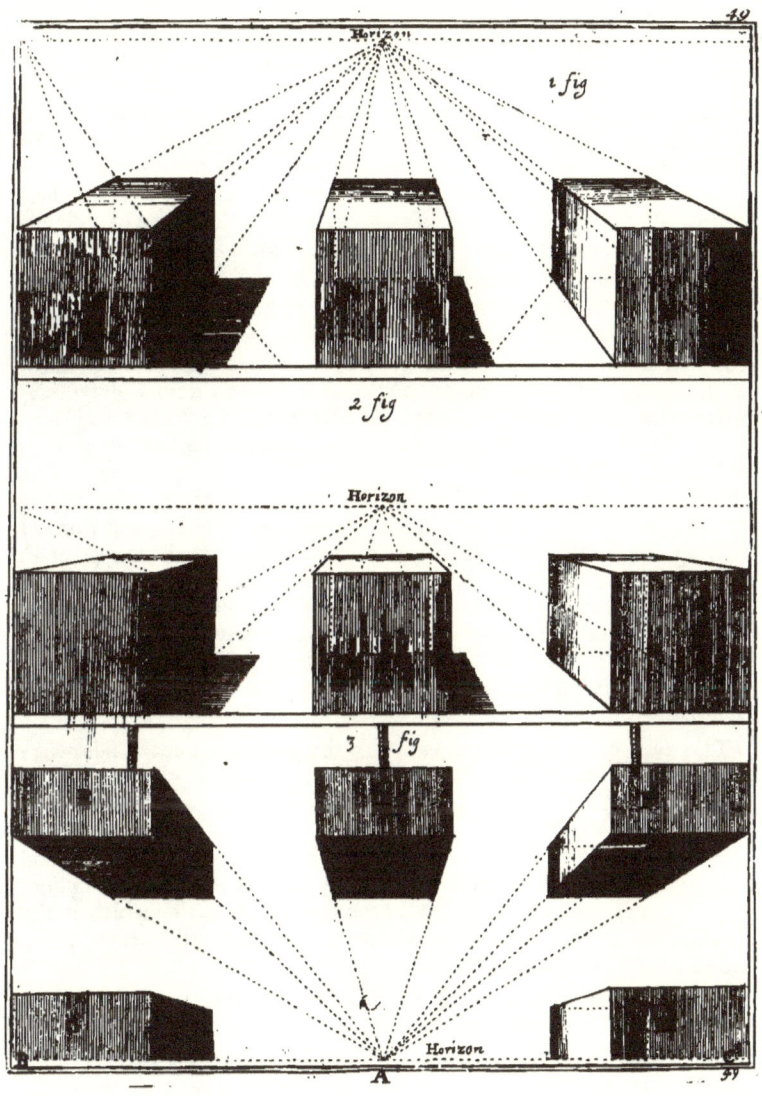

Elevation *of* Objects *viewed by the Angle.*

I HAVE fhewn in pages 19, 20. that in the projection of oblique plans, the lines are always to be drawn to the point of diftance, not to the point of fight, unlefs for finding the diameter. The fame rule is to be obferved in raifing the elevations, as is evident from the firft figures, all the lines whereof are drawn towards the points of diftance B and C, and none of them to the point of fight A.

The firft figure D fhews that though there be a multiplicity of parts in any object feen angle-wife, they are all to be drawn to the points of diftance B and C. To perform the operation, the rule is this; having projected a plan, and raifed occult perpendiculars, as already directed, fet the given height on the firft angle, as E F, and from F draw lines to the points of diftance B C, for the heights of the fecond and third angles, in the points of interfection G G, then from G G draw lines to B and C, and you will have the fourth angle of the platform. The other leffer pieces are raifed after the fame manner, namely, by fetting the heights on the firft perpendicular, as from F to H; and from H drawing lines to the points C and B, as before done from the point F. By fuch means you will have the heights of all the angles, and the points I and K will give the thickneffes of all the leffer pieces, and the platform of the middle, by ftill continuing to draw lines to the points B and C. The reft is evident from the figure, which may ferve for a caftle defended with four fquare towers, or for a palace cantoned with four pavilions.

The two other objects on each fide the great one are feen fide-wife; the manner of drawing them is in all refpects like thofe viewed in front. Thus, raifing perpendiculars from all the angles of the plan L, and giving the neceffary height to the firft of them, as M N, and drawing a line from the point N to the points of diftance B C, you will have the fecond and third angles in the points of interfection O O; then drawing lines from O to the points B C, you will have the fourth angle, which is the elevation of the whole. This is according to the firft method; the fecond would have given the fame.

The fecond figure underneath is produced the fame way; all the difference is, that in this the horizon is fomewhat lower.

The third fhews the bottom of the objects; but the method is ftill the fame as in thofe that fhew the tops, the lines being drawn to the points of diftance Q R in the horizontal line.

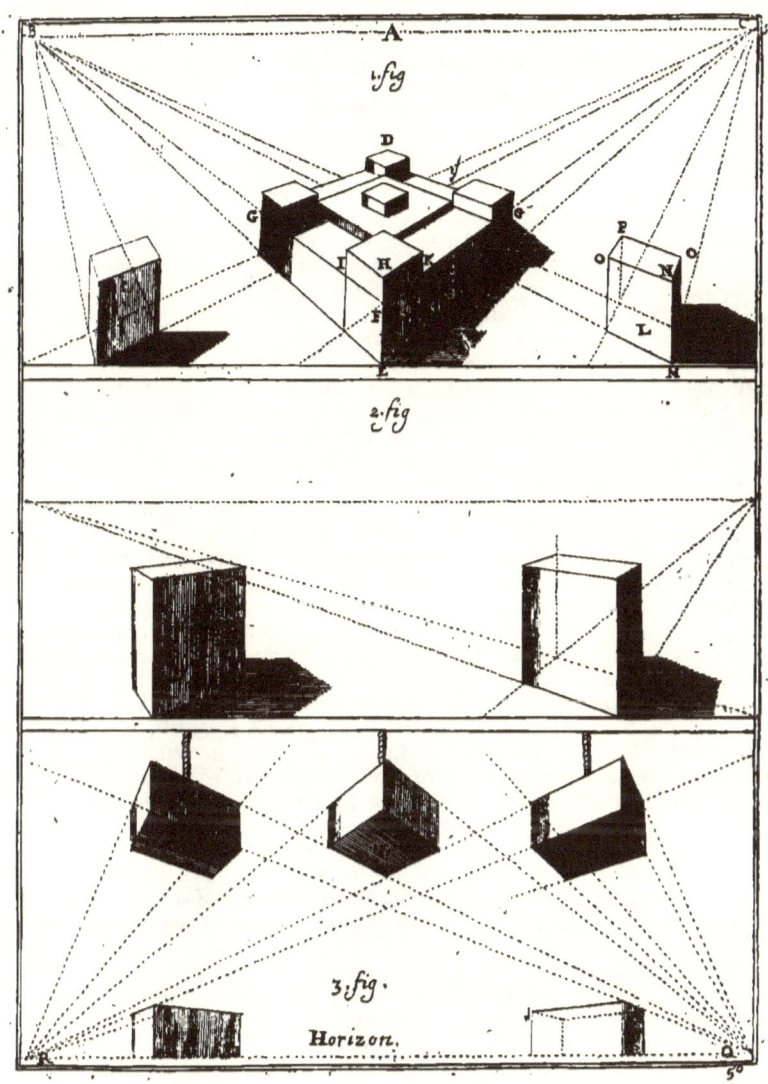

1.fig

2.fig

3.fig

Horizon.

S

To raife objeƈts of any heights, and remove them to any diſtance at pleaſure.

SUPPOSE it be required to have an objeƈt two feet high, one foot broad, and one foot deep; and another three feet high, one foot broad, two feet deep, and two feet diſtant from the firſt objeƈt; and another a foot broad, five feet deep, four feet high, and three feet diſtant from the middle objeƈt; your method of proceeding will be thus. Having formed a plan of fquares, fuppoſed each equivalent to one foot, by means of the points of fight A, and diſtance B C; from the firſt angle D ereƈt a perpendicular according to the fecond method, page 48, which perpendicular is to carry the proper meaſures to all the objeƈts, as here D E, wherein the meaſure D F, is fet four times, by reaſon the higheſt objeƈt is not to exceed four feet. From the feveral angles of the firſt fquare F I G D ereƈt occult perpendiculars; and having fet the proper meaſure, namely two feet, on the firſt of them, D, from the point 2 draw a line to the point of fight A, and it will cut the perpendicular of the angle G in the point H, through which a line is to be drawn parallel to the baſe, cutting the perpendicular of the angle I in K, and another parallel to be drawn through the point 2, cutting the perpendicular of the angle F in the point L; then connecting the four points H K L and 2, by right lines, you will have the firſt objeƈt. Now as you would have a fpace of two feet between the firſt and fecond objeƈt, two fquares are to be left vacant between them; and on the firſt angles of the third, perpendiculars are to be raiſed, and the fame operation performed as to the firſt objeƈt, with this difference, that the height of the fecond is to be taken from the third point of the line D E, by reaſon it is to be three feet high, and that it muſt take up two fquares, fince it is to be two feet deep. Between this fecond and the third objeƈt the fpace of three fquares is to be left, by reaſon there is to be three feet diſtance from the one to the other. From the firſt angles of the fourth fquare perpendiculars are to be raiſed as for the firſt objeƈt, and five fquares farther, another perpendicular for the line of the depth, and the bound of the five feet, which is the depth of this third objeƈt. The fourth point of the line D E gives its height, four feet, by cutting the perpendiculars, as in the firſt objeƈt. The objeƈts on the other fide are raiſed in the fame manner, and on the fame proportions as thefe; but the wall in the middle is of an equal height every where, namely, three feet, with an aperture of four feet in the middle.

In the fecond figure are three walls of equal height; whereof that in the middle is a fquare deeper than the two extreme ones. Between each is an aperture of three feet, for doors or windows. On the other fide is a continued wall fourteen feet long, and of an height anfwerable to the reſt. The method of elevating all thefe, is the fame with thofe above. What we call a wall may likewiſe ſerve for a hedge, palifade, &c. of a garden.

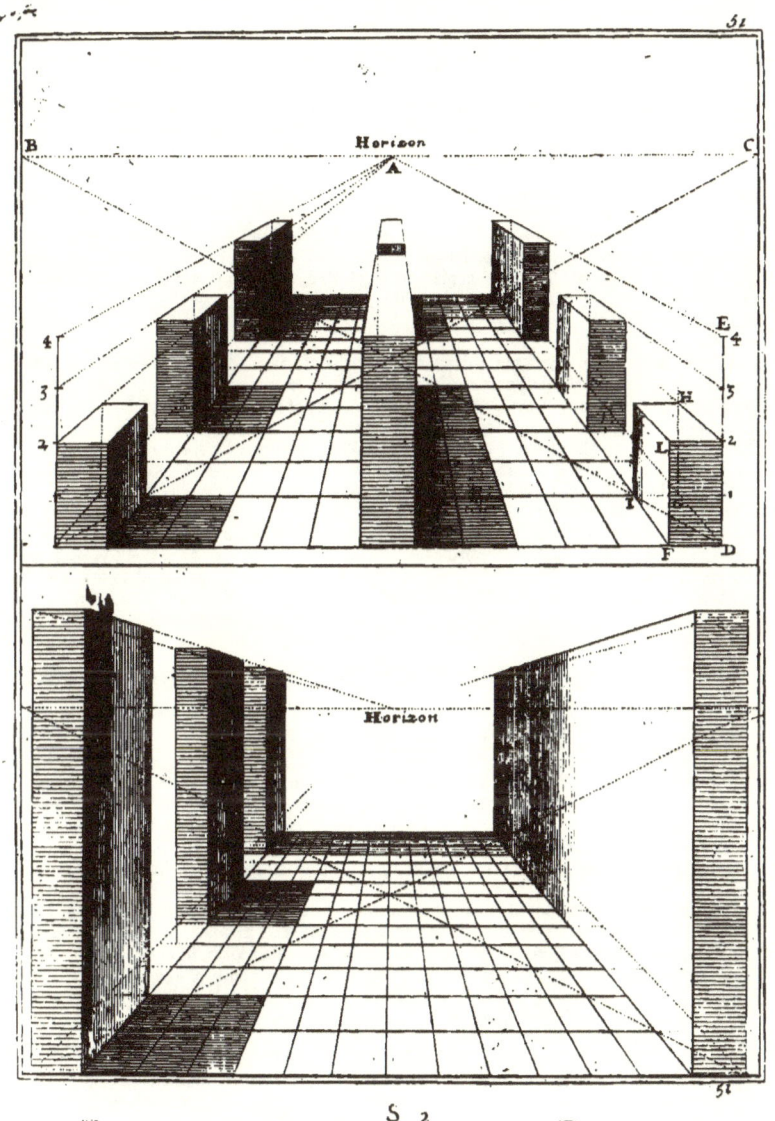

Of WALLS *viewed in Front.*

FROM what has been faid one may raife walls of all kinds in any oblique views ; and though the fame method may ferve for the fame walls viewed in front, I have thought proper to add this figure on two accounts : 1*ft*, by reafon it is not always that plans are made, and on fuch occafion a man would be a little to feek for the thicknefles. 2*dly*, To give the thicknefles to gates and windows, which might occur in fuch walls.

To make walls parallel to the bafe line, or the horizon, on a plan, one may give them any length at pleafure on the parallels to the horizon. To adjuft their breadth, you may take that of a fquare, from the angles whereof A B, you are to erect perpendiculars to any height, as C ; from C draw a ray to the point of fight D, and C D will give the diminution of the wall.

When there is no plan, the thicknefs of the wall, as E F, is to be fet on a parallel to the bafe line in the firft corner of the wall ; then from F a line is to be drawn to the point of fight D, and from E, another to the point of diftance G ; and from the interfection of the two in the point H, a perpendicular to be raifed, and another from the point F. Then the height of the wall F I is to be taken, and from I a line to be drawn to the point of fight D, the interfection whereof with the perpendicular H, will give the diminution of the wall. For the length, you may give it at pleafure on the firft parallel E F. For the doors and windows, in the fame walls, mark the width and height as here K L M N, and fet the thicknefs required on a parallel, either above or below the doors or windows, in the corner next the point of diftance, as here N O or L O ; laftly, from the points L and N draw lines to the point of fight D, and from the points O to the point of diftance G, and from the interfections of thofe lines in P, &c. draw the thicknefles.

Other WALLS *viewed by the Angle.*

WHEN the wall is to be raifed on a plan, you have nothing to do but erect perpendiculars from the angles already determined, and to mark the heights on the perpendicular from the angle next you, as on the line Q R ; and from the point R, to draw lines to the points of diftance S T ; the interfections thofe lines make, with the perpendiculars raifed from the angles of the plan, will give the length and thicknefs of the wall. If you have no plan, fet the meafures both of the breadth and depth of doors and windows on the bafe line, as in this example, V X is the breadth, X Y the depth, and Z I the height of a window ; then from all thefe points draw lines to the points of diftance S T ; firft from X, which is the ray of the bafe ; then from V, a little occult line cutting the ray X S in the point 5, which is the thicknefs of the wall. As to the depth, the ray Y S will give it by its interfecting with X T in the point 6 ; and Z 1 will give the breadth of the windows in the points 7, 8 ; from which points X, 5, 6, 7, 8, perpendiculars being raifed, and the height 2 being fet on the firft of them X, and from the point 2 drawing lines to the points S T, the interfections with the perpendiculars will give the height of them all. From the height of the window, marked 3, 4, draw lines to T, and where thefe interfect the perpendiculars 7, 8, lines are to be drawn ; and from the corners 9 to S, for the depth 10, draw lines to T, and from the point of interfection 11, draw a perpendicular. This may alfo ferve for a palifade as well as a wall.

9

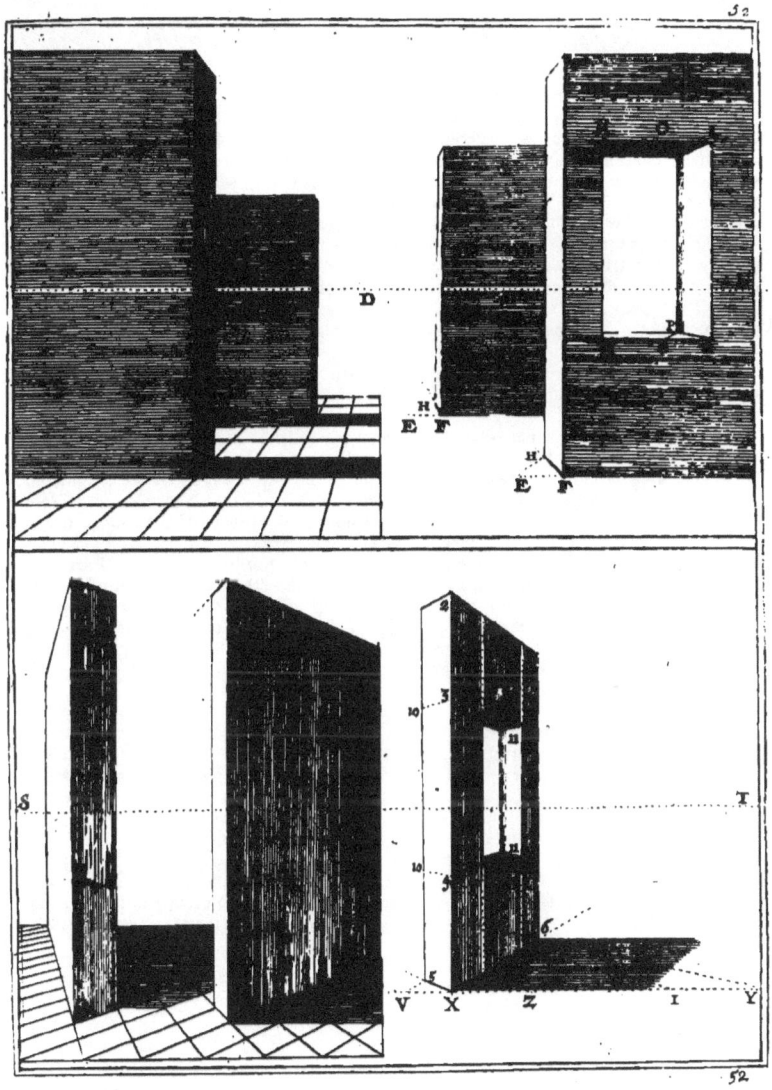

To place a Door in any part of a Wall at pleasure.

A WALL being raised one, two, or three feet thick, on the points H I, and carried on of the same height, as already directed; in order to place a door in any part thereof, observe the following method. Suppose the door required is to be three feet wide, and all its dimensions to correspond with that of the lower figure. To place this door in the middle of the end wall, set the breadth on the base line, as here in A B, and on the side of A and B set the breadth of the frame, or band, D and C, and from A B C and D draw lines to the point of sight K; and where they cut the parallel M N in the points O O, &c. erect perpendiculars of any heights at pleasure. Thus is the width of the door procured. For its height, D F E is to be transferred from the door underneath to the corner of the wall I, and lines to be drawn from the points F E to K; and where they intersect the perpendicular M P in the point Q, draw Q R parallel to M N, which will give the height of the door, and the band or frame at top. Its thickness, or depth, will be the same with that of the wall, which is G F. And if from G you draw a line from the point of sight K, it will cut the perpendicular M P in the point S, through which drawing S T parallel to Q R, you will have the thickness of the door V.

To make a door in a side-wall, the instructions given in page 17. are to be well remembered; importing, that all the measures are to be put on the base line; and, that lines being drawn from these measures to the point of distance, will give all the diminutions desired. For an example, a door four feet broad is desired in a chamber. Set off four equal distances from I to C, and draw lines from the dimensions of the door C A and B D to the point of distance L; where the ray I M intersects those lines, erect perpendiculars X Y, which will give the breadth of the door. For its height, draw lines from the point E and F to the point of sight K, and the intersections with the perpendiculars will give the height. As to the thickness of the top and bottom, draw the thickness of the wall, G H and F I, to the point of sight K; then drawing a little parallel to the terrestrial line, through the lower corner of the door X, and another through the upper corner, you will have X Z, the thickness of the top and bottom, to be joined by a perpendicular, as you see in the figure.

If you would have a door on the other side, you have nothing to do but draw parallels to the base line from the point X to the ray I N, and then raise them as already directed. The rest is the same as on the other side. The gate is not here represented in the middle; it is designedly placed elsewhere, to obviate the error of such as without any other measures, draw two diagonals through their painting, though of ever so great a size, and make all their objects equally distant from the intersection of those lines, that is, from the middle of the painting. So that, on their principle, a body should always be mounted to shew their work in all its advantage; which is a palpable oversight. For though painting should be forty feet high, and it should be placed on the ground to be seen, the horizon should never be above five feet high, but rather less than more; whereas in their way the horizon should be twenty feet high.

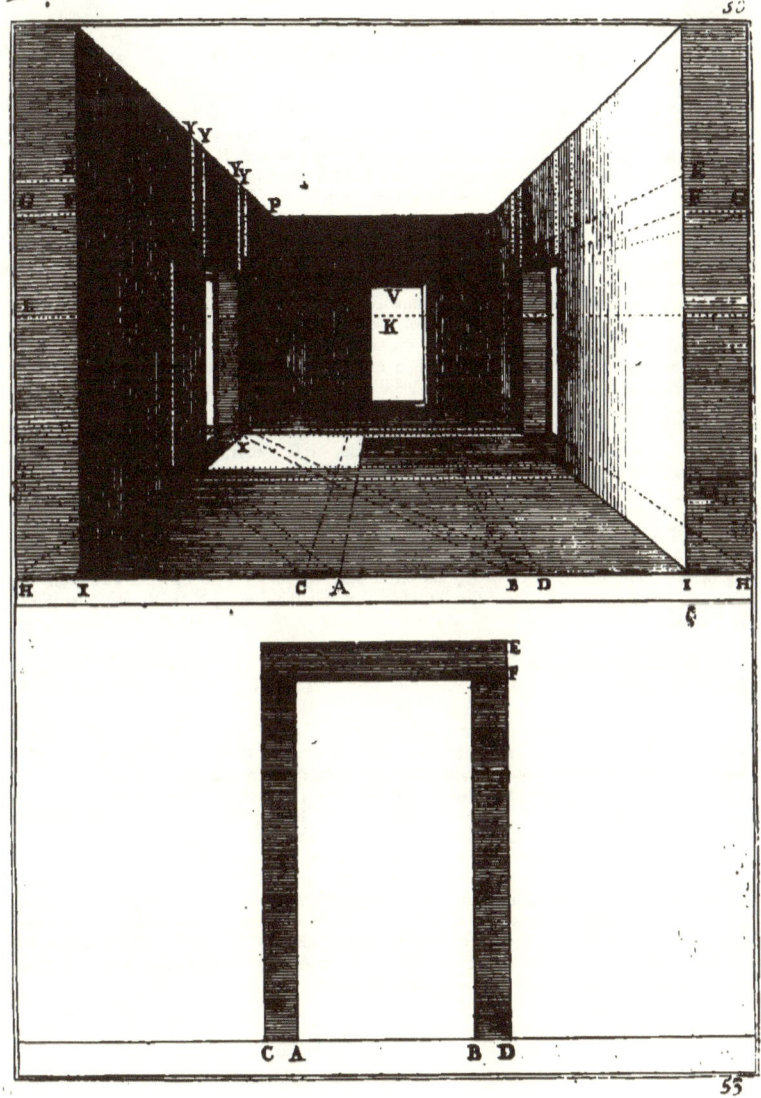

To draw WINDOWS in Perspective.

THE method of describing a window is perfectly the same with that of a door ; therefore by learning to make a single and double crofs, you are a master of windows. Suppose now it be required to make a window in the wall A B, of any breadth at pleasure, lay down its breadth on the base line, as D E, and from the points D and E draw lines to the point of diftance F, and from the interfections G G, of those lines with A K, erect perpendiculars G H, G H giving the width of the window, which is here only two fquares, or panes. As to the height, it is ufually raifed as near the ceiling as may be, but the breaft-part fhould not be above three feet and an half ; this meafure therefore is to be fet on the perpendicular A B, as from A to I, and drawing a line from I to K, where that line interfects the perpendiculars G H, will be the breaft-part. After the like manner drawing a line from L, the top of the window, to the point of fight K, its interfection with G H, will be the top of the window ; by which means we fhall have a long fquare, or parallelogram, to which a crofs being added, will form a window. To make this crofs, the fpace D E muft be divided into two equal parts, each being about half a foot ; then drawing this breadth M to the point of diftance F, and from the interfections thereof with the ray A K, erect perpendiculars N O for the upright poft, or ftancher in the middle of the window. As to the crofs pieces, you may add as many as you pleafe, only obferving that their thicknefs muft be equal to that of the upright piece ; therefore taking the meafure M, fet it off upon the perpendicular A B, as is P, and drawing lines from P to K, the points wherein they interfect the perpendiculars G H, G H will give the crofs bars, and of confequence the window is finifhed. For its thicknefs, it is here only to be half that of the wall ; to accommodate which, occult lines muft be drawn from the point Q to K, and little parallels to the bafe being drawn from the corners of the window S, the point wherein they cut the line Q K will give the thicknefs required.

This window ranges even with the wall on the infide, which is not very ufual, windows being now frequently made with embrafures, or niches entering into the wall a foot, or lefs.

The method is precifely the fame in both, only that inftead of taking the interfections on the line A C K, they muft here be taken in another line, re-entering into the wall as much as the window is made to re-enter, as appears from the lower figure, where the ray O K receives the meafures laid on the bafe-line ; and that all the reft muft be drawn to the point of diftance F, as in the former cafe, taking the thicknefs of the window between the perpendicular O, and the other F, which is the laft. Laftly, when the window is finifhed, on the ray O K, and from the breadth of the wall O F, raife the perpendicular A, and draw it to the point K ; then from the lower corner of the window, in the points P P, draw a little parallel cutting A K in Q, which will give the thicknefs of the wall, covering the window a little, and fhewing the thicknefs R P ; then from the point R erecting the perpendicular R V, cutting the ray T K in E : which will be the thicknefs of the top of the window. From the meafures here laid down, one may make as many as one pleafes, ftill obferving the fame order.

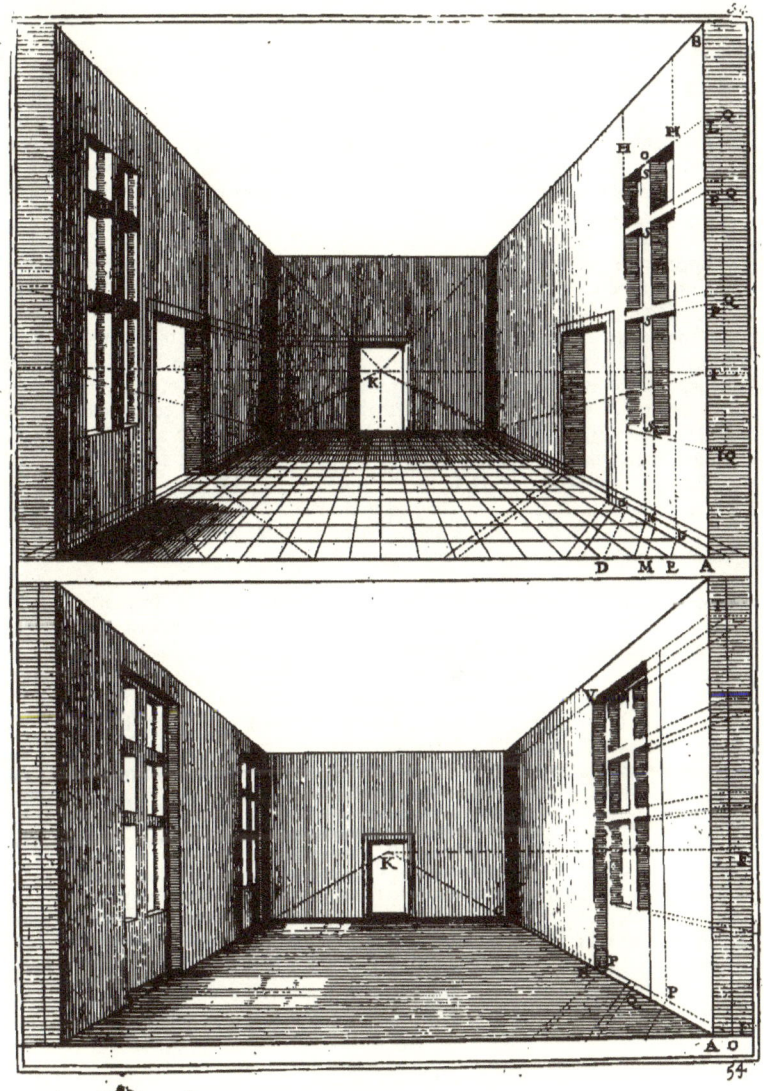

T

Of Cielings.

IN forming perfpective reprefentations, there are many inftances in which we muft obferve a method, fomewhat analogous to the order practifed by mafons in raifing a building from the ground. The pavement, or ground-work, is their foundation, whereon they raife walls, which they pierce in as many places as they pleafe for doors and windows.

Suppofe the walls A B raifed, on which beams are to be laid, and over them joifts or quarters. Having meafured the fquare of one of the joifts (which we here fuppofe a foot) it is to be carried to the top of the wall, as C D, and from the points C and D occult lines to be drawn to the point of fight E, which will give the rays C G D F. The fame meafure C D is likewife to be fet on a parallel to the horizon D H, on which line the meafures of all the intended joifts are to be difpofed, as will be fhewn prefently when I come to direct the drawing them. The meafures of three joifts are here placed at I, K, L; then drawing lines from all thefe meafures to the point of diftance M, and from the interfections with the line D F, in the points O, O, &c. letting fall perpendiculars, cutting the rays C G in the points P, P, &c. and laftly, drawing parallels to the horizon through the points O and P, you will have the beams, or girders, orderly laid : as in the firft figure.

Now, to lay the joifts upon the beams, or, more properly, to mortaife them there, the line Q R, *Fig.* 2. is to ferve as a bafe line whereon to lay the joifts in fuch number, and at fuch diftance from each other, as fhall be judged expedient ; the rule being ufually to be twice their thicknefs apart from each other. To mortaife them, take their thicknefs within that of the beam Q S, fuch as Q T, and draw an occult line T V ; then between Q R, and T V, range the joifts X, X, &c. and from all their angles that are vifible, draw lines to the point of fight Y. And that they may not exceed the half of the further beams, from the middle of the firft, which is the point T, draw an occult line to the point of fight Y, which will cut the other two beams in the middle of their depth, in the point Z ; laftly, from the point Z draw parallels to the horizon, which terminating the lines drawn from the angles of X X X, &c. to the point of fight, will fhew the joifts mortaifed in thofe beams anfwerable to the others, in drawing lines from the joifts to the point of fight. If you do not care to take fo much pains, fet the joifts Z on the line Q R, as they are underneath ; then draw lines boldly from one beam to another, from all the angles of X, X, &c. to the point Y, and you will have what you require.

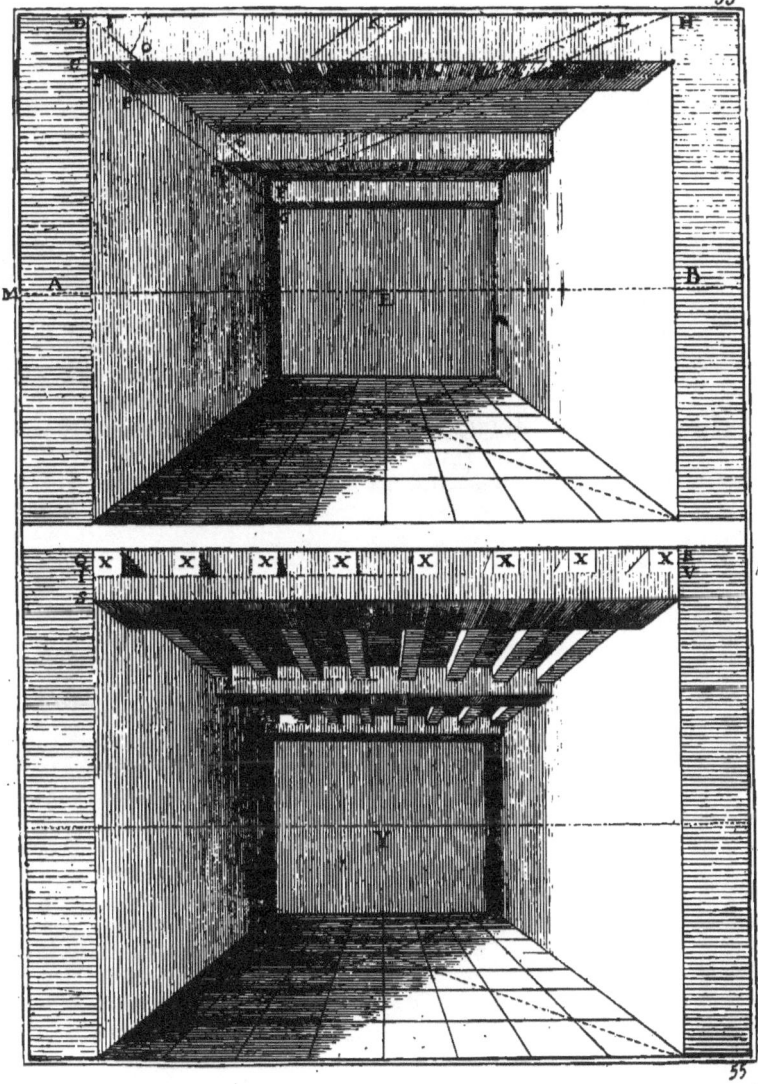

✿✿✿✿✿✿✿✿✿✿✿✿✿✿✿✿✿✿✿✿✿✿✿✿✿✿✿✿✿

The CIELINGS *of two* Stories, *ſhewn in Perſpective.*

THIS FIGURE is only added to ſhew the effect of the method juſt now laid down ;
wherein it is obſervable, the number of ſtories does
not render the practice at all the more difficult.

The joiſts are not mortaiſed in the beams of
the upper ſtory, as they are in the lower.

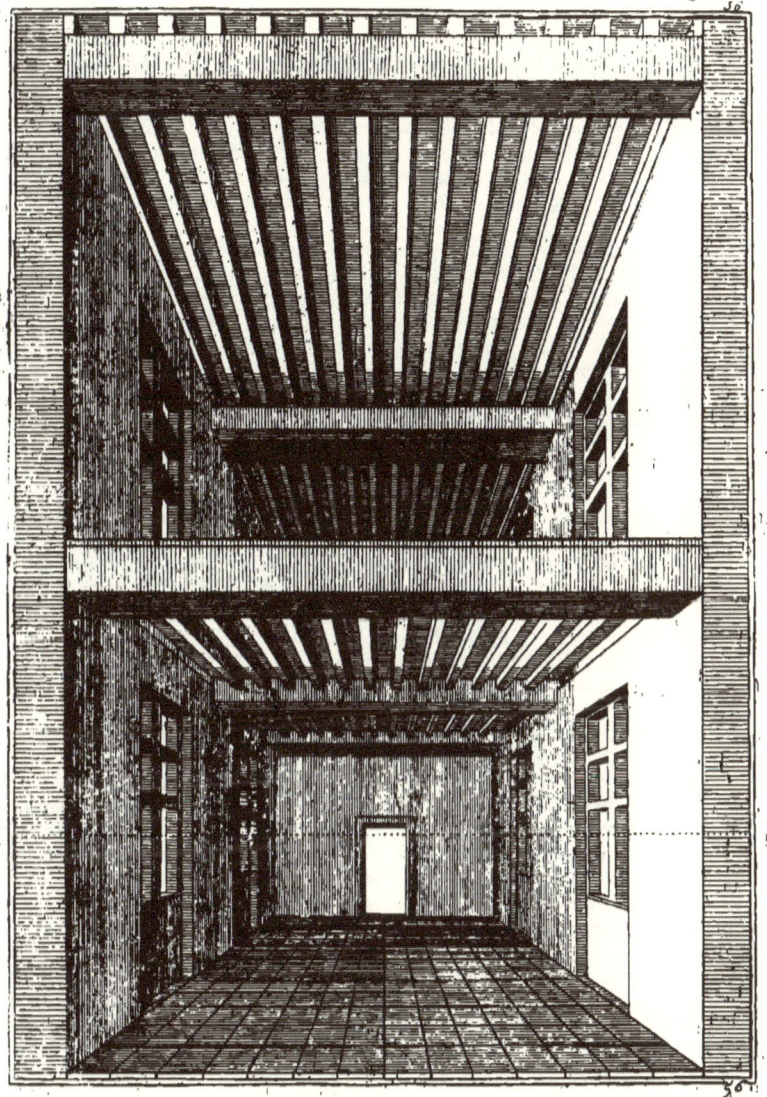

Another Difpofition *of* Cielings *in Perfpeſtive.*

THIS method is performed in all refpeſts like that juſt defcribed, only that the difpofition of the members and pieces that compofe the cieling is to be changed; that is, the beams are laid long-wife, tending towards the point of fight, and the joifts acrofs, which is the reverfe of the former.

Suppofe the walls A B; on thefe, or on confoles jutting out from them, fet the thicknefs of the beam C D, and through the points C and D draw parallels to the horizon C E and D F, between which you may put any number of beams at pleafure, in the manner that three are placed in this figure, namely G H and I, from all which, lines are to be drawn to the point of fight K; then through the point P, wherein D P interfeſts the perpendicular L P, draw a line parallel to the horizon P M, this will be the bound of all the other rays, as G N, I M, &c. laſtly, from the point N ereſt a perpendicular N O: and fo of the reſt. Thus much for the beams.

To lay the joifts acrofs the beams, fet their thicknefs on the line Q R, as V V V, *Fig.* 2. and from the extremes of V draw lines to the point of diſtance S; and through the points of interfeſtion with the ray Q T draw parallels to the horizon, as far as the beam of the other fide. If you would mortaife them in the beams, take the thicknefs of the rafters within the beam, as Q X; and from X draw a parallel to the bafe line, as far as the other fide X X; and between the two lines Q R and X X fet the divifions V V, &c. which will form Y Y, &c. And from all the points Y drawing lines to the point of diſtance S, you will have the thicknefles of the bottom and fides given by the interfeſtions with the ray X T in the points Z Z, &c. through which drawing parallels to the horizon, the cielings will be finifhed; as in the fecond figure.

Thus it is that fimple timber cielings are put in perfpeſtive. If, after thefe, or in lieu of thefe, you would have a handfome platform of painting, or enrichments of other kinds, the inſtruſtions given in page 35 for exhibiting the plan of a garden, are applicable to thefe purpofes, for by making ufe of the line Q R for a bafe line, you will eafily fhew on the cieling the perfpeſtive appearance of any defign: and making ufe of the line Q R for a bafe line, you may do what you pleafe therein.

As to floors and pavements, fuch full inſtruſtions have been given for them in pages 30, 31, 32, 33, and 34, as to make the operation for fhewing them very familiar and eafy, and to open the mind for inventing what variety of them it pleafes. Thus far we have had to do with the rooms, as hall, chamber, or the like, the feveral parts whercof are fufficiently defcribed: the moveables therein fhall be fhewn hereafter.   2

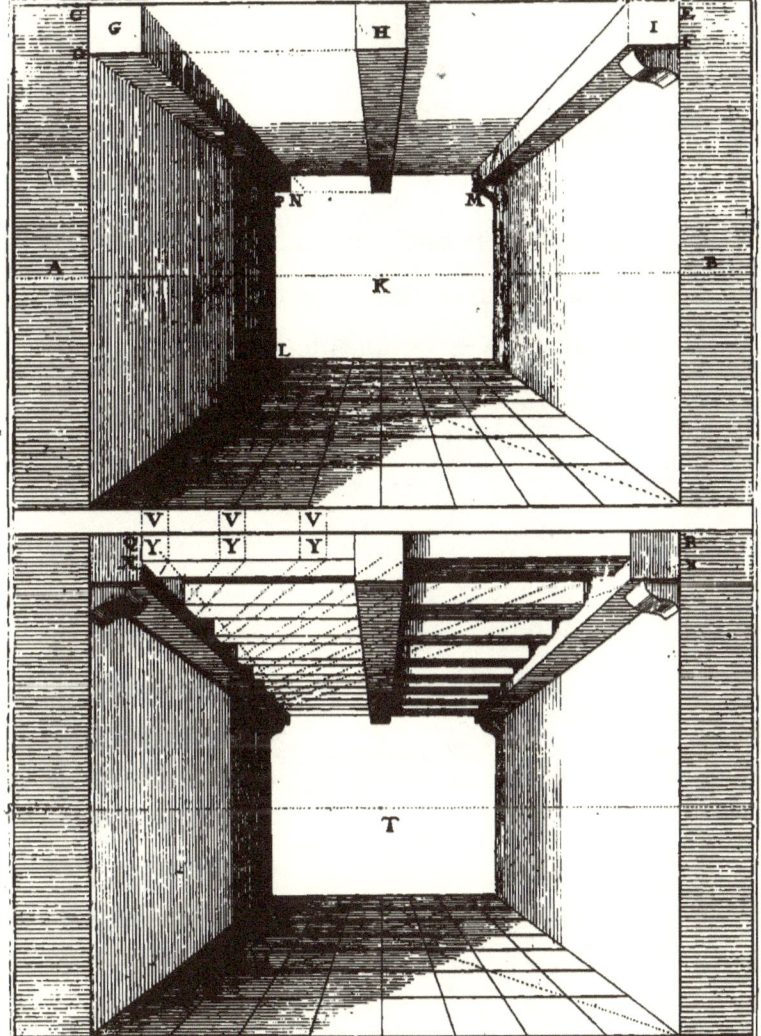

❀❀❀❀❀❀❀❀❀❀❀❀❀❀❀❀❀❀❀❀❀❀❀❀❀❀❀❀❀❀❀❀

THIS figure fhews the cieling juft now defcribed, diftinct and clear of the lines where-
with the former was embaraffed.

The conftruction of the gate fhall be fhewn
hereafter.

U

To deſcribe Circular G A T E S *and* A R C H E S *viewed di-reċtly in the front, or partly on the ſide.*

HAVING given ſufficient inſtruċtions for halls, cham-bers, windows and *ſquare* doors, or gates, we pro-ceed to the praċtice of *round* ones.

Suppoſe then A B C D E F to be pilaſters on a plan, in or-der to place arches thereon, divide the upper breadth G H into equal parts, in the point I, on which ſetting one leg of your compaſſes, with the other deſcribe a ſemi-circle G H, for the firſt arch.

To make all the other arches of the ſame height and breadth, draw lines from the points G H to the point of ſight K, and through the two points L, L, where thoſe rays cut the perpendiculars C, D, draw parallels to G H. Theſe parallels being divided into two, and ſemi-circles ſtruck from them, as in the firſt, you will have the ſecond and third arch. To find the middle of thoſe parallels M, you have only to lay the ruler in the firſt center I, and draw a line to K, which will cut them all preciſely in the middle M M, and give the points for the ſemi-circles to be drawn from. The arches viewed in front, and thoſe by the ſide, are all performed the ſame way ; as appears from the two firſt figures, and K is the point of ſight both for the one and the other.

If it be required to make an edge, or band about them, of equal thickneſs, you are only to uſe one center as O, from which the thickneſſes N P of the lower figures are formed. The reſt is all performed as already direċted, by drawing lines to the point of ſight K. The laſt figures ſhew how all kinds of ſimple vaults, only conſiſting of a ſemi-circle, are to be formed. As to the enrichment thereof, we ſhall have oc-caſion to ſpeak hereafter.

2

To defcribe Circular A R C H E S *over* Pilafters *viewed as in the preceding plate.*

THE out-line of the laft plate readily directs how to perform this operation, the method being the fame in both. In the prefent cafe there are a few more lines, but not any thing more of difficulty. For, drawing parallels to the bafe line over the tops of the feveral pilafters, and dividing the firft of them into equal parts, from the middle E as a center, defcribe the firft femi-circle A C, without removing the compaffes, from the fame center defcribe the band or thickneffes A G F C; laftly, from the center E, drawing lines to the point of fight H, the ray E H will give the middle points of all the parallels for defcribing femi-circles over them all, from B D to the laft, I. The method is the fame for that in the fide-view.

✿✿✿✿✿✿✿✿✿✿✿✿✿✿✿✿✿✿✿✿ ✿✿✿✿✿✿✿✿✿✿✿✿✿✿✿

To defcribe the GOTHIC ARCH, *or* Arch *in the* third Point.

THE drawing of this is as eafy as that of the circular arch. Having laid down the breadth K L, fet one foot of your compaffes in K, and directing the other to O, ftrike the arch L O; then removing your compaffes to L, defcribe the arch K O, and you will have an arch *in the third point*, K O L. Do the fame from M and N, and you will have the *fecond*, or *inner arch*, M P N. The fecond figure, *in the third point*, has a band or lift all round it, which is defcribed from the fame centers: thus, for example, from the center R the arches S X and T V are fwept; and from the point S the arches Q V and R X. All the reft is drawn to the point of fight Y.

Another *third point*, or *terzo acuto*, is reprefented in the figure +; the diameter or chord whereof, *a b*, being divided into three equal parts, and one foot of the compaffes fet in one of the divifions, as *c*, and with the other the aperture *c b* taken, the arch *b e* is ftruck therewith; then removing the compaffes to *d*, the arch *d a e* is ftruck, which is an arch in the *third point*, as well as the former; and either of them may be ufed at difcretion. Thofe in old *Gothic* churches come neareft the former kind.

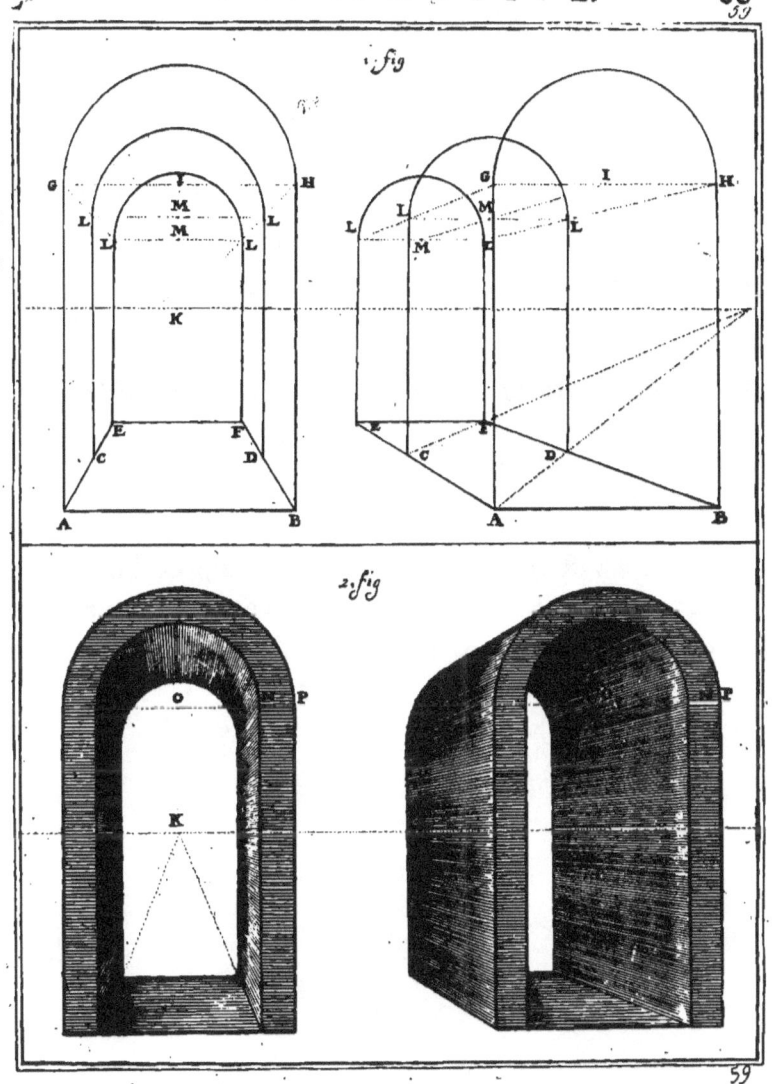

Sequel *of the former* FIGURE.

WE here add an arbour of a garden, the performance whereof is in all refpects the fame as that of arches viewed in front.

✻✻✻✻✻✻✻✻✻✻✻✻✻✻✻✻✻✻✻✻✻✻✻✻✻✻✻✻✻✻✻✻

Sequel *of the foregoing* RULES.

THE rules given in the two former pages, are applicable to a vaft variety of defigns. In this plate I fhew one inftance thereof in the perfpective reprefentation of an arbour, compofed of five arches, of equal chords or diameters, and placed at equal diftances behind each óther. Thefe are exhibited by the method laid down in pages 59 and 60.

To defcribe, and put in Perfpeêtive, femicircular Arches
and Doors.

THE circle being fomewhat difficult to put in perfpeêtive, requires a number of previous lines and points : to fhew the method of procuring them
is the defign of *Fig. 1.* which ought to be well underftood. To defcribe a femi-
circle upon a diameter A B, there needs no more than to fet one foot of your
compaffes in the middle thereof, in the point C, and with the other to fweep a
crooked line from A to B. And thus is the femi-circle to be upon the elevation
D E, *Fig.* II. for a circular gate or arch.

Now to put it in perfpeêtive, it is to be divided into any number of parts,
and the more the better ; as already obferved in page 28. and as I fhall hereafter
have occafion to fhew, when giving direêtions for the exhibiting of crofs vaults.
The prefent femicircle I fhall only divide into four, and that by circumfcribing
it with a parallelogram, or long fquare, and drawing two diagonals interfeêting
each other in I, and the femicircle in K K, and laying a ruler over C I, bifeêt-
ing the arch in F ; laftly draw the line K K, cutting the parallelogram in L,
which line L K is to be transferred to *Fig.* III. to put it in perfpeêtive.

Firft then draw a line from the angle E to the point of fight M, fet off the
meafures of the diameter of arch D E. on the bafe line as E N, N O, and from
the point N draw a line to the point of diftance P ; which cutting the ray E M
in the point Q. E Q will be the width of the front arch D E in perfpeêtive.
Then drawing a line from O to the point P, where it cuts the ray E M, in
the point R, will be the width of the fecond arch. As there is no more room
on the bafe line to take the third arch, there muft be drawn from N to the point
of fight M ; and through the point R a parallel to the bafe lines R S. Now
as R S is under the fame angle with E N, it is the fame breadth in its proper
diminution, as has been already proved in the beginning of the book ; therefore
drawing a line from S to the point of diftance P, it will cut the ray E M in
the point T, which gives the third arch.

Proceed then to raife perpendiculars V V , *&c.* from the three points Q R T,
which interfeêting the ray H M, will give the higheft of the arches ; then from
the ray B M, which gives the bottom of the femi-circle, draw diagonals B V,
H X, which interfeêting each other, give the place of the perpendicular Y F,
that divides the arch into two ; and drawing the ray L M, it will cut the diagonals in two, and the arch in four ; laftly, conneêting the points B Z, F Z X,
with curve lines, you will have the firft arch : and this method will give you infinite others. The fame ferves not only for arches and doors, but alfo for vaults,
bridges, and other things that require the femi-circle ; for which reafon it is that
we decline fpeaking any thing farther of the two latter.

The fame method may likewife ferve for church windows, only one or two
upright pofts are to be added to faften the glafs to.

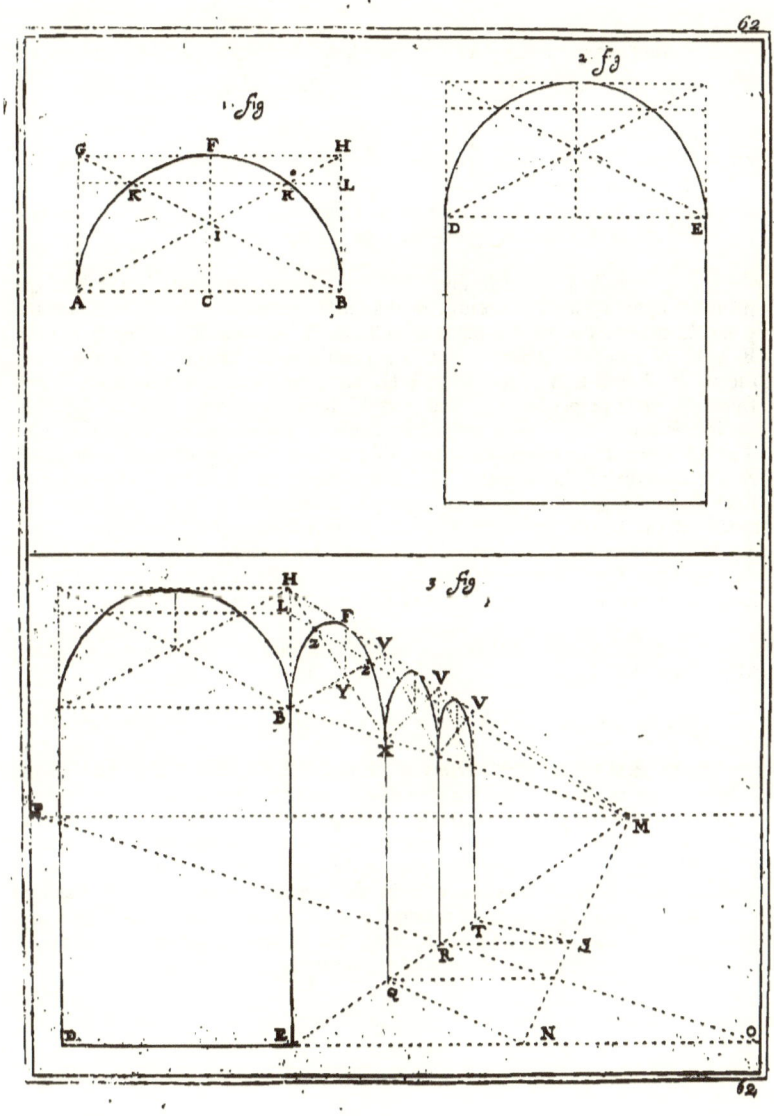

X

To defcribe, and put in perfpective, double ARCHES *and* GATES, *that is, fuch as fhew their* thickneffes.

THE former page only fhews the formation of the out-line: I therefore now proceed to the method of compleating the fame and exhibiting the breadths and thickneffes of the arches, and their fupporters, by only connecting the interfections of each by right lines: for example,

Having defcribed the firft line D E, and drawn lines from D and E to the point of fight A, fet the breadth or thicknefs on the bafe line E C. From the point C draw a line to the point of diftance B, and where it interfects the ray E A in the point F, draw the line G F parallel to the bafe line, which will cut the rays D A and E A in the points F G, and give the thicknefs required. Then from F G erect perpendiculars, and from H draw a line to the point of fight A, the interfection whereof with the perpendicular F I gives the height of that fide. To find the chord or line of the center of the inner femi-circle, draw a line from K, the extreme of the diameter of the femi-circle feen in front, to the point of fight A, which gives the point L, a parallel drawn through which will have the center of the hinder femi circle upon it, as N is the center of that before. This line M L is to be divided into two equal parts, by drawing a line from N to A, through O. Then fetting one leg of your compaffes in O, with the other defcribe a femi-circle M L, to be divided like that in the preceding figure. Laftly, draw right lines from the divifions of the one to the other, that is, from the fore femi-circle to the hind one, to connect the two into one; as in the figure, M is joined to P Q, to R S, to T V, to X L, to K.

For circular arches, &c. viewed in front, as D E F G, there is no need of fo many divifions, it being fufficient to find the line M L, in order for the defcribing of the femi-circle, which refers to the firft N P Q; but I have made them defignedly to avoid confounding the letters with the lines of the lower figure, where the arches are viewed obliquely, tending all towards the point of fight Y. Such arches would give their thickneffes by repeating the operation already laid down for *Fig.* I. twice over, and joining the divifions of the one to the other, as already obferved, and as is expreffed in the prefent figure, to which having given the thicknefs E Z, I have drawn the line E in dots, and Z a full line, in order to avoid confufion, and to intimate, that whatever is done with dots, is not intended to be feen when the draught is finifhed.

2

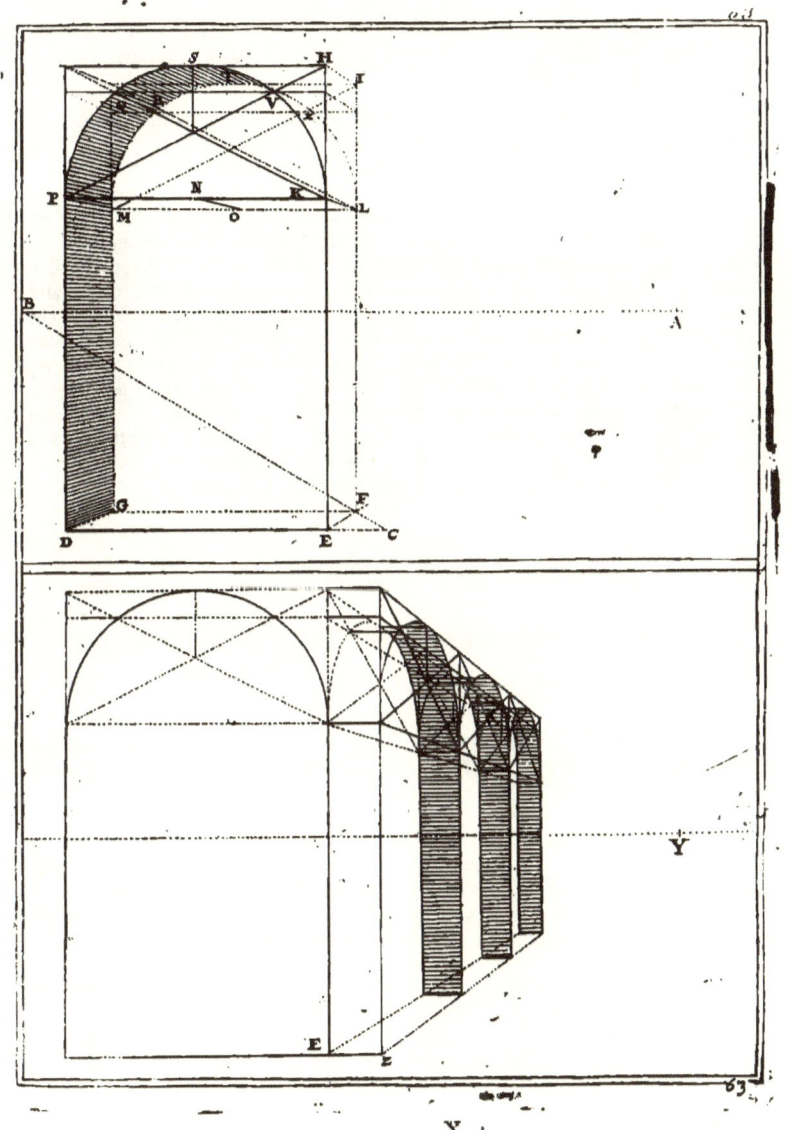

Another METHOD *of defcribing* Circular Arches.

THE arches in front, which I have hitherto defcribed, are all performed to the laft exactnefs ; but the procefs is a little long and tedious : I fhall now add another, equally juft, but much more expeditious.

Having defcribed a femi-circle, or a whole circle, B H I, from the center A, from the fame center and the extreme of the diameter B, draw lines to the point of fight C ; then fetting the breadth, or thicknefs required, on the line B I, as here D A, from the point D draw a line to the point of diflance E, and through F, the point where D E and A C interfect, draw a line parallel to the bafe, till it cut the ray B C in the point G ; this done, fetting one leg of your compaffes in F, and in the other taking the diftance G, defcribe a femi-circle, or circle, which will be the thicknefs of the arch, or fweep : as is feen in the four different figures, which are all performed by this eafy procefs. All the lines K K, &c. in the third and fourth figures are to be drawn to the center A, and the others, L, to the point of fight C. The fame method may ferve for circular windows built of ftone, in which cafe the lines will reprefent the joints ; as alfo for tons, vats, &c.

An expeditious method for ARCHES *viewed* obliquely *in perfpective.*

THE following method may ferve when a perfon is ftraitned, and does not defire to be fo very exact ; as alfo to avoid a multiplicity of lines, which in the preceding method is indifpenfible.

Having formed the fi ft arch N O as already directed, acrofs it draw little parallels to the bafe in any number at pleafure, as here Q Q. &c. then with your compaffes take the bread h of the fpring of the arch, as P O, and fet it off on the little parallels Q, by this means you will have the points R R ; through which a curve line being drawn, will form the thicknefs of the arch.

It is certain, that, according to the rules of perfpective, objects appear the larger as they are the nearer to us ; of confequence, therefore, the line O P fhould be the fmalleft : but the difference is here fo very fmall, that it is not worth the minding. Befide, I do not give this as a conftant rule, but only for an expeditious fhift in cafes of neceffity.

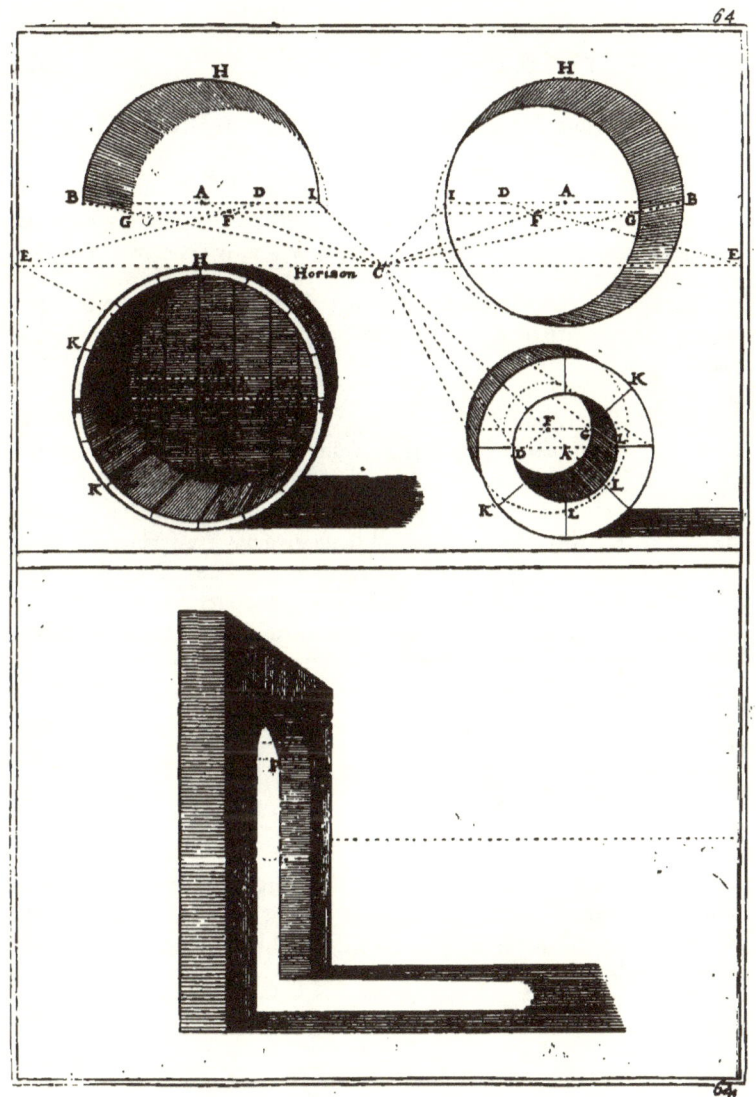

To exhibit ELLIPTICAL *or* FLAT ARCHES.

T H E method of putting thefe arches in perfpective, is the fame with that of the femi-circular, as appears from the figure A B, All the difficulty is in finding the out-line, which is done two ways.

The firft by two centers and a ftring, the method already mentioned page 4, for defcribing an oval; thefe flat arches being, in effect, femi-ovals.

The fecond method is thus: Suppofe the line C D given you to raife a flat arch upon of the height E F, from the center F defcribe a femi-circle C G D, and divide it into any number of equal parts at pleafure, as is here done into twelve; and from all thefe divifions draw lines to the center F; then again, from all thefe divifions draw perpendiculars to the diameter or chord C D, as are here the lines O I; this done, defcribe a femi-circle of the given height of the arch, as here H E K; and through the interfections made by this leffer circle on the divifion-lines of the greater, draw little parallels to meet the perpendiculars which fall from the fame divifions, for inftance L O, L O, &c. and the feveral points O connected together, as is here done, will give you the arch required.

The other figure makes the arch ftill flatter, and by the fame rules it may be made of any lownefs at pleafure.

The figure underneath fhews one of thefe arches in perfpective, fuch as it fhould appear, when finifhed, in a front view. I fay nothing of the method, as having already intimated it to be the fame with that for the femi-circle.

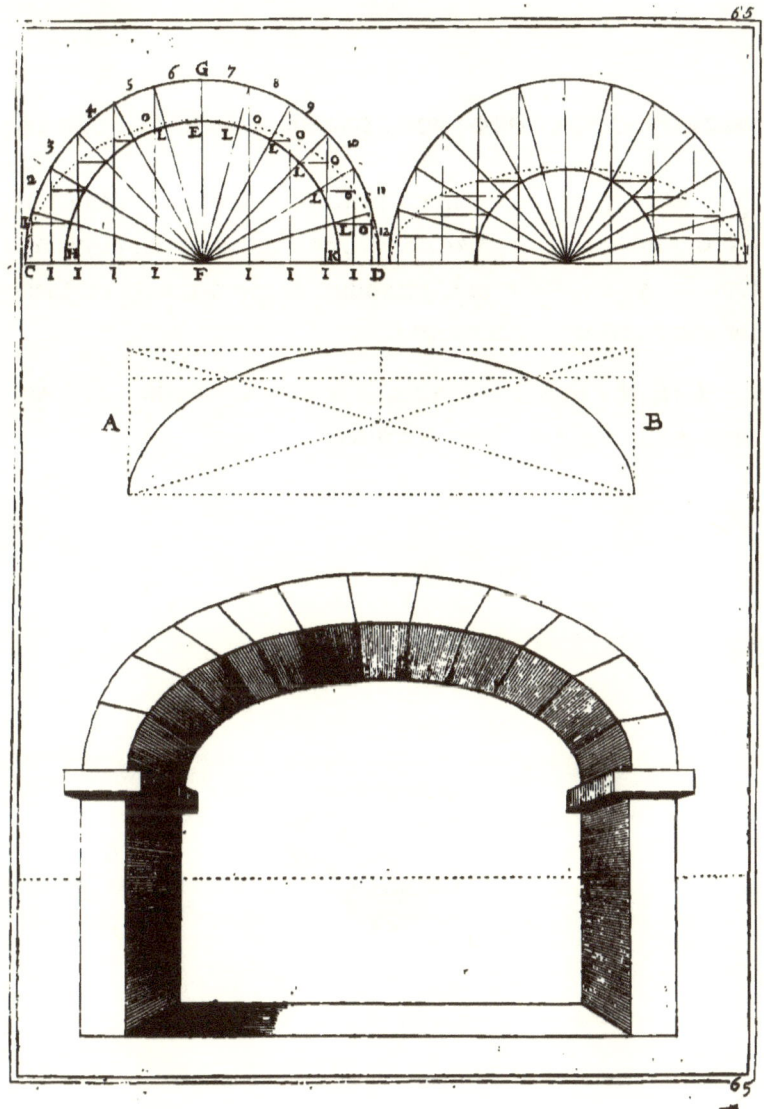

@@@

I N the figure here reprefented, you have an inftance of
the fine effect of Arches when they are well centered,
that is, when their juft rotundity is given them, in their
different perfpective fituations.

As for the fteps and figures, I fhall have occafion to treat
very particularly of them hereafter.

Y

To raise ARCHES *upon* Pilasters *or* Columns.

IT looks as if there were no pilasters formed in the last figure, for which reason I determined to add this, which may shew, that the method is precisely the same, and that all required farther, is to leave room for the breadth, &c. of the pilaster between every two arches, which is done by means of the plan, or base line; as already directed for *circular arches.*

❀❀❀❀❀❀❀❀❀❀❀❀❀❀❀❀❀❀❀❀❀❀❀❀❀❀❀❀❀❀❀❀❀❀❀

GOTHIC ARCHES.

GOTHIC ARCHES and VAULTS, called also arches in the *third point,* see page 60, are performed in the same manner as the semi-circular; so that having done one, you will do the other with ease. The figure shews the rest. As to the out-line, I have already shewn that nothing is more easy. The breadth A B being given to form an arch of, open your compasses to the breadth, and setting one leg in A, with the other describe the arch B C; then removing them to B, describe another arch A C; and the point wherein the two intersect, will be the point or apex of the arch C.

As the other arches seen on the side view are performed after the same manner as the semi-circular, page 62, I shall not repeat it. All the business is, that here are pilasters between each two, that are not in the other. This may serve to confirm and exemplify what I have already said, that all that is to be done is to draw lines from these divisions on the base to the point of distance O, which will cut the ray D E in the points F F, &c. on which points perpendiculars are to be raised; then setting off the thicknesses G, and drawing the ray G E for the breadth of the pilasters H, from the same point H erect perpendiculars, to be connected to the other by the right lines, &c. as in the semi-circle.

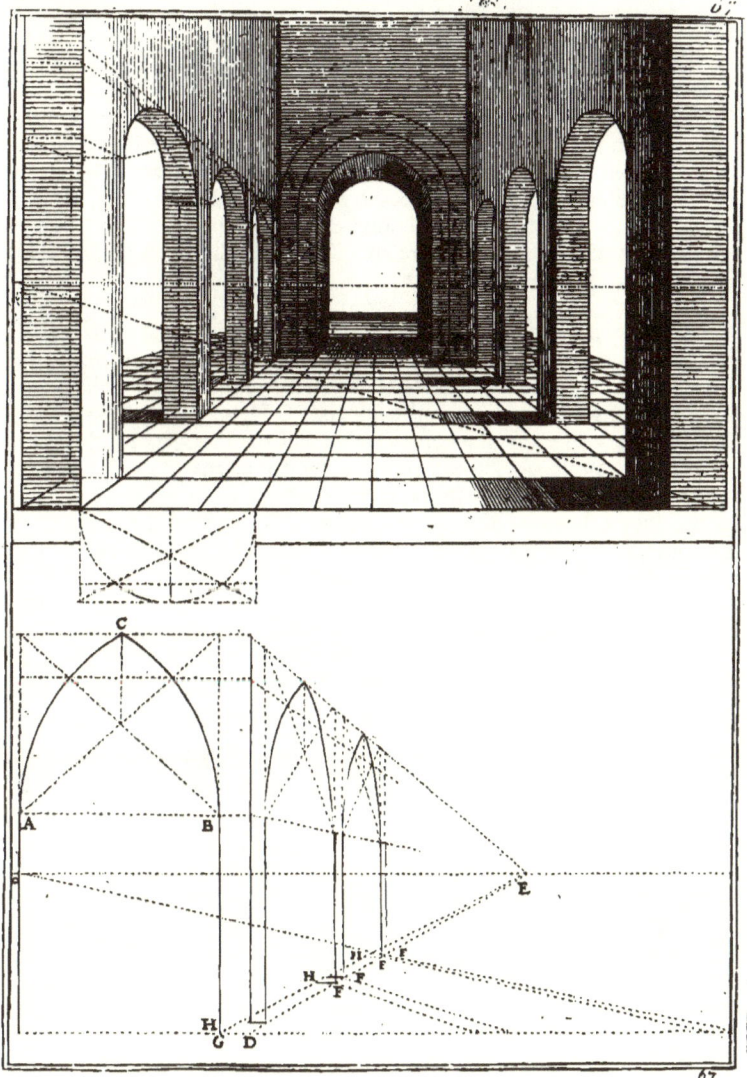

To find Cross Vaults *in perspective.*

THE reader muſt remember, or have recourſe to, what I have
ſaid in page 28. where, ſpeaking of putting a circle into perſpective, I divided it, for the greater exactneſs, into ſixteen parts ; but as in
ſuch a diviſion there neceſſarily occur a great number of lines, I have
here choſe to take up with a diviſion of eight parts, which if it be the
leſs exact, it will be the leſs confuſed. The other diviſion I ſhall reſume
in the following page.

Having then formed a plan of a circle divided into eight parts, 1, 2,
3, 4, 5, 6, 7, 8, parallels to the baſe line are to be drawn through the
ſeveral diviſions thereof, as far as the ray B A, which will give the points
C C, &c. on which erecting perpendiculars C D, C D, &c. the firſt of
them, B D, being the line of elevation, all the meaſures of the ſemi-
circle B E F muſt be ſet thereon, by which means you will have the
points D H G ; from which rays are to be drawn to the point A, and
in the interſections of the perpendiculars C D, you will have the ſame
diviſions as in the firſt, ſecond, third, fourth, and fifth Plans. For
a ſemi-circle, draw curve lines as in the arch of the firſt ſide, the diviſions whereof are to be transferred to the other, in order to have two
collateral arches from the center M ; the other in the bottom 5 L, from
the center N. And thus you have the four arches ordinarily found in
croſs-vaults. All that remains is, to make the croſs, or crooked diagonals, reſting on the corners G 5, K L, and paſſing through K or the groin O.

Now as the circle is divided into eight parts, the arches, which are but
halves of circles, are only to contain four parts ; the ſemi-circle G K,
therefore, is to be divided into four parts, in the points G P Q R K,
which are to be drawn to the point of ſight A, as far as the bottom of
the circle 5 L. Now what follows is the great ſecret of the croſs, namely
that parallels to the horizon are to be drawn from all the interſections of
the circle on the ſide 1, 2, 3, 4, 5, in ſuch ſort, as that G, which is the
firſt diviſion of the circle, touch the interſection 1 in a point ; that from
2 a parallel be drawn to the ſecond diviſion P, and the point S to be
marked ; that from 3 another parallel be drawn to the third diviſion
which will give O, the place of the key or groin ; and from 4, another
to the point T ; laſtly, connecting G S O T L with curve lines, you will
have a diagonal ; and doing as much for the other ſide, you will have
the entire croſs, and the vault compleat.

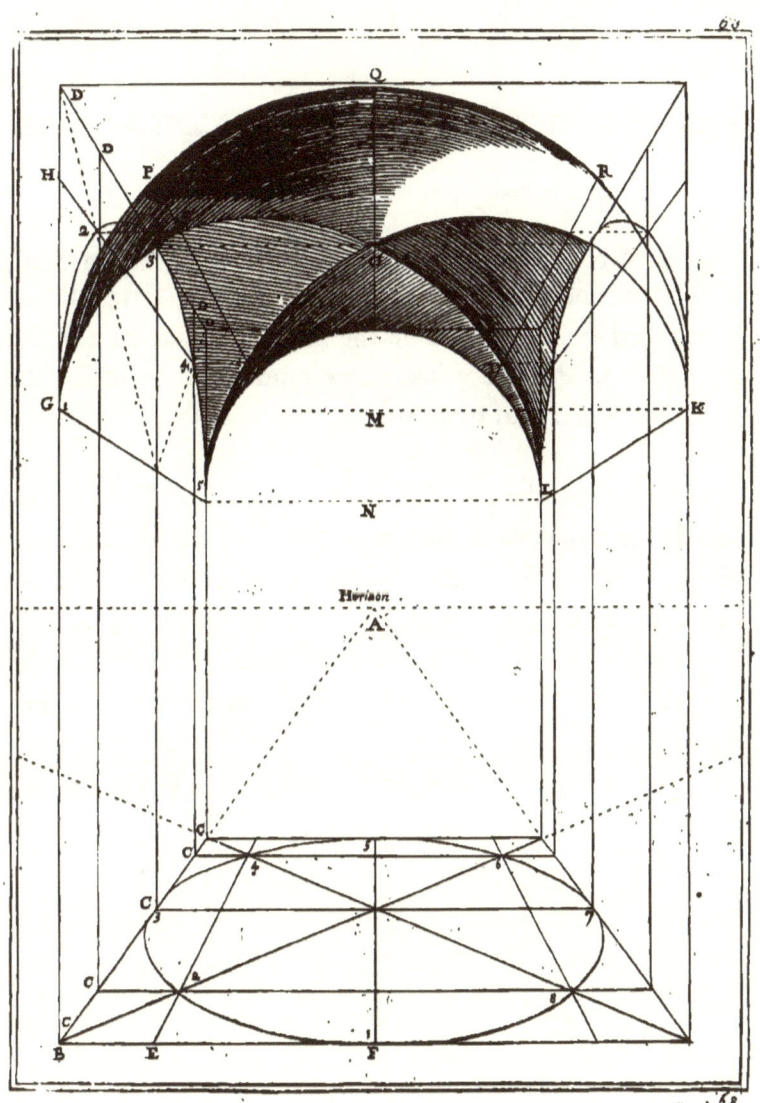

⊛⊛⊛⊛⊛⊛⊛⊛⊛⊛⊛⊛⊛⊛⊛⊛⊛⊛⊛⊛⊛⊛⊛⊛⊛⊛⊛⊛⊛⊛⊛⊛⊛⊛⊛⊛⊛

To draw the fame VAULT *more accurately.*

A MAN who has a good notion of the former method, will find no great difficulty in managing this ; all that is required being to double the lines, and take care of the interfections, which are here more numerous, by reafon the circle is divided into more parts.

How to form the plan is taught in page 28. Having produced the circle, and obtained the divifions on its periphery, from thefe divifions draw parallels to the ray B A, and their interfections will give the points O, O, O, &c. from which perpendiculars are to be raifed. The reft of the procefs is the fame with the method laid down in the preceeding page, over which this has the advantage of exactnefs, and enabling you to draw the vault more eafily, becaufe the divifions are clofer to each other. .

3

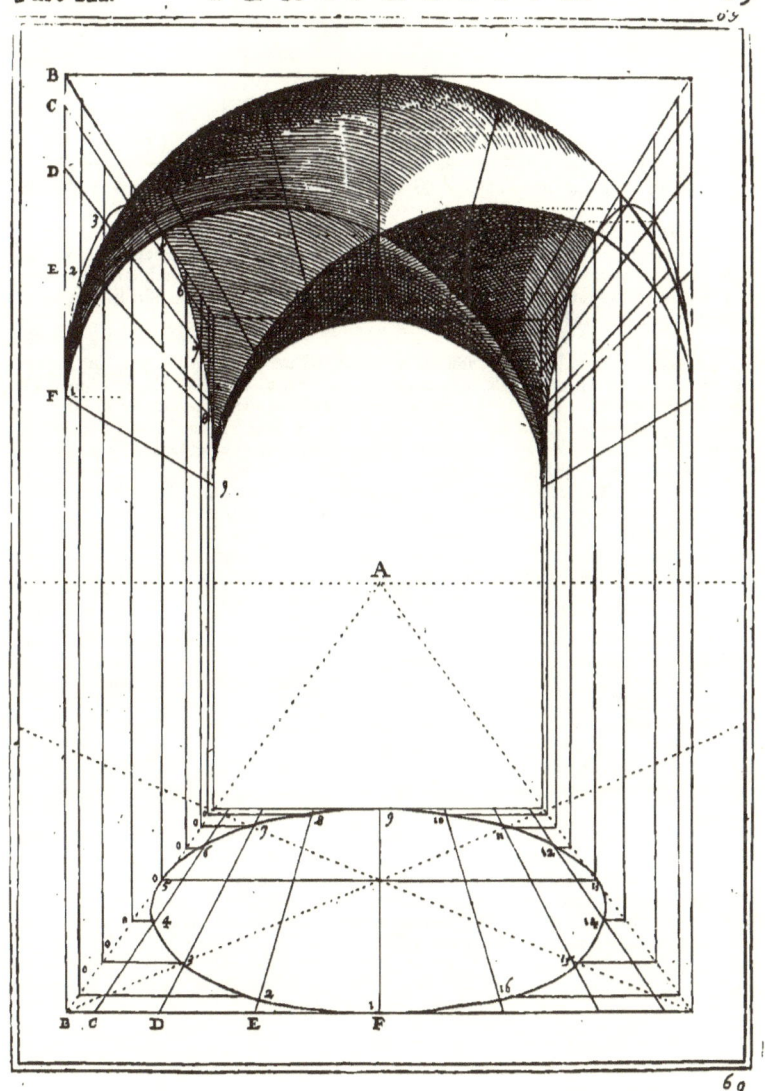

To form narrow VAULTS.

T HE R E are two proceſſes in this figure; the one for contracting or ſtraitning ſide-vaults; the other for giving the thickneſs to the croſs. I ſhall begin with the firſt.

The two methods for vaults already laid down, ſuppoſe them perfectly ſquare, that is, that their breadth and depth, or diſtance, is equal; both in thoſe repreſented in front, and thoſe in ſide-views. But a perſon only inſtructed in theſe, would find himſelf ſtrangely at a loſs were he put to conſtruct a church, where the ſide-arches are uſually much narrower than thoſe in the front or middle.

I proceed, therefore, to offer you an expedient whereby you will be enabled to make the ſide arches of what dimenſions you pleaſe, and that by means of the baſe line A Q. Suppoſe then the front arch A Q forty feet broad, and the ſide-arches limited to fifteen or twenty, you are now, according to the inſtructions in page 17. to ſet this meaſure on the baſe line, and to draw a line from the ſame to the point of diſtance, by which you will have the depth of the ſame figure in A E. Thus, in the preſent example, A C being ſuppoſed twenty feet, a line drawn from C to the point of diſtance, (which here is ſuppoſed beyond the limits of the paper) cuts the depth twenty feet in the point E; then returning to the baſe line, an arch or ſemi-circle is to be ſtruck on the line A C, and divided into as many parts as the larger arch F G has diviſions, namely, eight; and from the ſeveral diviſions perpendiculars H H to be let fall on its diameter A C, and from the points H, lines to be drawn to the point of diſtance, interſecting the ray A E in O, O, &c. Perpendiculars O P, O P, &c. are to be raiſed; then the plan of the ſemi-circle F G is to be made in ſome ſeparate place, and the diviſions thereof transferred from F to B. And ſince the plan of the preceding figure, ſee plate 69, is equal to F G, take the diviſions of half of it, B C D E F, and transfer them upon the perpendicular A F; and from the points E F D C B draw lines to the point of ſight D, and through the interſections which theſe rays B C D E F make with the perpendiculars, O P, draw curve lines, which will form the ſide-arch. Then drawing parallels through the interſections 1, 2, 3, 4, 5, 6, 7, 8, 9, to the diviſions of the arch F G, you will have points F R S T V X Y Z, to form the croſs after the manner already mentioned.

For the thickneſs of the nerves, or branches, a little line of elevation muſt be made, *a b*, which I have here added at the top of the perpendicular raiſed from Q. This line A B, being drawn to the point of ſight D, cuts all the other perpendiculars in the point *c d*, and this gives the proportionate heights to each perpendicular raiſed from the interſections of the croſs, that Is, from the interſections made to find the out-line of the croſs : the firſt elevation *a b*, for inſtance, gives the firſt perpendicular G *e*; the ſecond elevation *c d* gives the ſecond perpendicular F *e*; and ſo of all the reſt in their order, which all give points *e e*; and which being connected by a crooked line, give the thickneſs of the nerves or reins of the vault: as is ſeen in half the adjoining figure.

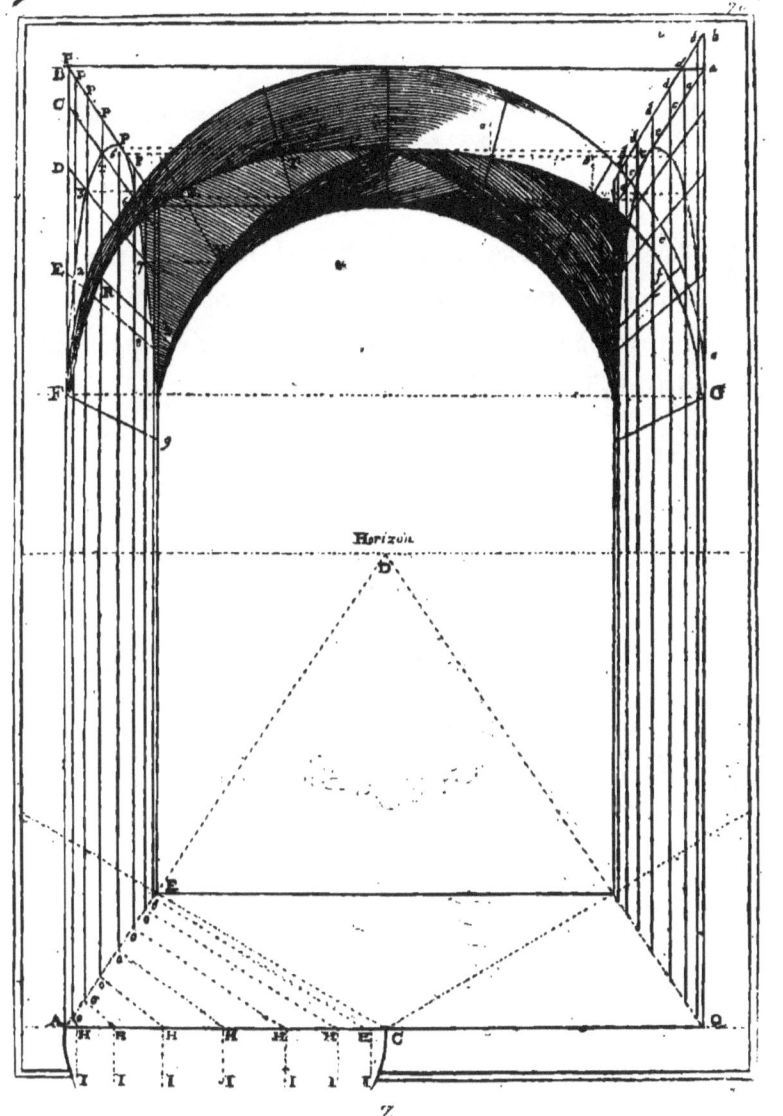

❖◈❖◈❖◈❖◈❖◈❖◈❖◈❖◈❖◈❖◈❖◈❖◈❖◈❖◈❖◈❖◈❖◈❖◈◈◈

A V A U L T *on the Principles of the preceding Rules.*

T H E ſeveral rules already dilivered, ſuffice for the con-
ſtructing the various arches of a complete V A U L T,
as that hereto annexed. The rules for the columns, or im-
poſts, I ſhall have occaſion to ſhew hereafter.

Z 2

To exhibit ARCHES *with* three Sides.

THERE is another fort of cieling which fometimes ferves for a
vault over doors and galleries, and even churches, having a pretty
good effect in perfpective, and eafy enough to perform. I have added
it here after the circle, by reafon it is formed of a femi-circle divided
into parts.

Having raifed the walls A B, defcribe a femi-circle including the whole
breadth C D; then holding the compaffes open to the width of the
radius E C, and fixing one point in C, with the other ftrike an arch
upwards, cutting the femi-circle in G, and another arch E H from the
point D; then connecting the four letters C D G H by right lines, you
will have a femi-hexagonal arch. A femi-circle is likewife to be drawn
upon the breadth I K, for the bottom of the arch; and to divide it, lines
are to be drawn from the angles of the former to the point of fight F;
at the interfections of thefe rays with the lower femi-circle, right lines
being drawn, will form the arch I L M K.

To exhibit an ARCH *with* five Sides.

THIS arch is performed after the fame manner as the former; all
the difference lies in the divifion of the circle, the firft being into
three, and this into five. Accordingly the femi-circle L M being divided
into five parts, N O P Q, and lines drawn from all thefe points to the
point of fight R, the reft is performed after the manner already laid
down.

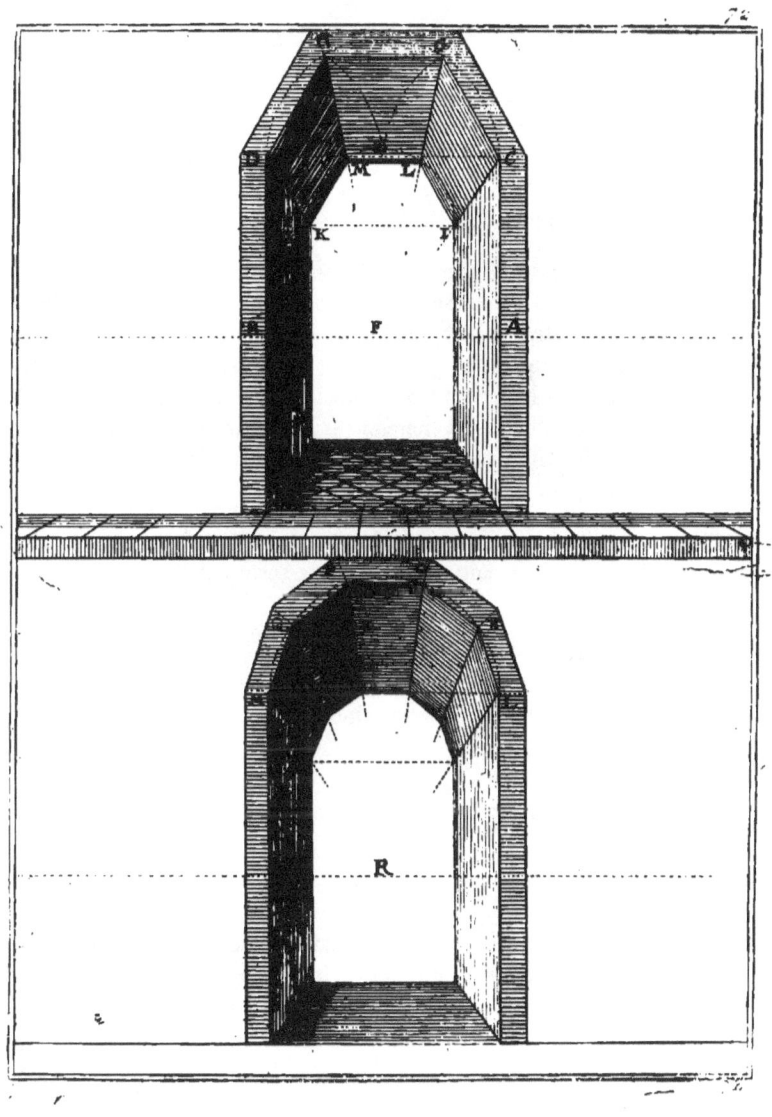

To exhibit the Elevations *of* Round Objects.

T H E defire I have of enabling my reader to put all kind of objects in perfpective with the utmost eafe, has induced me to fhew the method for raifing circular figures to any height at pleafure; and the fame rule may ferve for exhibiting all other rotundo's, as cupola's of churches, amphitheatres, towers, &c. &c.

Having put the plan of the round in perfpective, as already directed, and raifed the line of elevation A B by the fide thereof, from the feveral angles of the plan, which are here the feveral points whereof the round confifts, namely, 1, 2, 3, 4, 5, 6, 7, 8, 9, &c. parallels are to be drawn to the ground line, and from their interfections with the line A O perpendiculars are to be raifed thereon, as already taught, and the lengths of thofe perpendiculars transferred upon other perpendiculars, raifed from the points 1, 2, 3, 4, 5, 6, 7, 8, 9, &c.

The front part of the femi-circle has but half the height of the hinder part, and both the one and the other are mere out-lines without any thicknefs.

There is no round figure but may be put in perfpective by this method. Round figures, I mean, that are parallel to the horizon : for as to fuch as are perpendicular thereto, they are already taught in the rules for vaults.

❀❀❀❀❀❀❀❀❀❀❀❀❀❀❀❀❀❀❀❀❀❀❀❀❀❀❀❀❀❀❀❀❀❀❀

For the Elevation *of* Pilasters.

T H E circle muft be drawn in the plan double, as already fhewn in page 29. and between the two circular lines muft be placed the plan of the parts or members to be raifed, as thofe here marked A B C D, which all tend towards the center E ; then perpendiculars are to be raifed from all the angles of thefe plans, and their proper heights fet off from the line of elevation F G ; as already fhewn in the firft figure.

2

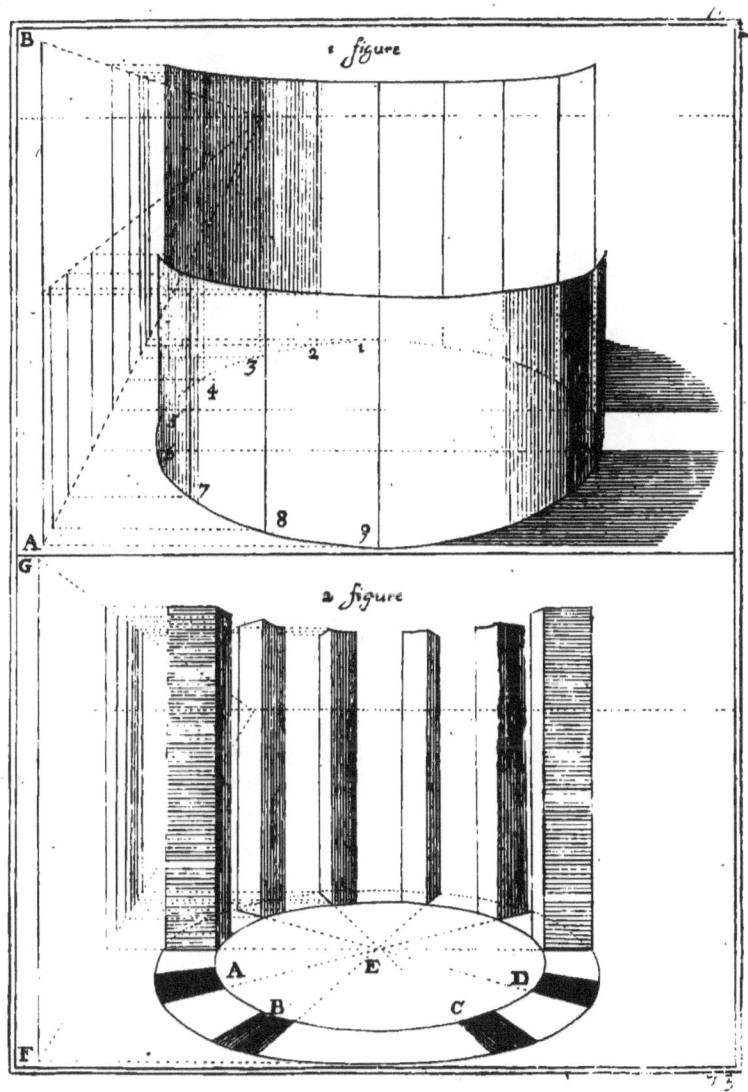

1 figure

2 figure

❀❀❀❀❀❀❀❀❀❀❀❀❀❀❀❀❀❀❀❀❀❀❀❀❀❀❀❀❀❀

A Vault *in form of a* Shell, *in* Perfpective.

THIS figure, with little variations, will either ferve for the *hollow* of a church, or grotto, a *nich*, or the like. The elevation is performed after the manner already directed.

To draw the plat-band, or border A B, which might ferve for a cornifh, its diminution is to be taken on the line of elevation in C D, and transferred thence to the pilafters.

For the vault, take the firft arch E F, as before taught, and in the middle of the infide defcribe a femi-circle O, to which draw curve lines fpringing from the pilafters, and you will have the ribs or reins of the vault, as in G H I K. The heights of the windows muft be taken on the line of elevation between L and M. For the reft, fee the figure.

To exhibit open D O M E S, *o* V A U L T S, *in Perspective.*

HAVING made the plan of a double circle according
to page 29, and marked the places of the pilasters
between the two circles, the lines of all of them tending to
the center A, set off the height intended from the ground
to the cavity of the dome, as the line D E, which is to serve
for a base line, upon which the measures already laid down
on B C drawn parallel to the ground line to touch the circle,
are to be placed. Then from the same point of sight G make
another plan at the top, like that at bottom, all the places
of the pilasters tending towards the center H. To form the
pilasters, all required is to draw lines from the places opposite to each other, which will thus give the breadth and
thickness. I have drawn no lines for the three front pilasters, both for the conveniency of shewing those behind, and
to instance that the plan of them must be drawn both at top
and bottom.

To give the thickness of the rotundo from 1 to H, and
from K to L, set the intended height on the line of elevation
D M, from whence draw lines to the horizon in the point
F ; and from the several points of the upper circle draw parallels to the line D F, at their interfections erect perpendiculars, as D M, which are to be transferred thence, with
the compasses, to the perpendiculars raised from the points
K L, N O, P Q ; and so of the rest.

If instead of a round you require a square, or polygon,
the same method is to be observed.

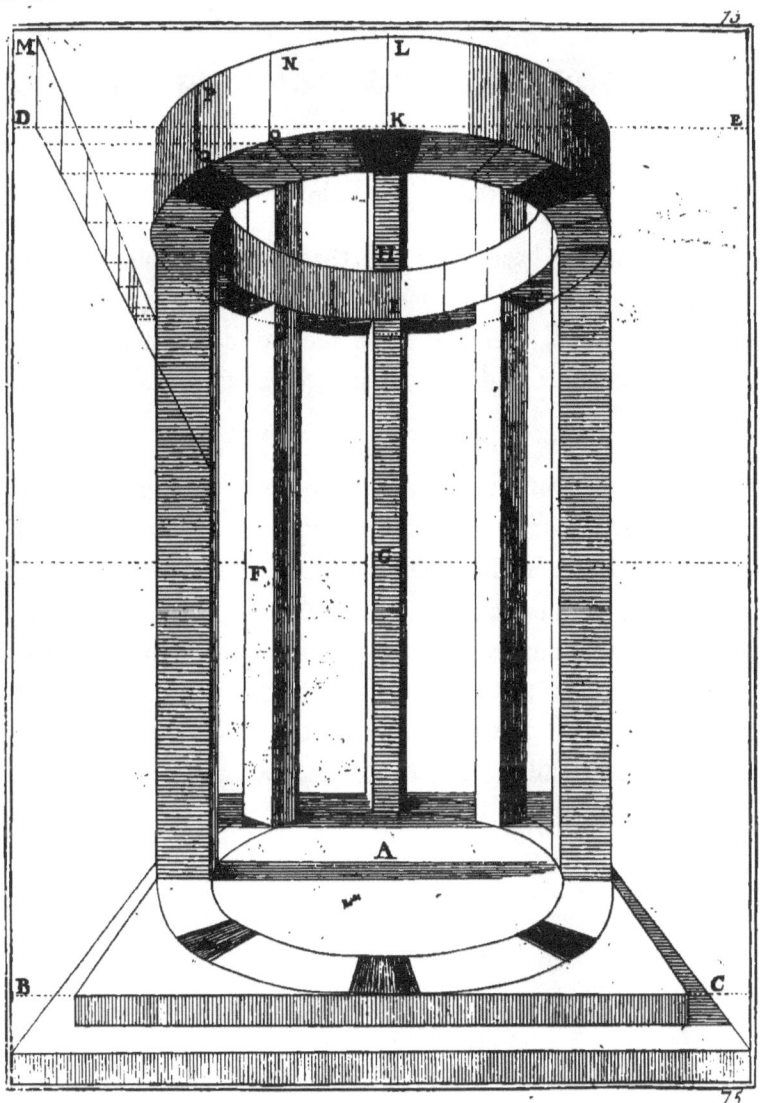

✿✿✿✿✿✿✿✿✿✿✿✿✿✿✿✿✿✿✿✿✿✿✿✿✿✿✿✿✿

That a Number of OBJECTS, *and Plurality of* STORIES,
only admit of one Point *of* Sight.

IT has already been obferved, that only one point of fight
is ever to be ufed in a picture, and that the ignorance of
certain painters is publifhed to all the world, by their making
as many points of fight, and horizons, as they make lines.

It is not long fince I remember to have feen a painting,
wherein there were feveral rooms one over another, each of
which had two or three points of fight; and yet the painter
wonderfully efteemed his performance. The prefent figure
may ferve to correct this error, and to fhew, that there
fhould only be one fingle point of fight, to which all the
objects, and all the rooms, though they were a hundred
over or afide of one another, are to tend. As the three
apartments do all here tend to the point A. The reft is
performed by the rules heretofore directed.

x

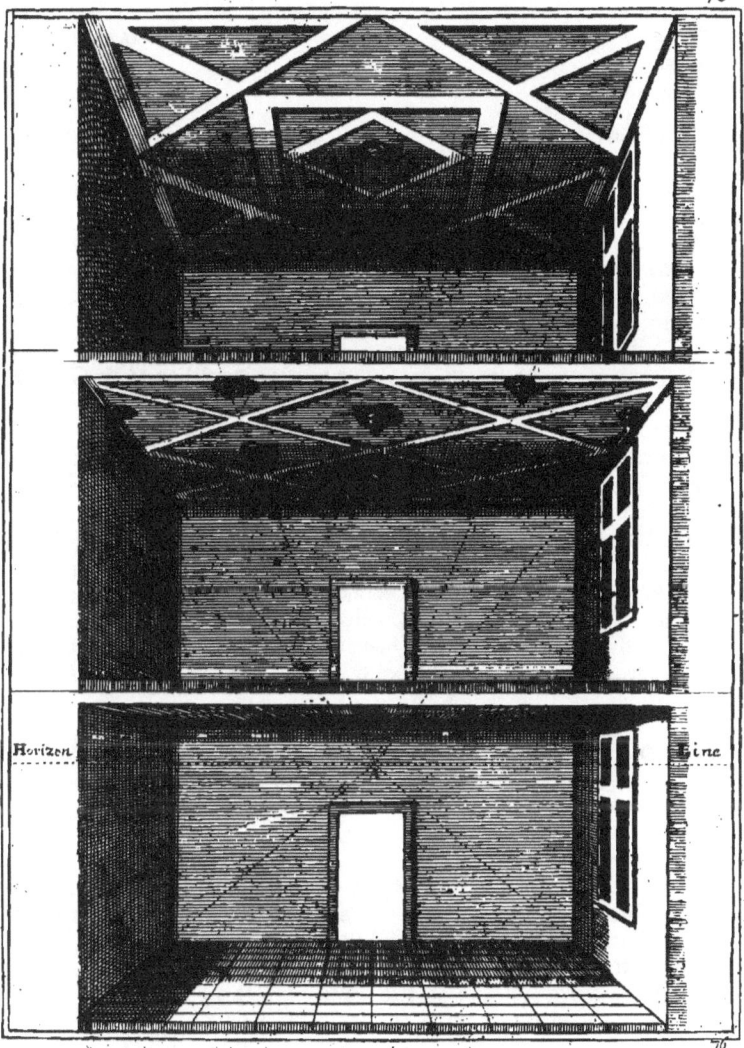

To put CHIMNEYS *in perfpective, either in the front*
or fide-view.

THE meafures are to be taken on the bafe line A B, which, to that
end, muft be divided into equal parts. The divifions may be accounted any thing at pleafure. The prefent is divided into eighteen,
which we call feet.

To make a chimney, or fire-place, in a wall, A, three feet within
the room, take three divifions as A, R, C, and from the point C draw
a line to the point of diftance D, which cutting the ray A E in the
point F, gives a depth of three feet. Proceed to fet the thicknefs of the
jaumb from C, for inftance, to G ; then drawing a line from G to D,
it will give the thicknefs of the jaumb in the point H. Then fet the
breadth of the chimney from G to I, four feet and a half ; and half a
foot; namely, from I to K, for the thicknefs of the jaumb ; then drawing lines from I and K to the point of diftance D, you will have their
meafures on the ray A E, in the points L M : and from the four points
F H L M draw little parallels to the bafe line, as F N, H O, L P, M Q.
For the breadth of the jaumbs take a foot and a half, namely, A R,
and the ray R E will cut the little parallels in the points N O P Q; from
which, and from F L raife perpendiculars. For the height of the mantle-
tree, take five feet on the bafe line, and fet them off on the corner of
the wall from A to S ; and from S to T fet off the cornifh. All the
reft is obvious from the figure.

The other chimney oppofite to the firft is done after the fame manner.
For thus the jaumbs are in all cafes to be managed. And of the jaumbs
may occafionally be made columns, termins, or, as we have here done,
confoles.

To find the hole, or aperture of the chimney, with the depth of the
jaumbs, which are a foot and an half, draw a line from 7 to the point
of fight, cutting the line of depth in the point 5, which will be a foot
and a half, then, from the point of diftance V, draw a diagonal through
5, cutting the ray 2 E in the point 6 ; and from this point draw a parallel, cutting the four rays 1, 2, 3, 4, in the points 9, 6, 9, 9: from
which perpendiculars are to be raifed, and the reft conducted, as above.

The fecond figure reprefents what I have been fpeaking of free and
unembarraffed with lines.

7

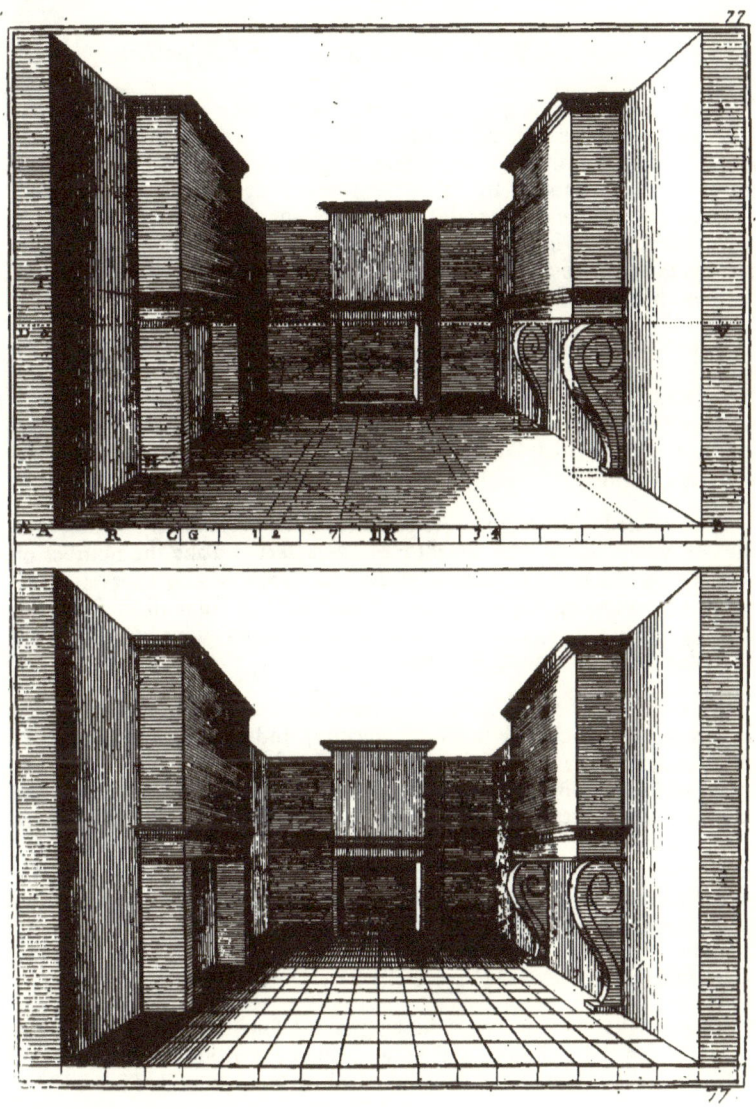

To exhibit Steps *or* Stairs *in Perspective.*

THERE is nothing gives a perspective so much grace, or deceives the eye so easily, as a number of returns and breaks; by reason these introduce a number of different lights and shadows, which give the objects such a force, that they seem to project or stand out from the ground. Now *stairs* have this advantage, that what way soever you place them, they have always a variety of shades, and of consequence are agreeable to the sight. I shall add a few instances of steps in different positions by way of specimen.

If you make use of squares, there will be the less difficulty, all required being to raise perpendiculars of as many squares as you would have steps; then to set the line of elevation, divided into any number of parts, on the first square, and from the divisions to draw lines to the point of sight, which will intersect the perpendiculars in the places where the steps are to be.

It is desired, for instance, to construct a stair-case of eight steps, the last of which to be the breadth of three feet. Take the number of squares of the plan, beginning at B, and proceeding 1, 2, 3, 4, 5, 6, 7, 8, and allowing three for the last marked 11, from all these angles erect perpendiculars, to be cut according to the divisions on the line of elevation B D, in manner following.

The first division, which, supposing the square to be a foot, is four inches high, will cut the first perpendicular, and must be continued to 2, which makes the top of the step; and so of the rest. The steps you may make as long as you please, by supposing the square a foot. Accordingly the uppermost here, taking three divisions, is three feet. Perpendiculars should likewise be raised, as in this instance, on the side B: but that trouble may be saved, by taking the height of the last step H, and that of the first I, and drawing the line H I, raising the angles on the side I, as E K does on the side B; for this done, you need only to draw parallels to the base line from all the stairs from the side B, to cut the line H I in L M N O P Q, &c.

One might likewise do without making squares; for laying all the measures on the base line, and drawing lines from them to the point of distance, the same measures would be had on the line A B.

The other figures we are silent upon, this much being sufficient for the understanding and executing them all.

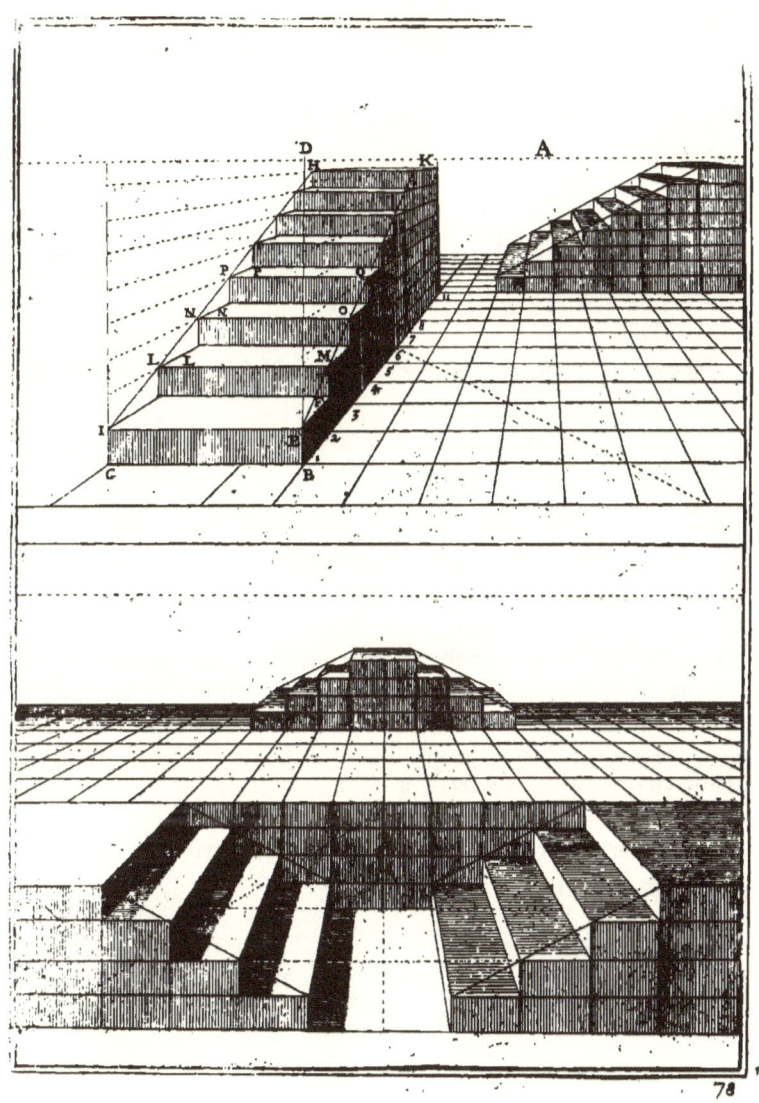

B b

STAIRS *open or perforated underneath.*

THE method of managing thefe ftairs is the fame with that already defcribed.

As to the aperture, a bare fight of the figure is fufficient to fhew how it is to be put in perfpective. Thefe two may give occafion to the inventing many others.

✿✿✿✿✿✿✿✿✿✿✿✿✿✿✿✿✿✿✿✿✿✿✿✿✿✿✿✿✿✿✿✿✿✿✿

STEPS *or* STAIRS *viewed in Front.*

THIS method is founded on the ufe of the line of elevation : the fame number of perpendiculars are to be raifed from the angles of the fquares of the plan, as there are required fteps, for example, C D E F ; and from the fame angles parallels are to be drawn to the ground line meeting the line of elevation A, the interfections whereof give the points O O O O, from which perpendiculars are to be raifed till they cut the occult rays of the divifions of the line of elevation. Thefe meafures are to be taken in your compaffes, and fet off on the perpendiculars raifed from the angles of the plan, each in its order; the firft for the firft ftep, the fecond for the fecond, &c.

To find the returns P P, &c. from the fame angles P, &c. lines are to be drawn to the point of diftance Q, and notice taken where they cut the line of the plan, or the bottom of the ftep ; for inftance, over the fourth ftep is the plan of the fifth : now to find its return P, from the point P draw a line to Q, and the point S, wherein it interfects the parallel R R, will be the line of return S T ; and fo of the reft.

To exhibit STEPS that shew four Sides.

THERE are various manners of ordering such steps, two of the easiest of them follow. Take the length of the first step, and set the number of steps required upon the same; as on the line A B are here set the points C C C C, for four steps. From these points draw rays to the point of sight D, which rays are to be cut by the diagonals A F and B E in the points I I I, from which perpendiculars are to be raised, and parallels to the ground line drawn to the line of elevation G, which give the points H, to be raised as H K.

On this line of elevation G, as many equal parts must be marked as there are steps desired, for example, four, here marked 1, 2, 3, 4. From these four points of division rays are to be drawn to the point of sight D, to cut the perpendiculars H K, and give each its proper height.

These measures must be taken in your compasses, and transferred one after another, beginning with the first G, which is to be set on the first perpendicular on the angle A, namely A L; then a parallel to be drawn to the other side B, (though here I only give half of it, to have room for the plan in the other.) For the second stair the second measure H 2 is to be taken, and set off on the second perpendicular I; and a parallel is to be drawn as before; and so of the rest.

Another Manner;

THE side M N being given, make a parallel O P over the same, for the thickness or height of the first step. From the two points O P draw two rays to the point of sight Q, and again other lines to the points of distance R S; which last will give a square after the usual way, and form the first step. For the second, set the intended breadth on the line O P, for example, O T, and from T draw a ray to the point of sight Q; which line or ray T Q will cut the diagonal O in the point V, the place where the second step must be raised. The height of this second degree must be half of V X, as M O is half of O T. The point Y thus gained, a parallel must be drawn through it as far as the diagonal of the other side drawn from the corner P; then from Y and Z draw lines to the points of sight and distance, to form the square, as for the first stair. For the third, set the measure V X on the line Y Z, extending, for example, from Y to A; and from the point A draw a ray to the point of sight Q, which intersecting the diagonal of the point Y, will give the point B for the third step. Its height will be half of B C, which is always that of O T in perspective. The rest the same as in the first and second.

The third figure shews these stairs free of all the confusion of lines and letters.

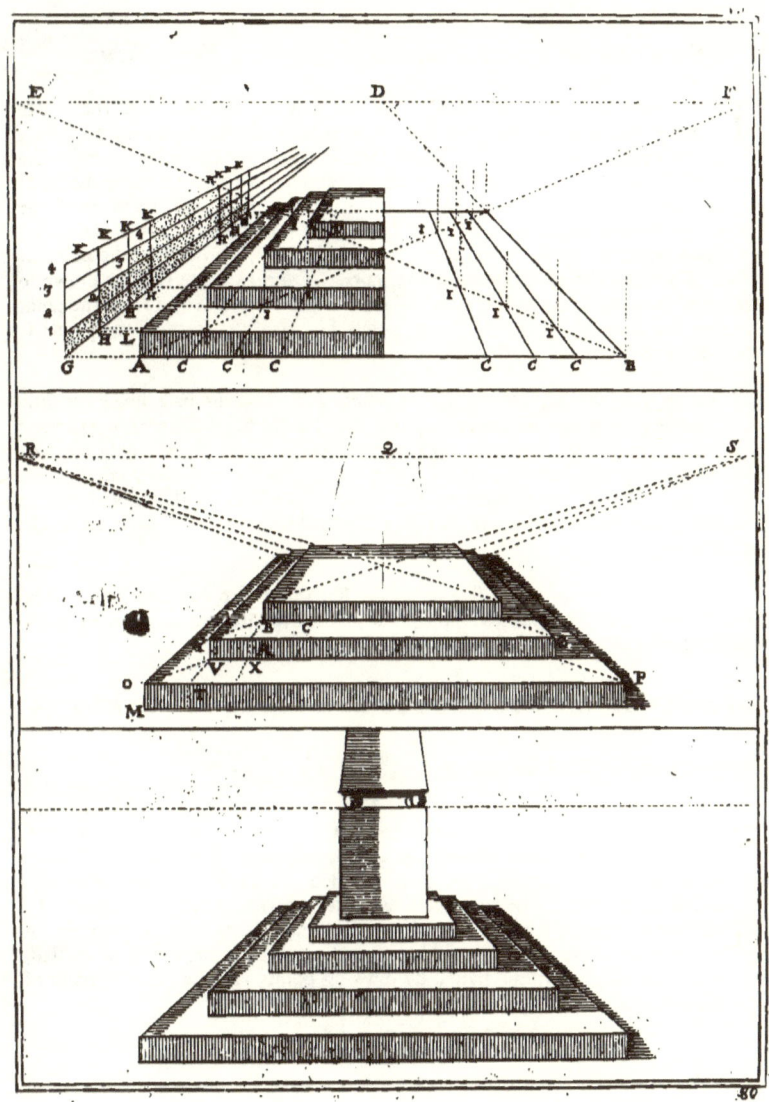

Stairs *or* Steps *viewed fidewife in Perfpective.*

THE number of ftairs is firft to be laid down on the bafe line, that is, fo many points are to be made thereon at equal diftance as you intend fteps; as in the prefent cafe A B C. From thefe points lines are to be drawn to the point of fight D; then from the point A, another is to be drawn to the point of diftance E, which diagonal A E will give the plan, and the place of the ftairs, by its interfection with the rays B D, C D in the points I; and by its interfection with the ray F, which is the foot of the wall, it will give the point G, which is the middle of the plan of the ftairs. From G a line is to be drawn to the other point of diftance H, which gives the angle of the laft ftair in the point K, and the place of all the reft in the points I I. Laftly, from all the points I, erect perpendiculars.

Now to give the heights; from the points A B C on the bafe line erect little lines, ferving for a line of elevation; on thefe lay the heights according to their number. The perpendicular A, for inftance, which is the firft, will only have 1; B, the fecond, will have 2; and C, the third, will have 3. From all thefe points 1, 2, and 3, draw lines to the point of fight D, and you will cut the perpendiculars raifed from the plan in the points O, which will give the height of each ftep.

The draught on the other fide fhews the fteps free of points and lines. The fame method may ferve for divers purpofes; as for the fteps of an altar, a throne, the front of a church, a gate, &c.

❀❦❀❀❀❀❞❀❀❀❀❀❀❀❀❀❀❀❀ ❀❀❀❀❀❀❞❀❀❀❀❀❀❀❀❀❀

Stairs *in a* Wall *in Perfpective.*

MAKE as many divifions at the end of the bafe line as you intend ftairs, as in this cafe, three between A and B, and from A and B draw lines to the point of fight C; then, having determined the fpace the ftairs are to take up, as D E, a parallel to the bafe line E F muft be drawn, which in the points I I will receive the interfections of lines drawn from the points G H to the point of fight C; and from the fame points I I, perpendiculars I K, I K are to be erected, to receive the heights of the ftairs, by drawing points 1, 2, 3, to the point of fight C, as appears from the figure.

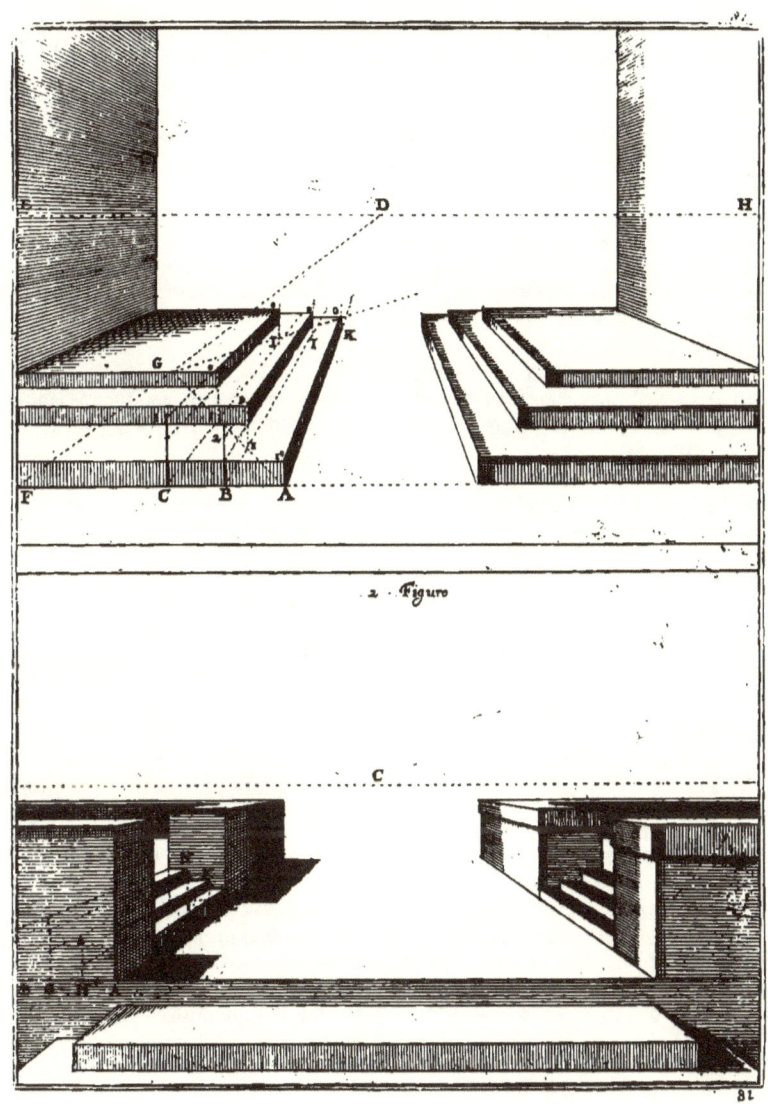

2. Figure

To exhibit a STAIR-CASE *with* Landing Places *in Perspective.*

D O but recollect the preceding methods, and you will find it exceeding easy to construct such stair-cases. However, to save the trouble of too irksome a retrospect, I shall explain the whole here.

By reason stair-cases of this figure usually run over a space equal to twice their width, to raise one of them in perspective, the horizon must first be disposed at pleasure; then a square to be made according to the common rules, and this to be doubled, as directed in page 16; then divided by an unequal number of small squares, that the wall, which is supposed in the middle, may be the measure of a square.

In this figure each square has nine sides, or squares, on either hand, which being doubled, give eighteen; of these, four being left at each end for the landing-places, remain ten squares, or stairs, each whereof we suppose equal to a foot every way.

At the distance of four squares from the point A, erect the perpendicular B pretty high, then a second perpendicular C at the other angle of that square, and a third D; and so onwards on the other angles of the squares, to the number of ten. This done on one side, the same must be repeated on the other; and such perpendiculars will give the depths or breadths of the steps.

For the heights, if they be a foot broad, they must be half a foot high, or half the little square A O; which height being taken in your compasses, set it on the first angle, which is to serve for a line of elevation, beginning at the bottom, or the point A, and making as many divisions thereon as you intend stairs, namely ten, from the bottom to the first landing-place; where you begin to mount up the opposite side, and the series of numbers is continued to twenty-three.

From all these twenty-three points, lines are to be drawn to the point of sight E, and care taken to cut the perpendiculars in their order; that is, having laid your ruler from the first point to the point of sight, cross the first perpendicular B to C with a little stroke, for the first step. For the second step, from the second point draw a line, crossing the second perpendicular C to D. And so of all the rest on both sides.

From the angles of all these little strokes between the perpendiculars draw parallels to the horizon, as far as the wall F erected in the middle; such are the lines I I I I, which I have only added on one side, to avoid confusion: It is these parallels alone that form the stairs. All the other lines hitherto drawn should be occult, and not to be seen when the figure is finished.

The landing-places should contain all the vacant spaces between the last perpendicular and the wall, as from G to H. Their height, or thickness A K, is half a foot, the same as that of a stair.

The lower figure is the same with the upper, only that one has the apparatus of lines, &c. necessary for the performance, which the other is without.

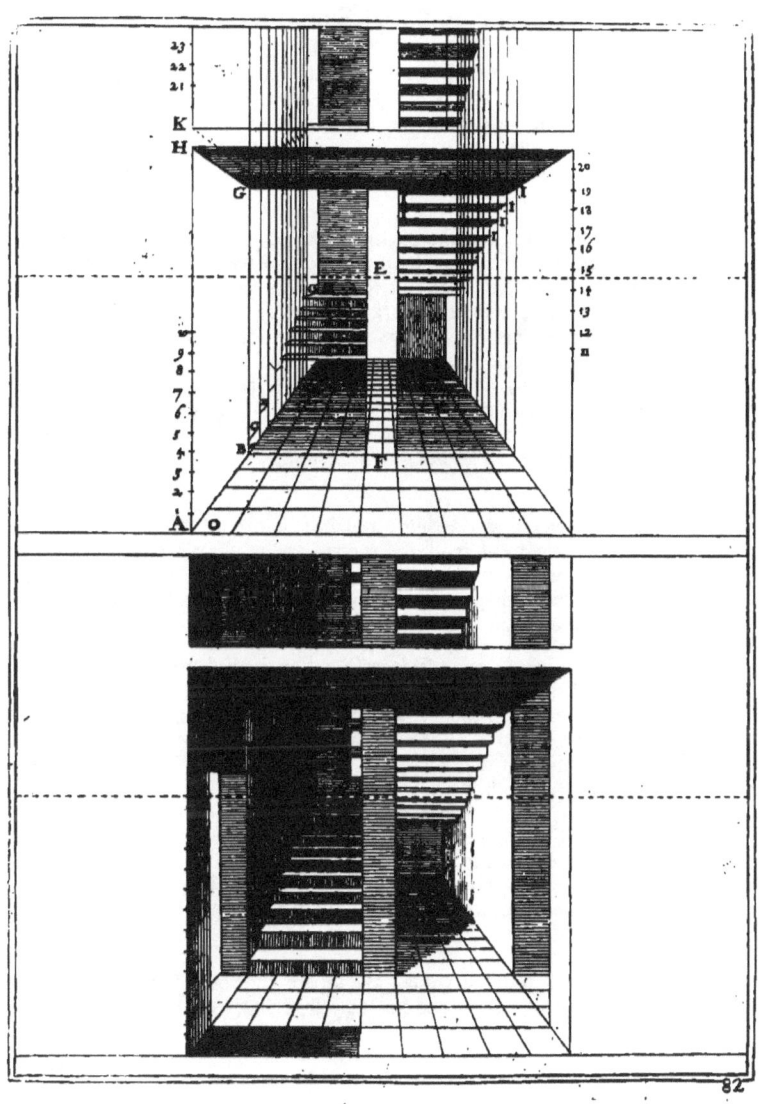

Cc

To exhibit Winding *or* Spiral ST AIRS *in Perfpective.*

ONE fide of the flight, or afcent, is to be fet on the bafe line, and divided into as many parts as you require ftairs. Suppofe, for inftance, A B the fide of the ftair cafe, and fixteen fteps required in the whole circuit of the fquare; each fide, in this cafe, will contain four; confequently A B being divided into four, a fquare is to be formed thereof, as here reprefented, divided into fixteen, according to the ufual rules.

From all the divifions on the fides of the plan, perpendiculars muft be raifed to give the bounds of the ftairs. Suppofe then the perpendiculars A A, B B, C C, D D, E E. Thus E E ftands for three of the perpendiculars, by reafon the point is in the middle, and ferves as a newel, * or common center of them all. On the firft perpendicular A, which is to ferve for a line of elevation, the height of a ftair Q A muft be fet, and from the point Q a line be drawn to the point of fight X, which by its interfections with the perpendiculars Q R S T V, gives the dimenfions of all the ftairs. Thus A Q is the height of the firft, F R of the fecond, G S of the third, H T of the fourth, and I V of the fifth. This laft is the height of all thofe at the bottom, as A Q is of thofe in the front.

Since G S is the meafure of the third, which is that in the middle of the fide, it muft likewife be the meafure of the center, and of the newel of the flight: for this reafon, having taken the meafure G S in your compaffes, fet it off in the center of the fquare or the newel as many times as you would have ftairs in the flight; for example, eighteen times for eighteen ftairs.

All things thus difpofed, the reft is eafy. For the firft ftep you are to take the divifion A Q, and fet it off upon the perpendicular D in the point 1, and from 1 to draw a parallel to the perpendicular B; then from the two points 1 1 draw lines to the third 1 at the newel or center of the fquare. Thefe three 1 1 1 will form the firft ftair. For the fecond, fince its angle reaches to the perpendicular B, which is on the fore-fide, it muft have the fame meafure A Q, which will be 1, 2; then from the point 2 a line is to be drawn to the point of fight X, cutting the perpendicular P in the point 2; from which points 2 and 2, lines are to be drawn to the 2 at the newel. Thus will you have formed the fecond ftair. For the third, fince it is found on the perpendicular P, the meafure F R muft be taken for its height; and the fame procefs obferved as in the former.

If you would have them round withal, the fquare muft be reduced to a circle; according to the preceding rules: and for the reft, the fame method will ferve for both.

---

* The newel is the upright poft which a pair of winding ftairs turns about.

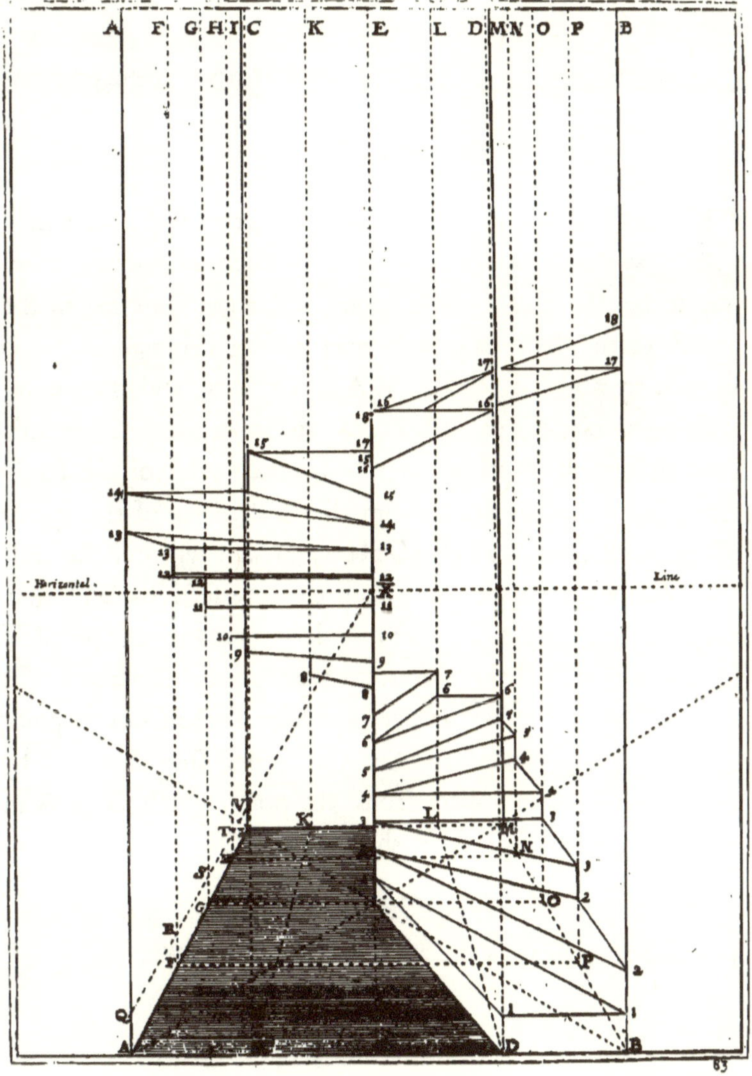

83

WINDING-STAIRS.

THIS figure is the fame with the preceding one, which
was not fhaded, that the method of the operation
might be the more confpicuous. For the fame reafon the
newel of the ftair cafe was referved for this figure. It is
formed by affuming the point A as a center, and thence defcribing a circle; or rather a femi-circle, as B C, becaufe
only half of it is to be feen. To the center of this femi-
circle lines muft be drawn from all the divifions of the fquare
of the firft plan, as DEFGHIK, which will cut the arch
B C into eight parts; and from the interfections O O, &c.
perpendiculars are to be raifed ; taking care they cut precifely
in the points, where the fteps are placed ; the ftep I, for
inftance, to be cut by the perpendicular raifed from its point
in the femi-circle, as in A ; the fecond ftep to be cut by
the perpendicular raifed from the point which K gives in
the femi-circle : and fo of the reft.

The doors, windows, &c. in the figure, are all conftructed according to the rules already laid down.

To exhibit ROUND STAIRS *in Perfpective.*

TO raife thefe three round ftairs or fteps, in a front
view, make a plan of three circles within each other,
after the manner already directed in page 28, and from the
feveral points that form the circle draw lines parallel to the
bafe, as far as the ray A, which is the foot of the line of
elevation A B. This gives the elevations, which are to be
taken thence with the compaffes, and fet off on perpendiculars raifed from the feveral points of the plan.

❀❀❀❀❀❀❀❀❀❀❀❀❀❀❀❀❀❀❀❀❀❀❀❀❀❀❀❀❀❀

ROUND STEPS *viewed fide-wife.*

THE rules for objects viewed by the fides I have often
obferved are the fame with thofe for objects in front.
However to fhew we are not always obliged to obferve the
divifion of the circle into fixteen, thefe of the fide-view we
have divided into eight. For the reft, it is the fame as in
the preceding cafes, the line of elevation is C D, drawn to
the point of fight E.

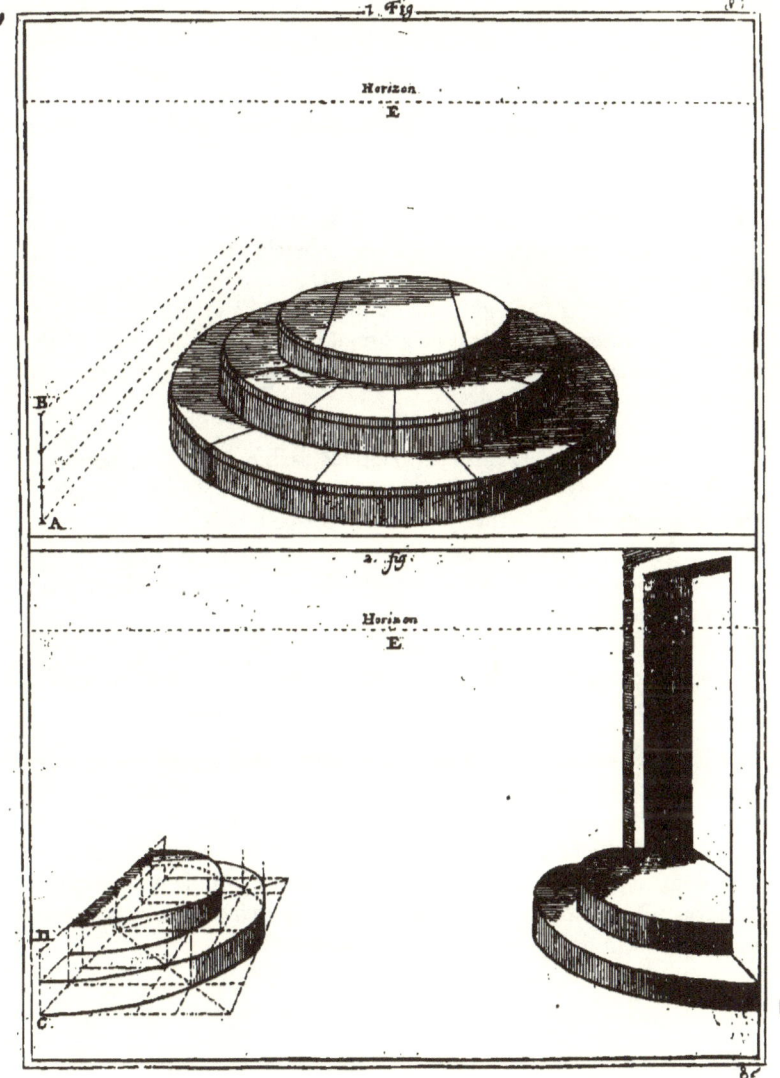

To exhibit S QU A R E S, *with* Circles *therein, in Perfpective.*

THE method for this procefs, is the fame with that delivered for putting planes in perfpective. The circle, for inftance, is to be divided into eight parts, as in figure A, wherein the circle on the front of the cube, gives the diminution of that on the top ; and that in the front, with that at top, give the diminutions of all the other fides ; as in figure B, where the circle is alfo diminiflied on the fide, and in the figure C, where it is diminifhed on three fides of the cube, I mean both on the outer and inner fides.

The three figures D E F are perforated each on two fides, according to the plan of the circle A. Thus the cube D is pierced through its fore-fide ; and through that perforation the bottom is feen. Thus alfo E is perforated on the fides, and F through the top and bottom, though the latter perforation be not diftinguifhable, by reafon the object is not fuppofed tranfparent.

The three figures underneath reprefent the pieces cut out of each cube. G, for inftance, out of the cube D. H out of E, and I out of F.

Upon the whole, the method of difpofing fquare figures in circles appears very eafy ; nor can the attentive reader find any difficulty in placing columns under any difpofition whatever. The reafon why I have yet given no directions for them, is, that I chofe to render the raifing of elevations as eafy to conceive, and the practice as little embarraffed as poffible. Thus much may ferve for the beginning of columns ; how to carry on and finifh them fhall be fhewn hereafter.

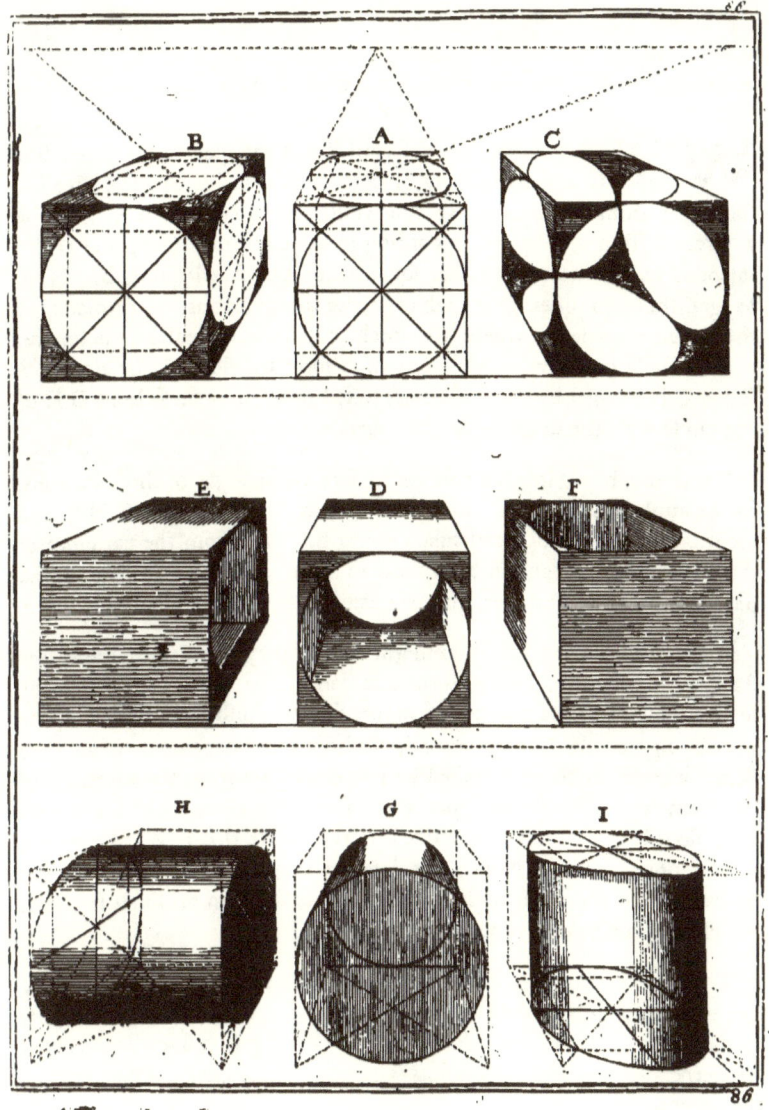

D d

To exhibit Columns *in Perfpective.*

WHAT has been juft obferved is not confined to the cube, but extends equally to any objeƈt which is to be rounded. For inftance, if from the fquare, A, you would raife a column A B, defcribe a circle within the fquare, according to the common rules; and at the intended height defcribe another fquare with a circle within it, B. Now to get the two lines D E, which make the thicknefs, or diameter of the column, obferve where the circle cuts the diagonal of the fquare, and on thofe points raife the lines which form the fides of the elevation. Thus C is formed by perpendiculars raifed from the interfeƈtions D E of the circle with the diagonal of the fquare.

Thus much regards the column in fide-views. As to thofe in front, for example, the figure F, they always fhew the femi-circle G H I, and for this purpofe the perpendiculars are to be raifed from the extremes of the diameter G H; and in both thofe in front, and thofe in fide-views, perpendiculars to be raifed from the center, to give the diminutions.

As to the three columns underneath, as they fhew the former inftances more clearly, and with the addition of fhadowing, they likewife ferve to point out the manner of proceeding to finifh the *columns.* The middle figure, K, is quite round, without any ornament at all, and being viewed in front, is raifed by perpendiculars from the extremes of the diameter. The fecond, marked L, fhews, that when a bafe is required, a double circle muft be defcribed on the fquare that ferves as a plinth, whofe upper part is M N; the interval between the circles to be the projeƈture of the bafe, and the inner circle the plan of the bafe, from which perpendiculars are to be raifed.

The third figure, O, is a column with its ornaments; which every one is to make at his difcretion; taking care the abacus anfwer, as it ought, to the plinth. Thefe two columns L and O being feen fidewife are raifed by perpendiculars from the points where the circle cuts the diagonals of the fquare.

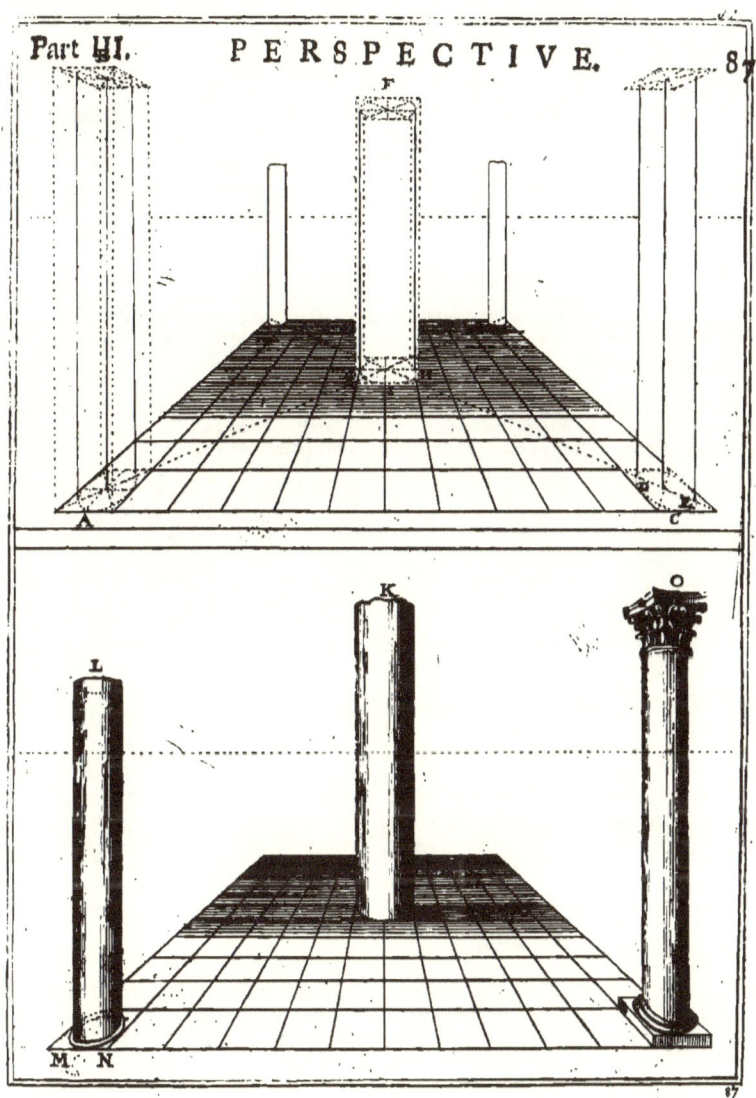

Cornices and Mouldings in Perfpective.

AFTER the *columns*, which are the chief ornaments of architecture, we proceed to the *cornices*, or *mouldings*, with their projectures; which have hitherto been omitted, for fear of rendering our elevations perplexed.

There is fcarce any building but has fome moulding or projecture by way of enrichment, and to render it pleafing to the eye: for this reafon, it is proper to give the rules for thefe; not the rules for their conftruction, nor their meafures and proportions, for in that cafe I fhould be obliged to give all the orders of architecture, and a thoufand other inftances; which the reader will find elfewhere: but rules to put them in perfpective, when any particular ornament or order is pitched upon.

To put the pilafter A B, with its ornaments or members in perfpective : its breadth being taken, and a fquare plan made as ufual, erect perpendiculars from all the angles thereof, and you will have the body, or fhaft, of the pilafter.

Proceed now to take the projectures, or jettings, as for example, the bafe of the pilafter C, and lay down the feveral meafures thereof in D E. To put this in perfpective all round the pilafter, from the point of diftance F draw a diagonal to the point E, and farther at random, as to G; then from the point of fight A draw a line to the bottom of the projecture H, and in the point I, where this cuts the diagonal, will be the jet, or projecture, of the whole bafe. The fame line A H gives the projecture of the bottom, by its interfection with the other diagonal in K. For the projecture of the front, from the point I draw a parallel to the bafe line, till it cuts the diagonal in L : this gives the other corner of the projecture of the front. Then drawing lines from the top of the bafe to thefe points, as from M to L, and from N to K, you will have the breadth and height of the whole bafe. The fame method ferves for the capital.

The figures underneath fhew the reft, and even the effect of what is faid, free of confufion. For the pilafter O, regard muft be had to that above in P, where the line D H has upon it all the interfections of the bafe. For this reafon lines are to be drawn from the point of fight A, which paffing through the divifions of D H, will exprefs the fame on the lines D I and N K; then parallels being drawn from·the points D I to M L, nothing remains but to draw the out-lines. When there happens fquares, or fillets, either at top or bottom, they are formed by perpendiculars. Thus, for the plinth, perpendiculars muft be raifed from the points L I K, and·from the point of fight A a line to be drawn through the angle of the plinth to Q; this will give the height of the perpendiculars I and K. Laftly, L is to be made equal to I.

This inftruction for the bafe will fuffice for the capitals ; the operation being the fame in both. The laft pilafter R, is only meant to fhew one clear of lines. They are all broke in the middle, that there might be room to exprefs both the bafe and the capital ; the page not allowing them to be reprefented whole.

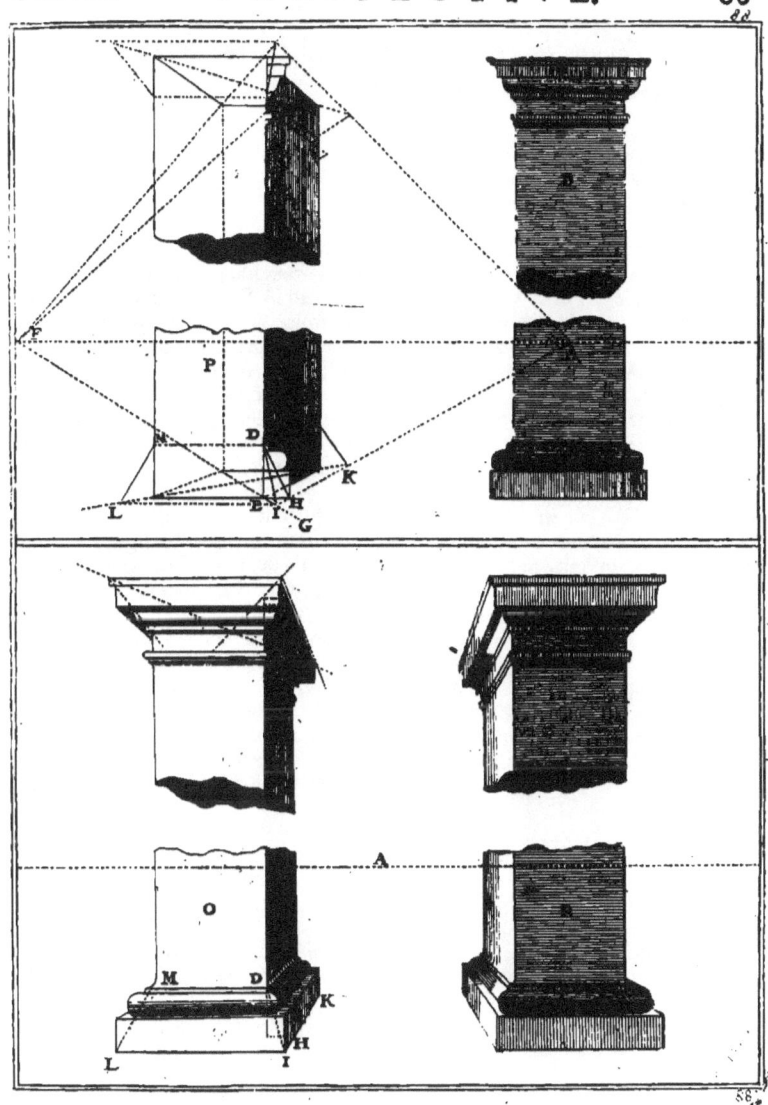

To exhibit a large Cornice *above the* Horizon, in *Perſpective.*

THE method is the ſame as that juſt delivered; but being ſomewhat trouble-ſome by reaſon of the number of lines, I have judged proper to repeat it again here, in order to avoid confuſion.

To the purpoſe then: having taken the profile of the cornice, and its pro-jecture, you are to transfer it to the place where the draught is to be made; as here the profile C, &c. is at the corner of a wall A B. To find what height it muſt.have, and to make it ſhew its bottom, from the point of ſight D draw a line through the extreme of the profile E, as the line D F; then draw a dia-gonal from the point of diſtance H, paſſing through the corner of the wall B, and prolonged till it cut the ray D E in the point F; from which draw the line F G, which is to repreſent the angle in perſpective, and to receive all the mea-ſures of E G. The corner of the other end of the wall, K L, is to be drawn to the point of diſtance I, as being the other diagonal.

In *Fig.* II. it is ſhewn, that all the figures which are on the line M N, are to be transferred, by means of viſual rays drawn from the point of ſight D, upon the line N O; in order for parallels to be drawn through all thoſe points, which are to give the cornice complete. But before we go farther, it is to be obſerved, as has been already hinted, that all plat-bands and ſquares are formed by per-pendiculars. Thus, for inſtance, to form the large ſquare of the cornice, having made the doucine, and the fillet; from the bottom of the fillet, which is the top of the ſquare, let fall the perpendicular P Q: then, to find the place it is to be cut in, to ſhew the bottom, a line muſt be drawn from the point of di-ſtance I, through the point at top of the quarter round R, to the perpendicu-lar P Q; and you will have your deſire. What has been ſaid of the large ſquare, holds equally of the leſſer ones; as the denticles, fillets, &c. which are all to ſhew their bottoms.

The third *figure* ſhews, that having found all the points, and drawn lines on the line of the angle S T proportional mouldings muſt be drawn thereon. I mean, that when they project much, as is here the caſe, by reaſon the point of diſtance is near, the mouldings muſt be helped out a little; that is, the quarter round muſt be inclined a little, the doucine be erected, the fillets enlarged; and the ſame done at one end as the other; for example, the ſame on V X as on S T.

This done, all that remains is, to draw parallels to the baſe line to form the front-ſide of the cornice.

The fourth *figure* is the cornice complete. In this we have drawn parallels from all the points of the line of the angle Y Z; and one end of the wall is made to paſs over the cornice, to ſhew that we are at liberty in ſuch matters; and that the rule is general.

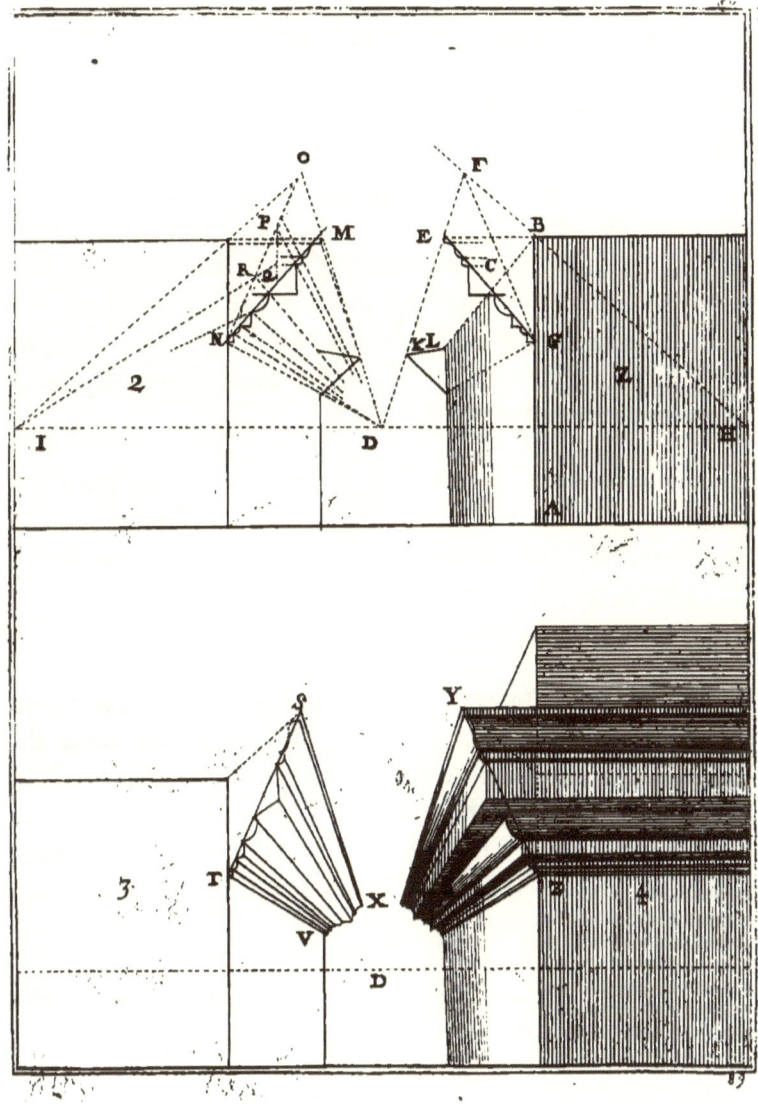

To find the Bottoms *of large* PROJECTURES.

TO find the projecture of the corona of the wall A; on the angle of the quarter round B, make a line equal to the length of the intended projecture, as B C; then from the point of fight D, draw a ray E, paffing to the extreme of the meafure C. This done, draw a diagonal from the point of diftance F, paffing through the quarter round B; and the point G, wherein it interfects the ray D E, will give the bottom on both fides, B H : as is more clearly expreffed in the oppofite figure K.

The projecture of the wall L, is formed after the fame manner as that of the former A. All the difference is, the projecture M N of the wall L, is half as big again as that of B C; to intimate, that the fame rule makes them as big, or as little as one pleafes.

It is likewife obfervable in the fame wall, how the return of the projecture, &c. is found. For inftance, from the point O of the quarter round in the fund of the wall, a diagonal is drawn to the point of diftance P ; and the interfection of that line with the ray C D will be a point, through which a little parallel to the horizon R Q being drawn, will give the return required.

The fame method may ferve for all fquares on cornices and mouldings both great and fmall.

The wall S fhews all the mouldings on that of L, more diftinctly.   2

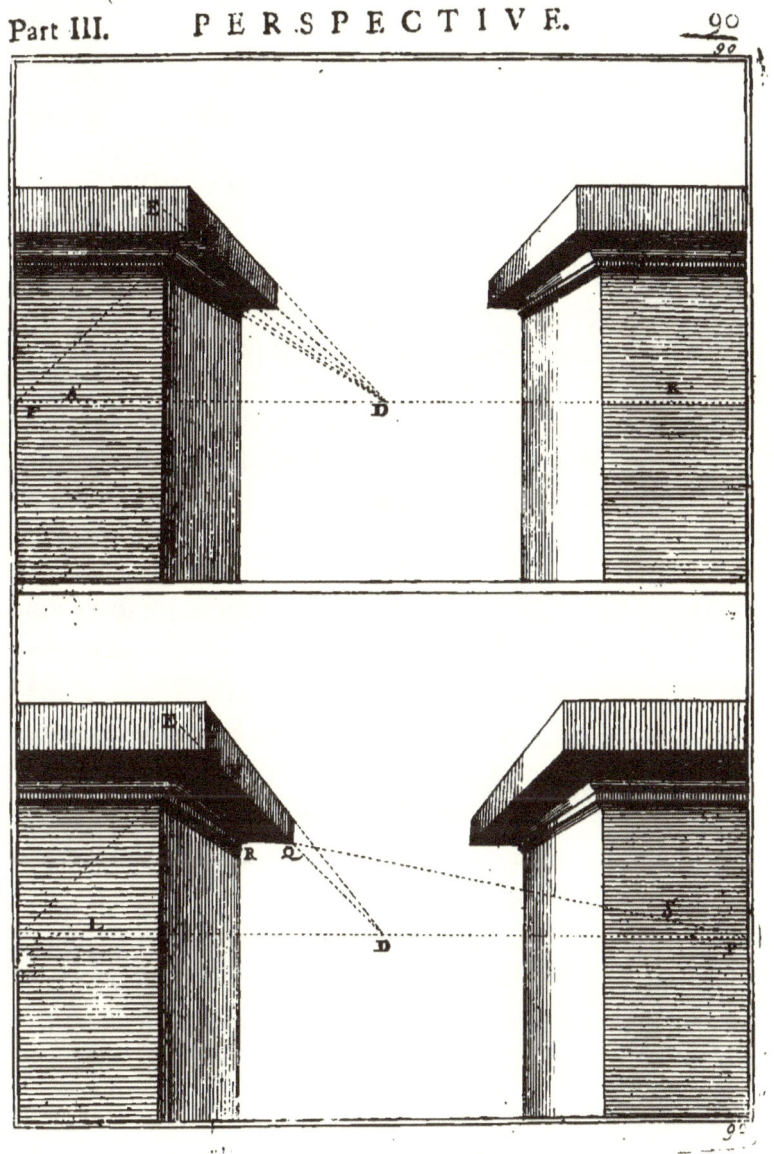

E e

To exhibit CORNICES *and* MOULDINGS *below the Horizon.*

T H E rules that obtain here are the fame with thofe of the preceding cafes ; though through an accident which fometimes falls out, namely, a diverfity of horizons, there arifes a little variation, which fuch as are unacquainted therewith might chance to be puzzled withal.

I obferve then that in viewing a cornice below the eye, and of confequence below the horizon, the projeétures hide fometimes half, fometimes more ; more or lefs of them being feen, according as the eye is more or lefs elevated.

To find precifely how much of the projeétion is to be co-vered, and how much not; fet the profile of the moulding on the corner of the body to be enriched therewith ; and having found the line of the angle, after the manner already direéted, draw the divifions of the profile upon the fame. Thus will you find that the fquare, or plat-band, covers the whole aftragal underneath, and only lets half the fillet be feen. For, drawing a line from the point of fight A, through the profile B C, it cuts the perpendicular from the line of angle in D, and fhews how much is to be covered. For the moulding at bottom the fame method ferves as for that at top.

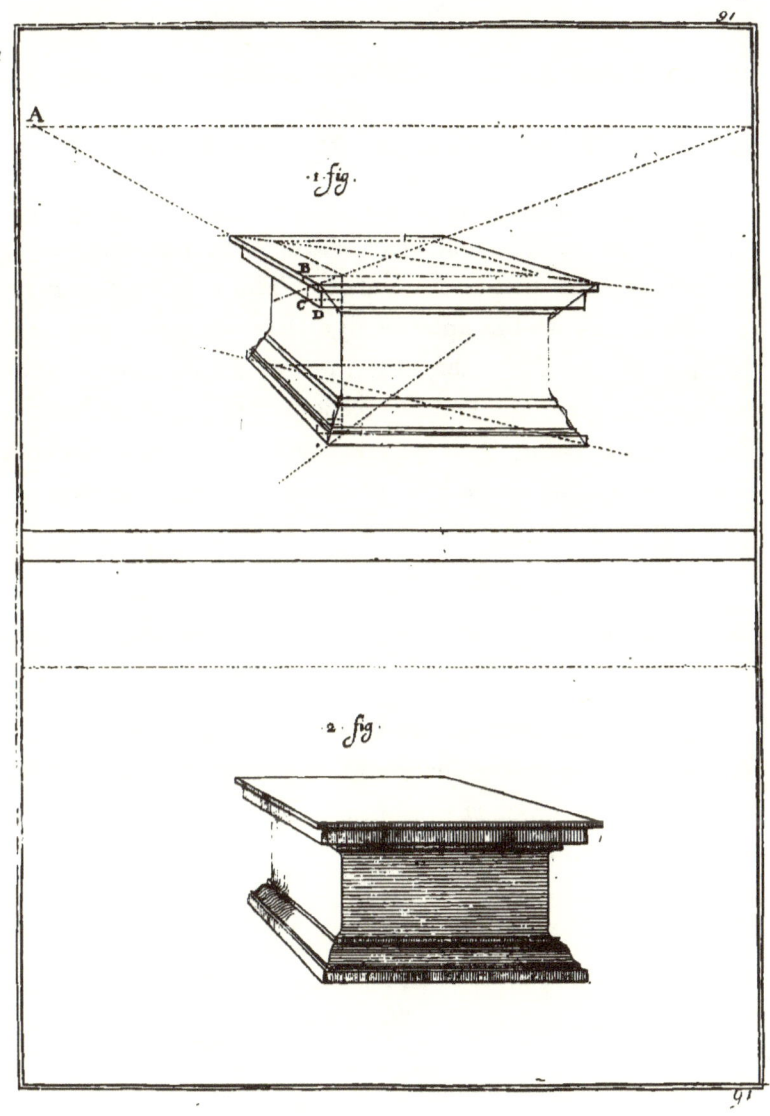

❀✿❀✿❀✿❀✿❀✿❀✿❀✿❀✿❀✿❀✿❀✿❀✿❀✿❀✿❀✿❀✿❀

To exhibit CORNICES *with several* Returns.

WHEN there happen divers turns and returns in the cornices or mouldings, their bottoms muſt always be taken from the point of diſtance. Thus, having drawn rays, A and B, to the point of ſight E; from the point of diſtance C, or D, a diagonal muſt be drawn through the angle of the quarter round O, till it cut the ray A or B in I. From which point, I, a parallel to the baſe being drawn, gives the bottom or projecture of the ſquare; as already ſhewn in page 90.

I would willingly have made a much bigger cornice; as that would not have been a whit the more difficult: but the compaſs of the page obliged me to be contented with this.

If you would have returns on the ground, in the manner as theſe are above the horizon; the ſame method is to be obſerved. For proof of this, invert the paper, and you will find it have the ſame effect.

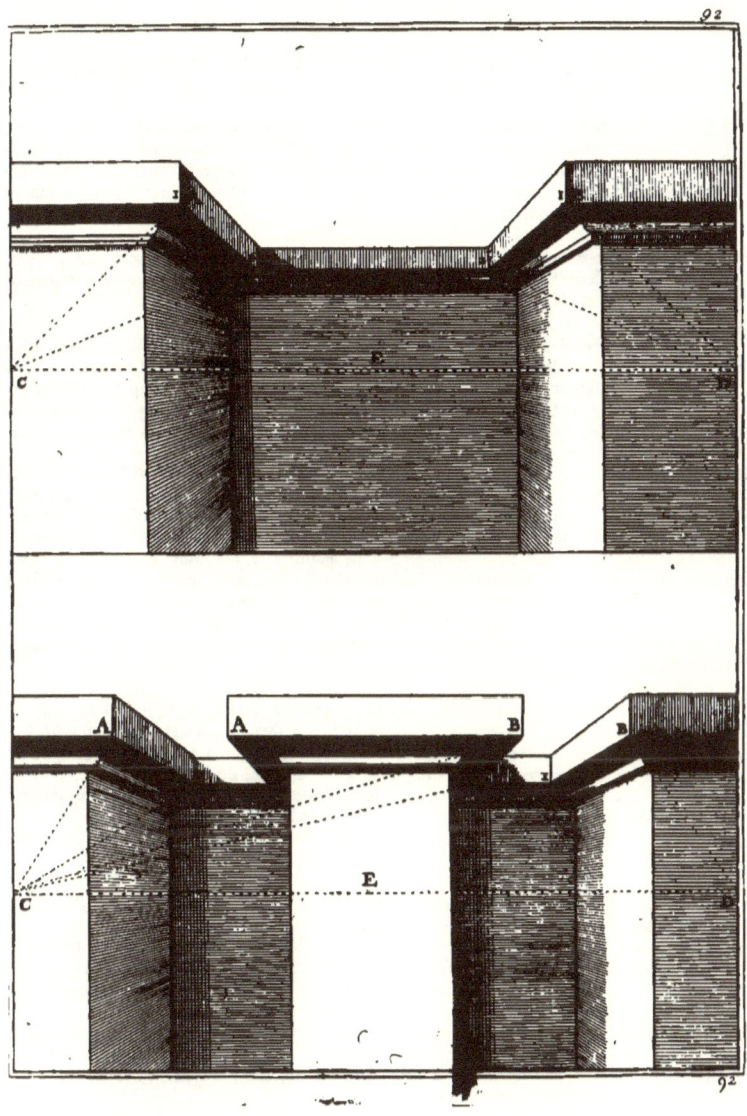

To exhibit the APERTURES *of* Doors *in Perfpective,*

IN my inftructions, I have kept pretty clofe to the order obferved in the actual erecting of buildings of all kinds. I now proceed to fhew how to furnifh and difpofe them for the reception of inhabitants. I begin with wooden doors; and hereafter fhall find occafion to fpeak of other apertures, as windows, cupboards, &c. then of moveables, as tables, beds, chairs, chefts, benches, &c.

All doors are to open and fhut far or little at the pleafure of the perfon who opens them. For this reafon I fhall fhew an eafy method of putting them in perfpective, at any degree of width or aperture at difcretion.

Now it is obfervable, that doors, windows, cabinets, chefts, and, in fine, every thing intended to open and fhut, always defcribe a femi-circle in opening. The reafon is, that the fide hung by hinges keeps its place, like the fixed leg of a pair of compaffes, while the other fide, like the other leg of the compaffes, fweeps its arch. Thus in the plan underneath the oppofite figure, the fixed fide A extending to B, if you open the door quite, the fide B muft defcribe the femi circle B C D, whofe center is A. Hence it follows, that if the door be three feet broad, as in the prefent cafe, the radius A C will likewife be three feet, and the whole chord or diameter of the femi-circle B A D fix feet. Of thefe fix feet in length, and three in breadth, a plan muft be made, confifting of eighteen fquares, wherein the femi-circle A B C D is to be defcribed, this method is directed to render the making of the fame femi-circles in perfpective the more eafy. Always obferving where the femi circle of the plan cuts the fquares, that thofe in the perfpective may be cut after the fame manner, and a femi-circle be drawn, taking up the fame fpace, traverfing as many fquares, and cutting them in the fame places. An inftance of which you have in the door E, where the interfections are marked the fame as in the plan underneath, 1, 2, 3, 4, 5, 6, 7.

When a door is to be reprefented open in perfpective, a femi-circle muft be ftruck on its plan, and the point of aperture placed on any part thereof at pleafure. Thus for the door E the point of aperture is fixed at 2. From this point 2 a perpendicular muft be raifed, as 2 H; and from the fame point 2, a line muft be drawn through the corner of the door F, and continued till it cut the horizon in the point G; from which another line muft be drawn through the other corner of the door I, and continued till it cut the perpendicular raifed from the point 2, in the point H. Thus will you have the door open F I H 2.

All apertures are performed by the fame rules as is farther feen in the doors K and L. The door K fhews its outfide, and that of L its infide; yet both are performed after the fame manner as the firft. The accidental point of K is drawn from the point M in the horizon, and that of the door L from the point of diftance O. If bolts, locks, or the like, be added on the doors, they muft all be drawn from the fame accidental point; as the bolts and lock of L tend towards O. What accidental points are, has been explained, page 12. Now all apertures have one fuch point in the horizon, excepting two forts. The firft, when the door is quite open; in which cafe its accidental point is the point of fight. The other, when its pofition is parallel to the horizon; by reafon the parallels, in that cafe, never interfect: as in the door N.

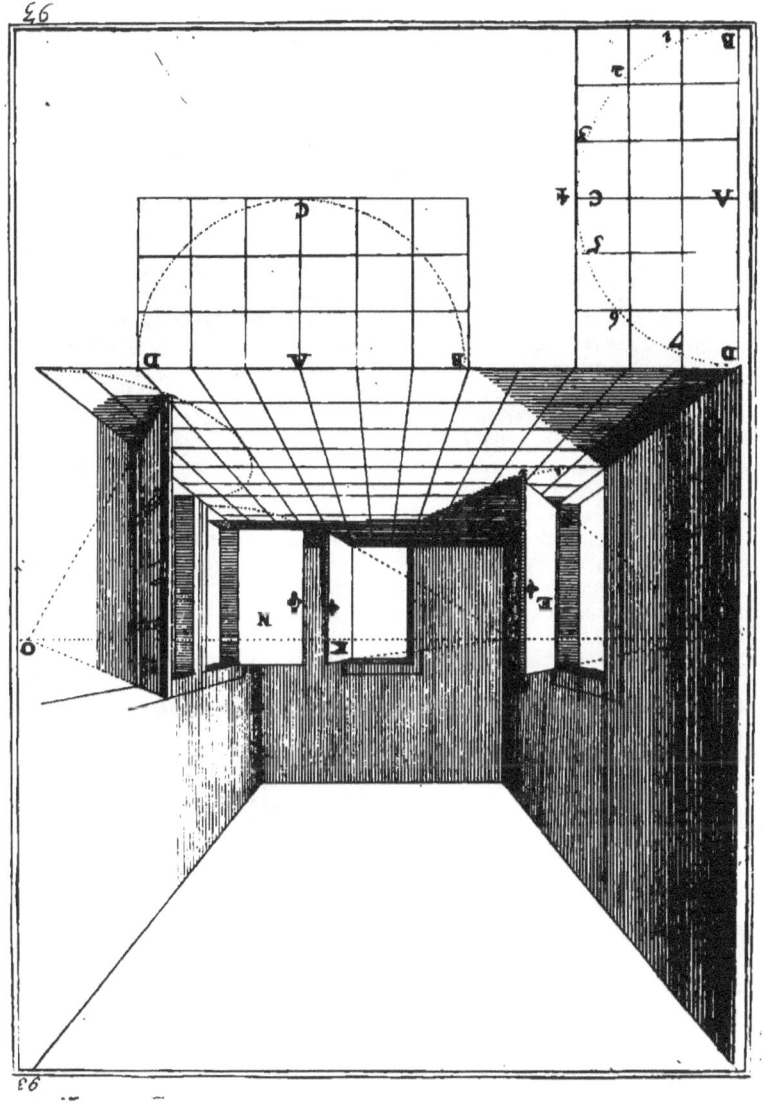

To exhibit APERTURES *of* Casements *in Perspective.*

ALL the difference between the *apertures of casements*, and those of *doors*, lies in this, that doors have their semi-circle of aperture on the plan, and casements in the air ; by reason windows are raised, and doors usually turn on the ground. On this account, the semi circles of casements may be either over or underneath them. And in such semi-circles is the point of aperture to be placed.

Thus, for instance, if a casement be two squares, or panes, broad, as A B, and it be made quite open, it will then take up two squares more C A, whereof A is the middle, and the center of the semi circle A B C. But by reason the window is raised above the ground, the semi-circle must also be raised; as is here actually done in the semi-circles of the windows D and E : whereof the same D and E are the centers ; and which are easily formed by erecting perpendiculars from the intermediate squares, till such time as they intersect the rays drawn from the corners of the casements D, E. From these intersections, lines must be drawn to the base line, and the measures of the squares of the plan 1, 2, 3, be set thereon. From the same points 1, 2, 3, lines are to be drawn to the point of sight F ; which cutting the parallels, will give squares to fix the aperture by. Proceed then to take the apertures after the same manner as those of doors. For example, the point G being given in the upper semi-circle, from the same G draw two lines ; the one, G H, perpendicular ; the other passing through the corner ·of the window E, and cutting the horizon in some point, for example, the point I. From this I, draw a line through the corner of the window K, till it cut the perpendicular in the point H, which gives the casement open K E G H. The same is to be observed with regard to all the rest ; and the point still to be taken in the horizon. Thus, L is the point for the casement M ; and N, that for the casement O. The casement P has none at all, as being parallel to the horizon.

The casements on the other side are performed after the same method, without any of the confusion of lines. Both the one and the other range with the wall, to facilitate the operation. The door at bottom is done after the manner already directed ; and the casements according to the method last delivered.

APERTURES *of* Casements *with* Embrasures.

THE rules for these are the same as for those that range even with the wall, excepting that these are not capable of being quite opened, by reason of the thickness of the chamfraining, or embrasure. On this account we never give them a whole semi-circle, but a portion answerable to the aperture they admit of. The accidental point should always be in the horizon, for upper windows, as here in Q and R ; that below is parallel to the horizon.

4

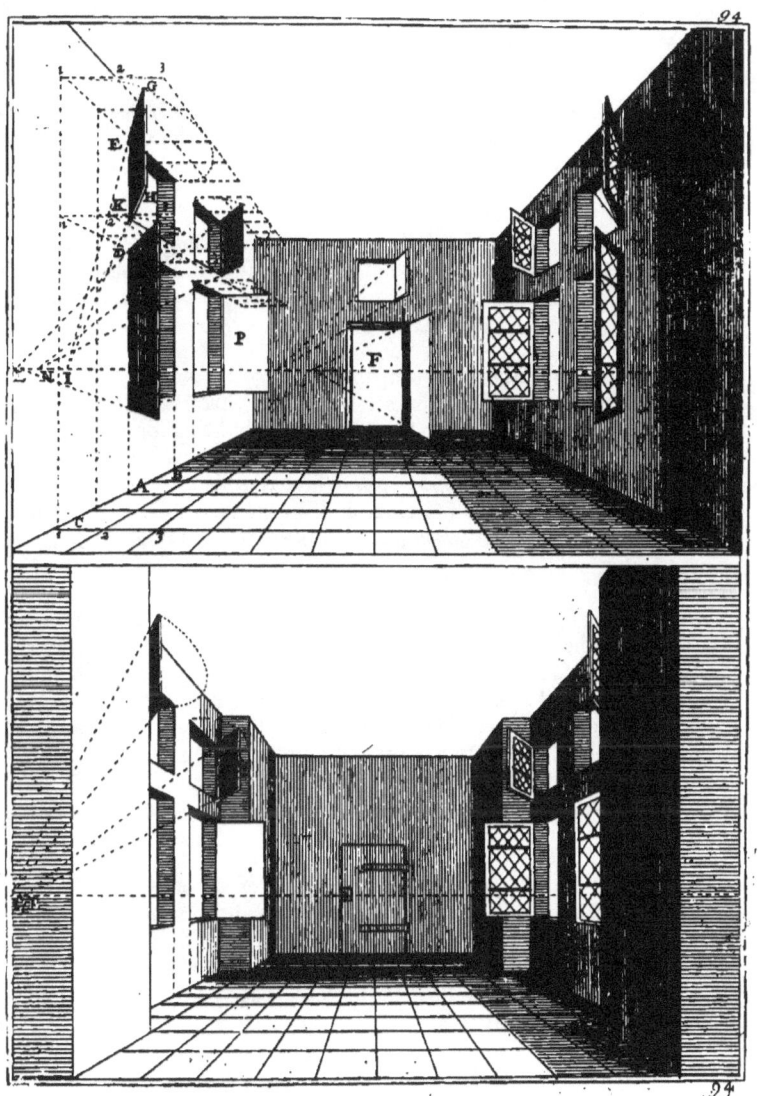

Divers other Apertures.

THE *openings of cupboards, preffes and chefts*, are at leaft as necef-fary as thofe of doors and windows; nor had the omiffion of the one been a whit more excufable than that of the other. Their doctrine will be difpatched in two figures.

The cupboards or preffes A A, are opened according to the rules de-livered for cafements, which it would be needlefs here to repeat. I fhall only add, that the uppermoft is parallel to the horizon; and that the latter tends to the point of diftance B.

The *ftop* on the other fide is opened by two leaves, one of them rif-ing upwards, and the other falling downwards. Each of them defcribes its femi-circle from the centers C and D; which being drawn with the compaffes, the apertures are fixed at any point at pleafure; as here in the point E; from which a ray is drawn to the point of fight F, till it interfect the femi-circles at the other ends in the points G. From thefe points E and G, lines being drawn to the centers C D, give the leaves opened in that pofition.

In the lower figure there are three *chefts*, differently opened. To open the firft, H, the quadrant M is put in perfpective, according to the meafures of the fquares of the plan. Thus, obferving the width of the cheft, which is two fquares, perpendiculars are to be raifed thence, and a femi-circle, or quadrant, defcribed for the opening, which is here fixed at the point N; and from this a parallel is to be drawn to the other qua-drant O; and from N and O lines to be drawn to the centers P P. If a greater aperture is required; a femi-circle is to be drawn in lieu of a quadrant.

The cheft I in that pofition has the eafieft of all openings, for hav-ing taken the breadth Q R, from the center R defcribe the femi-circle Q S; then take any aperture at pleafure, as T, and draw a line to the point of fight V, cutting the other femi-circle in X; and, laftly, from the points T and X, draw lines to the corners R, and you have the lid formed with that aperture.

If it is required to open the chefts farther, you have only to fix the point of aperture high in the femi-circle; as Y is in the cheft K. The reft of the procefs is the fame as in the firft cheft.

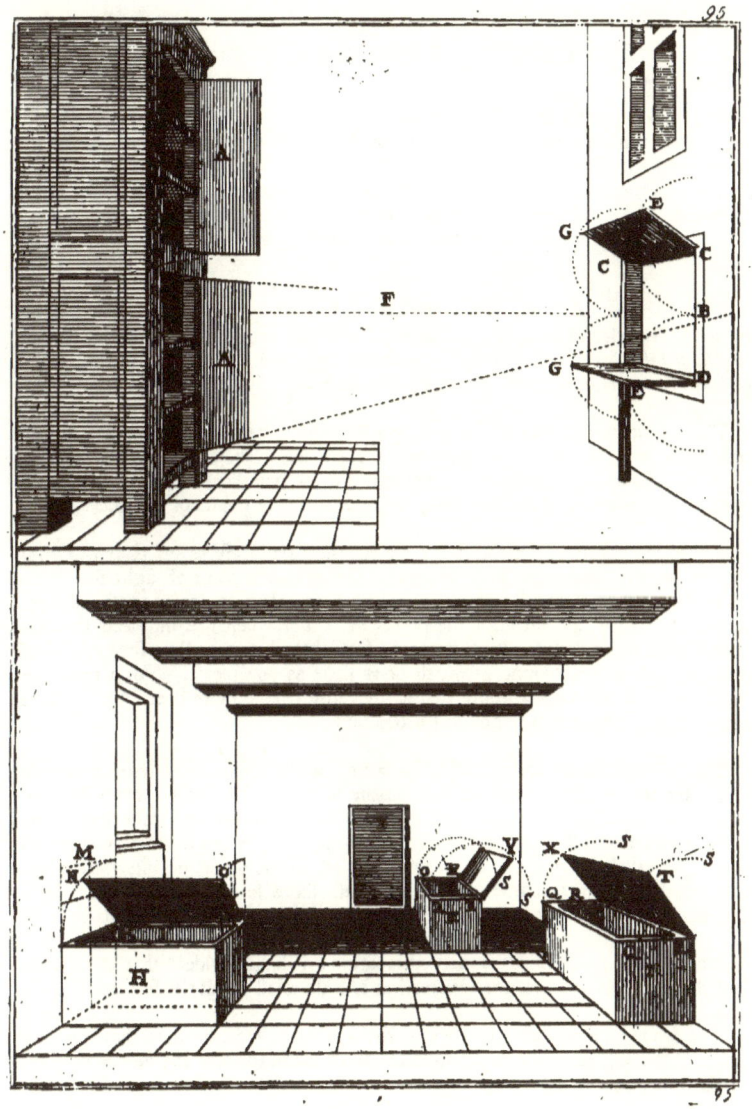

Plans *and first* Elevations *of Moveables.*

THESE plans I fhould have placed in their order among the reft, but for this confideration; that had I treated of them at the beginning of the work, without fhewing the neceffity thereof, they would have paffed for ufelefs, and accordingly have readily dropt out of remembrance. They now come in feafon, and cannot fail of being well received and learnt with pleafure; inafmuch as numerous forts of *moveables* or *houfhold goods* have a dependance upon them.

The firft plan, A, may ferve for *beds, tables, chairs, ftools,* &c. The other B, which is twice as long as it is broad, ferves for *long tables, cupboards, buffets, chefts, trunks,* &c. The third, C, which is long and narrow, ferves for *benches,* or *forms, couches,* and other pieces of furniture with fix legs or feet.

The acquaintance the reader is fuppofed to have with the other plans already treated of, will render the performance of thefe eafy; there being nothing more required than to lay down their dimenfions on the bafe line, draw lines thence to the point of view, and fhorten them by means of the points of diftances.

Thus, for example, for the firft plan A, the two meafures of E and D muft be fet on the bafe, and lines be drawn thence to the point of fight F. Then from one of the points of diftance, a line is to be drawn to one of thofe meafures, as from G to E; and through the points H and I, wherein it interfects the rays, parallels are to be drawn; by this means four little fquares will be formed, whofe meafure you may account as much or as little as you pleafe. For a table they muft be more than for a ftool, that is they muft have more breadth; the latter being ufually two inches, and the former four.

The plan B is performed after the fame manner; excepting that on account of its length, which is double its breadth, a line muft be drawn from B to one of the points of diftance, to find the half K. For if a line were drawn from L, it would interfect in M, and give a whole fquare; whereas we only want half of it. Parallels then muft be drawn from K to the points of interfection with the ray; and from the corner L, a line muft likewife be drawn to the point of diftance G, interfecting the ray: Thus will you have the four little fquares.

The third plan, C, needs no explanation; it being evident that it is formed like the firft A; and that the fquares muft be doubled to get the fix little fquares.

The figures underneath are intended to fhew that perpendiculars muft be raifed from all the angles of the aforefaid fquares, to begin to form the moveable pieces of furniture hereafter fhewn.

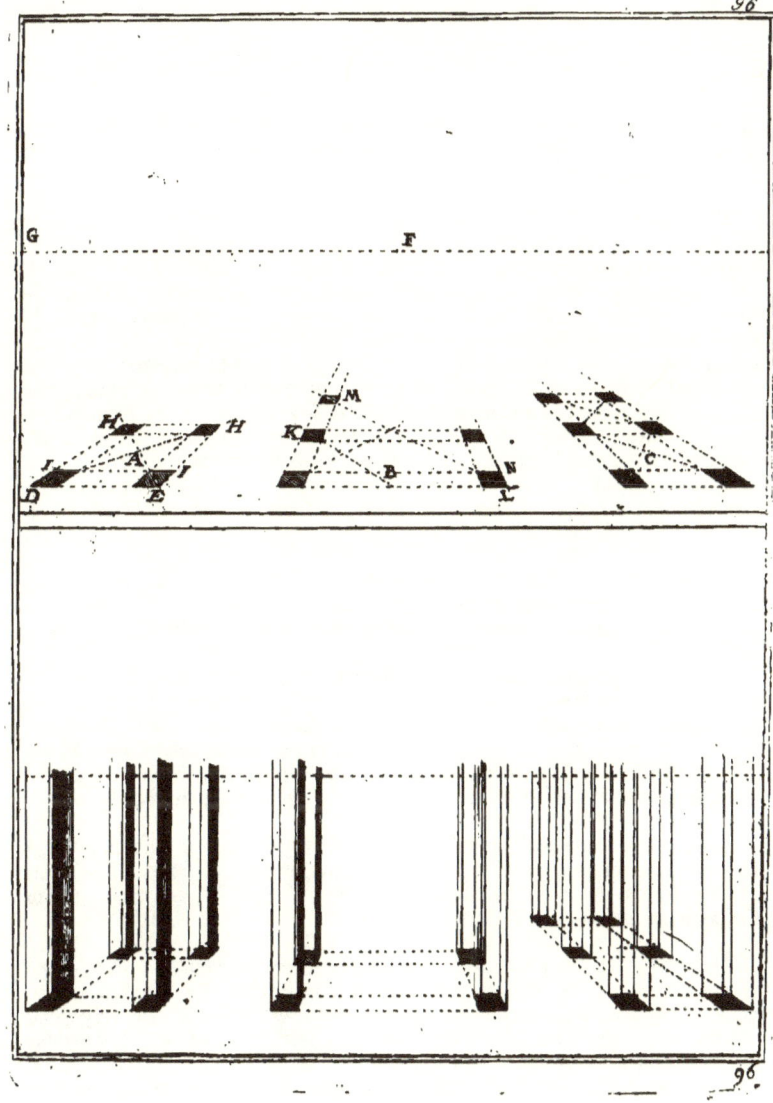

Elevations *of* Moveables.

HAVING raiſed perpendiculars from the plan, as already intimated; a line of elevation muſt be made in ſome part of the painting, on which the heights, crofs pieces, &c. are to be laid.

Thus the line C D being a line of elevation, and C E and D F breadths or depths of the crofs pieces; from thefe four points draw lines to ſome place in the horizon, as to the point G. . Then having erected perpendiculars from all the angles of the plan, as in A and B; from the angles draw parallels to the baſe line, till they cut the line C G. Thus will you have the points 1, 2, 3, 4; from which perpendiculars are to be raifed, and the interfections thofe perpendiculars make with the line D G, will be the points to cut the perpendiculars of the plans, as ſhewn in the figure; where a parallel being drawn from the point E, cuts the firſt perpendiculars of the plans A B in the points O; from which drawing lines to the point of ſight H, the other perpendiculars of the plans will be cut in the points P P, &c. And doing the like from the point F, &c. you will at length have a cube perforated on all its ſides. Which procefs being well underſtood, all the other pieces that follow, and even all that can be conceived, will be readily performed.

Inftead of parallels from the points on the line D G, to cut the perpendiculars of the plan, the meaſures of them taken with the compafſes and transferred to thofe perpendiculars will anfwer the ſame purpofe, as has been ſhewn elfewhere.

It is eafily obferved, that the two frames or ſtands of tables, I and K, are performed by the ſame rule as thofe above. All the difference is in the crofs-bar at bottom, which is higher in the line of elevation in this latter cafe, than in the former. In the latter, for inſtance, we find it in the line L, which gives M M. The feet of the ſtands or that part of the perpendiculars which are beneath the crofs bars, one may either leave them ſquare, or round them into bowls.

As to the laſt frames, N and Q, there is nothing in them more than in I and K; only that they are viewed by the angle, and the other in front. The plans of thofe ſtands, I and K, are drawn to the point of ſight R; and thefe latter to the points of diſtance S T.

The figures in this plate, with little variation, may be adapted to divers forts of moveables. Thus, for inſtance, to make a bedſtead of *Fig.* I or K, nothing more is required than to give it a proper height and breadth. In every thing elſe the operation is the ſame as for a couch, a ſtool, or the like. For a table you have only a top to add. For a joint-ſtool, befide the top, it muſt be made more in height than width, but the conſtruction thereof with four legs, and the four crofs bars, is the ſame as in this figure.

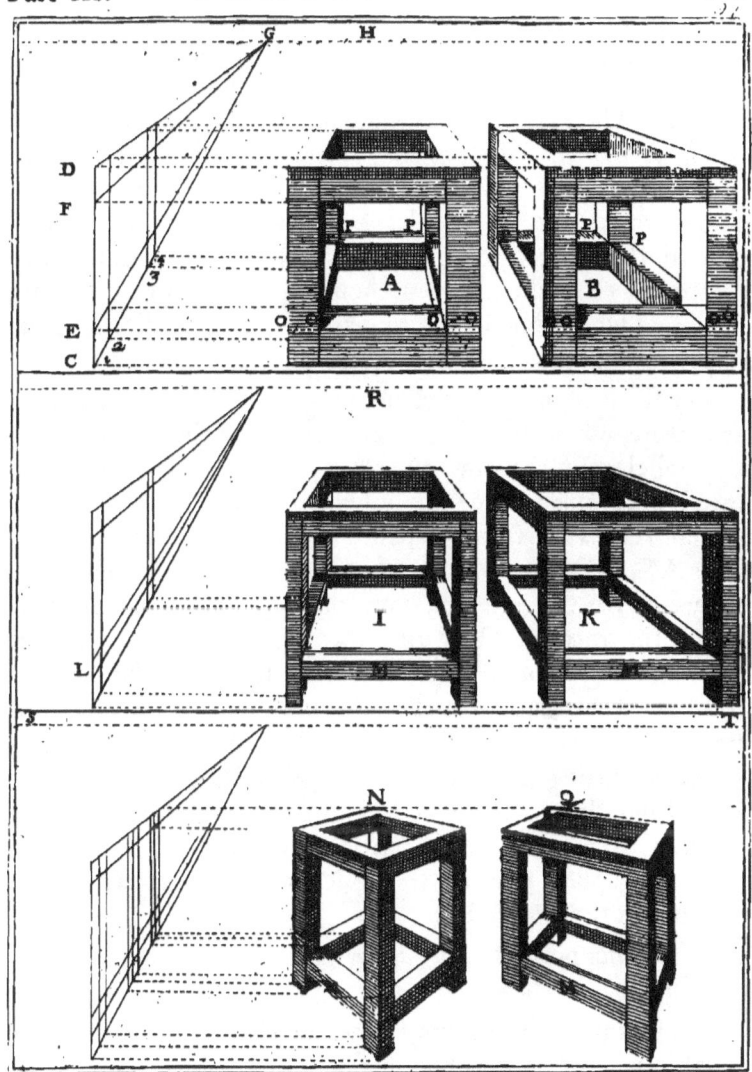

To exhibit the upper Part of Tables, Stools, *&c.*

HAVING raifed perpendiculars from the plan, as directed in the foregoing page, and fixed the proper
height thereon, the frame will be complete. Now to make
a cover to it perfectly on a level, and which fhall not extend
beyond the frame, there needs nothing more than to leave
the top of the cube plain, without expreffing any other lines
but thofe which bound the four fides, which will make the
upper part of a table, ftool, or the like.

But if it is defired the upper part or cover fhall have a
projecture, or ledge; from one of the angles of the frame
a parallel muft be drawn, as A B; and on this parallel the
meafure or quantity of the intended projecture muft be fet,
as here A B. Then from the points of diftance C and D, occult
lines A E, A E, *&c.* muft be drawn through the angles of the
fquare of the frame here expreffed by dotted lines. And to
make the meafure A B give the proper breadth to all the
fides and angles of the table; draw a line from the point of
fight F, through the point B, continuing it till it cut the
line C A E in the point G. From the point G draw another
parallel, cutting the other occult line in H. Then drawing
lines from the points G and H to the point of fight F, the
other diagonals will be interfected in I and K; which will
give the upper part of the table, with the projecture that
was fet on the line A B.

The thicknefs of this upper part of the table is fixed at
pleafure.

This fame method may ferve for the upper parts of any
objects, whether in front or in fide-views below the horizon,
and for the bottom of thofe that are above the horizon, as
particularly fhewn in pages 49 and 50.

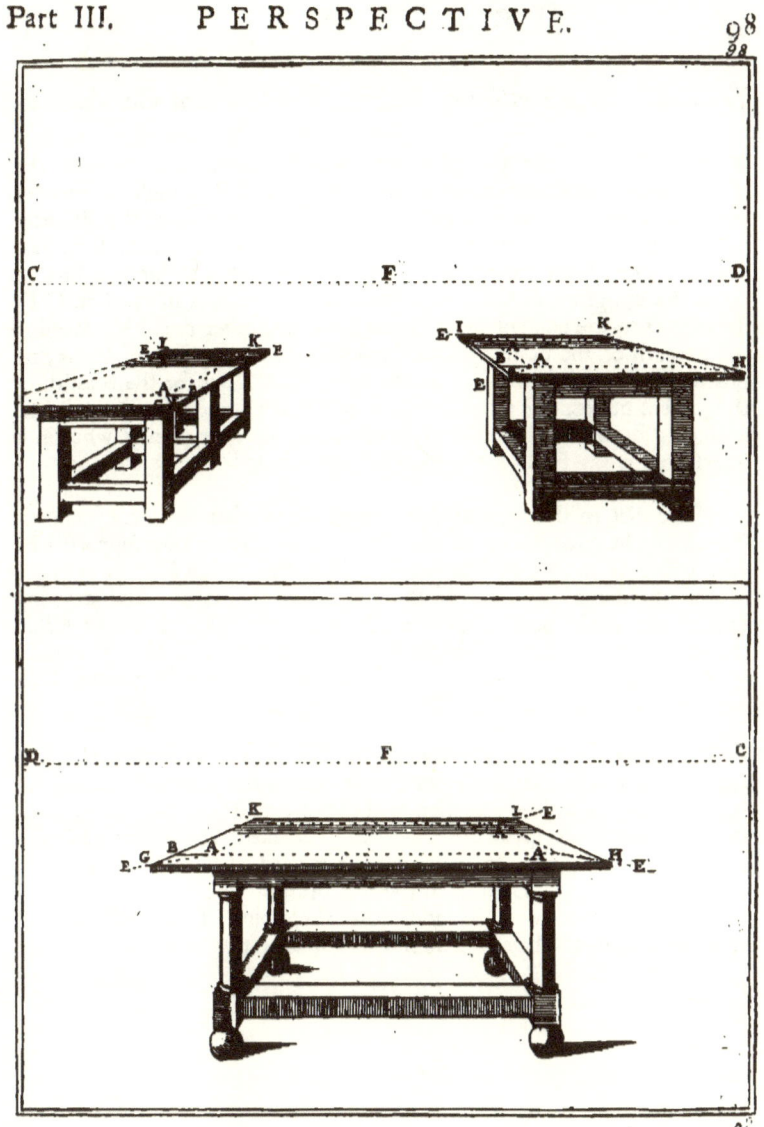

To exhibit the Elevation of Buffets, Preſſes, *and* Cup-boards.

HAVING made the plan, and raiſed perpendiculars from all the angles, as already taught ; upon the line A B, which is here to ſerve for a line of elevation, the meaſures or proportions of the diſtances of the ſhelves, with their thickneſſes, &c. as here C D E, muſt be laid down. Then from the points C D E, draw parallels to the baſe line, as far as the upright poſt G F ; and from the points thus marked on G F, draw lines to the point of ſight H ; as far as the other poſt I K, forming the breadth of the buffet. This breadth is fixed at pleaſure, by laying down the intended meaſure on the baſe line. Thus for the breadth of the preſent buffet, the diſtance F L is laid down ; and from the point L, a line is drawn to the point of diſtance M ; and the point I wherein it interſects the ray F H, is the place of the laſt poſt.

The buffet on the oppoſite ſide is performed after the ſame manner. To adjuſt the proportions of the little cabinet, or locker, ſupported by two columns in the middle thereof, take the points L P, which are in the middle of Q N, or of the breadth of the buffet ; and drawing lines thence to the point of diſtance O, where the ray N H is interſected thereby, draw parallels to the baſe line, cutting the ray T H in the points V V. And perpendiculars raiſed from thoſe points will give the little cabinet in the middle.

The *large preſſes*, or *cup-boards*, in *Fig.* II. are performed after the ſame manner as the buffets above ; only that in the middle being viewed in front, needs a little explanation to determine its depth. I obſerve, then, that its plan muſt be formed, as already directed, and as one half of it is here ſhewn. Then, to make croſs pieces equal to theſe in the front, occult lines muſt be drawn from the firſt upright poſt R, to the firſt per-pendicular of the depth S ; and from the points of interſection draw little parallels to the baſe. The reſt of the operation is plain.

6

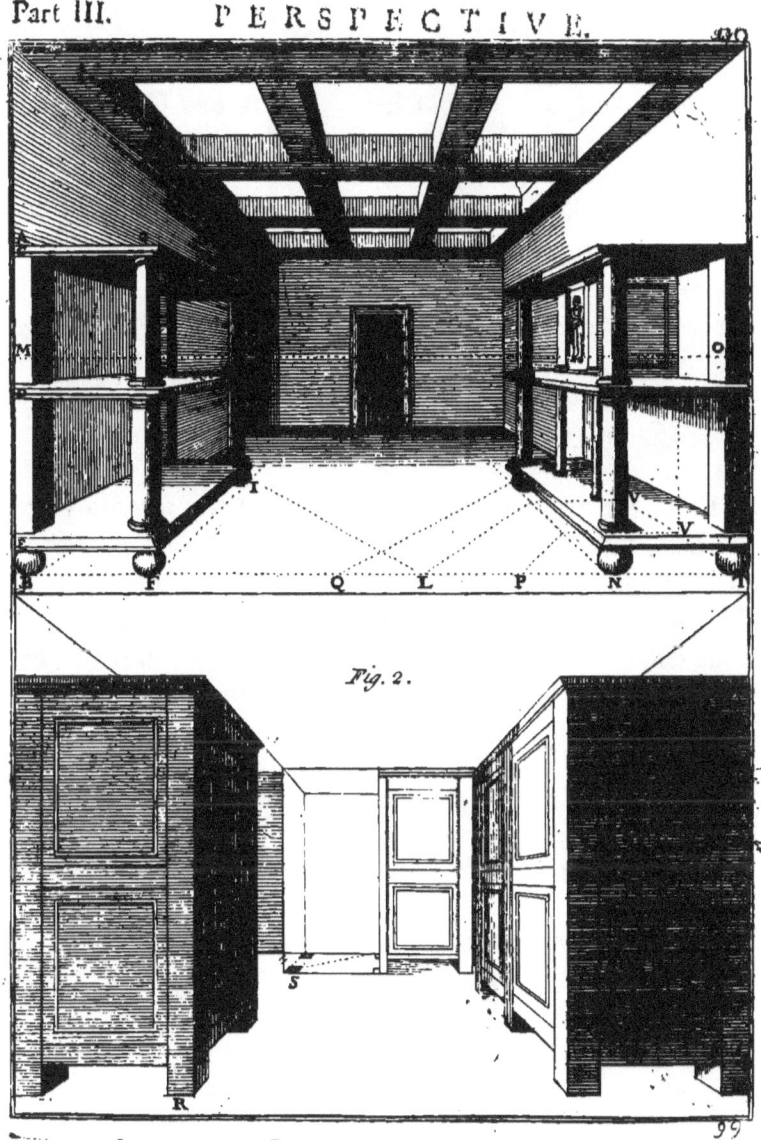

Fig. 2.

The ELEVATIONS *of* Chairs, Forms, *and* Couches.

TO *raise a chair*; from the dimensions A B C, erect
perpendiculars, and proceed in the same method already directed for table-feet, or frames without tops. All
that is to be done farther, is to procure the back of the chair;
which may be made of any height at pleasure. In the present case the height of the back is equal to that from the
foot A to the seat K. 'Which proportion may serve equally
for elbow chairs.

From the figure it appears evident enough, that to form
the back there is nothing needed but to prolong the perpendiculars of the legs, as here A E ; and from the point E to
draw a line to the point of sight G ; which cutting the perpendicular or post raised from the plan, or the foot H,
gives the point F. The rest the figure makes clear.

If elbows are required, you have only to raise the perpendiculars of the front legs higher, as the hind ones are for the
back, and to draw a cross piece, or bar, in the shape you
would have the elbow.

In the figure underneath, you see a form, or bench, covered with cloth, and two couches. The head of one is
turned back in the front of the picture, and the other is
viewed obliquely. It would be loss of time to dwell upon
the manner of making them ; the rules being altogether the
same as those already laid down for other moveables, mamely,
by making a plan, raising perpendiculars, &c.

Another Method of putting Moveables *in Perfpective.*

THERE are fome *moveables* that *fold*, or fhut down, and that ferve for tables, feats, beds, &c. very eafy to be put in perfpective.

As to the elevation, it is performed as that of a cube, as fhewn in ABCD, which is viewed in front; or E F G H. Then two diagonals, A C and B D, are to be made for that in the middle of the front; or E H, and F G for that of the fide: and thefe will ferve for the drawing of the two croffes; taking care that one enter half through the other, as G K does through H I; and both of them to be faftened by the middle to make them fold.

In the figure underneath we add a table upon treffels, that even the leaft confiderable moveable might not be wanting. To put them in perfpective, from the points A, and B, which are the interval between the feet of the treffels, draw a line to the point of fight C; then, laying down the thicknefs of the fame feet on the bafe line, as here D and E, draw lines from the fame to the point of diftance F, and obferve where they interfect the ray B C; and from the points of interfection draw little parallels to the bafe line; by which you will have the little fquares or plans of the feet, as in A and B: then between the diftance D and E, lay down the breadth intended for the top of the treffel, and drawing a line thence to the point of diftance F, it will cut the ray B C in the points G and H; from which points, perpendiculars are to be raifed to any height at pleafure, as here to I. Laftly, from the angles of the little fquares of the plan draw lines to I. The fecond treffel is performed after the fame manner as the firft.

The *form* K, and the *table*, or *feat* L, need not any explanation, to put them in practice, as having nothing but what is common with the pieces above-mentioned.

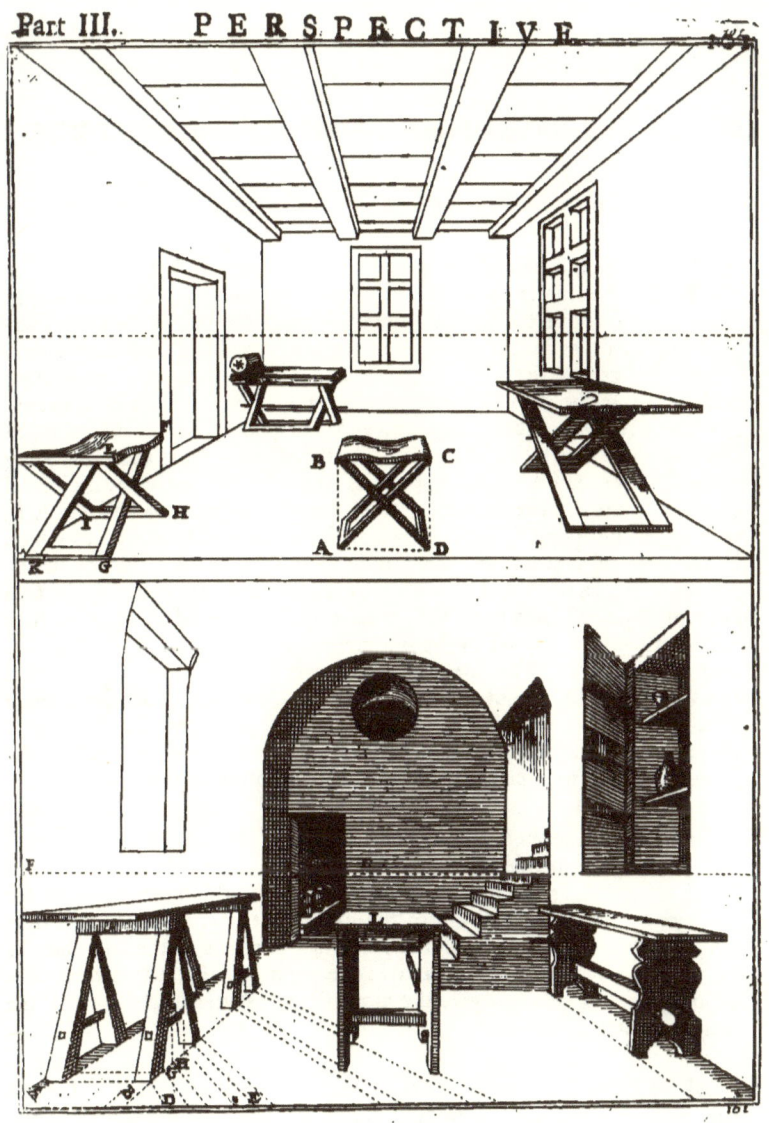

To exhibit MOVEABLES *placed without any Order.*

WHEN moveables are placed orderly along the fide of a wall, or in the direction of the rays and the bafe line, it is eafy to put them in perfpective by the rules already delivered ; but if they be irregularly placed, as in this figure, you are to proceed as I fhall now direct. Draw the geometrical plans, R, S, and T, for plans of three chairs ; which are to be diminifhed or put in perfpective by the rule delivered for the irregular figure, page 40, and the plans will be found fituated like the chairs, or rather the chairs like the plans. Now the plans being in perfpective, lay a ruler along one of the fides, to fee what accidental point it gives in the horizon ; thus, laying a ruler along the fide A B, you have the point C in the horizon for an accidental point, to which all the lines of that and the oppofite fide muft be drawn. In this manner you fee that A and D are drawn to the fame point C. It is true each plan placed irregularly fhould have two accidental points, but they are frequently fo far off in the horizon, that it is doubtful whether you find them both. The prefent plans have each of them one ; as A B has C ; and A D, the other fide, would have another, if our paper were broad enough. E F gives G for its accidental point, and I H gives K. As to the little fquares 1, 2, 3, 4, they are the plans of the feet of the fame chairs, as may be made broader and narrower at pleafure.

Proceed then to erect perpendiculars from all the angles of the plan, and on the fide of the picture add a line of elevation M N, whereon to lay the dimenfions of the crofs pieces ; as O, for the lower bars ; P for the bars of the feat ; and Q for the backs of the chairs. Things thus difpofed, from the angles of the plan draw parallels to the bafe line, as far as the line of elevation, and in the points of interfection erect perpendiculars. Thefe will give the dimenfions, as already obferved of the former figures.

All the lines of the fides are to be drawn to the accidental point of the plan. Thus, in the middle chair, all the fides are drawn to the point G, which is the point of the plan, as appears from the figure.

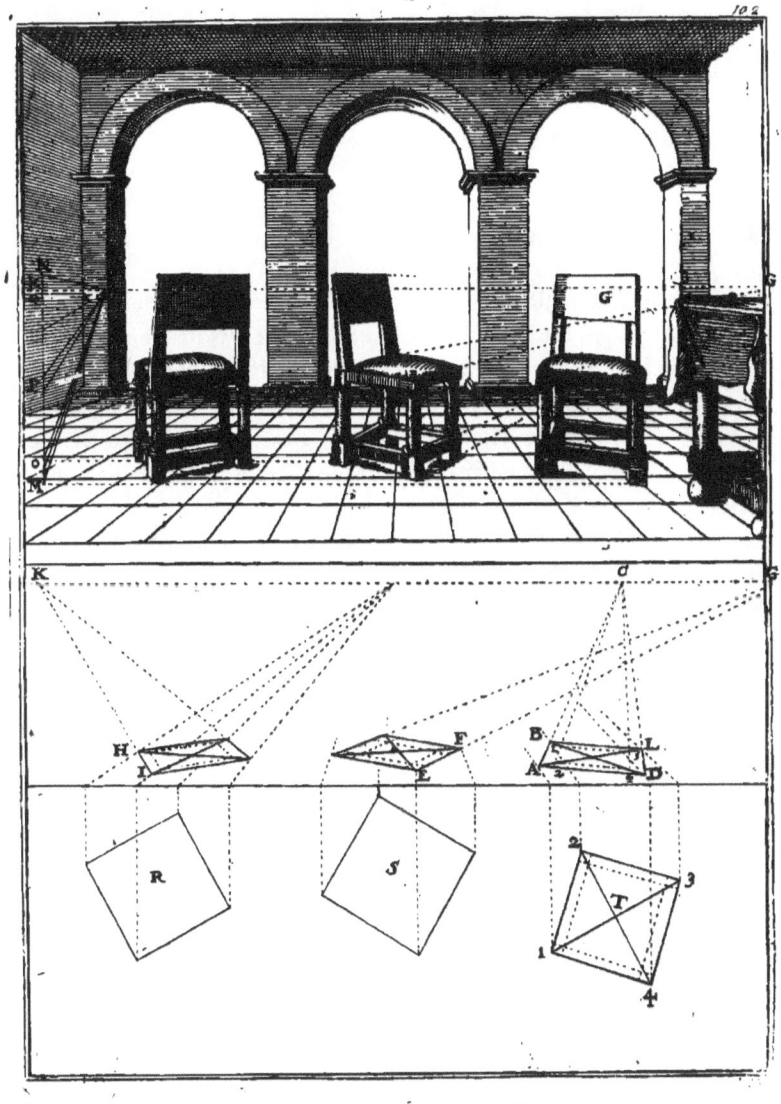

To exhibit M O V E A B L E S *laid or tumbled on the Ground.*

FROM the fame plan, which has been given for chairs ftanding on their feet, it is eafy to form thefe which are laid on the ground.

At the feveral angles of the plan erect perpendiculars, and give the fide on the ground the fame dimenfions as when it was ftanding above it. For example, having erected perpendiculars from the angles, you will have the breadth M in the chair laid on its fide, which is drawn to the point K. This meafure M, being doubled, gives O for the bar at the bottom of the chair; and the perpendiculars raifed from the plan, give the bar of the feat P: from which points, lines drawn to K, will cut the other perpendiculars of the front in the places required to fhew the fame bars on all the fides they are vifible on. As to the height of the back of the chair, make it the fame with the height of the feat ; but for the back of that in the middle, you are to draw a double diagonal, and obferve where it cuts the rays, or fides, R S. The reft is obvious.

The two other figures underneath, with their feet aloft, are eafily performed. One of them is drawn to the point of fight T, the other to the point of diftance Y, X. The line of elevation is Y Z.

The method of raifing them, is the fame as for elevating thofe upon their feet: that is, perpendiculars muft be raifed from the angles of the plan ; and from the fame angles, lines be drawn to the line of elevation ; by which you will obtain the dimenfions of each of the upright parts, and the places of the crofs parts both of top and bottom.

To exhibit A-L T A R S *in perfpective.*

THE method for raifing altars is the fame as that for frames of long tables, all that is farther to be done, relates to the circle in the middle, the edges of the cloth and the laces ; of each whereof in its place.

In raifing the *altar* here viewed in front, there is but little difficulty; for having adjufted its height and length, there remains nothing but to draw lines from all the points on the bafe line to the point of fight E ; and from the interfections thofe lines make with the bottom of the altar, erect perpendiculars, which being joined by a parallel at the proper height, give the front, and rays drawn to the point of fight E form the fides. As to the circle in the middle it is ftruck with compaffes. The reft is obvious.

For a *fide-altar* fet the intended breadth and height in the place where you would have it begin; as the breadth A B, and the height B D in the figure. Then, from B, D, and C, draw lines to the point of fight E : and fince B F on the bafe line is the length of the front altar, and we would make this equal thereto, from the point F, draw a line to the point of diftance G, and obferve where is interfects the ray B E ; and from the point of interfection raife a little perpendicular to touch the ray D in the point H. Then drawing a little parallel from H, it will give the point I in the ray C ; and by fuch means you will have the top of the altar, C D H I. For the two orna-ments that are on each fide the circle, they are found on the ray B E, by drawing lines thence to the point of diftance G. M gives the breadth of the border of the altar cloth. Now taking the meafure B M, fet it off from D to O, for the breadth of the cloth at the top. As to the circle, I need not repeat what has been already faid of the method of putting it in perfpective. I fhall only here obferve, that lines muft be drawn from all the divifions thereof on the bafe line to the point of diftance G ; and in the interfections with the ray B, perpendiculars to be raifed. Then, the fame dimenfions to be taken and fet off between O and B ; as P P P, and from thofe three points rays to be drawn to the point of fight E , obferving where they cut the perpendiculars raifed from the other divifions of the circle, and connecting thofe points with a circular line, which gives the circle in perfpective. The method of diminifhing would be the fame, if in lieu of laces and a circle there were an embroidery.

In the figure undemeath, the fame altar is fhewn free of lines and points, and farther adorned with a crucifix and two candlefticks. In order to this, the corner line of the altar muft be pro-longed, as Q R. Then, from the point of diftance G, a line to be drawn through the corner of the altar T, and continued till it cut Q R ; and the line Q R will be the length of the altar, equal to B F in the firft figure. Hereon muft the dimenfions of the crofs and candlefticks be laid ; for example, V for the crofs and S S, &c. for the candlefticks. From all the points S and V, lines to be then drawn to the point of diftance G, and through their interfections with the ray Q E, little parallels to be drawn; which cutting the ray S E, give fquares upon the altar, X X, &c. for the crucifix, and candlefticks. This fquare muft be left for the foot of the crucifix; and from the middle of the fquare, the crucifix is to be raifed. For the proportions of the arms of the crucifix, erect occult perpendiculars from the angles of the fquare, as here Y Y ; and draw lines to the point of fight E, for the candlefticks. Then turn the fquares, for their feet, into circles, and obferve where they interfect the diagonal : For perpendiculars erected from the points of interfection, give the breadth of the bafons or ftands ; and lines drawn to the point of fight, the height. Laftly, from the middle of the foot erect a perpendicular for the body of the candleftick, and the taper therein, which is to be made high or low at pleafure. To proportion them, draw a line from the top of the firft to the point of fight E. The reft as already faid. The figure will call to mind the methods.

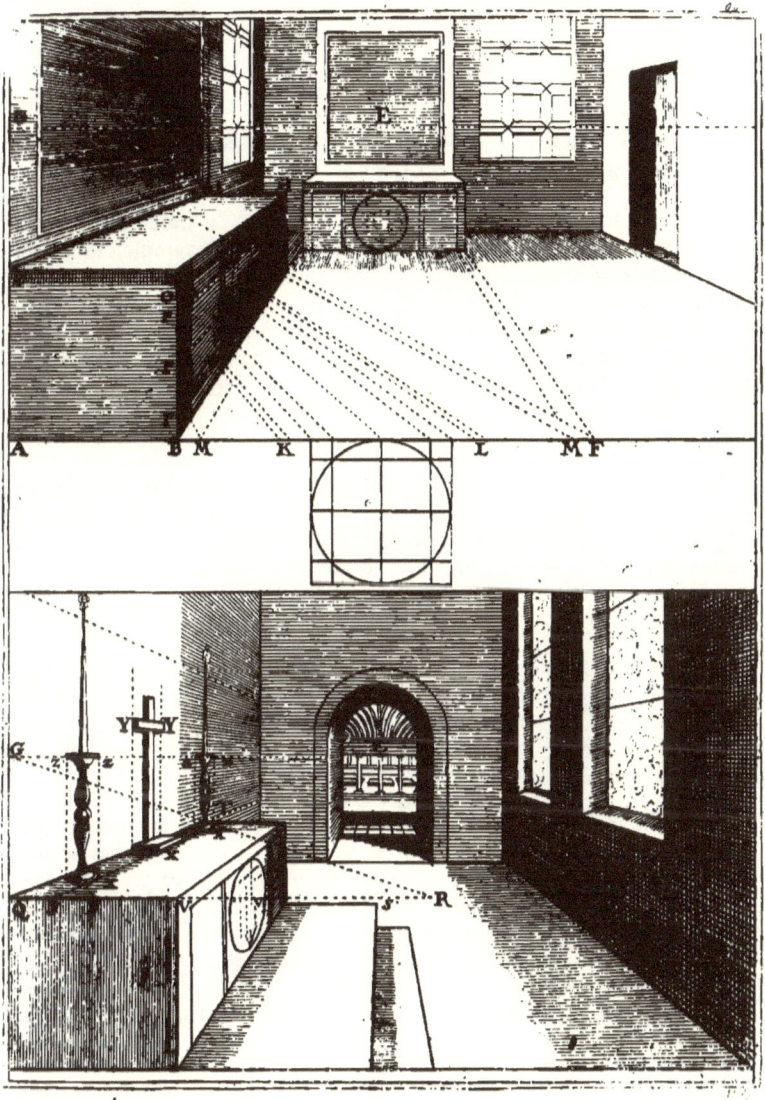

To exhibit the Fixtures of Shops *in* Perfpective.

TRADESMEN's fhops are ufually encompaffed with fhelves, boxes or drawers, wherein their goods are difpofed.

The rule for defigning boxes, preffes or fhelves, is much the fame as that already laid down for doors and windows ; for example, in lieu of the thicknefs of the wall ufed in making a window, you are here to put the board A B, and from the point B, to draw a line to the point of fight C. Then, for the width of the fhelves or preffes, having laid down the diftances on the bafe line in E F G, from thefe points draw lines to the points of diftance D. Thefe make interfections H I K, with the ray B : from which interfections, perpendiculars being raifed, will give you the upright divifions.

For the crofs boards, fet any number thereof at pleafure on A B, or only on the firft perpendicular B O ; fuch are here L M N O : from all which draw rays to the point of fight C, and at their interfections with the perpendiculars in the points P P, draw little parallels to the bafe line, which will fhew the top and bottom of each fhelf, and feparate them from the fides.

As to the *front* divifions and fhelves, there only needs to draw rays from the points of meafures E F, and in the points of their interfections with the lines Q S, to erect perpendiculars R and S. The crofs pieces are had, by drawing parallels from all the divifions on the perpendicular K ; as here, P 1, P 2, P 3, P 4.

As to the divifions on the oppofite fide, where there are fquare upright pofts to fuftain the fhelves, their depth is had by drawing lines or rays from the meafures T, G, to the point of fight C. And to get their plan, or fquare, lines are to be drawn from the meafures A E F on the bafe line to the point of diftance V, which give the interfection X Y Q on the ray T C. Through thefe interfections little parallels muft be drawn till they cut the ray C G in Z ; and from the angles of thefe little fquares, perpendiculars are to be erected, which give the upright pofts, as in the figure.

The figure underneath fhews a fhop quite fitted up, and ready to receive goods of any fort : for a bookfeller, it muft be ftocked with books ; for an apothecary, with drawers and gallipots ; for a draper, with pieces of cloth, ftuff, &c. 2

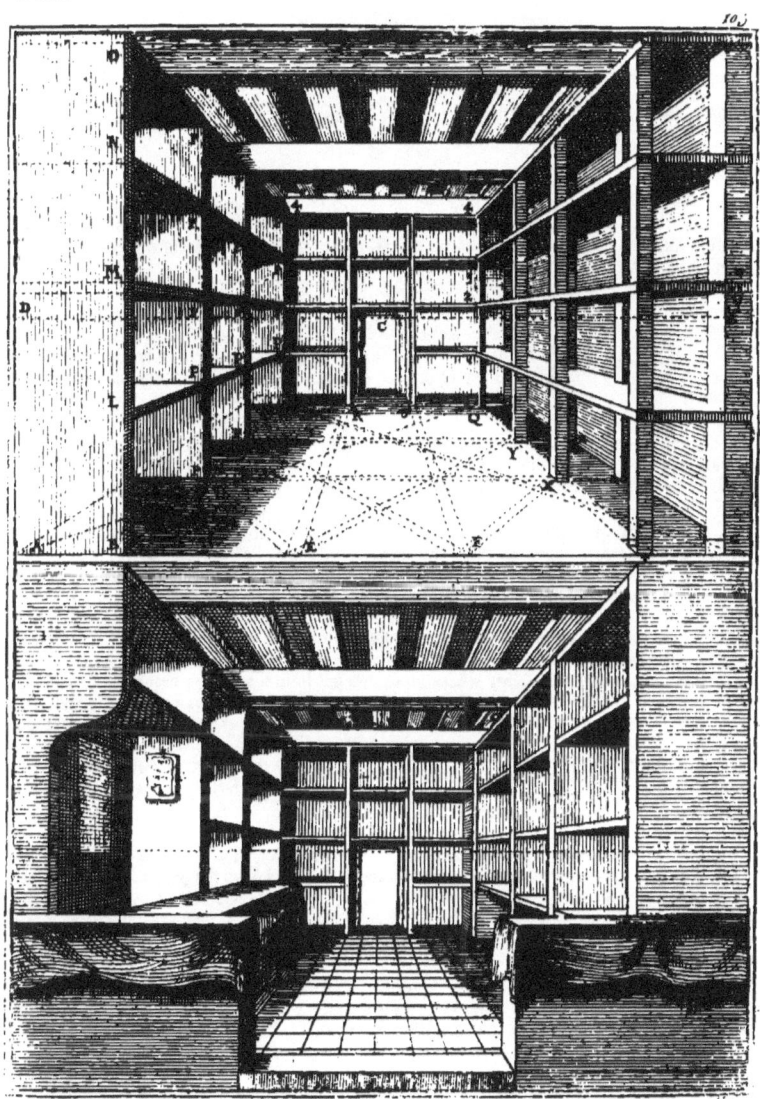

BUILDINGS *viewed en the* Outside.

HAVING now confidered every thing relating to the interior parts of buildings, I proceed to g ve rules for the exterior.

Many of the methods already laid down for the infides may likewife ferve for the outfides ; the procefs for the doors and windows is the fame in both ca'es, and as thefe are very material, and diftinguifhing parts of every ftructure, the reader is already in great meafure qualified for the elevation of buildings. If they be adorned with orders of columns or pilafters, inftructions have alfo been given for thefe.

Suppofe there be windows in front, as A, and it is defired to have others in the fame proportions on the other fide, the proportions A A A muft be transferred to the bafe line, as here B B B, and lines be drawn thence to the point of diftance C : and in the points F F F, where they interfect the ray D E, perpendiculars to be raifed for the *uprights* in the window.

For the *crofs pieces* ; thofe in the front window muft be continued to the perpendicular D, by which means you will have the points I I ; from which lines are to be drawn to the point of fight E, which cutting the perpendiculars F, give the crofs bars in the fide-window.

If the number of windows were much greater, nothing farther would be required but to continue their rays, in order to make the meafure and height of the crofs pieces the fame in all. An inftance of which we have in the houfe on the other fide, which has two windows from the fame rays. As to the breadth or thicknefs of the pofts or crofs bars of windows in front, it muft be fet on one of the travers, as here on K H ; and from the corner of the window K, a l ne be drawn to the point of fight E ; and from the point H, another to the point of diftance C, for the window A, and to the point of diftance L, for the window on the other fide ; and in the point, where thofe two laft lines interfect, a perpendicular, H M, muft be raifed. Then, from all the corners of the window lines to be drawn to the point of fight, and from the points Q Q, &c. where they interfect the perpendicular H M, parallels muft be drawn to give the thicknefs of the crofs bars. The thicknefs of the middle poft, N, will be had by drawing a line from the corner, N, to the point of fight ; and in the points Q Q, where it cuts the thickneffes of the crofs bars, erecting perpendiculars Q R, Q R.

To fix the thicknefs of the windows on the other fide, it muft be fet in the corner of the wall, on the perpendicular D, as the diftance I O ; and from the points O O, &c. lines muft be drawn to the point of fight E. Laftly, little parallels to be drawn from all the corners of the windows, as S T ; which, interfecting the ray O, give the thicknefs in the point S. Thefe rules may ferve for all kinds of windows, both high and low.

In the figure underneath is fhewn a door diminifhed according to the rules delivered heretofore. As, in effect, every thing belonging thereto is very eafily underftood, and readily practifed, on fome or other of the preceding methods.

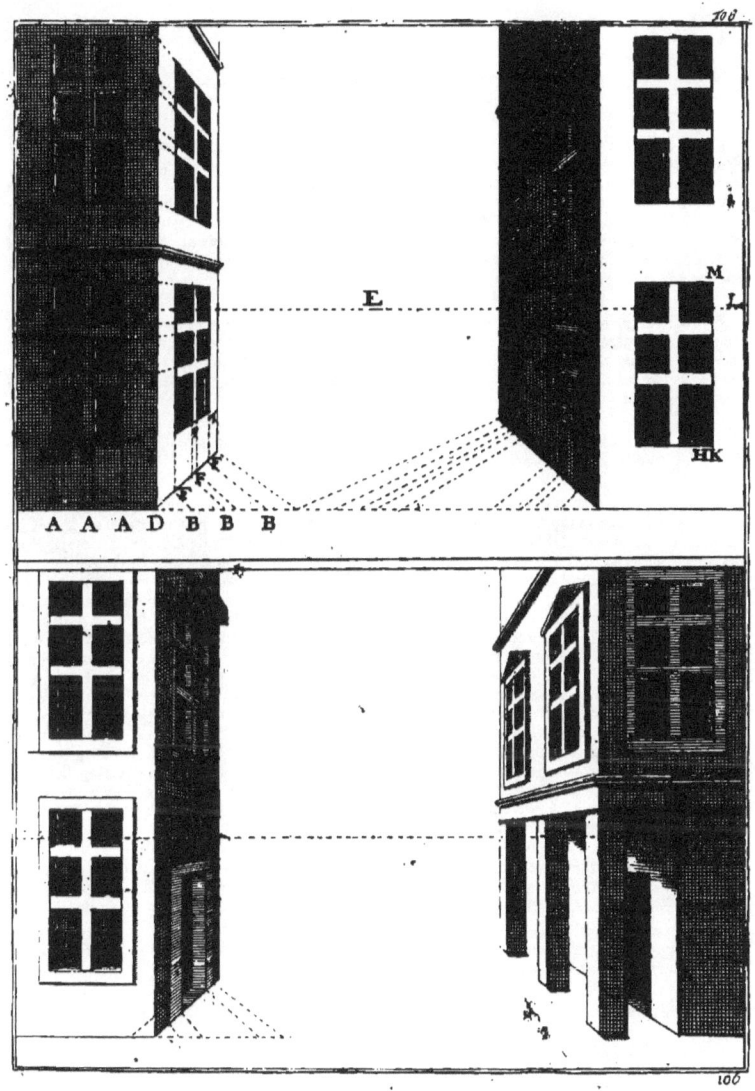

To exhibit Roofs of Houses in Perspective.

ROOFS are made of different heights according to the materials they are covered with. Those of *slate* are the moſt upright of all. Their uſual meaſure is an equilateral triangle; that is, their ſlope, or the declivity of the roof, is equal to the width of the houſe. Thus, in the little figure at the bottom of the preſent plate, C A, or C B, is equal to A B. Others make the breadth A B equal to the punchion, or middle top, D C, which is higher. But that practice is much leſs uſual than the former. For *flat tiles*, we only make the roof two thirds of the height of thoſe of ſlate, or the width of the houſe, as in A E B. For *thatch*, the height is uſually but half the width; and for *pan-tiles*, only one third; as A 9 B.

Before we go any farther it is to be obſerved, that what we call *punchion*, or middle top, is a timber raiſed perpendicularly on the beams that ſuſtain the ridge, and wherein the rafters are all jointed. *Rafters* are the pieces of wood which form the declivity of the roof, as H I. The other pieces in the corners, which go to the middle top, are called *ſtays*, and are uſually longer than rafters, as H K.

There are three kinds of roofs in uſe; pavilions, pinnacles, and pent-houſe-form. The firſt have four ſides, the ſecond only two, and the laſt but one.

To put a pavilion or turret, in perſpective, the place of the middle top muſt be known, that the ſtays may be drawn to the ſame. For this reaſon it was that I made the geometrical plan L M N O; to ſhew, that a ſquare, L M N P, is to be made of the breadth of the houſe L N, and two diagonals drawn through the ſame, interſecting in Q. Some put the punchion in Q, but that advances it too far, and renders the end of the declivity too ſquat. It has a much better grace when more upright. With this view, it ſhould be approached towards the wall L N a third part of the diſtance Q R, which will bring it to the point S; from which point a perpendicular, S, muſt be drawn upon the line N P. Then the meaſures L T and T M are to be ſet on the baſe line, and lines drawn from them to the point of diſtance, which is here more remote than uſual; and from the points, wherein they interſect the ray V, perpendiculars to be erected to the top of the wall, which will give the points X X; from which, parallels to the baſe line are to be drawn as far as the other ray I. Then, from the middle of the wall Y, a line to be drawn to the point of ſight, cutting the parallels in the point Z, Z, &c. from which points the punchions are to be raiſed. To give them the proper height regard muſt be had to the materials intended for the covering, and the height to be adjuſted thereby, according to the proportions already fixed. Thus, ſuppoſe the covering ſlate, an equilateral triangle, 1, 2, 3, muſt be made of the breadth of the wall; and from 3, a line be drawn to the point of ſight, cutting the punchion in the point 4. To which point, lines being drawn from the corners of the houſe, will give the form of the pavilion.

For *pinnacle roofs* there need not ſo much ado. You are only to make an equilateral triangle, 5, 6, 7, of the breadth of the wall 5, 6, and the like for the other end of the wall, which will give you the point 8, Then joining 7 and 8, you will have the form and meaſure of the roof.

The figures on the other ſide ſhew the ſame thing unembarraſſed with lines. The projecture ſtanding beyond the roof is made at diſcretion.

The front houſe is covered with a pavilion, performed after the ſame manner as that on the ſide.

In the preſent figure, where the letters are, the horizon is placed very high, to ſhew the tops of the houſes, and render the practice more eaſy and conceivable. But, as it is not often ſuch a caſe happens, I have added the other figure at the top, wherein the horizon is as low as uſual. Though the rule in itſelf is the ſame as that already delivered.

2

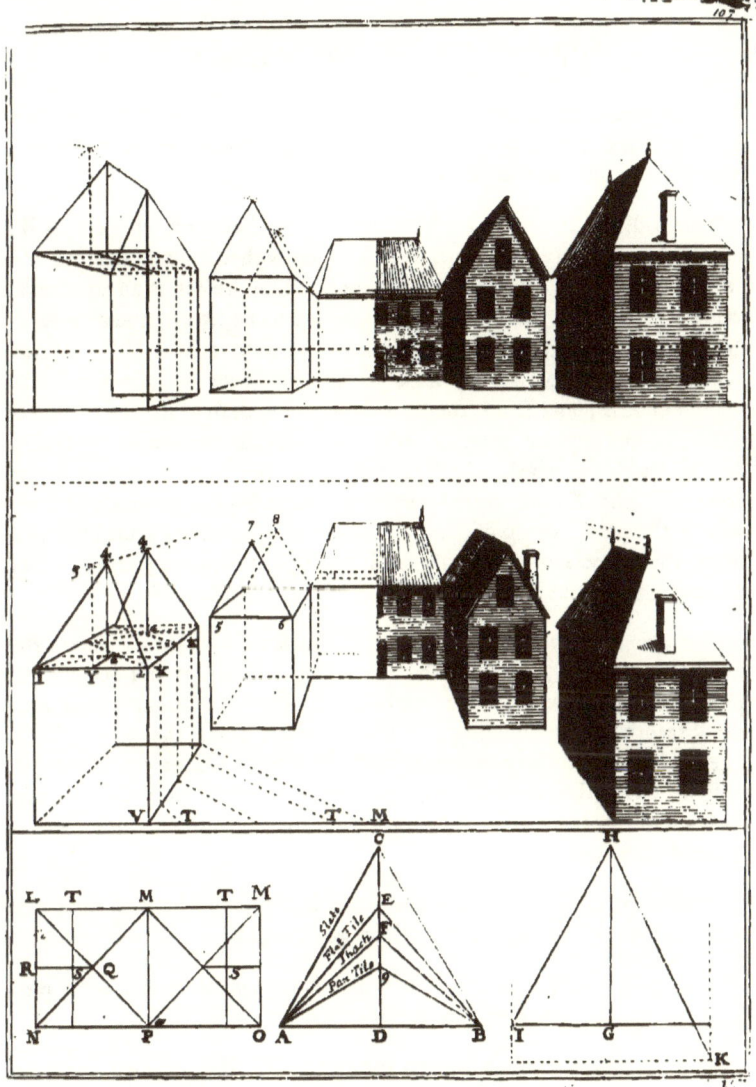

Sequel *of the* Roofs *in Perfpective.*

IN the preceding figure the *pinnacle roofs* are viewed in front, in this plate they are fhewn laterally; the method for conftructing them with their returns in the fide-views is now to be given.

The width of the houfe muft be fet on the bafe line, as here A B; and of this width a triangle is to be formed with the dimenfions of the fides according to the form of the roof. The prefent is an equilateral triangle, whereof C D is the height intended to be fet perpendicularly on the corner of the houfe, at the height of the wall, as here E F. Then half the breadth of the houfe is to be laid down in C, which is the middle of A B; and from thence a line to be drawn to the point of diftance; and in the point G, where it interfects the ray A, a perpendicular muft be raifed. Laftly, from F, a line is to be drawn to the point of fight X; the interfection whereof with the perpendicular H, will be the point, or tip of the pinnacle: to which lines muft be drawn from the corners of the houfe, E I. If you would have eaves, they are eafily added, as is feen in the figure K on the other fide.

For the conftructing of *pentices*, you have only to draw a line to the height of the roof, as here the line L M, and give it any declivity at pleafure. In the prefent, the height of the roof M N, is the fame with the breadth of the building, N O. If then, from the points M O, lines be drawn to the point of fight X, the perpendiculars of the depth will be cut in the points P and Q; which being connected by a right line will form the roof. The figures on the oppofite fide fhew houfes covered after fuch manners.

The uppermoft figures are only intended to fhew that the fame rule is to be obferved, though the horizon be changed.

A church is feen in the middle, which is covered or roofed with pinnacles; and the wings with pentices.

There is alfo a pavilion viewed end-wife; mention whereof has been made in the preceding page.

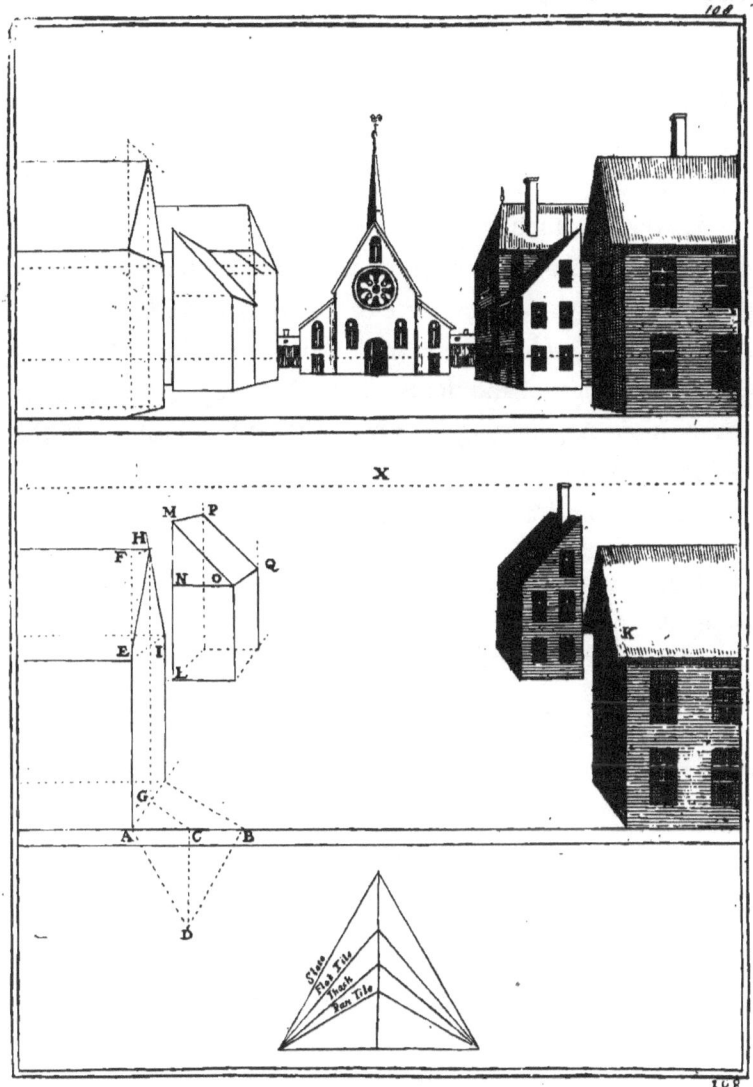

To exhibit Rows of Buildings, *or* Streets *in Perfpective.*

A Bare fight of the figure muft fuffice to fhew the method, which is exceeding eafy.   All you have to do
is to make a plan of fimple fquares, the common way ; and
to take one, or two, or three of the fquares for the breadth
or length of each houfe ; and on fuch breadth, &c. to fet
off the meafures of the doors, and windows ; and to get the
diminutions by drawing lines from the feveral meafures to the
point of diftance ; as here from BCDE and F, the lines are
fuppofed to be drawn to the point of diftance A.

The firft angle of each houfe may ferve for a line of elevation, as the angle G for the firft houfe.   As to the roofs, I
have already faid how they are to be managed.

If you require any crofs ftreets, one, two, or three fquares
are to be left vacant, and nothing upon them, as here H
and I.

The figure underneath is to fhew, that where houfes are
to advance beyond others, or fall further back, you have
only to put their elevations forwarder or backwarder on the
plan of fquares.   Thus L advances a fquare farther than K,
and M farther than L ; and fo of the reft.

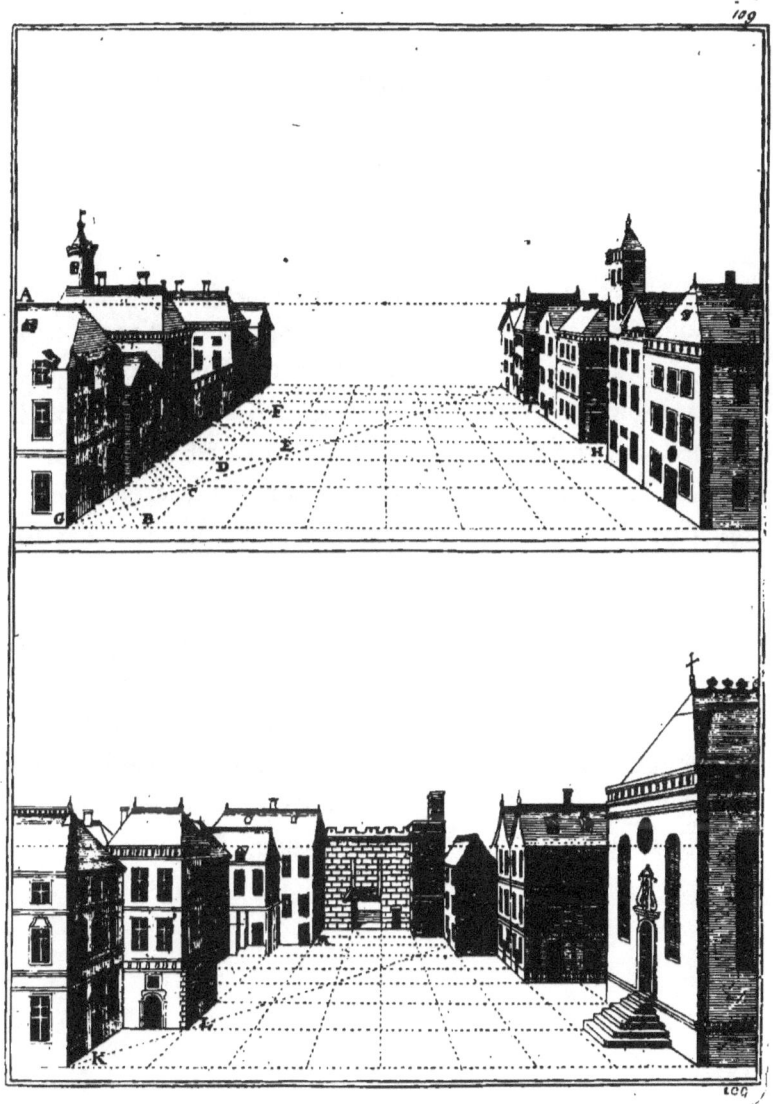

A Demonſtration that remote Objects *do not ſhew*
their Thickneſs.

IT muſt be here remembered, that objects near the horizon, that is, ſuch as are extremely remote, are not to
ſhew any thickneſs when viewed in front. Thus, for example,
the windows and doors of the houſes A, B, C, D, ſhould
not have any thickneſſes ſhewn, but be expreſt only by mere
lines. The reaſon is, that the viſual rays proceeding from
the front parts of the object become united in the eye with
the collateral ones.

I ſhould have given a ſtrict demonſtration hereof, had I
apprehended it any way neceſſary. But as I do not ſee of
what uſe it would be, and as I ſtand engaged from the beginning of the book not to enter into ſuch demonſtrations,
by reaſon I ſuppoſe I have to do with people who are but
indifferently prepared to underſtand them, I decline it.

K k

To exhibit BU I L D I N GS *viewed by the* Angle.

OF thefe two buildings feen angle-wife, the firft is performed after the manner already delivered for fquares viewed by the angle, and elevations of other objects in fide-views. However, to fave the trouble of recurring to the one and the other, I fhall here obferve, that to perform fuch buildings the meafures muft be fet on the bafe line, and from each of them, lines be drawn to the point of diftance, and from the points of interfection perpendiculars to be raifed; the perpendicular raifed on the firft angle ferving for a line of elevation. Thus, in the prefent building, the breadth being A B, and the length, B C, double its breadth; from A and B, lines are to be drawn to the point of diftance D; and from B and C to the point of diftance E; and from the interfections B F and G, perpendiculars to be raifed for the corners of the houfe. As to the dimenfions of the doors and windows, they muft be laid down on the bafe line between A B and B C; and lines be drawn from them all, to the points of diftance D and E. Then, obferving where B D or B E are interfected thereby, raife the pofts of the windows therein. The perpendicular of the firft angle B ferving for a line of elevation, will give the crofs pieces, and the height of the windows. The reft is obvious.

As to the figure underneath, the method is the fame as for chairs placed irregularly, fee page 102; that is, having made the plan, put it in perfpective as irregular objects are put. Then, laying a ruler along each fide of the plan, obferve where it cuts the horizon, and marking thofe accidental points, draw lines to them from each part of that fide of the building. Every fide or face of a building has its particular point. Thus the plan being put in perfpective, the fide H I, gives the point K on the horizon, to which all the rays on that fide muft be drawn. The other fide I L, fhould likewife have its point; but for want of paper-room, we could not here exprefs it. Thefe two points found, a ruler muft be laid thereon, and an occult line drawn over the other fide of the building parallel upon the plan to that which gave the point in the horizon, and continued to the bafe line; as from R, through L to M; and from the other point continue an occult line through H to N. Then fetting the number of windows of the fide H I, between N and I; and between L and M, fetting the number of windows on ● fide I L, draw lines from all thefe points, or meafures on the bafe line to the points in the horizon, and proceed as in the figure above.

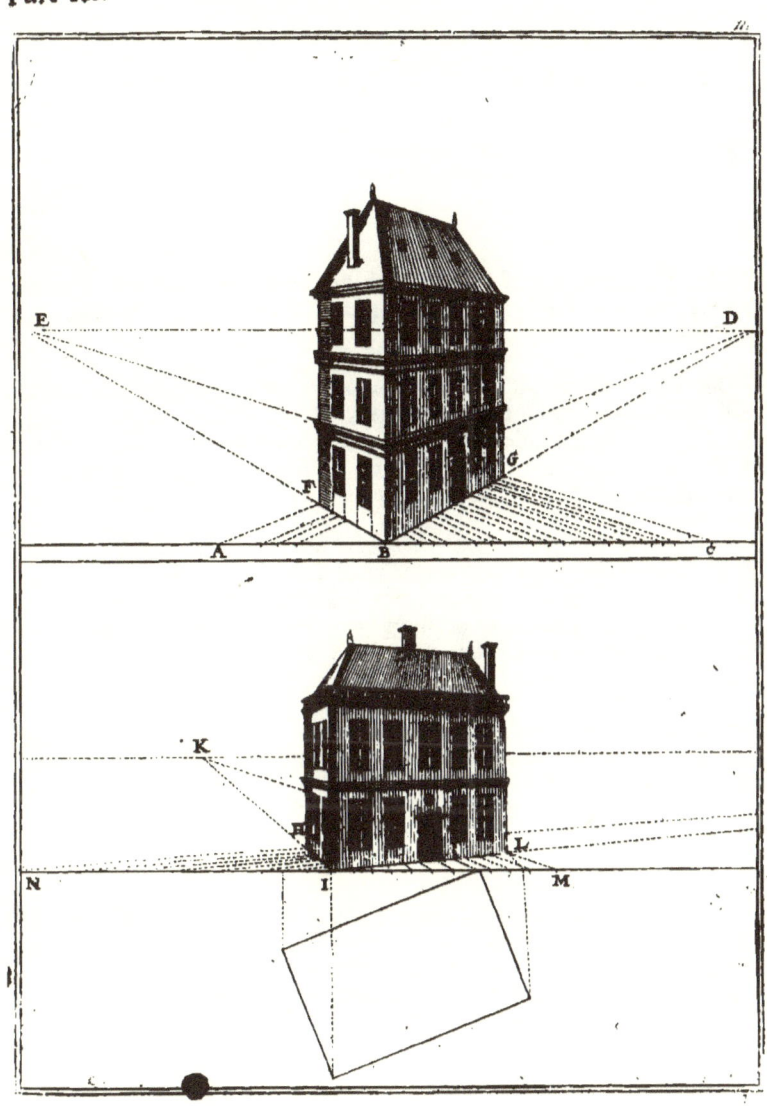

To exhibit Walks, *with Rows of Trees,* in *Perfpective.*

THOUGH the preceding rules might furnifh fufficient inftructions for putting walks with trees in perfpective; I have judged
it not amifs to add a particular rule which may render the method ftill
more eafy.

If only a fingle row of trees on each fide be required, there is no need
for making a plan of fquares, or chequers: what is directed in page 17,
will fuffice.

But where a number of walks are to be fhewn, I think it advifeable
to form a plan in occult lines, as already taught in page 31, and from
the diagonals of the little fquares, to erect perpendiculars, as is fhewn in
A B. If you defire to have the trees farther or lefs apart, increafe or
diminifh the diftances of the fquares on the bafe line.

When you have given the ftem of the firft tree its proper height, as
A C, draw a line from C to the point of fight D, which ray C D is to
bound the ftems of all the other trees. The firft tree, A B, fhews that
you may give what turn or form you pleafe to the body of it between the two perpendiculars A B, for it fhould not be drawn with the
ftraightnefs of a ruler.

The figure underneath is performed as that above, all the difference is,
that the fquares of the upper are direct, or in front; and thofe of the
under are viewed angle-wife: whence the meafures on the bafe line, in
the latter cafe, muft be all drawn to the points of diftance E and F. Perpendiculars are to be raifed from the angles of the little fquares; and the
reft as above.

In the fame perfpective, wherein are walks drawn to the points of
diftance, one may add others, drawn to the point of fight. Thus the
middle walk tends to the point G, which is the point of fight; and the
others to the points E F, which are thofe of diftance.

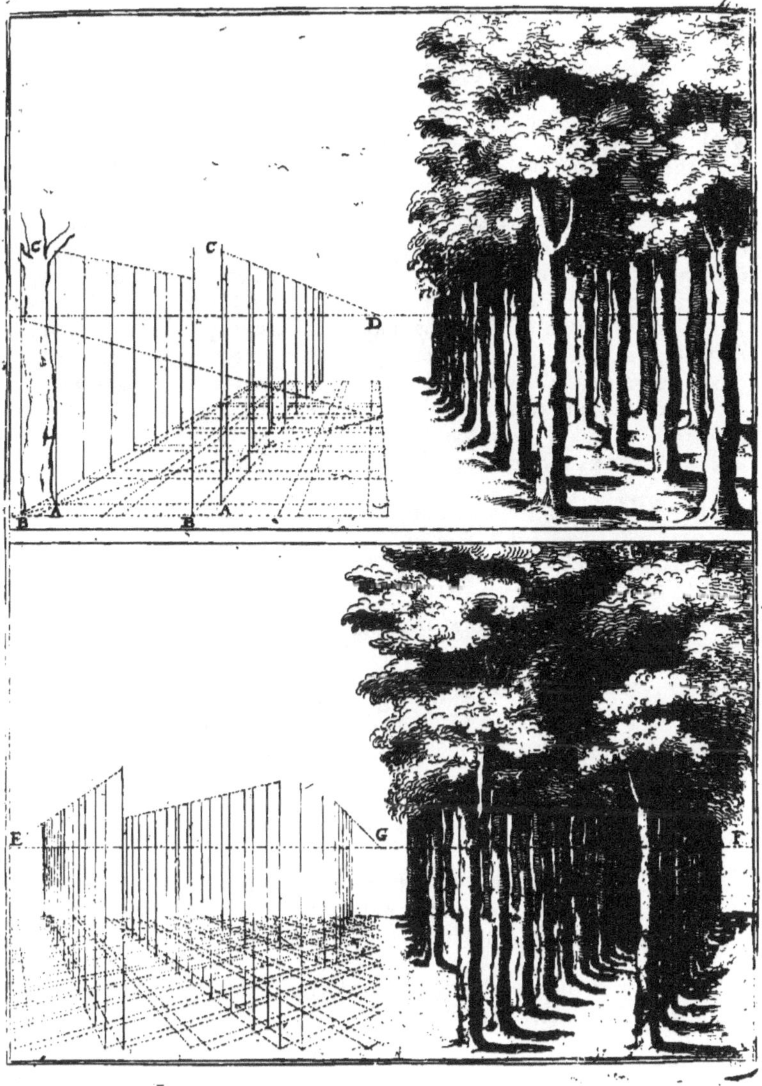

To put Gardens *in Perſpeɛ̃ive.*

IN the doɛ̃rine of plans was ſhewn, page 35, the manner of dimi-
niſhing, or putting the plan of a garden in perſpeɛ̃ive, by an eaſy
rule; ſuppoſing that you have the plan thereof. But, as I always endeavour to avoid geometrical plans, by reaſon it takes up too much time
to make them, I have added the preſent figures; whereby it appears,
that having made a chequer, or plan of ſquares, you may take as many
or as few of them as you pleaſe for the beds of the garden. As here,
A and B have each of them three ſquares every way; the reſt ſerving
for walks, as C C. If you would have compartments, or knots in the
beds, you are to uſe the little ſquares or diviſions of each bed; cutting
them, and forming them into the figure required; as is ſhewn in the
ſquares of A and B; and thoſe of the other ſide, D and E. The pali-
ſades and arbours are cut through the breadth of the walks.

✿✿✿✿✿✿✿✿✿✿✿✿✿✿✿✿✿✿✿✿✿✿✿✿✿✿✿✿✿✿✿✿✿

To exhibit Beds with Borders, Arbours, and Groves.

WHEN Borders are to be given the beds, the intended heights
and breadths muſt be ſet on the corner; and from thoſe meaſures
lines muſt be drawn to the point of ſight. Thus, in the lower figure,
F G being the breadth and depth of the borders of the bed H, lines
muſt be drawn from the angles of the little ſquare F and G, to the point
of ſight I; and go on with the reſt, as aboveſaid.

To exhibit *arbours,* raiſe upright poſts, or perpendiculars, O O, from
the angles of the ſquares of the walk, and perform the reſt as already
direɛ̃ed for arches viewed ſide-wiſe, in page 60.

The *grove* in the middle is performed by ereɛ̃ing perpendiculars from
all the angles of a chequer, &c.

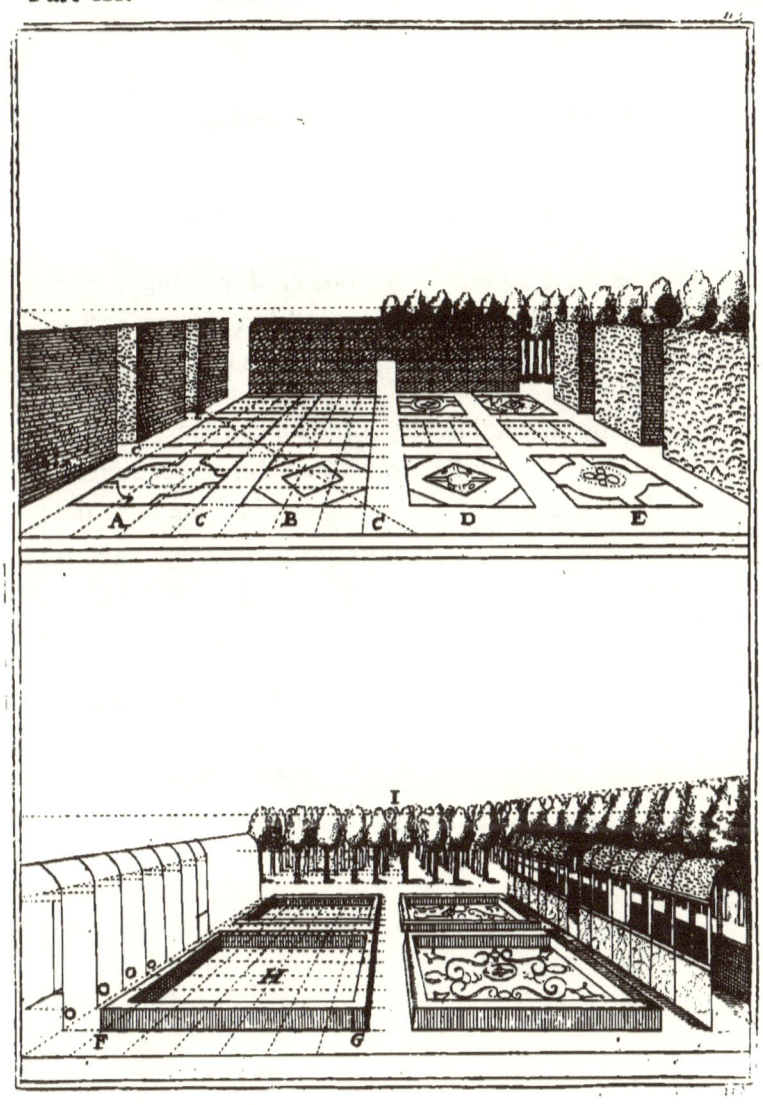

✿✿✿✿✿✿✿✿✿✿✿✿✿✿✿✿✿✿✿✿✿✿✿✿✿✿✿✿✿✿✿✿✿✿✿✿✿✿✿

To put Fortifications *in Perfpeɛive.*

I Need not here repeat the method of diminifhing, or put_
ing in perfpeɛive, the plans of all forts of fortifications :
what has already been faid in page 39, is clear enough.

There is no more difficulty in raifing them than in the
elevation of a bare wall; only more time is required, by
reafon of the greater number of angles which are to be drawn
all to the line of elevation, to give their heights thereon;
as has been mentioned over and over in treating of other
works.

The little line of elevation is divided into four parts. The
firſt, from 1 to 2, is the height of the *parapet of the covered
way.* From 2 to 3, is the height of the *rampart.* From 3
to 4 is the height of the *parapet of the rampart*; and from
5 to 1, the depth of the *ditch.*

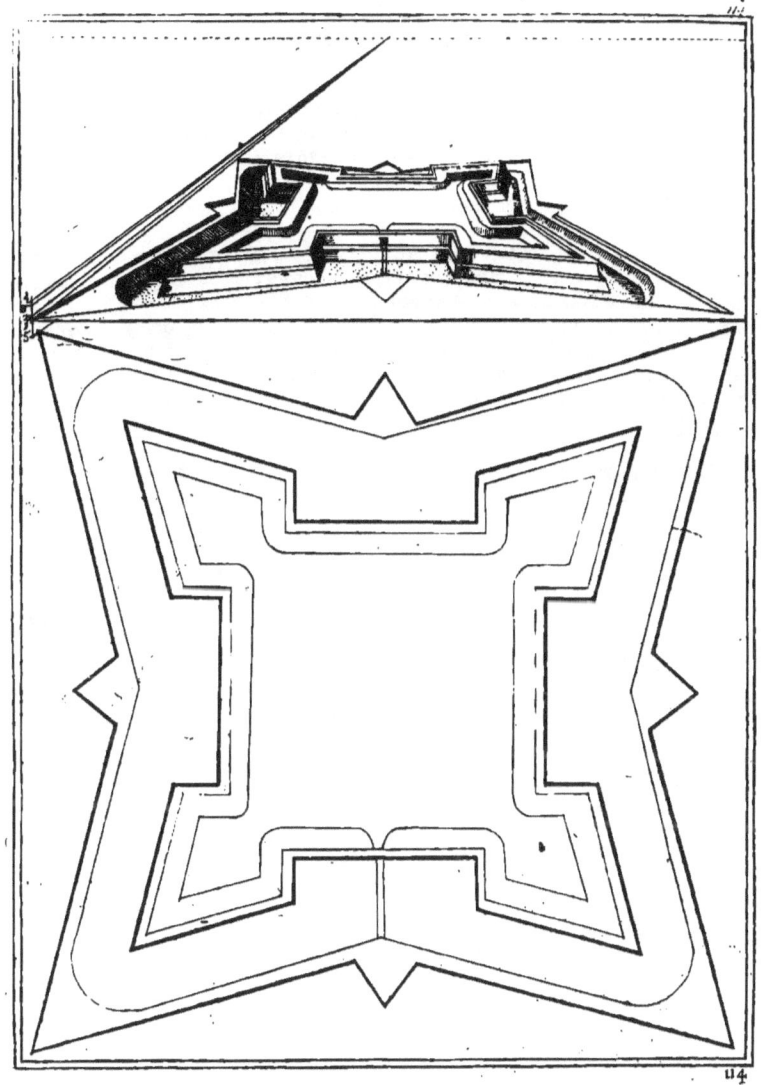

To make Defigns *in Perfpective.*

THERE is no mafter fo excellent, but he makes defigns of the works he would fucceed in. If this be ufual in moft arts, it is neceffary in this, by reafon of the great number of points and lines to be ftrictly obferved, and nicely managed, without which nothing is to be done correctly, or in any wife pleafing to a perfon that has tafte or fkill.

Since then there is a neceffity of making defigns, we are to look out for what may be affiftant therein. And as every body knows that the length and tedious-nefs of fuch works lie in the drawing of parallels and perpendiculars, I have fought, both in authors and in experience, for a method of doing the fame as expeditioufly as poffible. The refult is, that nothing of this kind has appeared to me worth the recommending, but the plate and fquare, which *Viator* has left us in his writings; which are inftruments fuch people as have occafion to fpend much time in defigning will find a deal of eafe and benefit from.

The figure gives a tolerable notion of the inftrument, and the method of ufing it, but it may be convenient to give fome defcription thereof. The plan A B C D, then, is to be perfectly on the fquare, a foot and half long, fifteen inches broad, and half an inch thick. The wood to be dry, firm, and fmooth. To make it the fofter, and favour the pen, a fheet of paper may be ftruck on it.

The fquare E F is a ruler a foot and a half long, an inch broad, and a quar-ter of an inch thick, fitted at right angles in another ruler G H, eight inches long, one broad, and three quarters of an inch thick. Now to draw lines, this laft ruler, G H, is held clofe to the board A B C D, in which cafe the other ruler E F, is certainly parallel to the bafe line, provided the board and ruler be exactly formed.

When you go to work, faften the fheet of paper I K L M, on the board with four little pieces of wax, N O P Q; then may you draw lines from any point, fecure that they are right. And for raifing perpendiculars, you have only to lay the handle of the ruler, G H, on the fide G D, in which cafe E F will be perpendicular to C D.

For myfelf, I find a wonderful eafe herefrom. The truth is, without fuch a contrivance, a man muft never be without the compaffes in his hand. All the trouble now remaining is for the vifual rays. And for thefe, fome ufe a ruler perforated at one end, and faftened by a needle to the point of fight. But this is to run into a trouble greater than what you would avoid. The common ruler does every whit as well.

S R *is a common ruler.* T *a pair of compaffes.* V another *pair of compaffes,* with a drawing pen therein; for circular lines.
Thefe are all the inftruments neceffary for making of defigns in perfpective.

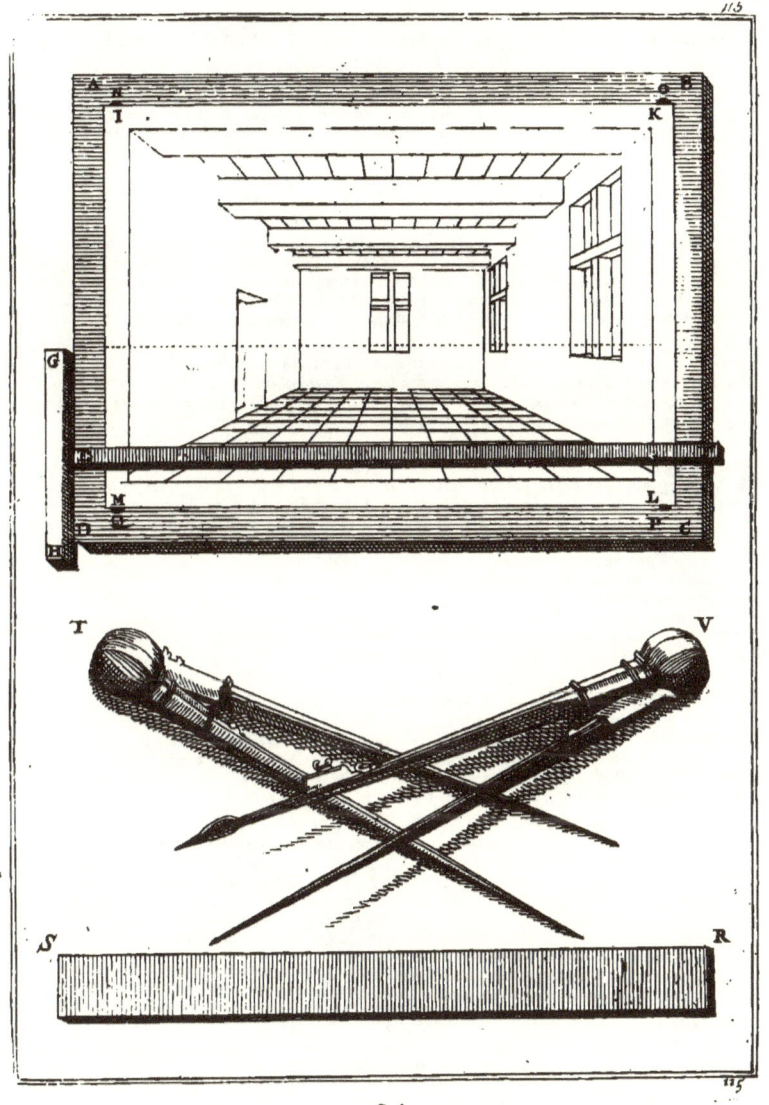

The Method of enlarging perspective Draughts out of Small into Great; and of reducing great Ones, into lesser.

A S designs are more easily made of a small, than of a large size, it is but reasonable they should always be so made. This has put me on giving a method of enlarging small designs on the canvas.

The method commonly used by the painters is to divide their little design, and the canvas they intend the large ones to be on, into an equal number of little squares, and to transfer what is in the squares of the design, into the correspondent squares of the canvas. This way some greatly approve of.

Here follows another, which, in my opinion, is easier and surer. Provide a scale proportionate to the little design, and another proportionate to the canvas. To make a design the first thing to be determined is the scale, which is to fix the measures of all the parts of the work. Thus, in the little design A, the scale B C of five parts, which we may call feet, is the first thing made. From this scale are taken the horizon, the height and distance of the trees, the breadths of the walks, &c.

To *enlarge this design* the method is this. Consider whether or no the draught is to have its natural horizon, that is, whether, when the bottom of the painting is on the ground, the horizontal line be the height of the eye, which is about five feet. Then, of the five divisions between B and C, make a scale of five feet F G, that thus, having taken all the measures and proportions in the small one, you may transfer them to the great one, after the following manner.

The two scales thus fixed, the first thing to be done is, to take in your compasses the distance between the base line D and the horizon E, and to apply the compasses thus opened, to the little scale B C, noting what number of parts it includes, as here it does five. Take therefore five divisions on the large scale F G in your compasses, and set them on each side the painting, or large design, beginning at the bottom of the cloth H H, and ending in I I. From the points I I, strike, or score a line with a chalked or blackened packthread. This line I I, will mark the horizon in the large draught. Then take the distance, or depth, K L, of the little design, which gives the bottom of the house, note how many divisions it includes, and take the same number from the large scale, and set them on the edges of the canvas, H M, H M, which you must strike with a pack thread for the bottom of the house. Proceed to take the distance N O, which includes two parts of the little scale; accordingly two parts are to be taken on the great one, and set off from H to P, which must be struck as before, for the depth of the second tree. Do the same for all the parallels to the base-line, as the other trees, windows, roofs, &c.

The method is the same for the perpendiculars as for parallels; only that they are to be struck or scored not from the side, but from the top and bottom. Thus, for the two corners of the house, the interval between them and the side of the draught being taken in the compasses, and found on the little scale equivalent to seven divisions and a half, as many divisions must be taken from the great scale, by which you will have H S, T S, to be struck as before. And the like must be repeated for all the other perpendiculars, as buildings, trees, palisades, &c.

To find the visual rays, which are the lines proceeding to the point of sight V, fasten a pack-thread to this point V, of the length of the painting, and with this strike or score all the rays very exactly. Thus, for the two rays D X, which give the breadth of the trees in the little design, take the distance D X, set it one the little scale B C, and take an equal number of divisions from the great scale, this will give you H Y; to which points H and Y, lines are to be struck with the pack-thread, from the point V. For the ray of the palisades, take the distance D Z, and set it on the little scale, and take as many divisions from the large scale; by this means you will have H †, which are to be struck from the point V, as before.

Every thing in a perspective ordinarily comes under one or other of these three sorts of lines, parallels, perpendiculars, and visual rays: and having shewn how to describe these with a good deal of ease on the canvas, there remains nothing difficult in the process of enlarging a small design.

As to the reducing *great into little*, you have only to invert the process; that is, take the measures first on the large scale, and diminish them proportionally on the small one. Thus, if the horizon of the large design were five divisions of the large scale, five divisions of the small scale were to be taken for the height of the horizon of the small design. And so of the rest.

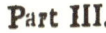

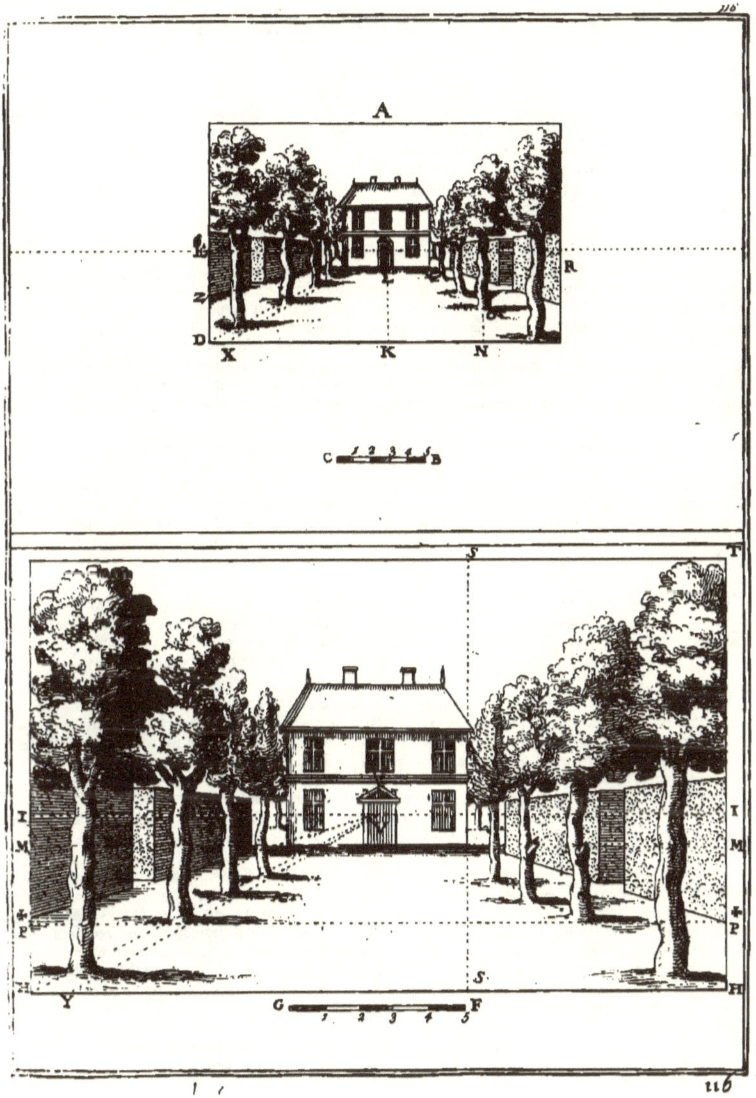
A
R
D
X
K
N
C
1 2 3 4 5
B
S
T
I
M
P
H
Y
G
F
1 2 3 4 5

Apparatus *to the univerfal Method of the Sieur* G. D. L.

AS feveral, for whofe benefit I intend this work, may not be fufficiently fkilful to fee clearly into this univerfal method of the Sieur G. D. L. the author, I believe will allow me to make it as eafy as I can, that they may be the better enabled to reap the benefit thereof. For this reafon I have added the two following figures, which will call to mind what has been already touched upon in the fecond, third, fourth and fifth obfervations, pages 16, 17. The defign whereof was to facilitate this method, and accordingly in them is fhewn how to take all the meafures on the bafe line ; and that as many rays as cut the diagonal C F, fo many fquares are formed in the depth of the draught ; which fquares may be made of any magnitude at pleafure.

Now, not to have fo far back to feek, view the firft figure, where the bafe line is A B, the point of fight G, and the points of diftance E, F. This bafe line I divide into twelve equal parts, which I fuppofe equivalent each to one foot, from all thefe divifions draw lines, or rays, to the point of fight, where-of A and B are the laft. Now, if a line fhould be required that is funk a foot deep in the draught, draw a line from the firft divifion B D, to the point of diftance F ; and where this line D F cuts the ray B G, will be the point for a line to be drawn through, that is funk a foot. If another three feet deep were required, take three of thefe parts on the bafe line, and from the third draw a line to the point of diftance F, and the point where it interfects B G, will be the place for that line. Confequently, if from C a line be drawn to F, the point where C F cuts B G will be a line fix feet deep.

If of the other fix parts remaining of A C, you make twenty four, by dividing each into four, and yet account each divifion a foot, you will have twenty four feet between A and C ; fo that if a line fhould be required eighteen feet deep in the draught ; I would reckon eighteen little parts from A, and from the eighteenth would draw a line to the point of diftance E, which by its interfection with A G would give a point for that line. If a line were required twenty four feet deep, the whole line A C muft be taken, and from C a line be drawn to E, and from H, the point wherein C E cuts A G, the line H I muft be drawn, to appear twenty four feet deep in the draught.

In perfpective, the line H I is equal to that of A C, that is, contains as many parts, or feet. So that if from I, a line be drawn to E, the interfection of I E with A G, will give the line K L forty eight feet deep. And if from the point L, a line be drawn to the point of diftance E, by its interfection with the ray A G, you will have a line twenty four feet farther off than the other.

If you would have a line thirty feet deep, from the point A reckon fix fmall divifions, and from the fixth draw a line to the point of fight G, obferving where it cuts the line H I, as here in the point M. Then from M draw a line to the point of diftance E, and the line M E will interfect the ray A G in the point N, through which the line required muft be drawn. If a depth of forty feet were required, from A fixteen divifions were to be reckoned, and the reft to be done as before. If fixty feet be required, twelve divifions muft be taken, and from the twelfth a line be drawn to the point of fight G, as far as the line K L, which will give the point O. Then from O, a line to be drawn to the point of diftance, and its interfection with the ray A G, will give the line.

As to the fecond figure, from what has been faid it is eafy to find a point of any depth or diftance at pleafure. It remains to fhew how the fame is found within or without the rays A G or B G. In order to this, the line B C is to ferve as a fcale of fix feet, one of which we divide into twelve inches ; that we may have the half, third, fourth, &c. of a foot. Things thus difpofed, if it be required to fhew a point feventeen feet diftant, and a foot and half within the ray A G, a line muft be drawn from the feventeenth divifion of the bafe line, to the point of diftance E, and where the ray A G is interfected thereby in P, the line P Q to be drawn. Now fince a foot and half is required within the ray A G, I take the extent on the fame line N Q in my compaffes, and fet it off from P to R, which point R is the point required. If a point twenty nine feet diftant, and feven and a half within the ray A G be required, a line muft be drawn from C to the point of diftance E, and through the point where it cuts A G, a line being drawn, gives twenty four feet. Then, from A taking five leffer parts, a line muft be drawn from their extent to the point of fight G, till it cut that line in the point S ; and from S a line is to be drawn to the point of diftance E, and from the point wherein it cuts the ray A G, a line T V muft be drawn. And fince feven feet and an half are required beyond the ray A, that fpace muft be fet on the fame line from T towards V to the point X, which point X will be the point defired. After fuch manner, may any diftance at pleafure be determined.

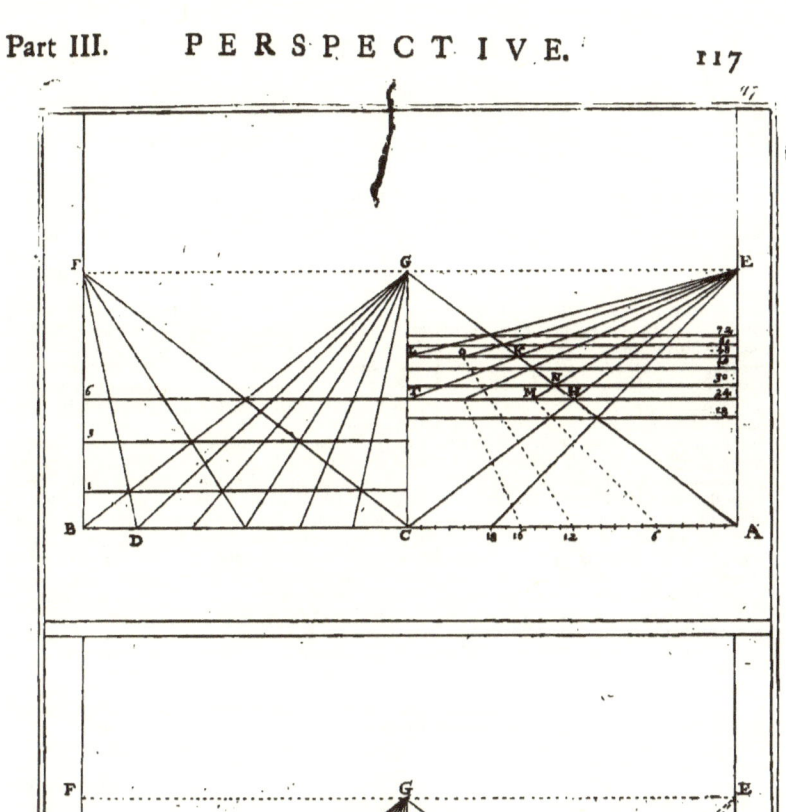

An univerſal method of perſorming Perſpective without having the point of diſtance out of the painting, or Ground of the work; made public by the Sieur G. D. L.

IN this method a geometrical plan is required, or at leaſt a ſcale of meaſures both for the plan and the elevation, in order for the one or the other to be put in perſpective.

For an object or ſubject, we ſhall take the author's own example, which is a ſquare cage, terminating at top in a point, or a building with a pavilion roof. The meaſures whereof ſhall be given by a ſcale.

Now having made the plan of the cage M I L K, which is here added at the top of the figure, a line *a b*, muſt be drawn at the diſtance the object is to appear at in the draught, as here the line *a b*, 17 feet, which is to be the baſe line, or bottom of the piece, and to be placed accordingly to the aſpect the object is to be viewed in. Then, from the two extremes of the line *a b*, two indefinite lines muſt be drawn parallel to each other, as the line *a g*, and *b g*. On one of which lines, as *a g*, you are to draw little parallels to the baſe line, proceeding from the angles of the plan, and by means of the ſcale ſee how far each angle of the plan is removed from this line *a g*, and mark the ſame on each line. Then, from the place the painting is intended to be viewed from, which is here the point *c*, five feet diſtant from *b*, deſcribe a perpendicular to *a b*, namely, the line *c t*; and to this line allow as many little parts of the ſcale, as the ſpectator is to be diſtant to view the painting, namely, 24 feet. At the extreme of which 24 feet, which is the point *t*, erect a little perpendicular of the height of the eye, namely, the line *t ſ*, equal to four feet and an half.

The cloth, wall or paper thus diſpoſed for putting the plan in perſpective, and making the elevation on the plan, divide the baſe line A B, in o as many parts as *a b* in the plan is divided into, namely twelve, each accounted a foot; and over the points A and B, ſet the height of the line *ſt*, namely four feet and a half; that is, taking in your compaſſes four and a half of the diviſions of A B, ſet them perpendicularly over the points A B, by which means you will have the points E and F. Draw the line E F, therefore parallel to A B, and it will be the horizon. Then, as in the plan, the point C, which is the place the draught is to be viewed from, is five diviſions diſtant from *b*, you are to reckon as many parts from B; and from the fifth C, erect a perpendicular to A B, which cutting the horizon in the point G, gives the point of ſight G, to which all the rays A G and B G, repreſenting the parallels of the plan *a g* and *b g*, muſt be drawn.

As to the point of diſtance, it will be the point F, and as the line *c t* is 24 feet long, 6 diviſions muſt be taken from the line A B, namely, from A to D, and each ſubdivided into 4: which 24 parts are to ſerve as a ſcale for the depths or diſtances, being ſufficient for the ſame; though they were infinite. And the 6 parts remaining between B and D, will be a ſcale for the feet, according as the lines drawn from the points found for the plan, ſhall cut the rays drawn to the point of ſight G. For as this ſcale is a pyramid, whereof B D is the baſe; the meaſures diminiſh in proportion as they are farther off. One of the parts is divided into inches, that all the meaſures may be there, as on the plan.

By the ſcale of diſtances, the points of the plan are found, and by the ſcale of meaſures the lengths of the lines both of the plan and elevation.

Now to put the plan in perſpective, all the meaſures of the geometrical plan muſt be obſerved. The firſt angle of the plan *r m* is 17 feet diſtant from the point *a*, on the line *a g*. For this reaſon we reckon 17 parts, beginning at A, and from the ſeventeenth draw a line to the point F, cutting the ray A G in R. From this point R, a parallel to the baſe muſt be drawn: and by reaſon the point *m* is within the ray *a g*, by a foot and an half, therefore, on the ſide B D of the line R, muſt a diviſion and an half be taken, and ſet off within the ray A G, which will give the point M, repreſenting the angle of the plan *m*. As to the angle *l*, which is 26 feet diſtant from the point *a*, a line muſt be drawn from the point D, which is 26 feet from A, to the point F; and where the ray A G is interſected thereby, namely, in the point *y*, a parallel is to be drawn. Now as the point *y* is not remote enough by 2 feet, a line muſt be drawn from the ſecond diviſion of the ſcale to the point G, and where this ray cuts the parallel *y*, namely in the point Q, the line Q F to be drawn, which will give the point H on the line A G: from which point H a parallel to A B muſt be drawn, and on the ſide B D of the ſame line H, muſt the diviſions for 14 feet and an half be taken, namely, from the point H to L.

For the point *k*, which is 29 feet diſtant from A, a line muſt be drawn from the fifth part of the ſcale A D, to the point G, and where this ray interſects the parallel *y*, namely in the point O, the line O F muſt be drawn, which gives the point N on the line A G. Then from N draw a parallel, the ſide whereof of B D, 7 feet and an half, muſt be taken, to be ſet off without the ray A G, namely, from N to K.

For the point *i*, which is 38 feet from *a*, take 14 diviſions on the ſcale A D, and from the fourteenth draw a ray to the point G, which cutting the parallel in the point S; from that point draw a line to F, cutting the ray A G in T, which is 38 feet from the point A, inaſmuch as the parallel *y* is 24; to which, 14 being added, gives the whole 38. And ſince the angle *i* is 4 feet and an half within the ray A G, that extent muſt be ſet on the ſide D B of the parallel T, namely, from T to I.

To form the plan, thoſe four points M L K I muſt be connected by right lines, and perpendiculars erected from their angle, as M *il*, L *ſſ*, K /*r*, and I /*p*; each of which will be ſeventeen feet, as is expreſſed in the plan of the line X. Then, from the extremes of theſe perpendiculars, draw two diagonals *il*, *ſp* and *ſſ*, /*r*, which interſecting in Z, from the ſame point Z erect a perpendicular Z Æ, thirteen feet and an half. Laſtly, drawing lines from all the four angles *il*, *ſſ*, *ſp* and *ſr*, to the point Æ, the cage will be formed in perſpective. If you would have it ſunk a foot under ground, add a foot underneath each point of the plan, and connect them by lines.

M m̄

To give any precise diſtance required, without removing the point of ſight out of the piece.

SUCH as are diſpoſed to make uſe of this univerſal manner ought to know, that the number of feet you take on the baſe line are to have a regard to the point of diſtance propoſed.

To make the propoſition underſtood : in the firſt figures are put two points of diſtance, the one ſix, the other twelve feet, which have an eaſy ratio to each other ; inaſmuch as the ſix parts being each divided into two, you have twelve.

Suppoſe then the line A B divided into twelve parts, and from each diviſion lines drawn to the point of ſight C ; take half theſe diviſions A D, and from D to the point E, which is the diſtance of ſix feet, draw D E. It is certain its interſection with the ray A C will give the diminution of the ſquares viewed at ſix feet diſtance. And if from D a line be drawn to F, which is the diſtance of twelve feet, the line D F cutting the ray A C will give the diminution of ſix ſquares, viewed at twelve feet. And if the diminution of twelve ſquares, viewed at twelve feet diſtance, were required, from the point B, which is the whole baſe line, a line muſt be drawn to F, and its interſection with the ray A C, in the point H, will give the thing required. Or from I a line I F is to be drawn, which will give the ſame point H, the line H K, in each caſe, being the depth of twelve ſquares, viewed at twelve feet diſtance. Hence we obſerve, that twelve ſquares, viewed at twelve feet diſtance, meet in the ſame line H K with ſix ſquares viewed ſix feet off, and that all the lines of the ſix ſquares, given by the interſection of the diagonal D G, have a relation two by two to thoſe given by the diagonal D F. The reaſon why the diagonal D F gives two lines for one of thoſe D G, is, that the diſtance is double. If it were triple, it would give three, and four if quadruple. Now, to find the ſame interſections, and the ſame number of ſquares on the ſide B D, as are on that A D, without having the point of diſtance out of the piece, you have only to divide each of the ſix equal parts between B and D into two, by which means you will have twelve parts : then draw occult lines from each diviſion to the point of ſight C, and drawing parallels to the baſe line through all the interſections the diagonals make with all thoſe rays, you will have twelve ſquares depth in the ſame line as if the diſtance were twelve feet, though in reality G be but ſix. The reaſon is, that in multiplying the rays you multiply the ſquares, and multiplying the ſquares you remove the diſtance farther. Such is the reaſon why having made twelve parts of the ſix that were between B D, there are procured twelve ſquares, which have the ſame depth as if at twelve feet diſtance. And if a diſtance of twenty four feet were required, you have only to divide each of the parts between B and D into two, which making twenty four parts, from the twenty fourth draw a line to the point D, and the point K, wherein it interſects the ray B C, will be the depth of twenty-four feet.

In the ſecond figure the ſame meaſures are laid down on the line L M, as on A B of the firſt figure, and the ſame depth and diſtance on the ſide M N, as on the ſide A D, which gives the line H K ; to ſhew, that if a line were drawn from the fifth part, as Q G, or from the ſeventh, as R G, the true depth would not be had, which is at K. For R G would not ſink it enough, and Q G would ſink too much ; even though thoſe five or ſeven parts there were made twelve or twenty-four.

For this reaſon you are always to obſerve to take a number which may be multiplied by the diſtance, as here the diſtance of 6 may ſerve for 12, 18, 24, 30, 36, 42, 48, &c. the diſtance 5 may ſerve for 10, 15, 20, 25, 30, &c. and the diſtance 8 for 16, 24, 32, 40, 48, &c. In this way you cannot fail ; for ſuppoſing the point of diſtance cannot be nearer the point of ſight than G is to C, it follows, that if G be ſix, ſeven, eight, or ten feet from C, that then half the baſe line will have the ſame number, which is to be divided proportionally to the diſtance intended. For inſtance, if there be eight feet from N to L, and I require a diſtance of thirty two feet, without moving G out of its place ; I divide each of the eight parts, or halves of the baſe lines, as L N, into four, accordingly, four times eight makes thirty-two rays. So that the diminutions of the ſquares will be thirty two feet diſtant.

Theſe little diviſions do none of them remain after the painting is finiſhed, only the principal diviſions of feet, which are drawn to the point of ſight, and the diminutions, that is, the parallels to the baſe line, which ſtill ſtand.

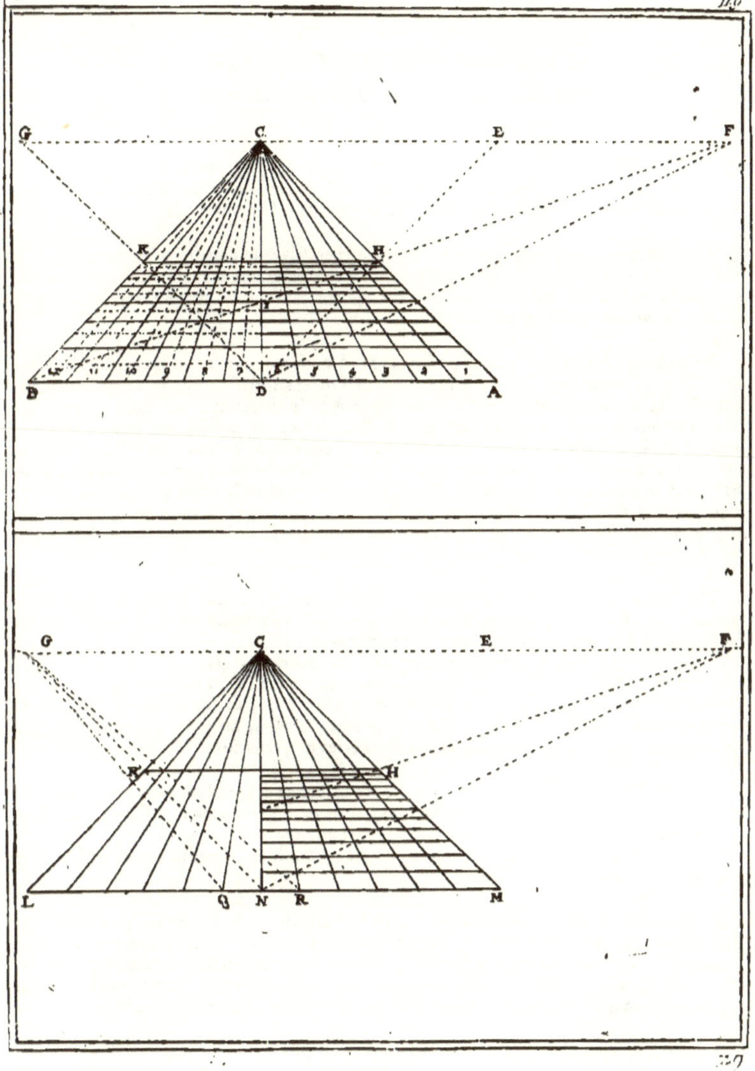
G
C
E
F
K
H
I
B
D
A
G
C
E
F
K
H
L
Q
N
R
M

A very curious Method of drawing all Perſpectives *in the moſt natural Manner, without obſerving the rules.*

HAVING given you all the neceſſary rules for drawing perſpectives in the exacteſt manner, I have thought fit to add this and the following method of drawing very correctly after nature, without being tied to the proceſs of any one rule.

Many lovers of painting, and who entertain themſelves in drawing after nature, would willingly be excuſed the trouble of opening the compaſſes, or taking up the ruler, and in this method neither the one nor the other are required ; and yet the proportions and diſtances of objects will be exactly preſerved.

Before I come to the method of performance, I muſt deſcribe the inſtrument uſed therein. The principal requiſite is a large piece of fine clear glaſs, fitted in a wooden frame, expreſſed at the bottom of the plate by the letter A. This frame is to ſlide between two cheeks or pieces of wood an inch and a half thick, which are raiſed at the two extremes of a board the breadth of the frame, that is, about a foot broad, as ſhewn in B C, the cheeks are groved to receive the frame A. In the middle of the board ſquare holes muſt be made as in E, to receive the ſlit ruler F, ſo as it may be raiſed or lowered at pleaſure. At the top of which ruler is a circle of three or four inches diameter, but very thin, being made of tin, or the like, and having a little aperture about the ſize of a pea in the middle. The whole is repreſented put together in G.

The figure of the inſtrument ſhews the application, yet I ſhall deſcribe the method of proceeding. Place the inſtrument G before the object you would draw, look through the little hole or ſight F, and if you ſee all the propoſed objects repreſented on the glaſs, the inſtrument is rightly fixed, otherwiſe bring the ſight nearear the glaſs, till you ſee the whole of what is required. The piece thus rectified, draw on the glaſs every thing that you ſee thereon through the hole F ; which has the ſame effect here, as the point of ſight in the other methods. And it is certain, every thing thus drawn on the glaſs, the eye being fixed to the little hole, will be according to the ſtrict rules of perſpective.

It is well known how to take off or copy what is thus deſigned on the glaſs. One method is to draw on the glaſs with pen and ink, then wetting the backſide of the glaſs a little, and laying a moiſt ſheet of paper on the ſide that has the deſign, rub or preſs the paper gently thereon with the hand, and the whole draught will be impreſſed or transferred from the glaſs upon the paper.

Some adviſe to make uſe of a hair pencil and colours, but every body is left to his own diſcretion. It is enough to know the method in general. The draught of a palace is as eaſily taken this way as a landſkip, and a church as a houſe or chamber. All required in any of them being to pitch on a ſituation where the whole object intended to be repreſented, may be ſeen, and to bring the ſight to a proper nearneſs to the glaſs.

A painter may uſe the ſame method for the drawing of figures or poſtures, from nature, ſtatues, relievo's, and every thing elſe. It being certain, that a little practice will render the method exceeding eaſy.

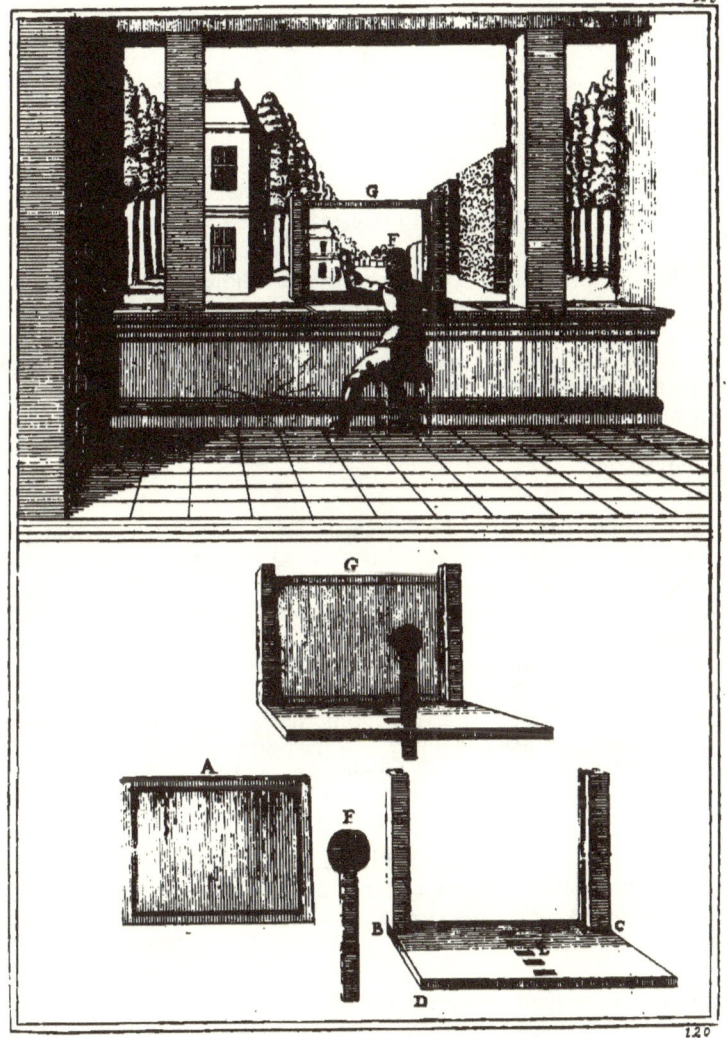

Another curious Manner of practising Perspective, with-
out understanding the Rules.

THIS method is as curious as the former, and some even prefer it, because a double draught is required in that, one on the glass, and a second copied or imprinted from it. Whereas in the present method only a single draught is made, and that as exactly as the former.

I shall not describe the structure of this instrument, it being the same with that already mentioned; excepting that the frame, instead of a glass fitted in it, must be divided into a number of little squares by fine threads, drawn at equal distances from each side of the frame, across each other, forming what we call a *reticula* or lettice. As to the number of squares, it is left to discretion. But they must not be too large that you may work the more exactly, nor too small for fear of being confused.

For the practice, place the instrument H in such manner as that you may see all the objects you intend to draw, through the hole of the sight I. If your draught is to be larger than the compass of the frame or *reticula*, squares must be made on the cloth or paper, larger than those of the frame. If your drawing be intended smaller than the frame, make the squares less. But in all cases make the same number of squares on your paper or cloth, as you see in the frame when you look through the sight I. Then, transferring proportionally from the squares in the one, to the corresponding squares in the other, the perspective will be as just as if you had gone by the strict rules, and used the compass and ruler.

The two figures shew how the instrument H is to be placed, in order to draw on a table. The expedient is of excellent use in painting, and serves to draw very exactly any perspective from nature, or to copy from paintings.

Some people will be apt to urge, that the method is not new; there being few painters but what know how to enlarge or diminish paintings by means of the chequer, or squares. All this I allow, but must take the liberty to say, that I do not know of any that ever yet used the sight-hole, which, however, is of very great advantage to the artist.

I

M E A S U R E S

A N D

P R O P O R T I O N S

O F

F I G U R E S

F O R

Perſpective Draughts, Paintings, and Relievos.

P A R T IV.

Figures in perfpective.

HAVING fhewn how to draw all kind of views in perfpective, I proceed to give directions for adjufting the height of figures.

I would here make one obfervation concerning the altitudes of figures. Thofe which are placed at the end of a gallery, hall, or in a garden at the termination of a walk, with a defign to deceive the eye, and appear at a diftance to be real life, are beft reprefented in attitudes which do not fuppofe a progreffive motion. Whereas thofe figures which are introduced as part of the compofition of a picture, admit of every kind of attitude to the defign of the piece.

The number of horizons which our painters frequently introduce in the fame piece, leads them into innumerable faults, in not being able to give the figures their proper heights, proportionate to their horizons. I fhall therefore here give a fingle rule, which may prevent their failing, be the horizon what it will.

For Figures that have the Eye in the Horizon.

IN perfpective draughts placed at the end of a gallery, hall, or walk, to deceive the eye the horizon fhould always be its natural height, that is, five feet, which is that of an ordinary fize.

And figures intended to appear there the fize of life muft have the eye in the horizon. For, having the eyes in the fame horizon with ourfelves, they will be of our own height. This might pafs as fufficient inftruction; but to make the point more clear and obvious, I fhall inftance in thefe three figures, inftead of twenty others which might be brought.

The firft figure A is the natural height, and has its eye in the horizon. If a fecond figure be required in the place B, from the point B a perpendicular muft be raifed to the horizon, and it will appear of the fame height with the former. If you require a third at C, let his eye likewife be in the horizon, and he will be the fame height with the reft, in appearance. In effect, though there were a thoufand, there need no other rule be regarded, when the horizon is the natural height. I muft not here be underftood as including children, which are to be made in proportion to the large figures, according to the difcretion of the painter.

For Figures that have a low Horizon.

IN painting for halls, which are ufually hung pretty high, the horizon muft be lower, to bring it as near the eye as poffible.

Now, to give each figure its juft height and proportion in whatever part of the painting it be, fome one muft be drawn of any height at pleafure, in any part of the piece, as the figure D F, which is here to do the office of a line of elevation.

And to find the height of the other figures in the painting which are to appear as high as the firft, draw lines from the head and feet of this figure D F, to a point in the intended horizon, as E, and within this triangle D E F, will be found the heights of all the reft. Thus, for example, if the height of a figure in the point G be required, from that point G draw a parallel to the bafe G H, till it interfects the line or ray F E in the point H, and the perpendicular H I gives the height of the figure, which is to be taken in the compaffes, and fet off in the point G. If another be required in the point K, the fame operation is to be repeated, and we fhall have the perpendicular M N for the juft height. And fo of whatever number of figures you pleafe.

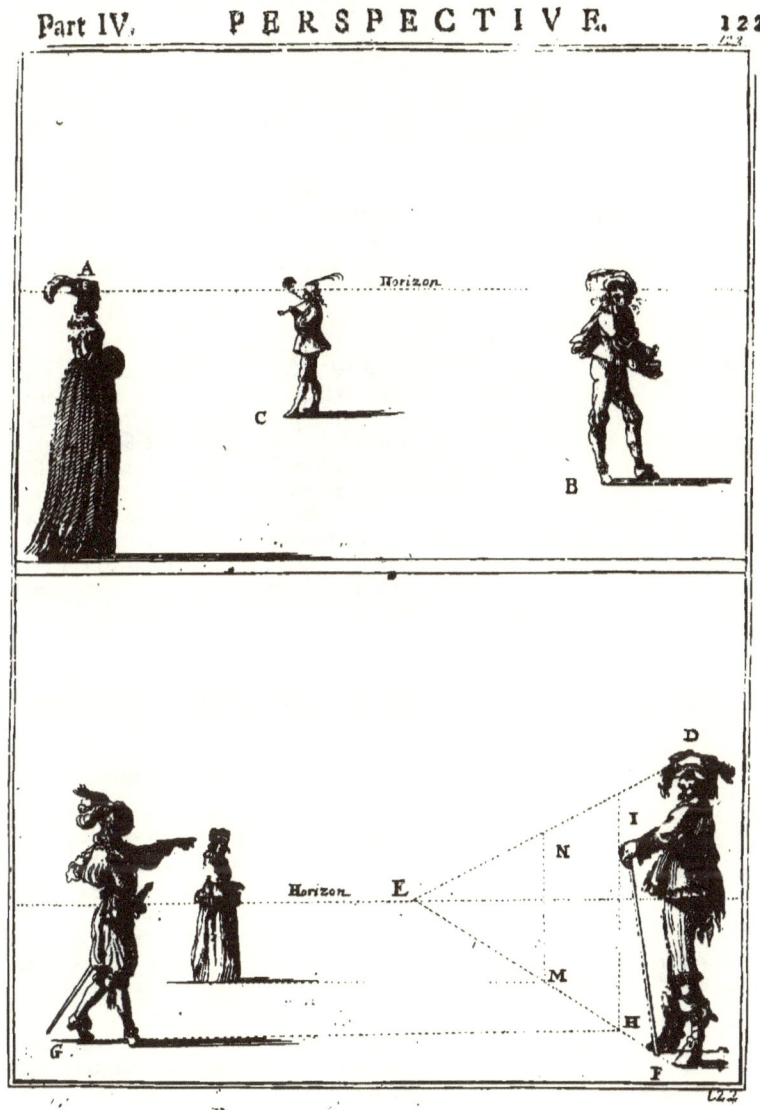

To exhibit Figures *that have a high Horizon.*

W HE N the horizon is high, as it neceffarily is when objects are viewed
from an eminence, the fame rule already laid down for the remote figures
in a low horizon, muft be obferved ; as in that cafe, the hindermoft figures
are placed higheft, and are moft diminifhed, fo in the prefent cafe, their diftance
is expreffed by raifing them further off from the bafe line, and diminifhing them
in proportion to their diftance.

Having drawn the firft figure A B, draw a line from the top of its head,
and another from the bottom of its feet to fome point in the horizon, as the
point C, then will all the heights of the other figures be taken within this triangle A C B. For example, if you would have the height of the figure in the
point D, from D draw a parallel to the bafe line, D E, as far as the ray A C,
which will give the point E, from which a perpendicular is to be raifed as far
as the line B C, which will give the point F. This perpendicular, E F, will be
the height of a figure in the point D. If a figure be required in the point G,
the fame is to be done as for D, and you will have the perpendicular H I, for
the height of the figure G. By the fame method the heights of all other figures
in any other places may be taken.

✿✿✿✿✿✿✿✿✿✿✿✿✿✿✿✿✿✿✿✿✿✿✿✿✿✿✿✿✿

For Figures *that have their feet in the horizon.*

I T is but rare that figures are made above the horizon, but where there is a
neceffity for it, thofe intended to appear the foremoft muft be made the
largeft ; that is, they muft be made the natural height, and all the reft being
made lefs, as they are more remote, will appear equal to them. Thus the
figure K L is here the biggeft and the neareft, and M N the remoteft. All the
fecret here, is the painter's finifhing the front figures more than thofe behind,
and ftill the farther off they are, the fainter and lefs perfect muft they be.

The rule for thefe figures, and for thofe which have their eyes in the horizon, is no other than reducing their height, and making them fmaller and
fainter, as they are thrown farther behind.

To exhibit Figures *raifed a fmall Matter above the Plan.*

THERE are fome who plead, that objects raifed above the ground are more diminifhed than if they were on the plan; and, of confequence, a figure mounted four or five feet fhould therefore be fmaller than if placed on the earth. The rule is good for figures at a great height, as fhall be fhewn in its place: but an elevation fo fmall as that juft mentioned, can only make an infenfible diminution. For fuppofing fuch an object or figure may be feen at one fingle view, that is, without raifing the eye, it muft be the fame height when fo inconfiderably raifed, as when ftanding on the level ground. Thus, the figure A muft be the fame height as B, and the figure C as D, and F equal to G.

The fame reafon holds for figures a little below the plan, which are to be reprefented of the fame height as thofe above it, as as fhewn in figure E, which is equal in height with H; and I is as big as K. Thefe two examples may ferve for all cafes, where the variation of the figures is as fmall as in thefe inftances, the diminution of figures occafioned by high elevations will be the fubject of future inftructions.

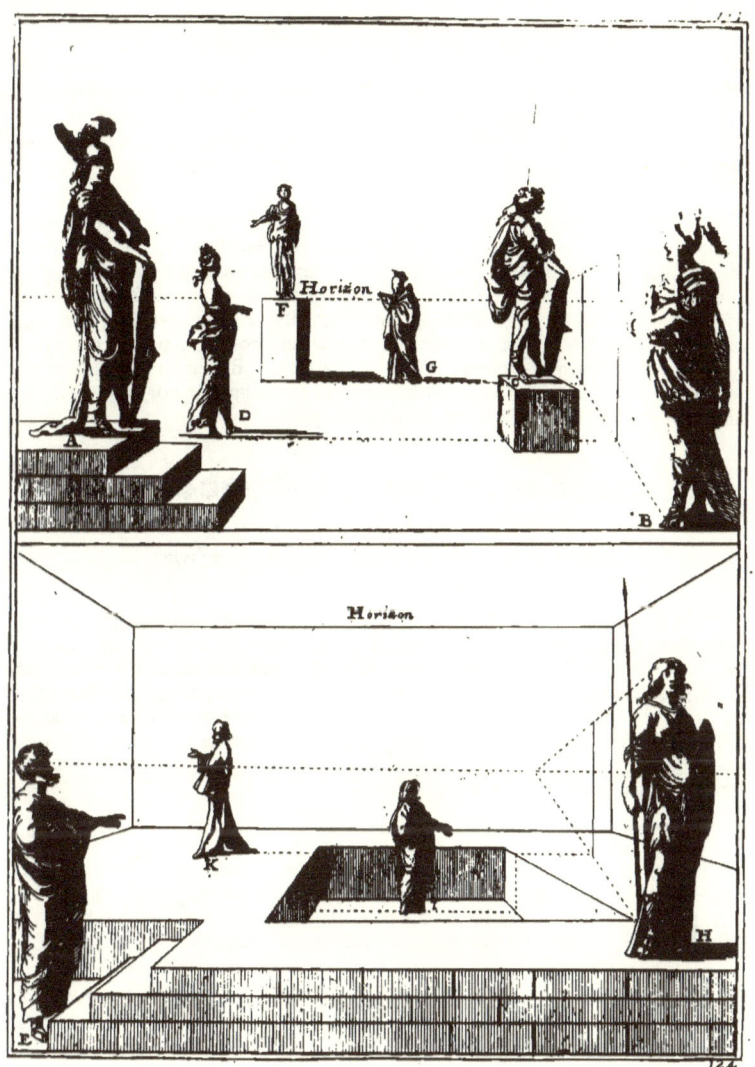

The Postures *of Figures in Perspective.*

THERE must be a judicious choice in the postures, or attitudes of figures, when intended to deceive the eye. For all of them are not proper, as I have already observed. This consideration has determined me to add a few, which may pave the way for the invention of numerous others.

The first is a man who reads, sitting; the second is reading an advertisement posted on the wall; the third plays on a lute; the fourth is asleep; the fifth is lolling against the banisters; the group of two figures marked 6, are looking on a draught on paper; the remoter, marked 7, are in earnest discourse. One might add others, playing, speaking, or discoursing at table, writing, praying, &c. In effect, you have a choice of numberless postures, provided they be such as that a man may continue in them for a time. But never use such as are much in action; for you can never be deceived in seeing a leg or an arm in the air, or a person running without shifting his place.

❀❀❀❀❀❀❀❀❀❀❀❀❀❀❀❀❀❀❀❀❀❀❀❀❀❀❀

Beasts *and* Birds *in Perspective.*

THE same rules must here be observed as in human figures, giving each the height or breadth of the first, and from the two ends of this first measure drawing lines to the horizon from the measures of all the rest. For example, having intended the first horse, A D, to be the height of that other B, from the line A D draw a line to the horizon C, and from B draw a parallel to the base line B K, till such time as it cut the line A C, which will give the point K; from which a perpendicular K L being erected, will give the height of the horse in the point B.

As to birds: from the extremities of their wings F F, you are to draw lines to the horizon, and between those lines to take the dimensions of the rest, which we suppose of the same size. For example, to have the magnitude of a bird in the point G, draw a parallel to the base line G H, till such time as it cut the rays E and F, which will give the line H I for the magnitude of the bird G.

When beasts or birds are required, you must always make choice of such as are the stillest, or least active, as a dog sleeping or gnawing a bone, a cat watching a mouse, a parrot, &c.

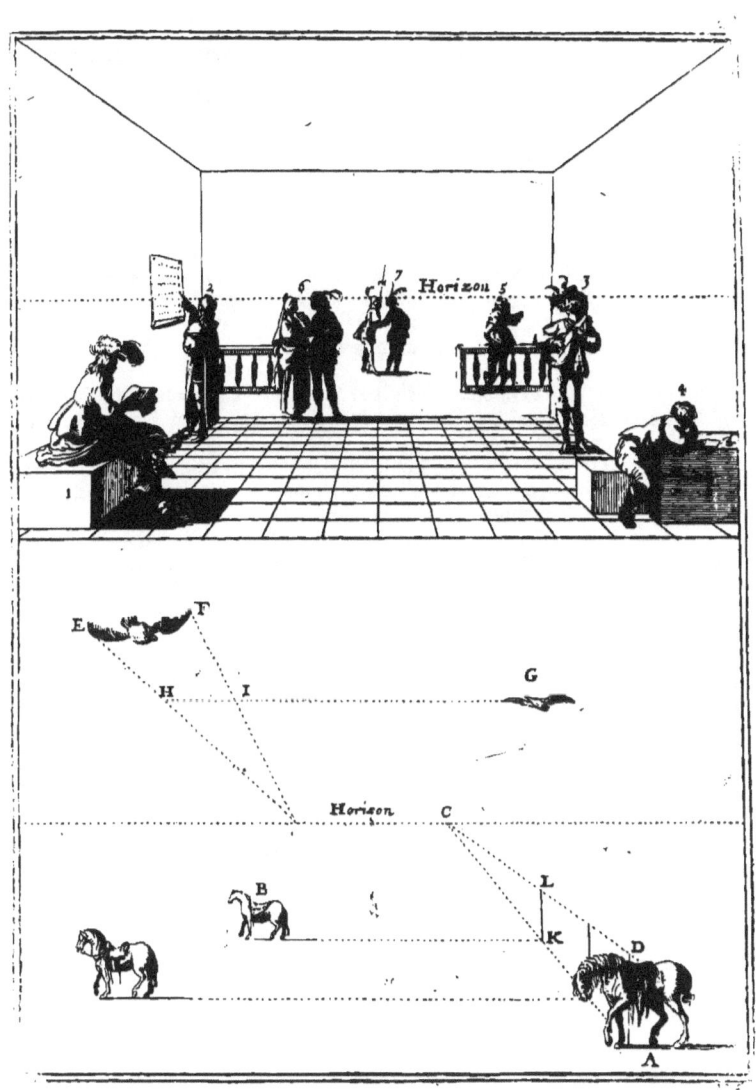

To find the Height of remote Figures, whereof the first
is on a Mountain near the Eye.

IT gives great satisfaction to the mind, when a person knows what he does to be right: on which account, no doubt, the reader will be pleased to have the following rule, with which but few practitioners are acquainted.

When figures are to be made, determine the hight, that is, the space of the ground you would have it raised ; and at that distance put another figure underneath, of the same height as the first ; and from the feet and head thereof draw lines to the horizon ; by which you will have the height of the other figures in the champain. To explain myself :

The figure A, for example, which is at the top of a mountain, is five feet high, which is the natural height ; and I suppose the mountain twenty-five feet high : If now a man be raised twenty feet, as is the piece in the middle, whereon the spectator is mounted (who himself is supposed five feet high) the horizon will be twenty-five feet as well as the mountain ; and consequently will reach the top of the mountain : as is expressed in the figure.

Now to find the height of the little people in the champain, make a figure twenty-five feet lower, underneath the figure A, or in some other place, as B C ; and from the feet B, and the head C, draw lines to some place in the horizon, as the point O ; and between those two lines, B and C, drawn to O, take the height of the little figures, in the manner already taught. Thus, for the height of the figure D, draw a parallel to the base line, till it cut the line B in the point E ; from which a perpendicular is to be raised, cutting the line C O in the point F : and take the height of this perpendicular E F, for the height of the figure in the point D. If you likewise require the height of the figures in the point G and H, proceed after the same manner as in the figure D, and you will have their heights between the lines B and C ; to be taken in the compasses, and set off in the points G and H. The same you are to do for any other figures, still diminishing, till at length you come to a mere point.

This is all I have to say as to the measures of figures in perspective. But as I have ingaged myself to give all the measures of this kind, the following rules come in my way, though they have no strict relation to that art.

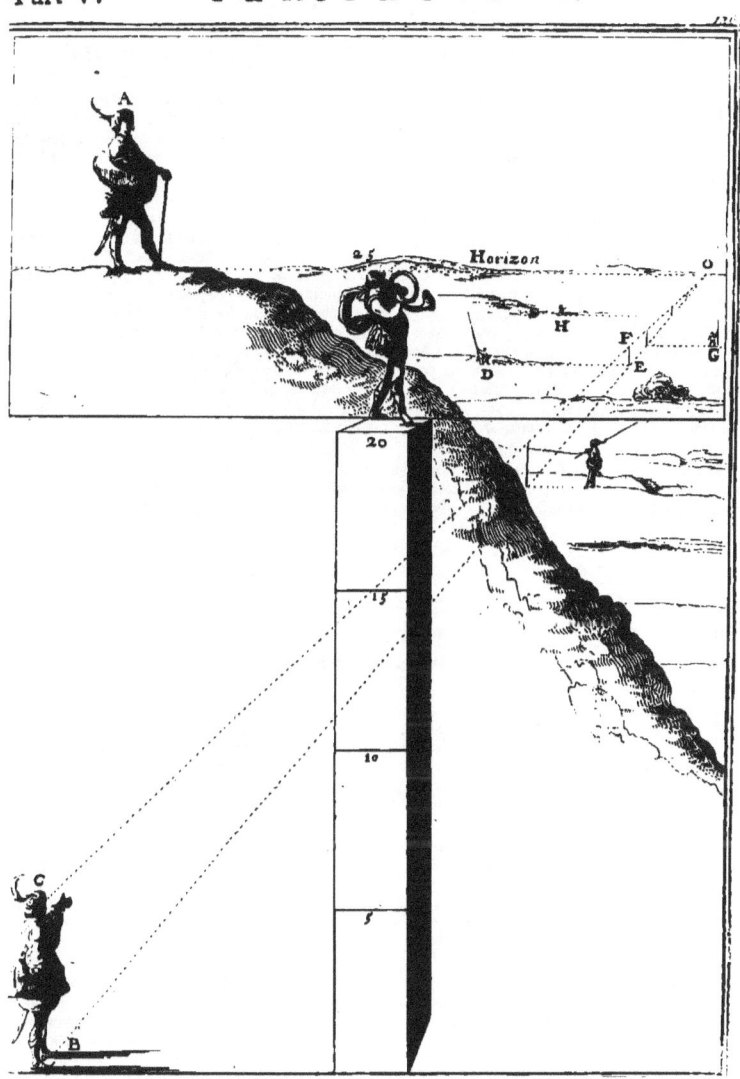

To give the natural or any other Height to Figures much elevated.

TO omit nothing relating to the heights of figures, I add the two following rules. The firſt given by *Albert Durer, Serlio,* and others, for adjuſting the ſize of letters in inſcriptions ſo as they may appear of the ſame ſize as others below. Which rule may be applied to find the meaſures and magnitude of figures placed at different heights to appear equal when viewed by the ſpectator placed at any height.

Thus in B there is a man five feet high, and fifty diſtant from the tower A, viewing the firſt figure C, which there appears of the natural ſize; and thirty feet higher another figure is to be placed, which ſhall appear of the ſame ſize as the other when viewed from the ſame place. Now, to find its dimenſions deſcribe a quadrant of a circle, or a leſſer arch, on a paper to be placed before the eye; then looking at the figure C, it will give the diſtance or angle, E F, on the paper. This done, without moving the quadrant, look at the point D, where the foot of the figure D I is to be; and obſerve what point it gives in the quadrant, namely G. And from this point G ſet off the ſame diſtance or angle, as that of the figure C, that is to ſay, E F, which being removed to G gives G H. Then looking through the point H, note what part of the perpendicular raiſed from D is cut thereby, namely, the point I; then will the interval D I, be the height required for the figure to be placed there. If you would have another ſtill higher, the ſame operation muſt be re-peated, and they will all appear of the natural bigneſs to the ſpectator, B.

If you require the reaſon thereof, you muſt recollect the principles already laid down, or recur to them again; and you will find that all objects viewed under equal angles appear equal. Now it is cer-tain, that the angle G H is equal to E F; conſequently the figure D I muſt appear equal to the figure C.

To find in what Proportion equal Figures grow leſs to the Eye, when placed over one another.

THE ſpectator K having a quadrant or part of a circle, like that of the former ſpectator B, looks towards the firſt figure M of the tower L; which there appears of the natural ſize, Then taking its meaſure from head to foot he marks the diſtance thereof on the quadrant, namely, N O. After this, without ſtirring out of his place, he directs his eye to the head of figure P, and marks the angle it gives on his quadrant Q R. And if there be others ſtill higher, he ſhould t.ke them all after the ſame manner, and lay them down on his quadrant.

Now to find the difference between the one and the other, take the angles or diſtances of each in your compaſſes, and you will find that the higheſt gives the ſmalleſt angle, and of conſequence appears the ſmalleſt to the eye; the figure P only appears half the ſize of the figure M, though in reality both figures are of equal magnitude. If you aſk the reaſon of this different appearance, I anſwer that the angle of the higheſt figure P, is only half that of the lower figure M; as you ſee that Q R is only half of N O, or nearly ſo.

By the knowledge of this rule we may arrive at that above, and by that above we can come at this. For if M and P be the ſame magnitude, and yet P appear to be only half of M, we may ſecurely ſay, that to make P appear as big as M, it muſt be twice its preſent magnitude. The ſame may be ſaid of the upper figure, where D, which is double to C, appears of the ſame ſize to a ſpectator in B. It might be added, that if the figure C was removed to D it would only appear half as big; ſo that one rule is the reverſe of the other. Both the firſt and ſecond rules are beſt put in practice by the little foot, as the figures hitherto have been; by which we come to the difference and proportion of figures as ſecurely as if they were taken from the life by a quadrant.

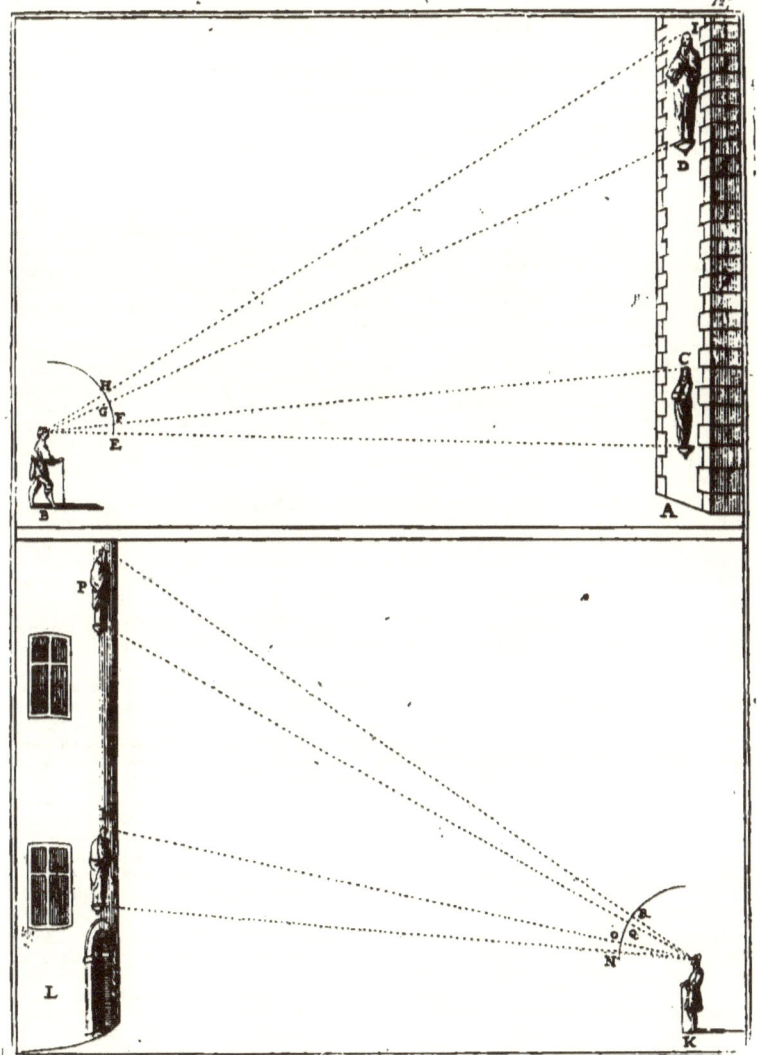

Meafures for elevated Figures.

FROM what has been faid concerning the diminution of figures when placed on high, we are to take our meafures in proportion, for fuch as are to be raifed in paintings, whether they be placed on mountains, the tops of houfes, or above the clouds in the air. The two rules I fhall now give, will render the method extremely eafy.

For the firft. Suppofe the man A to be fix feet; which height fet off feveral times on the perpendicular B, and from the feveral divifions 6, 12, 18, &c. draw lines to the head of the figure A. Then fetting one leg of the compaffes in the point A, with the other defcribe the arch C D, and the interfections that arch makes with the rays, are the meafures to be given the figures at thofe feveral heights or perpendiculars B. Thus, if you would have a figure appear forty two feet high ; take E D, which cuts the two laft rays, and fet it off to F, which is forty two feet above the bafe line A B. If another be required thirty feet high, the diftance G H muft be taken, which cuts the ray 30, 36, and gives the height of the figure P ; and fo of the reft. The main point is the approaching or receding of the line B ; which muft always be the diftance between the fpectator and the object, namely here, thirty feet, or thereabout.

For the fecond rule. Inftead of the perpendicular B ufed in the firft figure, I here put the divifion from fix feet to fix on the bafe line I T. The two firft points I and 6 are to be drawn to the point of fight K. Thus between the two rays I K, and 6 K, we have the meafures of fix feet, which is the height to be given the figures. Then from all the other divifions 12, 18, 24, 30, &c. draw lines to the point of diftance L, and in the interfections made with the ray 6 K, draw little parallels to the bafe line, between the rays I K, and 6 K. Thefe parallels will give the heights of figures of equal magnitude, but at different diftances. Which may be proved by comparing the meafures of the firft method with thofe of the fecond.

If it be afked how much each figure is diminifhed from the firft, which is fix feet high, you need only to take the height of the figure required in your compaffes, and fet it off on the little fcale M, and the queftion is folved. Thus having taken the height of the figure B, and fet it on the fcale M, it gives four feet ; which fhews, that a figure fix feet high, raifed thirty feet, will only appear to be four feet. The heights or diminutions of the reft are found by the fame operation ; provided the diftance be the fame with that of thefe. If the diftance be changed the procefs muft be begun anew.

The figures V, X, Y, placed in the clouds are of the fame height and proportion as the figures in the uppermoft draught. They are only here added to fhew, that though the method be different the effects are the fame.

What has been faid as to the diminutions of figures elevated over the bafe line A B in the firft method, and I T in the fecond, muft be obferved in proportion between thofe figures which are funk farther behind. Thofe of them which are placed on an elevation muft have the fame relative magnitude according to their heighth with the figure on the ground, on the fame line with them, as F and P have to A. Thus, in the fecond rule, if over-againft the laft figure N, another figure C, be placed on a tower forty eight feet high, its magnitude muft be in the fame proportion to N, as the figure at N has to that at I. And inafmuch as the figure at N contains only two and a half of the fix parts which I contains, this at O upon the tower muft only have two and a half of the fix parts in the figure N. If I would have another figure R, on another tower, forty eight feet high oppofite the figure Q, I take two parts and a half of the figure Q for the height of the figure. If another were required in S, which is thirty feet high, in the fame tower, he muft take four of the fix parts of the figure Q, that is, four feet ; as already mentioned in the firft method between the rays G and H.

What renders this rule the more valuable is, that all the proportions of figures may be learnt by heart. For whoever would be at the trouble of making this meafure, where he might add more parts, they would ferve him in all cafes ; and he would render them fo familiar, that in a little time he would tell you off hand, that if you are thirty-five feet diftant, and the figure fix feet, or fix parts high, when on the ground, another, that fhall be of the fame fize, will only appear five and a half when raifed to the height of twelve feet ; only five, if raifed eighteen feet ; only four and a half, if twenty four feet ; only four, if thirty ; only three, if thirty-fix ; and only two and a half, if forty-two : and fo on, by fix and fix, to any number at pleafure.

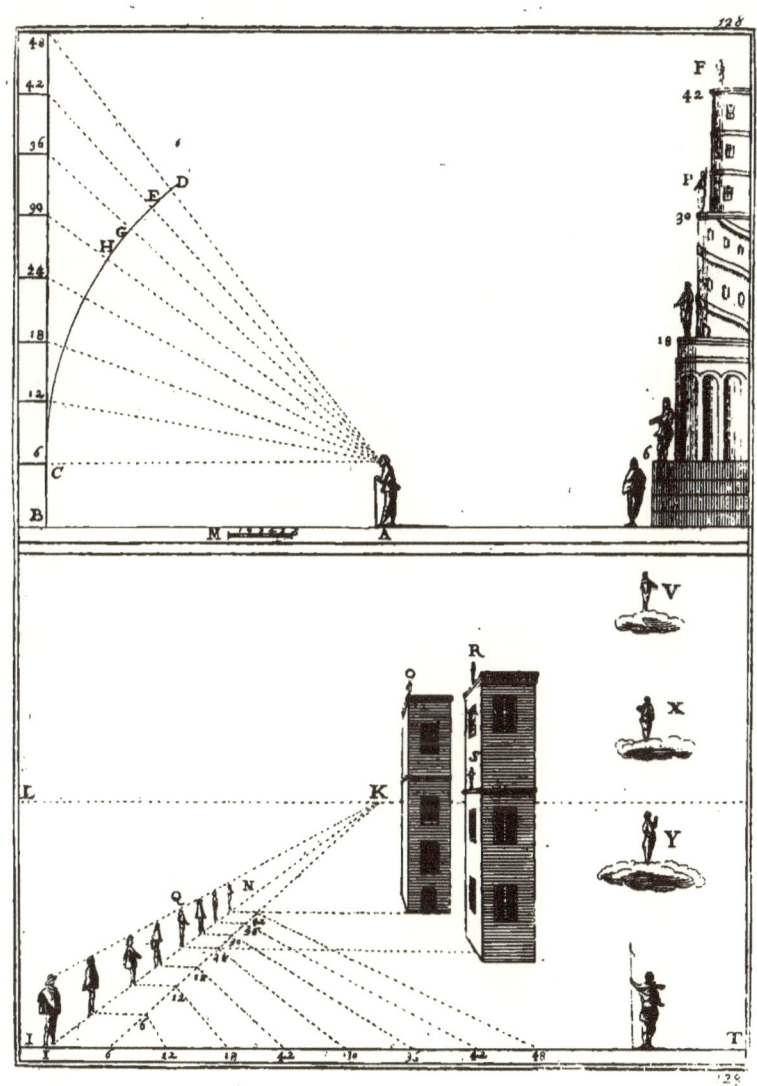

M E T H O D S

Of finding according to the Laws of PERSPECTIVE, the

N A T U R A L S H A D O W S

OF

O B J E C T S

Both by the

SUN, CANDLE, TORCH, and LAMP.

P A R T V.

The Origin of Shadows, *with the Laws of their Projection from opaque Bodies.*

TO *define a natural shadow,* we do not call it an absolute privation of all light, for this would be to form a perfect obscurity, wherein objects would be no more seen than their shadows : but by *shadow* is meant diminution of light, occasioned by the interposition of some opaque body, which receiving and intercepting the light that should be cast on the plane, gives there its own shadow. For the rays of light diverge, and diffuse themselves on every thing not hid therefrom, particularly on every plain and smooth substance, but where there happens the least elevation, a shadow is produced, which exhibits the figure of the illumined part on the plan.

The *diversity of luminaries* occasions a difference of shadows; for if the body that illumines be larger than the body illumined, the shadow will be less than the body. If they be equal, the shadow will be equal to the illumined, and if the luminary be less than the object, the shadow will be continually enlarging as it goes farther off.

The better to comprehend this, I here add three figures, which may serve as a foundation for all the rules to be advanced hereafter.

The first shews, that the luminous body A B, being larger than the illumined sphere C D, enlightens more than half the object, and gives a pointed or conical shadow, whereof the luminary is the base. This truth is evinced in an eclipse of the moon, which is rarely quite covered by the shadow of the earth, though the latter be above forty times bigger than the former. The reason is, that the sun, which is the luminary, is one hundred times bigger in diameter than the earth, which therefore it illumines more than half, and of consequence makes its shadow terminate in a point.

In the second figure, the luminous body F G is equal to the illumined sphere H I, therefore half of the object is enlightened, and its shadow projected parallel; H I K L, and it will be propagated in that form to whatever distance the luminary is capable of acting.

The third figure shews, that the luminary or light M, being less than the illumined N O, that object is not half enlightened. And of consequence the shadow N O P Q enlarging as it recedes farther from the object, makes a pyramid, whereof the luminary is the point or vertex.

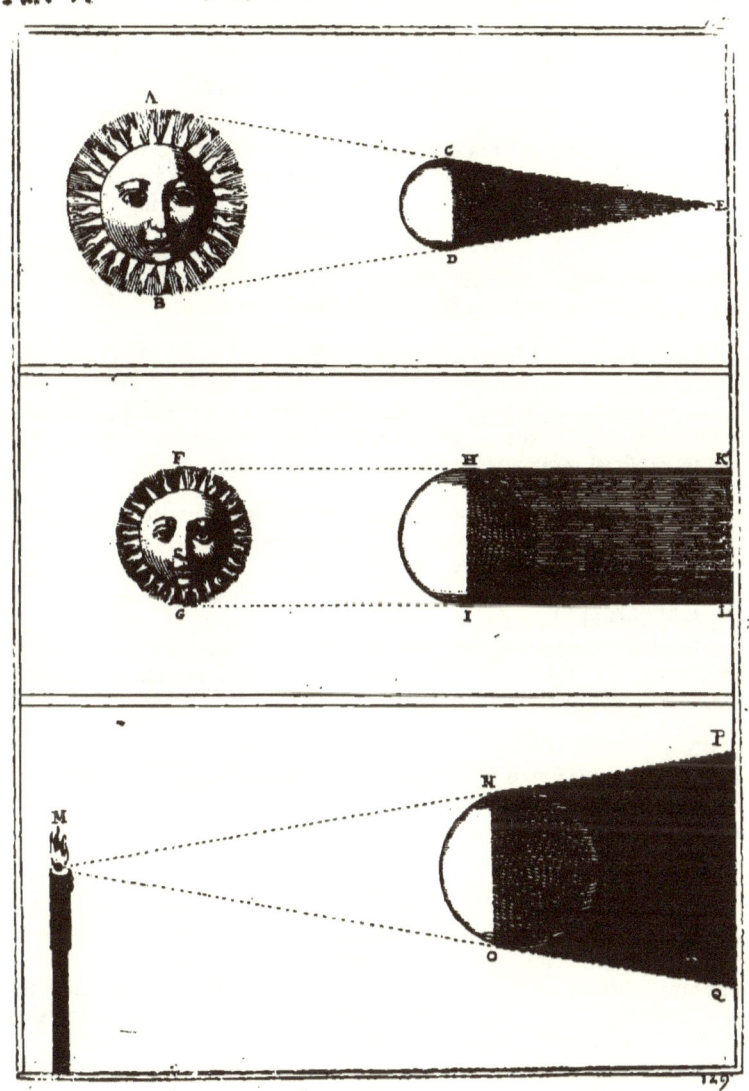

Of the Difference of Shadows.

FROM what has been obferved in the preceding page we draw this conclufion, that the fame objeĉt may projeĉt fhadows of divers forms, though ftill illumined on the fame fide; the fun giving one form, the torch another, and the day-light no precife form at all.

The Sun always makes the fhadow of breadth equal to the opaque objeĉt, that is, projeĉts it parallel-wife, as in the firft figure.

How this method is to be put in praĉtice, and every objeĉt have its natural fhadow, fhall be fhewn hereafter. It is certainly of confequence to all painters, engravers, *&c.* to obferve thefe rules precifely, and not indifferently to ufe the fame method for fhadows produced by the fun and by artificial luminaries, as is too frequently done.

The fhadow produced by a torch or flambeau is not projeĉted in parallels, but in rays proceeding from a center; whence the fhadow is always bigger than the opaque body, and grows bigger as it recedes the farther. this is fhewn in the fecond figure, where the fhadow is larger than in the firft, though the cube of the one and the other be of equal breadth and height. It appears, therefore, a grofs abufe, to reprefent the fhadow of a torch like that of the fun, and the fhadow of the fun like that of a candle, when the difference is fo confiderable.

There is a third kind of fhadow, neither produced by the fun nor a torch, but only a fine clear day, which wanting ftrength to finifh and define its form occafions a dimnefs near the objeĉt, as in the third figure. Now for this there is no certain rule, but every body conduĉts it at difcretion.

All thefe fhadows, both thofe of the *fun*, of the *torch*, and of the *day-light*, muft appear darker than the parts of objeĉts not illumined. Thus A is lefs dark than B, by reafon A receives the refleĉtion of the brightnefs around it, and B has no refleĉtion but from A, which itfelf is in obfcurity. It muft be obferved by the way, that the part of the fhadow moft remote from the objeĉt is ftill darker than that neareft it; as G is darker than H, by reafon A cannot communicate the little reflexion it receives, as far as G, though it does to H.

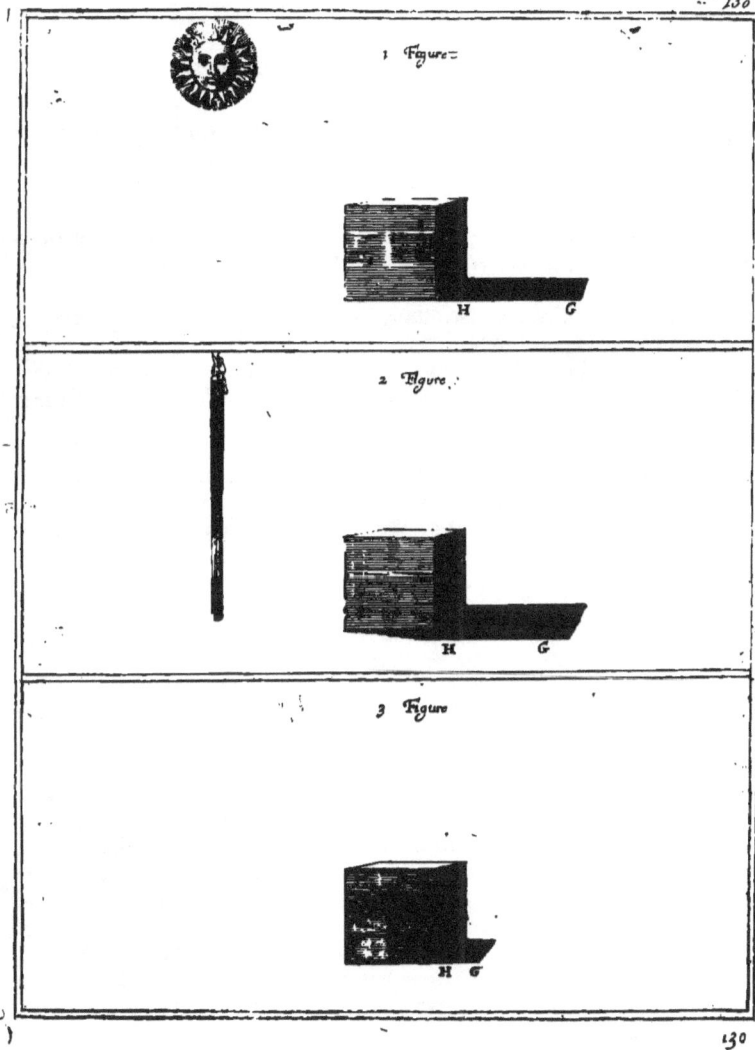

1 Figure

H   G

2 Figure

H   G

3 Figure

H G

To find the Form of the Shadows.

I·T may be remembered, at the entrance of this work, PERSPECTIVE was defined the art of reprefenting objeɛts which are on the ground or horizontal plane, upon a plane perpendicular to the horizon. But in the bufinefs of fhadows it is quite the reverfe, fince we there conceive a body raifed over the plan, which being illumined, cafts its own fhadow on the plan ; as the body A gives a fhadow B, on the plan.

To produce a fhadow, two things are fuppofed, namely, light and an opaque body. Light, though quite contrary to fhadow, gives it its being, as the opaque objeɛt gives its form and figure. *What we have here to con-fider is the fhadows, the reader has been already inftruɛted in what relates to putting the bodies in perfpeɛtive.*

To conceive the nature of fhadows more clearly, and render the prac-tice more eafy, it muft be obferved, there are two points to be made ufe of. One of them is the foot of the light, which is always taken on the plan the objeɛt is placed upon ; the other is the luminary. The rule being common to the fun, torch, or any other light, with this difference, that the fun projeɛts the fhadow in parallels, and the torch in rays, from the fame center. I begin with the fhadow produced by the torch, as leading to a more eafy underftanding of that by the fun.

Suppofe then, for example, it is defired to have the fhadow of the cube A here reprefented in B, lines muft be drawn from O, the foot of the luminary, through all the angles of the plan of the cube, as here O D, O E, O F, O G. Then other lines are to be drawn from the point of the light of the torch C, through all the raifed angles, till they in-terfeɛt the lines from the point O. Thus having drawn a line from O through the angle D, another muft be drawn from C through the raifed angle, interfeɛting the former in H, which point H will be the fhadow of that angle. And if from the fame point C, the fame be done through all the raifed angles, the lines of the plan will be cut in the points H I K L, thefe points being conneɛted together by right lines, you will have the fhadow of the cube, as is fhewn in the uppermoft figure of interfeɛtion, and more diftinɛtly in that below.   2

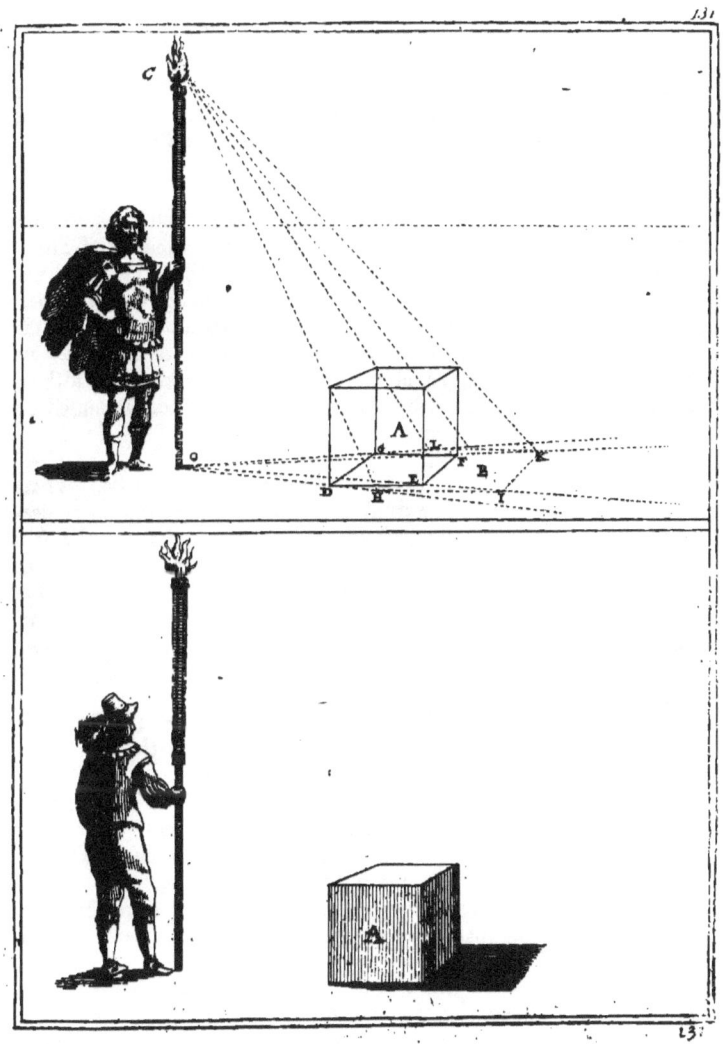

Shadows *from the* Sun.

THE fun, that magnificent luminary, being vaftly larger than the terreftrial globe, as has been already intimated, muft give the fhadow of that fphere pointed, by reafon it always illumines more than half thereof.

In confequence of this demonftration we might conclude, that all the fun's fhadows muft be lefs than the bodies that project them, and diminifh more and more as they recede farther. Now this would be true, were there any conceivable relation of magnitude between the illumined body and the illuminer; but as all objects on the earth are fo fmall, either in comparifon of that ftar or of the earth, the diminution of their fhadows is imperceptible to the eye, which fees them always of equal breadth to the body that forms them. On this account all the fhadows caufed by the fun are made in parallels, as is fhewn in page 130.

From the whole it appears, that to find the fhadow of any body whatever, oppofed to the fun, a line muft be drawn from that luminary perpendicular to the place where, according to former directions, the foot of the light is to be taken, and from this point an occult line is to be drawn through one of the angles of the plan of the object, and another from the fun through the raifed angle; the interfection of the two lines will exprefs how far the fhadow is to go. The other line muft be drawn parallel hereto.

For example, to find the fhadow of the cube A, the fun being in B. From the bottom of the fun C, which is, as it were, the foot of the light, draw a line through one of the angles of the plan, as C D. Then from the other angle E, draw a parallel to this line. The breadth of the fhadow being thus finifhed, to find the extreme thereof, draw a line from the fun B, through the raifed angle F, cutting the line C D in G. Then drawing a parallel to this line through the angle H, it will cut the line E in the point I; thefe two points G and I being connected by a ftrait line compleats the fhadow of the cube D G I.

If you defire to have the fhadows caft forward, or any other way, you have only to determine the place of the fun, and the point beneath it, to draw the lines of the fame angle, and the other lines parallel thereto. The method is the fame as in the former cafe, fo that it needs not be repeated. The figure fhews the reft.

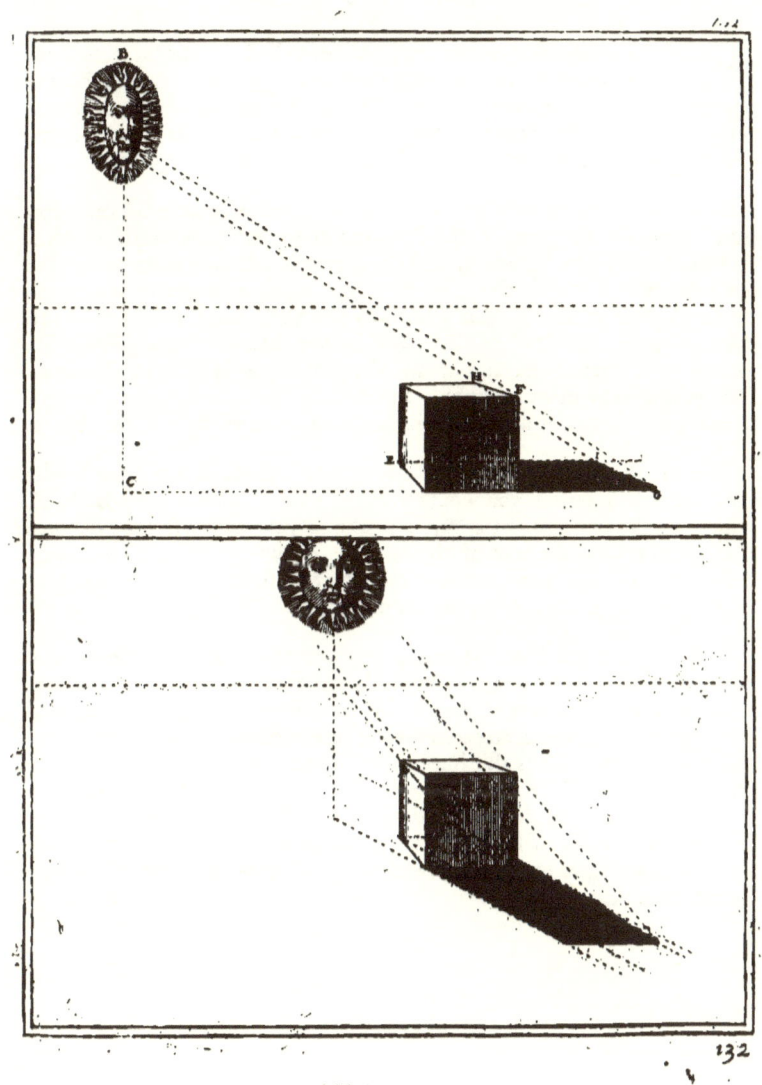

The Shadows *produced by the Sun are equal in all Objects of same Height, though at a Distance from each other.*

EXPERIENCE teaches us, that feveral elevations of the fame height, removed to a diftance from each other, do yet project equal fhadows at the fame time. I fay in the fame time, for the fhadows are lengthening and fhortning, in proportion as the fun comes nearer or recedes farther off; one or other of which he is continually doing.

For this reafon, when the fhadow of an object is to be produced, you muft determine the place of the fun, and the point underneath which I call the foot of the luminary, and draw two occult lines from them, for the extremity of the fhadow; as here the palifade A gives the extreme of its fhadow in B. And if from this point B, you draw a line to the point of fight C, this line B C will be the fhadow of the palifade D, as well as of that of A, and of all others of equal height in the fame line to the very point of fight. In effect, it muft be held for a certain maxim, that fhadows always retain the fame point of fight as the objects.

On the footing of this obfervation, that objects of the fame height give equal fhadows, if you would give the fhadow of the palifades E, F, which are the fame height as A, D; take in your compaffes the diftance A B, and fet it on the foot of the palifade E, by which you will have E G; then from G draw a line to the point of fight C. And thus you are to proceed, be the walks ever fo numerous.

If the light come from the fore-part, as in the figure underneath, the method muft not be altered; but only the foot, or bottom of the fun, is to be brought nearer or farther off according to the fun's place, and lines drawn from the center and foot of the luminary through the upper and lower angles. Thus the lines from H and I give the extreme of the fhadow of the palifade K, in the point L; and from L a line drawn to the point of fight M limits the fide fhadow. From the remote angles of the plan of the palifade, a parallel to the line H drawn as far as the ray L M, will give the extreme end of the fhadow, and the whole will appear natural.   3

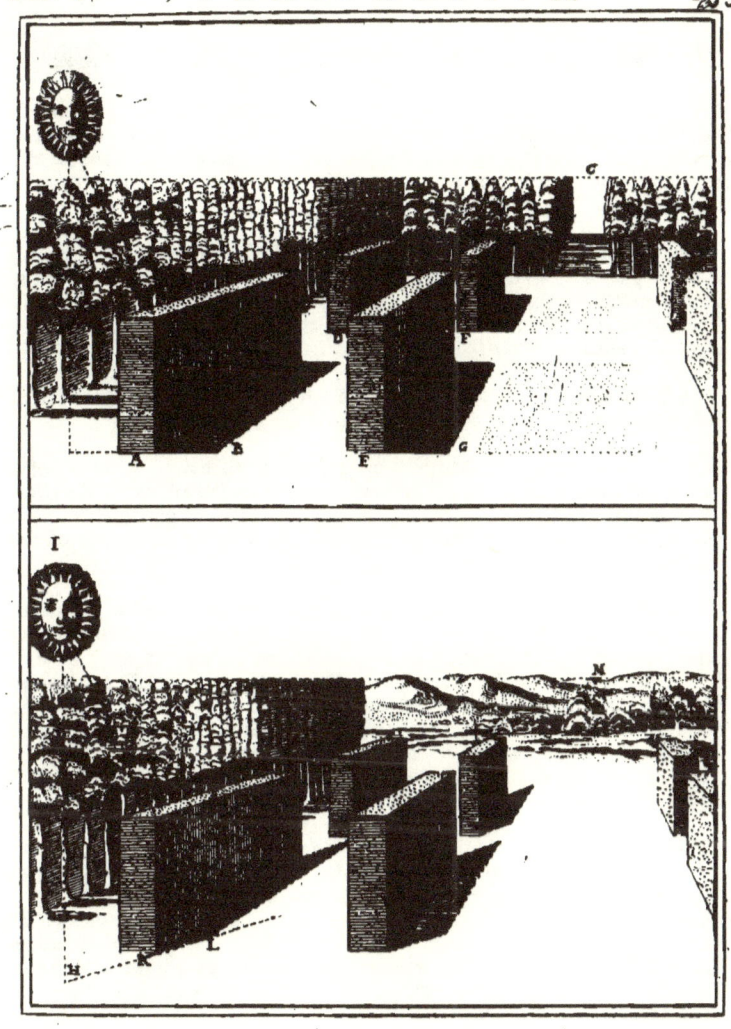

Q q 2

Of Shadows, *when the Sun is directly opposed to the Eye.*

AS often as the fun is before the eye, that is, directly over the point of
fight, the fides of the fhadow it produces will be parallels, as all the
vifual rays are. For this reafon, the point of fight is always to ferve for the
foot of the light when in that altitude, and the other ray, that is to determine
the fhadow, will be taken from the center of the fun.

Thus the fhadow of the cube A being required, draw lines through the angles of its plan B C, to the point of fight D, as the lines B E and C F. Then,
from the center of the fun G, draw two rays cutting the former in the points
K and L, and paffing through the raifed angles H and I. By this means the
fhadow of the cube will be found in B K L C.

The fhadows of the two other objects, M and N, are found by the fame rule,
and fo might the fhadow of any object whatever.

But my mind fuggefts, that there might be fome difficulty, if, inftead of a
cube, a pyramid were given ; by reafon the ray from the middle of the pyramid, and that from the fun, paffing through its vertex or point, only make
one line ; and of confequence cannot terminate any thing for the fhadow of the
vertex of that pyramid.

When this happens, draw a line from the point of fight P, through one of
the angles of the plan ; by which means you will have O Q. Then from O
erect a perpendicular O S, and from the point of the pyramid T draw a parallel to the bafe, till it cut the perpendicular O S in the point V. Draw the ray
of the fun through this point, and continue it till it cut the ray O Q in the
point X ; from X draw a parallel to the bafe, as far as the ray of the middle of
the pyramid, which will be cut thereby in the point Y, the extreme of the
fhadow. To Y draw lines from the angles Z and O ; and the triangles Z Y O
will be the fhadow of the pyramid.

The like you are to do for the oppofite face, if it be perpendicular to the
plan ; and the fame rule will ferve in all cafes. For example, if the point, or
apex correfpond to the center of the plan, draw a line from the fame center
parallel to the bafe, and of any length at difcretion ; and from the end of the
line, as here from O, draw a line to the point of fight, and proceed as before.
Which will be a ftanding rule, whether the pyramid be viewed in front or
fide-wife. And hence you will eafily judge what is to be done, if the point or
vertex correfpond to any other ray of the middle of the plan.

The walls in the front of each figure have their fhadows as already taught
in that of the cube A.   4

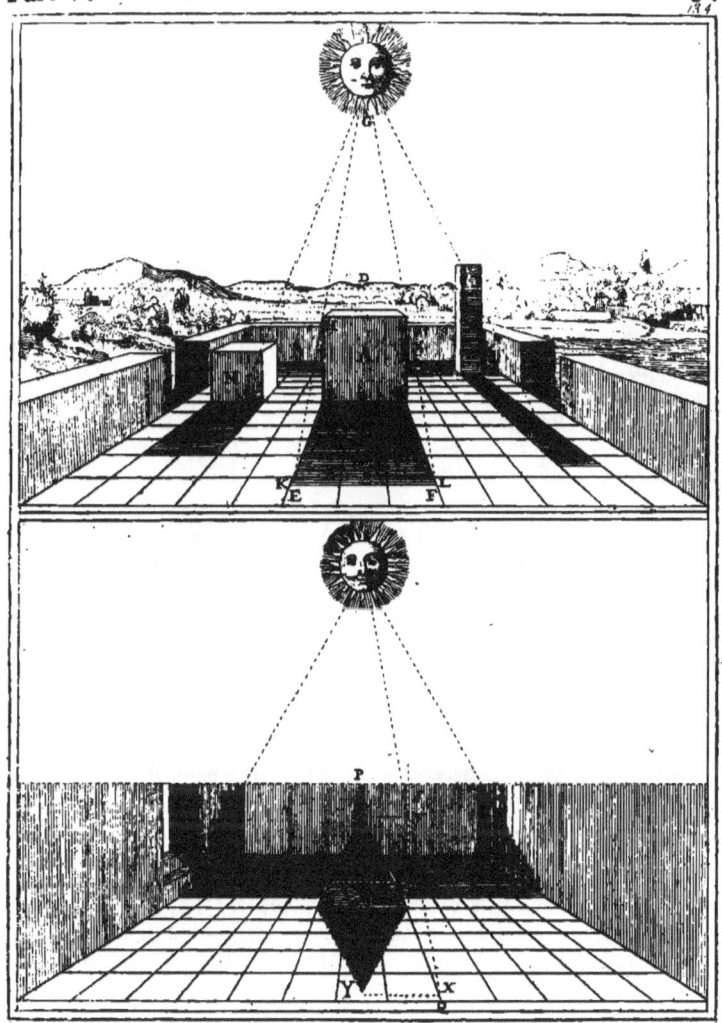

For the Shadows *of perforated Objects.*

WHEN the object is square or rectilinear, a line must be drawn from the foot of the luminary through the angles of the plan for one fide of the shadow, and parallels thereto for the other fides; then from the middle of the fun B, draw a line through the raifed angle C, which will cut the line from A, in the point D; through which point a line must be drawn to the point of fight, till it meet the remoteft line from the plan F. To find the reft of the shadows; draw parallels to the line B C D, through the angles G H I; and inafmuch as the fun illuminates two fides of the object, and makes the shadow broader, as is shewn in the figure, where G C and H I are the diagonal of the fquare pieces; where thefe lines drawn through G C and H I cut the line A, a line must be drawn to the point of fight E; and you will have the whole projection, or shadow of the object.

If it be a round object, as reprefented in the fecond figure, a circle muft be defcribed, according to the rule given for arches in pages 62, 63, by erecting of perpendiculars, &c. And when the circle is formed, and its thickneffes given, from the bottom of thofe perpendiculars, parallels to the bafe muft be drawn; as here K, L. Then taking L, which is the parallel of the middle of the circle, for the foot of the luminary, from the middle of the fun M, draw a line paffing over the circle N, and continue it till it cuts the parallel L in the point O; which will be the extremity of the shadow. The vacuity or aperture of the rotundo is found by drawing a parallel to N O from the point P, which is the top of the object oppofite to the fun, till it cut the line L O. The reft of the rotundo will be found by drawing another little parallel to N O from the point R, which will give S. The reft of the round object is found by drawing parallels to N O, through all the points of the circle of perpendiculars, which are to be continued till they cut the parallels to the bafe line; as is here done for that of the middle L O. I could eafily mark them all with points, but I forbear it to avoid confufion.

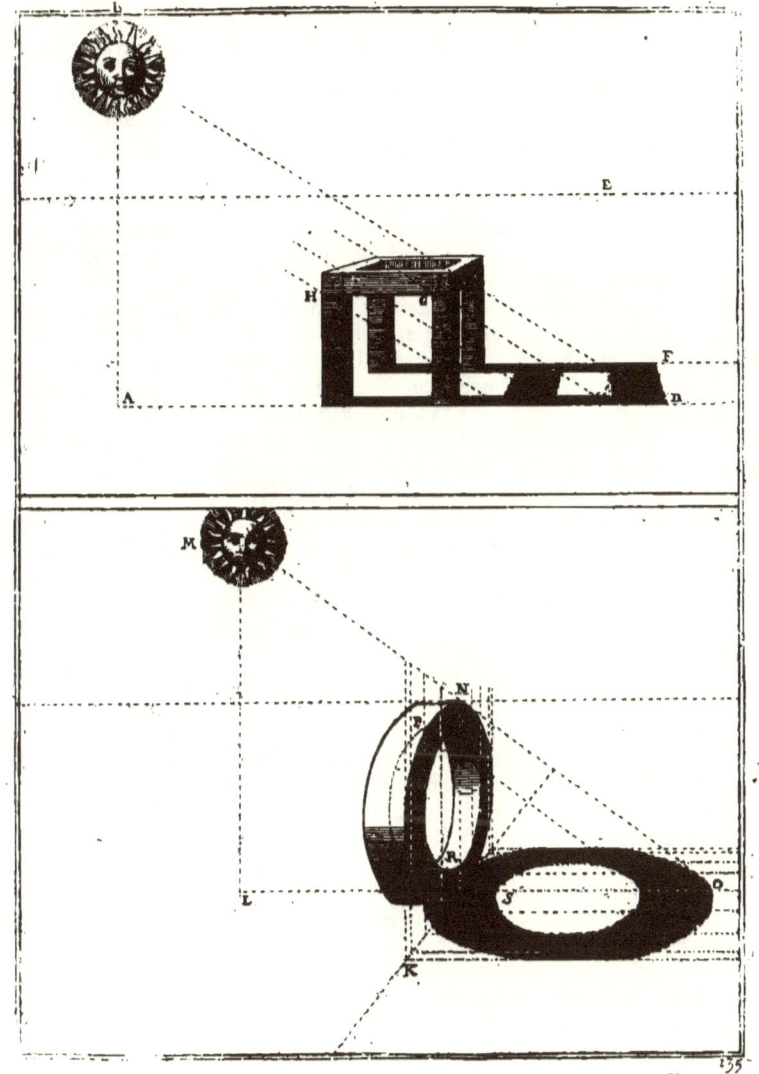

Shadows *aſſume the Form of the Planes they are caſt upon.*

HITHERTO I have conſidered ſhadows on the horizontal plane; being certain that a perſon who underſtands ſuch, will find no difficulty in the practice of the reſt which follow. For the rule is the ſame in all; and one ſingle inſtruction will ſuffice to ſhew how ſhadows ſink and riſe according to the planes on which they are caſt.

To ſhew that theſe ſhadows are formed by the ſame rule as thoſe preceding, draw a line from the foot of the luminary A, through the plan of the door B; and another from the ſun C, over the top of the ſame door at D; theſe lines will interſect each other, though without the limits of our page, and give the extremity of the ſhadow; as already is obſerved of the others on the horizontal plane. But the wall E preventing the line A B from being continued as it ſhould be if the plane was horizontal, obliges it to riſe, as we ſee in F G. For this reaſon the ſun's rays, which ſhould proceed to meet the line A B, cuts it on the wall in the point G, and there marks the form or ſhadow of the door; the top whereof is drawn to the point of ſight H.

The ſhadow of the object K is caſt in all its length K I, and paſſes over that other L. And it is to be obſerved, that the ſhadow ſtill preſerves its length, though it meets with a raiſed object in the way: and that the ſhadow which paſſes over any thing aſſumes the ſame figure, as here the ſhadow M and N takes the form of the object L, or rather is loſt in the ſhadow of L.

Though I have made the ſun to appear in all my figures, it muſt not be imagined that he is ſo near the objects. My intention was to ſhew that the rays proceed from him when at ſuch a height, though far without the limits of the paper, as in this ſecond figure, which yet has the line for the foot of the ſun A B, and that of the rays of the ſun C; by reaſon thoſe are always required for finding the extremities of the ſhadow.

The ſhadow of the object O is found by continuing the line A B, and making it riſe over the ſteps, and againſt the wall, till cut by the ray in the point S, by the rays paſſing over the corner of the object; and from S drawing a line to the point of ſight T.

To find the ſhadow of the object P, it muſt be remembered (as already obſerved) that the foot of the light is always ſuppoſed on the plan where the object is placed. Accordingly the ray C cutting the little line A B, ſhews how far the ſhadow of the little object P muſt go, to be thence drawn to the point of ſight T.

The object V caſts it ſhadow the uſual length, though in its way it deſcends into a pit and riſes again.

The ſhadow of the wall R, is found by the ſame rule as the reſt; as appears from the lines A B and the ray C.

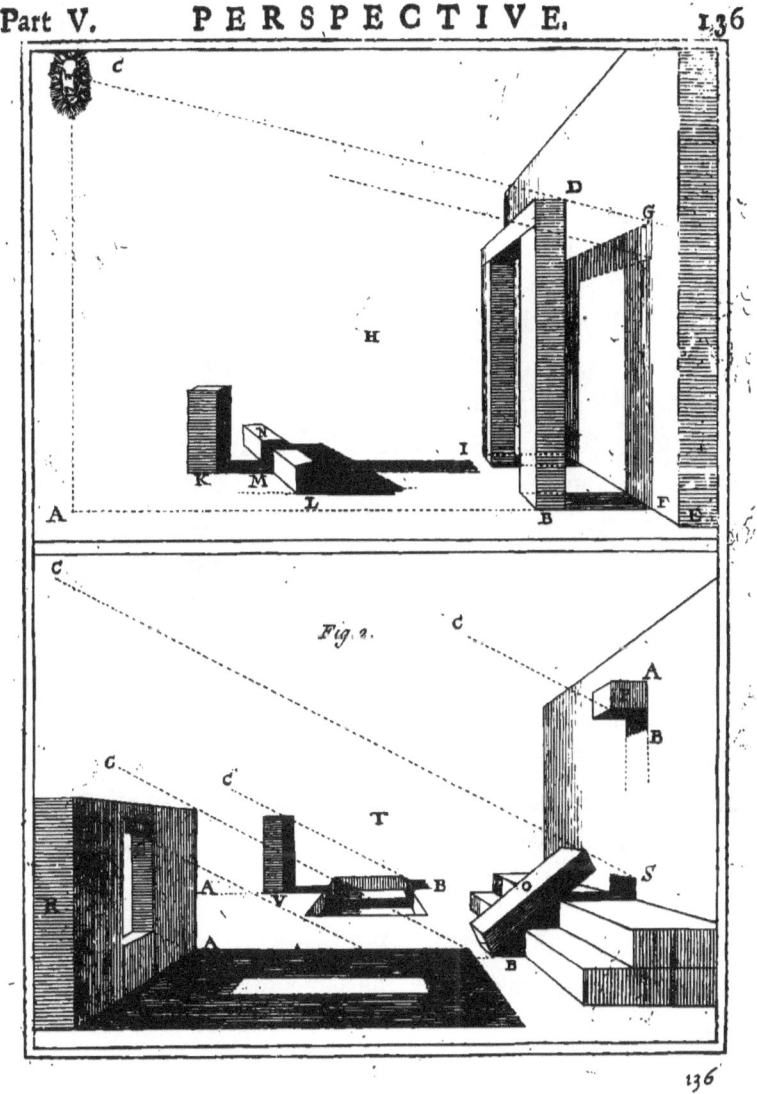

Fig. 2.

R r

❀❀❀❀❀❀❀❀❀❀❀❀❀❀❀❀❀❀❀❀❀❀❀❀❀❀❀❀❀❀❀❀❀❀❀❀❀

To find the Shadows of Objects broader at Top than at Bottom.

WHEN the projection or fhadow of a figure is required, whofe top is broader or wider than the bottom,
as in the two adjoining figures, the ufual method is, to
make a plan, and draw perpendiculars, as B A, B A, from
the fame. The plan finifhed, a line muft be drawn underneath the fun, as already mentioned, and parallels to this
line be drawn from all the angles of the plan. Then a line
is to be drawn from the fun C, through one of the angles
of the object, as D, till it cut the line of the plan of the
fame angle at F. Another line is to be drawn over the angle
A, till it interfects the line B A in the point F. Then drawing lines from E and F to the point of fight, you will have
the fhadow of the fquare of the top of the object. Laftly,
drawing lines from the point of the figure H, to the points
F and L, you will have the fhadow of the whole figure,
which is a pyramid inverted.

It is evident that the projection or fhadow of the crofs underneath is performed after the fame manner, which it is
unneceffary to repeat.

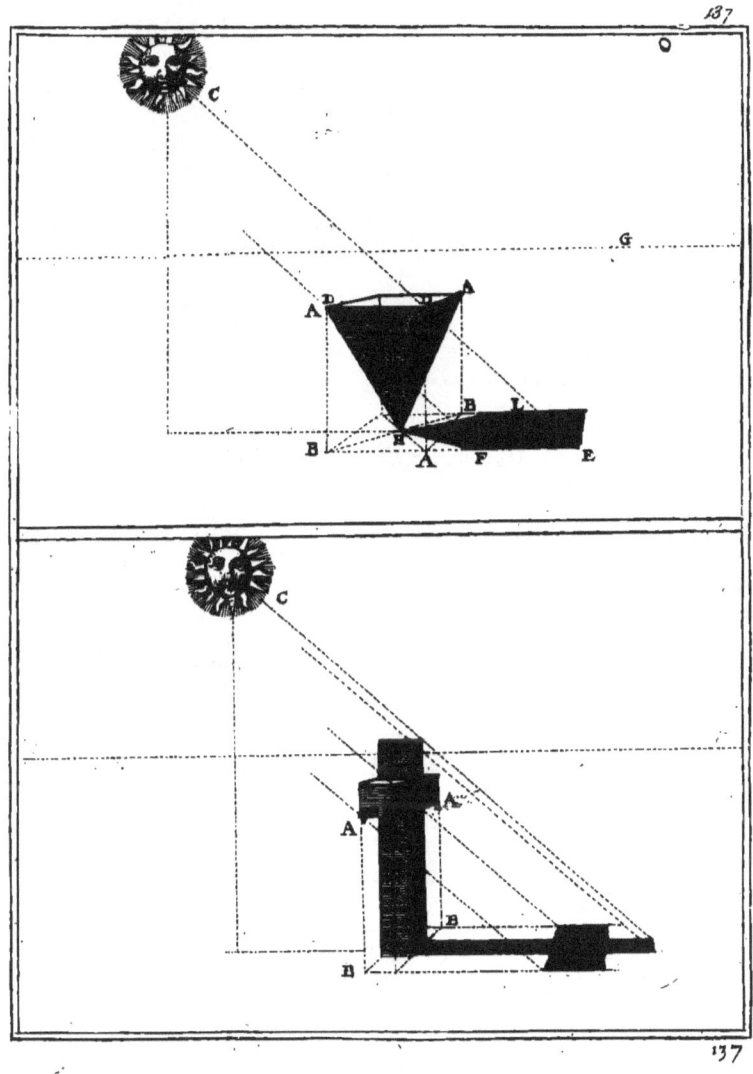

To find the Shadows of Objects suspended from the Ground.

THE method of finding the shadows of objects suspended from the ground is rendered very easy by the preceding rule: all you have to do is to find the plan, and from the angles thereof to draw parallels to meet the perpendicular line under the sun, and then, from the same angles of the objects suspended in the air, to draw other lines, cutting those drawn from the plan; by which means you will find the extremes of the shadows, as already mentioned under the preceding figures.

I am clearly persuaded, that my reader would easily conceive the method of these, or any shadows made by the sun, without farther explanation of the figures here annexed, they being all intelligible, and performed by the rules already taught.

However, as every instance has something particular therein, it may not be improper to take notice thereof, that there may be nothing but what is easily understood.

I observe then, that in the first figure the plan A B C D is alone made use of, to find the shadows of the objects E F, by reason they are both on the same line, and of the same height.

In the second, it must be observed, that the piece of wood G casting its shadow on the wall H, the shadow makes that same figure at the cornice I underneath. And the same is observable of the stick K, raised against the wall H.

To find the shadow of the board L, the rule already delivered for objects broader at top than at bottom, must be remembered; for having drawn the perpendicular M, where it cuts the ray N O, you must draw the line from underneath the sun M P. Then from the board L, drawing a line to cut the line M P; the point of intersection will be the extremity of the shadow.

The shadow of the globe or ball Q is likewise found by letting fall two perpendiculars, of which the plan is to be formed, then through the center of this plan drawing a line from beneath the sun R, and a tangent from the sun, as Q S, till it cut the line R in the point T, and lastly another, as V, cutting the same line R: this interval T V will give the extent of the shadow of the ball.

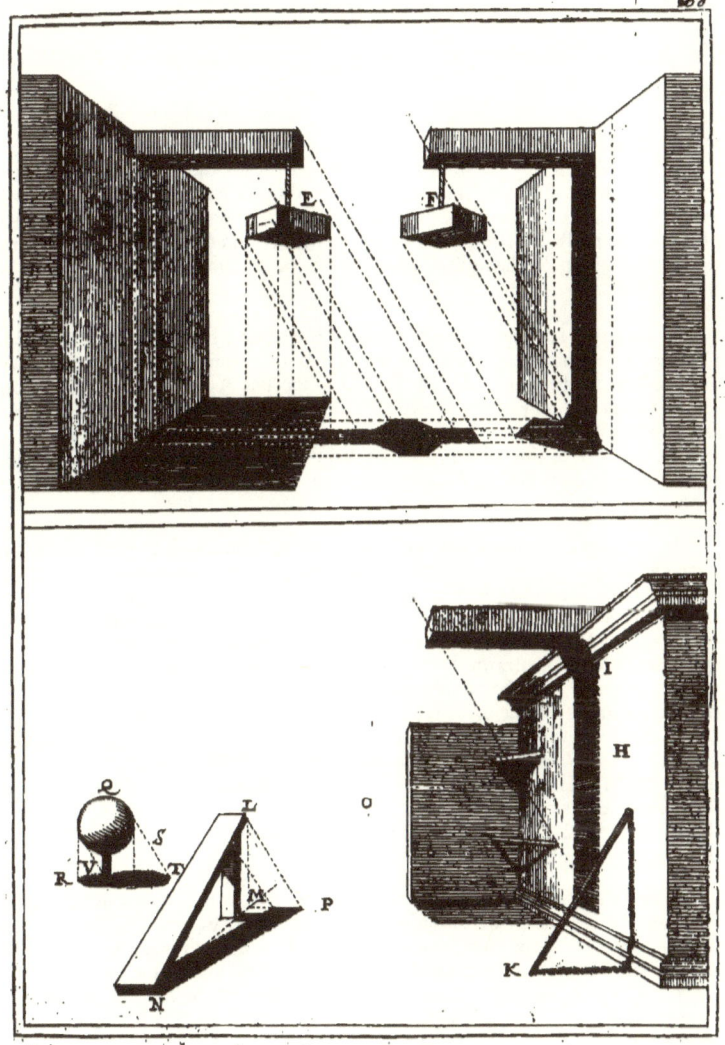

To find the Shadows *of human Figures, caused by the Light of the Sun.*

THE shadow of figures is found by the same methods as those of other bodies, that is, by parallels both from underneath the figure, and from the
sun; with this difference only, that the shadow of other bodies or objects is
found by means of their plan, whereas figures have none. But in lieu of such
plans, a line must be drawn underneath the figure, and on this line, the several
remarkable points of the figure to be let fall perpendicularly, which line is to
serve as a plan.

For example, *In a figure naked, or undressed without a cloak or gown,* as the first
figure hereto adjoining, with its back towards us; from under its feet, as A,
draw a line to the point of sight B, and to this line A B draw occult lines from
all the points that may contribute to the true shadow; thus from the hand C, let
fall a perpendicular, cutting the line A B in the point D, and from the elbow E
let fall another to the point F, and a third from the head G to the point H, and
from all these points D F H, as also from the end of the staff I, draw parallels to
the base line.

Then having determined the height of the sun, a line must be drawn from the
same, as K, passing over the edge of the hat G, and continued till it cut the line
H in the point L, which will be the extreme of the shadow. And again, from
the hind edge of the hat M, draw a parallel to K G L, till it likewise cut the line
H in the point N, these two points N and L will be the shadow of the hat. A
third parallel must be drawn through the point C, till it cut the line D in the point
O, this point O will be the shadow of the hand that holds the staff; drawing
therefore a line from the point O, to the point I, the line O I will be the shadow
of the staff. A fourth parallel is to be drawn through the point E, which cutting F in P, will be the shadow of the elbow. The same do from all the other
parts, as the knees, the feet, &c. These several points connected together, give
the shadow of the whole figure. The shadow of the little figure Q is done by
the same method. I have not expressed all the points and parallels therein, in
order to avoid confusion.

To find the *shadows of figures cloathed in long garments*; draw a line from under their feet to the point of sight, as here the line S R, and through the bottom of the robe draw two parallels to the base line, each way, as the lines T
and V, and between the two another line X for the middle of the figure. Then
from the top of the head draw a line Y, for the ray of the sun, to be continued till it cut the line X in the point Z; which point Z will be the extreme
where the shadow is to terminate. The rest of the shadow will be drawn between the two parallels T and V. If any thing comes over them, as the two
plaits or folds † and *, they must be drawn by parallels to) Z, till they cut
the line V. And thus † gives the shadow of the elbow, and * that of the folds
of the gown.

9

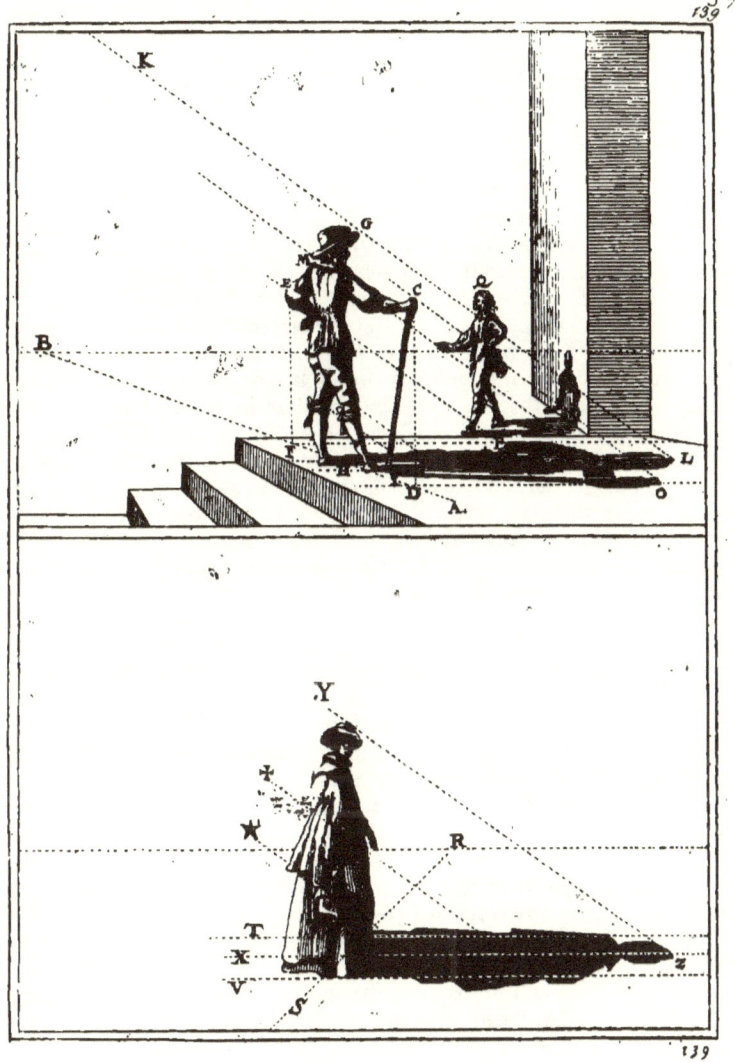

An eaſy Method of finding the Shadow *of a Body from the Sun.*

WERE I here to add the ſhadows of all the objeᶜts that might be given, it would be a work without end, objeᶜts being multipliable to infinity; in effeᶜt, beſides the greatneſs of their number, each particular one might furniſh out a whole book, as being capable to be turned, inclined, and diſpoſed in many and various manners, each of which has its ſeveral ſhadows. But the labour would be uſeleſs, inaſmuch as every body will be prepared to make any at pleaſure, provided he be maſter of two or three rules already laid down for the ſhadows of objeᶜts taken from the ſun, two kinds of lines have been ſhewn to contain the means for finding all ſhadows imaginable; one of the lines coming from under the ſun, and paſſing over the plan, and the other proceeding from the ſun itſelf, and paſſing over the objeᶜt, and cutting the former line in the place where the ſhadow is to terminate. But as theſe lines are to be all parallel, that is, thoſe from under the ſun parallel to each other, and thoſe from the ſun likewiſe parallels among themſelves, it may be neceſſary to give a method of drawing them with expedition and advantage.

I have already ſhewn how to draw parallels to the baſe by means of a ſquare board, as A, and a ruler B, which ſame may ſerve to draw the lines from under the ſun, when found direᶜtly over the face of the objeᶜt, as the line C D. But where he illuminates the objeᶜt from an angle, another inſtrument muſt be uſed, as that here repreſented E, which is a rule faſtened to the end of another piece of wood, well ſquared, and grooved quite through, ſo as the rule F G may be moveable therein with ſome force, and that having taken an inclined line, as H D, another parallel thereto I K may be taken by means of this bevel, which is the name the workmen give this moveable ſquare E F G. This inſtrument ſhortens the work exceedingly, when ſhadows are to be made by the ſun, on which occaſion there is no line of any inclination whatever, but parallels will be required thereto. The application will evince its uſefulneſs. For ſhadows by the candle or torch, it is of no importance, by reaſon all the lines are there drawn from a center.

8

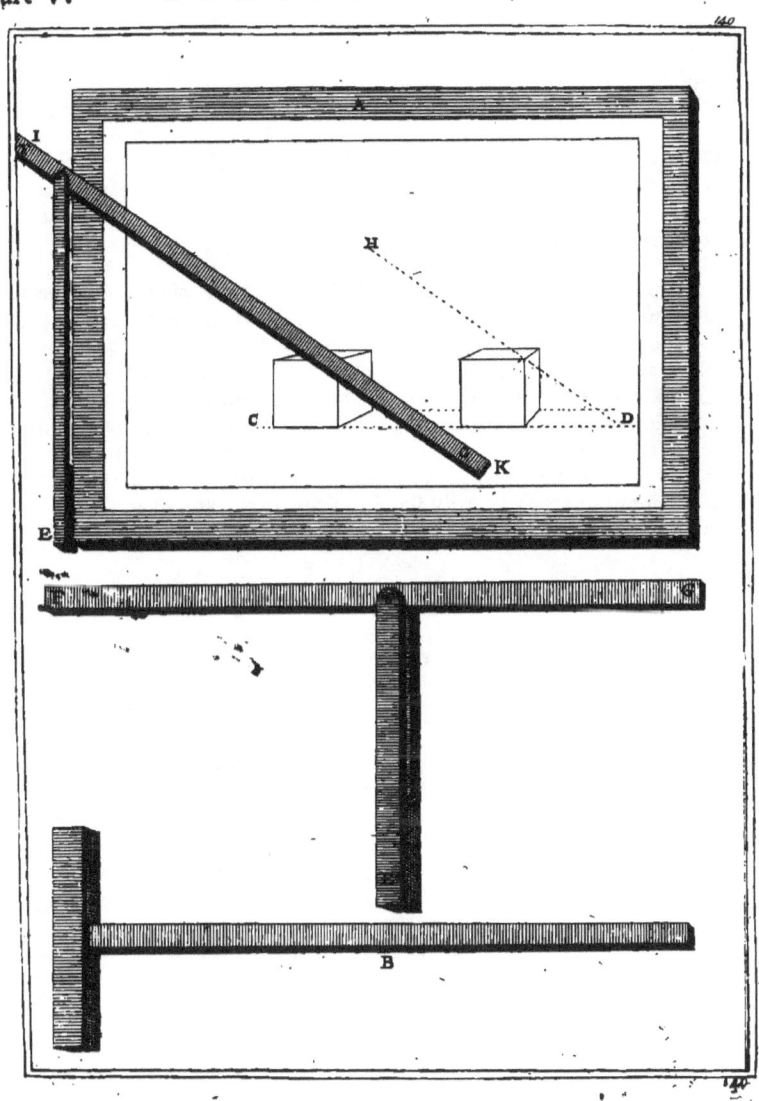

Shadows from a Torch, Flambeau, Candle, *and* Lamp.

IT has been already obſerved, that there are two points required for the finding of ſhadows; the one the foot of the flambeau, candle, lamp, &c. which is always found on the plane where the objeft.is placed, the other in the fire, or flame of thoſe luminaries.

From the firſt point, which is the foot of the flambeau, or beneath the lamp, &c. lines muſt be drawn through all the angles of the plan of the objeft, whoſe ſhadow is required; and the ſecond point gives other rays, which paſſing through the angles of thoſe objefts, inter- feft the former lines, and ſhew where the ſhadow is to terminate. I ſhall illuſtrate this by an example, wherein the ſame letters ſhall be uſed for all the three luminaries, from which it will readily appear, that the praftice is the ſame in all. With this only difference, that the foot of the flambeau or torch aftually ſtands on the plane, and that the others are only conceived to do ſo.

I add then, that if the ſhadows B of the cubes A be required, lines muſt be drawn from the point O, which is the foot of the luminary, through all the angles of the plans of thoſe cubes, as O D, O E, O F, O G, and then from the point C, which is the light or fire of the lumi- naries, other lines muſt be drawn through the angles of the objefts, and continued till they interfeft the former lines from O.

Thus having drawn a line from the point O through the angle of the plan D, drawing another line from C, through the correſpondent angle of the objeft P, this latter line being continued, will cut the firſt from the angle D in the point H, which point will be the ſhadow of that angle D P. From the ſame point C, do the ſame for all the other angles of the plan in the points H I K L, which points being connefted by right lines, give the ſhadow of the cubes, as in the three figures. From this inſtance it readily appears, that the method is the ſame in one as another.

In the following page we ſhall ſhew how to find the bottoms or feet of candles and lamps.

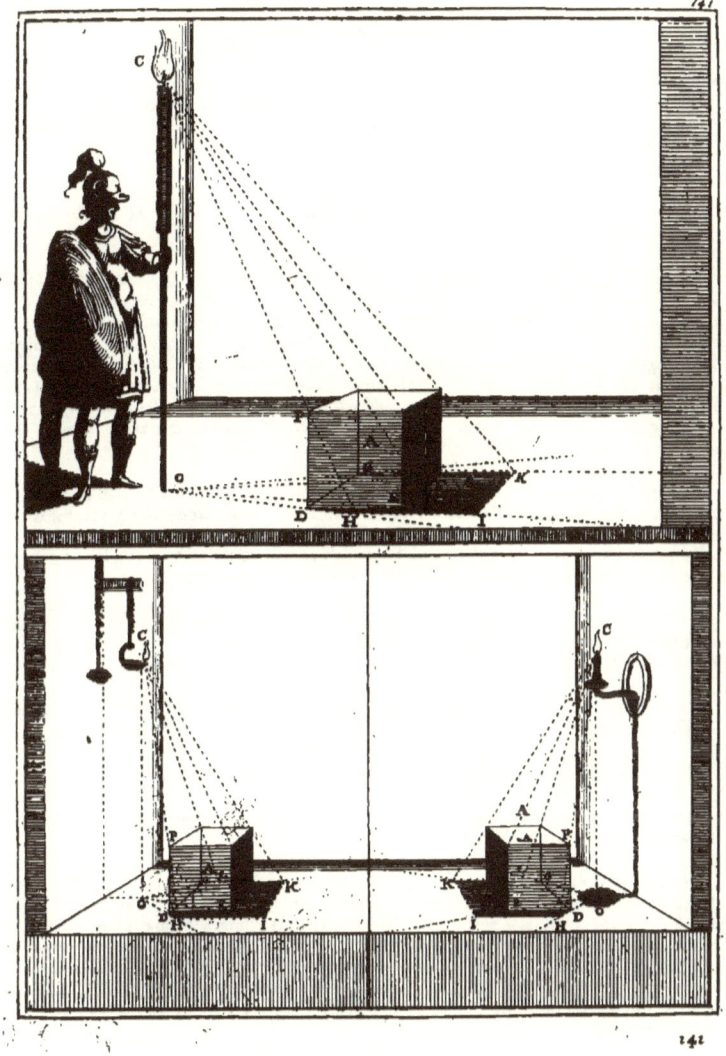

S f 2

Of the foot of the Luminary.

SINCE the method of finding shadows by the torch, candle and lamp is the same in all, as already observed, there is no occasion for distinguishing between them in any of the following rules. For when I put a candle, a torch or a lamp might as well be put in its place, the light of one having the same effect as that of any of the rest. So that for the future, we shall use the word light indifferently for all three.

As to the foot of these luminaries, which must stand on the plans where the objects are placed, it is found after the following method.

A lighted torch being in a chamber, whether in a corner, at a side, or in the middle thereof (instances of each hereof we have in the erected figure) we must consider all the parts of the room, namely, the cieling, floor, sides, &c. as having points wherein the foot of the luminary may be placed, and that from these points lines may be drawn through all the angles of the plan of the object whose shadow is required, as shall be expressed more at large in the following page, my chief design in this being to shew how that point is to be found. The torch then being placed in A, this point A is the foot of the light, and B the light or fire of the torch, which fire is there supposed immoveable, though the foot may be found on all sides.

To find the foot of the luminary on the side of the wall C, draw a parallel to the base line from the point A, till it cut the ray D E in the point F, from which point erect a perpendicular F G. Then from the point B, which is the fire, draw another parallel to the base line till it cut F G in the point H, which H will be the foot of the luminary; as if the torch were laid all along, its fire still remaining in the point B.

To find the foot of the same luminary on the cieling, from the point G draw a parallel to the base line, as G I, and from the point B erect a perpendicular to the same G I; this gives the point K for the foot of the luminary, as if the torch were turned upside down.

To find it on the other side of the room, the same method must be observed as for the side C, and you will have the point L.

To find the foot of the luminary in the middle of the room, draw a line from the point H to the point of sight, till it cut the perpendicular E in the point M. Then from M draw a parallel to the base line, intersecting the torch in the point N; this point will be the foot of the luminary for the middle of the room.

The foot of a candle is found after the same manner as that of a torch, taking the middle of the foot of the candlestick for the foot of the luminary; but when it is a plate, or an arm fixed in the wall, it is this arm or branch, that determines the line where the foot of the luminary shall be. For instance, in the plate P, through the arm Q draw a perpendicular to the base line, as R S. Then from the fire T, draw a little parallel to the base line, which cutting R S in the point V, gives the foot of the luminary for that side. The point X will be the foot for the floor, the point Y for the cieling, and Z for the front wall of the room.

As to lamps, it is the place they are hung in that determines the foot, as here the character *; from which place a parallel to the base line is drawn as far as the first ray, &c. The rest the same as in the torch or candle.

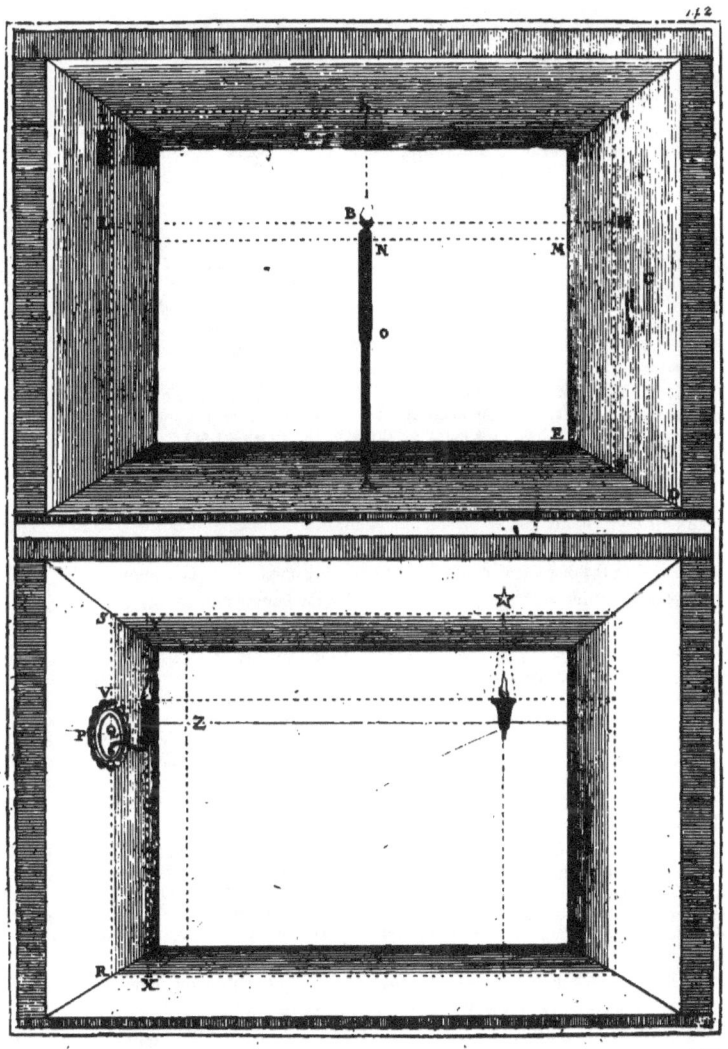

To find the Shadows of a Torch on all the Sides of a Room.

THE fhadows taken from the fun always tend towards the earth, by reafon that ftar never gives us any of its light, but when above our horizon, and of confequence raifed above our ordinary objects, and fo occafioning their fhadows to defcend. But the cafe is different in torches, candles, and lamps, which may be placed either above, below, or on the fides of objects, and therefore may yield fhadows on all fides, as we are now to fhew.

The preceding figure will help to find the fhadows of objects difpofed on all fides of the room, for having found the foot of the luminary as already directed, there is nothing difficult behind, the method throughout being the fame with that for the cube in page 141. to which recourfe may be had. However, to fave you the trouble of going fo far back, I fhall here obferve, that to find the fhadow of the table the torch is placed in, you muft draw lines from the foot of the torch A, through all the feet of the table C. Then from the point of light B, draw lines over all the points of the table I I I, &c. till they interfect the rays C C, &c. in the point O O, &c. which will give the bounds of the fhadow of the table.

The fhadow of the object D is found by drawing lines from the point A, through all the angles of the plan, as far as the angle of the wall D, and from that angle raifing them perpendicularly. Then from the point of the light B, drawing lines over the object D, and obferving the angles correfponding to the lines of the plan, you will have the fhadow F of the object D.

The fhadows of all the other pieces are found after the fame manner: fo that all we fhall here note, is the foot of the luminary, the fire itfelf being fuppofed to be fixed in the point B.

For finding the fhadow of figure G, the point L is the foot of the luminary.

To find the fhadow of figure N, the point H is the foot of the luminary.

To find the fhadows of the figures I and M, the point K is the foot of the luminary.

For the fecond figure; having found the foot of the luminary on all the fides of a room, as directed in the preceding page, the fhadows of objects are found in any place at pleafure by the rule now delivered. For example, having found the foot of the luminary Q and its fire P, if you would have the fhadow of the object R, draw rays from the point Q over the plan of the object, continuing them indefinitely. But inafmuch as they meet with the wall, or fide of the room T, in the places S and S, where they meet the fame, they muft all be raifed; then drawing other lines from P over the fame object R, they will cut thofe of the plan, and mark the place of the fhadow upon each, obferving that the angles refer to the lines drawn from the plan.

This method is fo univerfal, that a man who only knows how to take the fhadow of a cube, will make no difficulty of finding the fhadow of any other object whatever. For this reafon, having defcribed that method for the cube in page 141. and added this above, which in effect is the fame; I imagine I have given abundant inftruction for the managing of all fhadows, and may be excufed from repeating the fame in the feveral figures following. Wherein all I fhall note, is the point for the foot of the luminary.

To find the fhadow of the figure V, the point X is the foot of the luminary.

To find the fhadow of figure Y, the point Z is the foot of the luminary.

To find the fhadow of the figure +, the point & is the foot of the luminary. P is the fire, or light itfelf, for all the objects in the fecond figure.

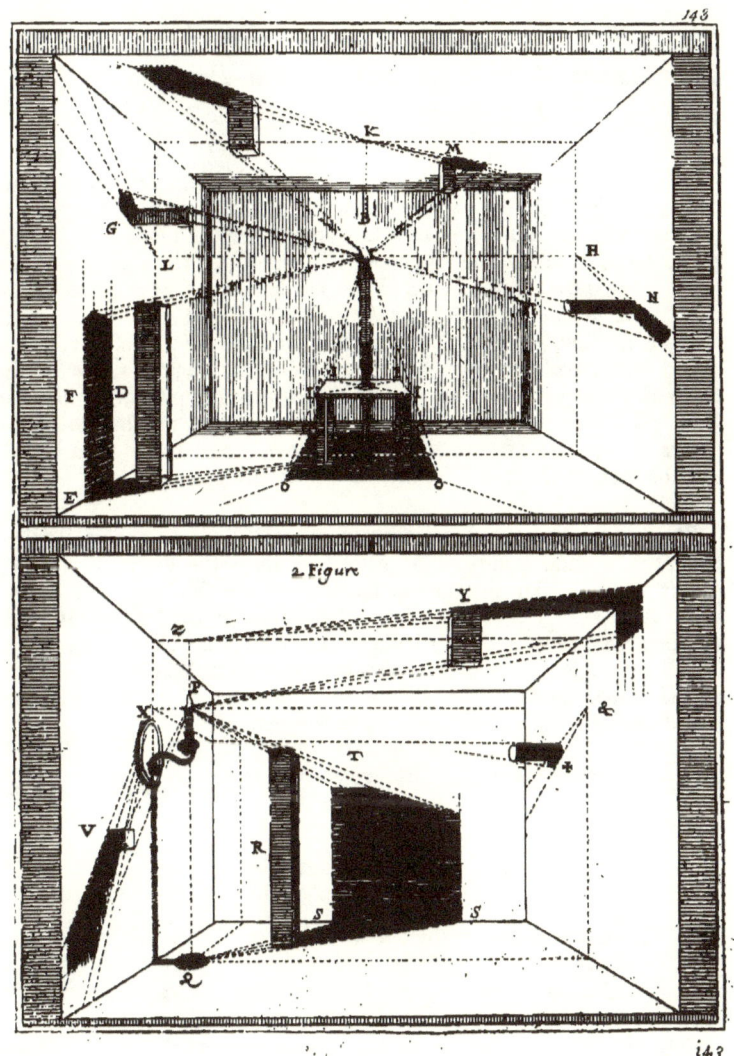

The Shadow of an erect and inverted Pyramid by Torch-light.

THE ſhadow of an erect pyramid by torch-light, falls as it would by the light of the ſun, and in both caſes there is but one line wherein the vertical point of the pyramid will be found. Upon the plane B C D E draw the diagonals E B and D C, through the central point F raiſe the perpendicular F A, and from the four points B C D E draw lines to the point A, and the pyramid will be erected. Then to find its ſhadow, draw an indefinite line from the baſis G of the illuminating body, paſſing through F, and from the central flame of the torch H draw another line over the vertex of the pyramid in the line G F, till it cut the point I, which point will limit the ſhadow of the pyramid. Laſtly, draw a line from C to I, and another from E to I, and the triangle C I E will be the ſhadow of the pyramid.

To gain the ſhadow of an inverted pyramid, draw perpendicular lines from the angular points of its baſe, and form the ſubjacent plane by means thereof, after the manner directed for the ſun, page 138. And from all the angles of this plane, draw lines to the baſe of the torch G, then from H, the central point of the flame draw other lines, touching all the angles of the baſe of the inverted pyramid, and dividing thoſe of the plane, whereby the ſhadow will be defined; as we before obſerved, in other inſtructions relating to the torch.

The Shadow of a Croſs.

WE before conſidered the ſhadow of a croſs by the ſun, let us now ſuppoſe the ſame object placed in the light of a torch, that we may find the difference between the two caſes. The conſtruction of the latter is obvious enough, particularly if compared with the method of finding the plane, delivered in page 137, and the other directions laid down for ſhadows by torch-light.

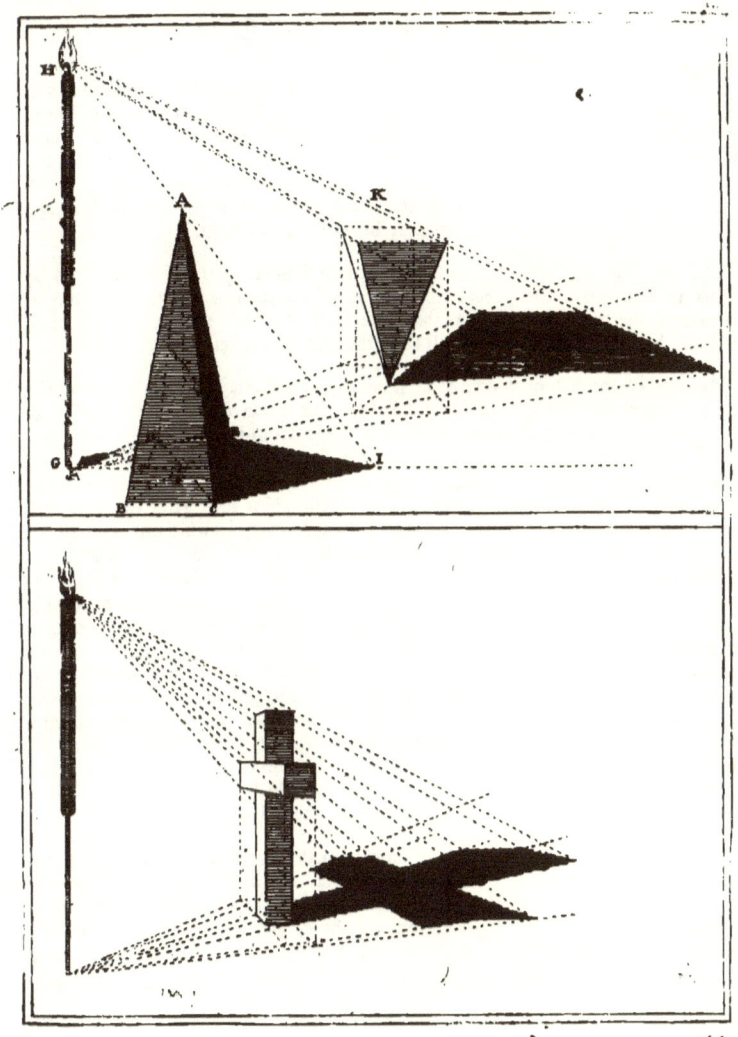

T t

To find the Shadows of round Objects by Torch-light.

THERE may feem to be more difficulty in reprefenting the fhadows of globes, bottles, drinking-veffels, and other bellied objeêts, by torch-light, than in thofe of fquare ones, but the direêtions already given will ferve for thefe alfo ; for there is nothing more. required here, but to reduce fquares to rounds, as we taught in pages 19, 20, 28, 29, and 86 ; which contain all the neceffary inftruêtions for giving the plans of round objeêts in perfpeêtive, whence all other cafes of that kind may be eafily underftood.

We gave in page 138, the method for finding the plan of a ball, and by means of that plan, the precife magnitude of the fhadow by the fun. But as the cafe of the torch differs from that, we fhall be a little more particular upon the ball, becaufe it will facilitate all the other direêtions relating to rounds.

Having by means of a pair of compaffes marked out the great circle of the ball A, draw its diameter B C, and below this circle draw a line parallel to B C touching the circle in the point H. Then from the extremes of the diameter B C let fall perpendiculars upon the line below, as B D and C E, and with thefe points D and E make a plan D E F G in the ufual manner, the diameter whereof F G, will divide D E at the point H. And this plan will ferve to find the fhadow of the ball A. Now, having drawn from the bafis of the illuminating body I, lines touching this plane on both fides, as I K and I L, and another I H M, through the center of the plane H, as alfo lines from the center of the flame N, which touching the ball between A and B, fhall divide the line I H at the point M : this point muft terminate the fhadow. To gain the firft part of this fhadow, draw from the fame point N another line, touching the fore-part of the ball, and dividing alfo the line I H at the point Q, then the diftances between Q and M will be the length of the fhadow. And for its breadth, draw from the fame point N two lines touching the extremes of the diameter of the ball Z Z, and dividing the lines I K at the point R, and I L at the point S. Now then, as R S is the breadth of the fhadow, and Q M the length of it, if the four points R S Q M be joined with curve lines, there will be an oval formed for the fhadow of the ball A.

I have been the larger upon this fhadow, becaufe I judge the direêtion given about it alone fufficient for finding the other fhadows of rounds, as of the objeêt V, for example, which having two unequal breadths, ought to have a plan of two circles. And the figure X having three, fhould have its plans correfponding thereto, one for the neck of the bottle, another for its belly, and a third for its foot ; all which are to be made as thofe for the ball.

An infpeêtion of the figures will render any farther explanation of them unneceffary.   2

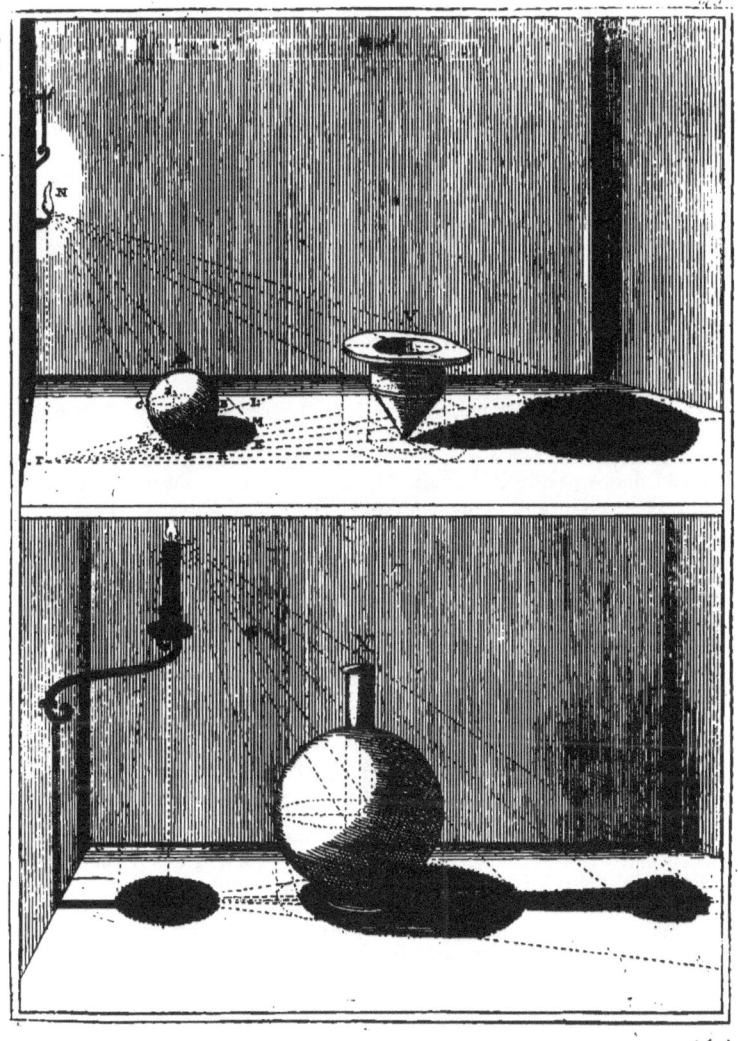

Shadows *on several parallel Planes.*

THE firft plane here is the floor whereon the chair A ftands; the fecond plane is the upper part of the table, parallel to the firft, and may be either above or below it.   There might alfo be more of thefe planes wherein to find the foot of the illuminating body, in order to come at the fhadow of the object.   Suppofe the foot of the illuminating body to be C, and the flame B; from thefe points C and B draw lines through the upper and under part of the object D; which will give the fhadow E upon the table.

To find the fhadow of the chair A, which is placed on the ground; determine the foot of the luminary on the table in C, on the ground: this is cleared by the inftructions following.

From the point of diftance, which is here fuppofed without the limits of the paper, draw a line through the foot of the table F; then from the angle G upon the table, let fall a perpendicular cutting the line F in the point H; and from H draw a parallel to the bafe H I, which is equal to the upper part of the table, and will direct us to the thing required.   For, drawing a line from the point of fight K through the foot of the luminary C, to the extremity of the table L; from the fame point L, let fall a perpendicular to H I, which will give the point M.   Then from M draw a line to the point of fight K; in which line M K will the foot of the luminary be found.   To determine the precife point let fall a perpendicular from the point C, which, cutting the line M K will give the point N for the foot of the luminary.   This point N thus found, there will be no difficulty in finding the fhadow of the chair A, the method being the fame as for the other objects taught in the preceding pages: that is, from the foot of the luminary N draw lines through all the angles of the plan of the chair, and other lines through the upper part of the chair, from the luminary B; thefe latter by interfecting the former exprefs the bounds of the fhadow.   For the reft the figure gives fufficient directions.

The fecond figure is not here added as if there were any particular circum-ftances different from thofe of the figure above, but only to put you upon re-collecting what has been already taught; namely, that objects caft their fhadows differently, according to their different difpofitions about the luminary.   Thus the little objects on the table project their fhadows this or that way as the lumi-nary is on this or that fide, as is found from the common rules relating to the foot of the luminary, and the light itfelf.   Moft of the objects here reprefented are broader at the tops than bottom; fo that it will be neceffary to make plans thereof, after the manner already fhewn.

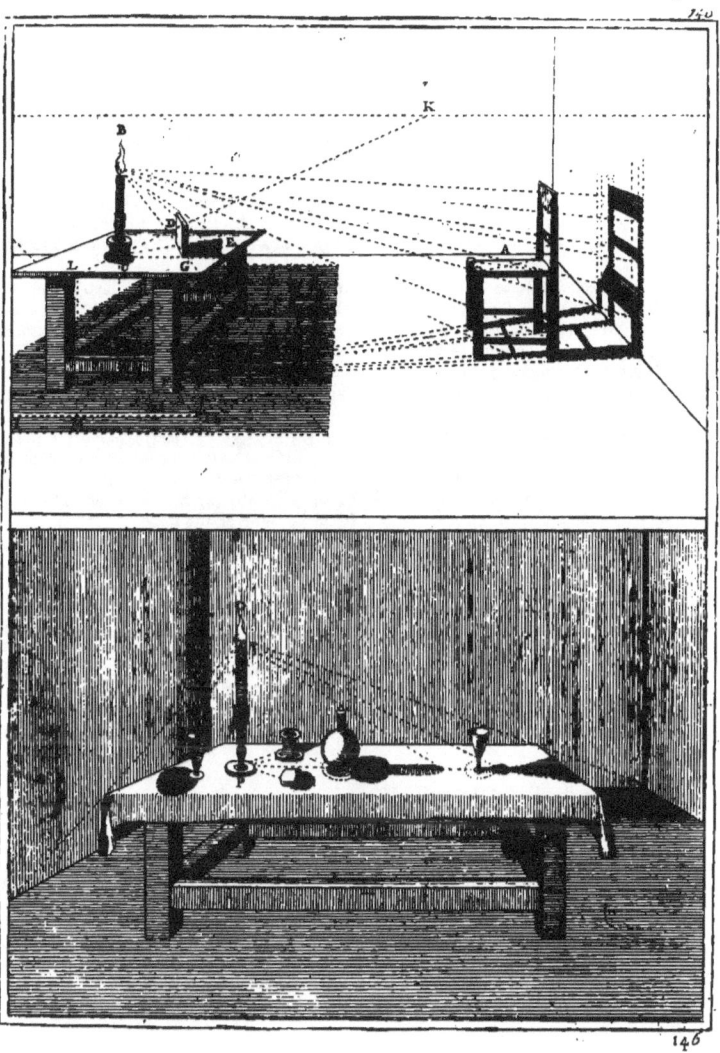

Shadows *of* Cielings *by Torch-light.*

THESE figures are not placed in the fun's light, becaufe that luminary is high above all the objects of the earth, and confequently can give no fhadow where the illuminating body is fuppofed to be under the object. If it be faid, though the fun's rays enter a room, yet the fhadows of bodies continue to appear; I anfwer, that fuch fhadows are not immediately caufed by the fun, but by the light reflected into the room from other objects; and that they cannot be reprefented by parallel lines, as thofe of the fun, but by rays iffuing from the fame center, as thofe of a torch, taking the reflecting body for the illuminating point, and proceeding in drawing fuch a fhadow as in the cafe of a torch.

The directions hitherto given, which turn upon the forming of plans, and drawing of lines from the angles of objects, to find the bounds of the fhadow, would be too tedious here, and the great number of lines neceffary to be drawn, would render the figure exceeding intricate, on account of the feveral beams, fupporters, and rafters that would occur. This inconvenience drove me to invent a fhort, eafy, practical method for the fame purpofe, without departing from the rules of art.

The floor being put in perfpective, as was taught in pages 55, and 57, and the illuminating body fixed, we muft find by means of the bafis of that body where the illuminating point ought to be. To find this point, when the illuminating body is at B, draw from the foot of it C, a parallel to the bafe D E, till it cut the ray E F in the point G, from this point G raife a perpendicular G L, and from the flame of the torch B draw a parallel to D E, dividing the perpendicular G L at the point L, and this point L will give the place and length of the fhadow.

For example; to find the fhadow of the band A, from the point L draw a line touching the vertex of the angle H, and obferve where this line L divides the firft rib, as at the point I, which is the place of the fhadow's ending. From this point draw a parallel I K, and mark upon the ribs the place of the fhadow O. And to find the fhadow of the fpace betwixt them, draw another line from the point L, touching the vertex of the angle of the firft rib M, which will divide the angle of the interval at the point N. Now then, from the point N draw a parallel N P, and you will thence have all the fhadow Q for the beam A.

To find the fhadow of the joifts, draw a line from the illuminating point B, touching the angle S, and dividing the bottom of the entab'ature at the point T. Proceed thus with all the other ribs, and the fhadow will appear to be longer the farther it is removed from the luminous body. Then mark upon one beam all the points T, and from the point of fight R, draw lines through each of thefe points, and then the fhadows of all the other ribs will fall exactly between the bands, as we fee in the points V V.

The fecond figure is the fame with the former, and differs from it only in being fhadowed, which would have obfcured the letters and the fine lines neceffary in the other: only here the fhadow of the jambs of the gate muft be taken from the foot or the illuminating body, as in X and Y.

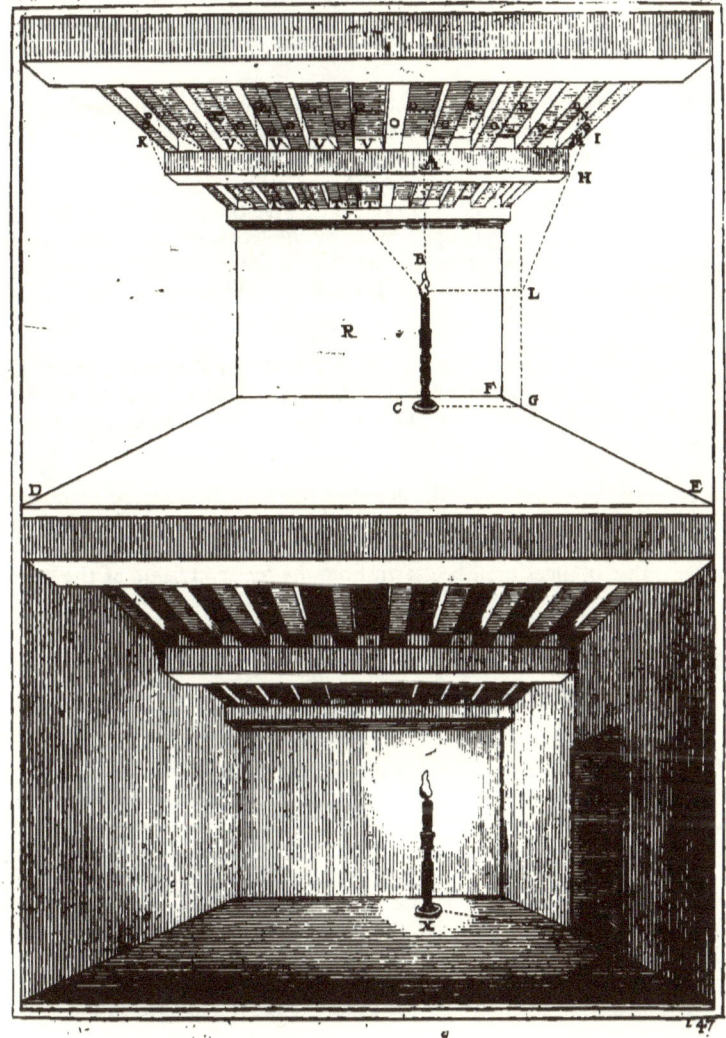

To find the Shadow by the Foot of the Luminary.

IF the objects be perpendicular to the bafe line, and higher than the flame of the candle A, we need only draw lines from the foot of the luminary B through the moft advanced angles of the objects; for example, C and D of the fkreen, *fig.* I. and others from the angle of the wall E. Thefe lines B C, B D, and B E, give the place of the fhadow in the points where the angles made by the leaves of the fkreen, meet the floor; as alfo the return of the wall in the point G, from whence perpendiculars muft be raifed, as G R, which will terminate the fhadows given by the candle A.

The reafon hereof is, that the line A B being parallel to the line C H, D I, K and E L, occafions the flame, in what part foever of the line A B it be found, whether on high in the middle or below, to give a like fhadow.

It muft here be obferved, that this rule only holds good of objects raifed above the flame, as thefe are in the prefent figure. For fuch as fhew their upper part, as here the object M, the preceding rules take place; that is, lines muft be drawn from the foot and flame of the luminary.

❀❀❀❀❀❀❀❀❀❀❀❀❀❀❀❀❀❀❀❀❀❀❀❀❀❀❀❀❀❀❀❀

The Shadow doubled.

WHEN two luminaries fhine on the fame object, two fhadows muft be produced, each by means of the luminaries occafioning the refpective fhadow, and that in proportion to the circumftances of the luminary. If fuch luminaries when at equal diftances be equal, the fhadows themfelves muft be equal; but if there be any difproportion, that is, if one of them be a little bigger than the other, or one of them a little nearer the object than the other, the fhadows will be unequal. Thus the object C being illumined by two candles, the one near at hand in P, the other farther off in Q, it is evident; the fhadow of the candle P will be deeper than that of the candle Q, as is expreffed in the figure.

The rules for fuch fhadows are the fame with thofe already given both for the fun and the torch.

✿✿✿✿✿✿✿✿✿✿✿✿✿✿✿✿✿✿✿✿✿✿✿✿✿✿✿✿✿✿

The Shadows *of human Figures by Torch-light.*

I HAVE reafon to hope that the advice already given, not to turn over the page to a new figure, before the preceding one be well underftood, has been carefully obferved. Suppofing therefore my reader to have maftered what was directed in page 139. for finding the fhadows of human figures by the fun; I have little to add as to thofe in the prefent plate; the line drawn under them, which I ufe as a plan, ferving indifferently in either cafe. But inafmuch as the fhadow projected by a torch is not equal to the body, as is the fhadow projected by the fun, a farther confideration muft here be added; namely, that inftead of drawing the lines parallel to one another, they muft here be all drawn from a center; that is, all the lines drawn over the plan muft proceed from the foot of the luminary A, and thofe over and about the figure from the point of the flame, in like manner as for the other fhadows of the torch; which it would be needlefs here to repeat, the figure itfelf giving abundant fatisfaction.

3

✿✿✿✿✿✿✿✿✿✿✿✿✿✿✿✿✿✿✿✿✿✿✿✿✿✿✿✿✿✿✿✿

The different Difpofitions and Heights of Shadows by torch-
light.

SHADOWS from the fun are all caft the fame way, and
have the fame difpofition ; it being impoffible the fun
fhould occafion one fhadow to tend towards the eaft, and
another towards the weft, at the fame time. True, in different times of the day it makes this difference : but never
in one and the fame hour.

But the torch, candle and lamp have always this effect ;
for in what place foever one of thefe luminaries be found,
provided there be a number of objects about them, the
fhadows will be caft various ways ; fome to the eaft, fome
to the weft, fome to the north, and others to the fouth,
according to the fituation of the objects around the luminary :
the foot of which, here reprefented by A, ferves as a common center from which they all proceed ; and the flame
here reprefented by B fhews where they are to terminate,
though at different diftances ; as the neareft produce the
fhorteft fhadows, and the remoteft the longeft.

Though in the fecond figure the luminary be not placed
in the middle, yet the fame rule obtains, with refpect to
the fhadows as in the former figure ; being all drawn from
the foot of the luminary C, and terminated by lines from
the flame D.

4.

F I N I S.

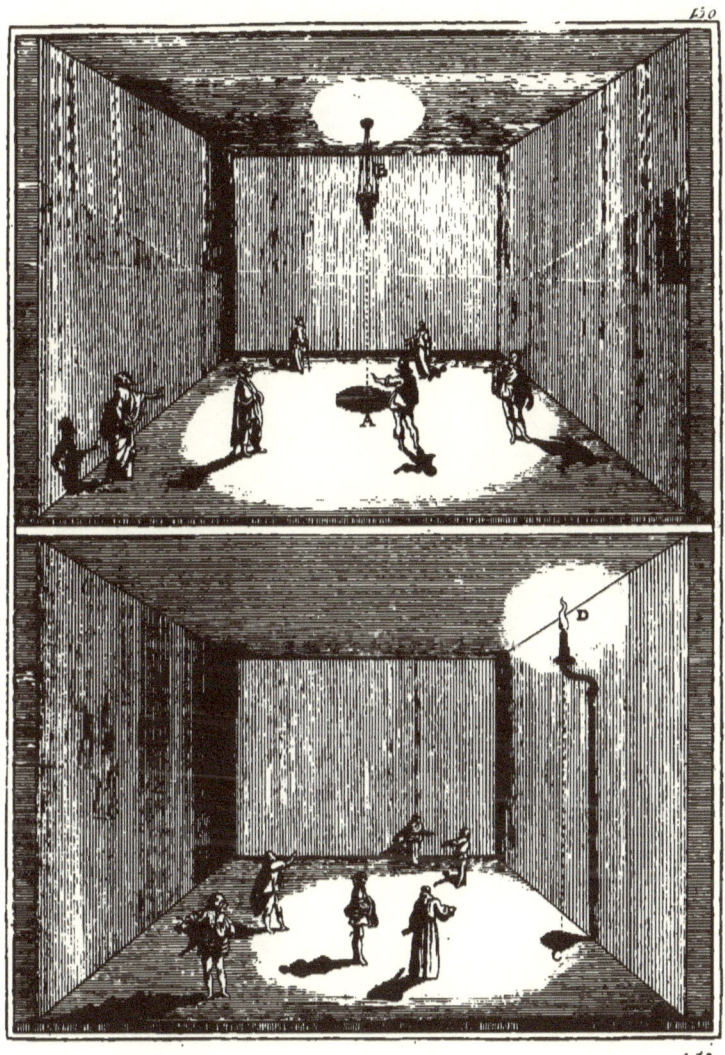